TEARS OF PKKHUUX
STORMS OF TRANSFORMATION
BOOK 1

DANIELLA BOVA

Cover design: Logotecture

ISBN-10: 1499306725

ISBN-13: 978-1499306729

STORMS OF TRANSFORMATION SERIES

ACKNOWLEDGMENTS

Seems that revising a series is harder than writing one, at least in my case. My husband Tom has been my rock through this entire journey. Without his support over the past two years this project would not have been possible. Special thanks to my dear friend and feedback reader John Earle, whose tireless support and encouragement kept me on track, and whose knowledge of the English language is second to none. I'm grateful to Kia Heavey for her constant friendship and support, and for helping me through numerous periods of writerly self-doubt throughout this process. A big thanks to Marina Fontaine for her friendship and writing tips over the past eight years, and also to Matt Margolis for his formatting and cover design skills. Finally, I would like to thank God, whom I lean on daily, and even hourly. He is the true author of all.

AUTHOR'S NOTE

If you have persevered to the end of this book, I thank you. I have been following current events closely, ever since September 11, 2001. What I have written is a worse case scenario, but still within the realm of possibility, if America continues on its present course.

The above is from my 2014 note to readers of Tears of Paradox. I began revising the series in the fall of 2019 after reflecting on critical reviews and gaining additional feedback from readers and other authors.

The characters, plot, ending etc. remain the same; the revised books simply make the series more enjoyable for readers. When I began the revisions I wasn't positive I would end up actually republishing the books. However the "worse case scenario" I mentioned in 2014 is becoming more real by the day, so I decided to go ahead and update the books in hopes that additional readers will find the series.

ONE

Jason

Some people are born as old souls. It's one of the few things I remember my father telling me. Just before he walked out when I was nine, he said I was an old soul just like he had been as a boy.

Michelle never wanted to face this fact. Because she was happy and carefree as a child she wanted to believe the same about me, but it wasn't so. She finally figured it out the year before I left town. That's when she put it all together. But maybe she knew deep down inside. She was an old soul, too.

Seems everything was predestined—the good, the bad, the happy, the sad, the joy and the laughter and the sorrow of our lives. Things have turned out the way they were supposed to, I guess. It's a paradox. Life is full of such things: paradoxes and ironies, good choices and bad.

I may as well start with a couple of ironies.

20 Years Earlier

I was in Denfield's Department store looking for a gift for my mother. I loathed shopping, especially at the mall. But her birthday was the next day, and I had waited until the last minute as usual. In hindsight I remember a feeling of foreboding along with a familiar sensation of water. At the time I attributed it to the thought of Mom's inevitable reaction to whatever I ended up purchasing. I didn't connect it to what followed until afterward.

I was standing in front of the jewelry counter searching through a display of bracelets when I heard the voice behind me saying, "Jason? Is that you?"

Oh my God.

The voice was low toned and lilting, soft and caressing, meaningful and expressive and mysterious and laughing, all at the same time. *It's her.* I'd been back in town for three weeks at that point. Memories of Brad and St. Bonaventure flashed through my mind like a bullet train, along with other memories. Wrenching memories of goodbyes. Sorrowful memories, dark and brooding, overshadowed by grief and loss.

I was afraid to turn around. *What if she's not alone? Why does it have to happen here? I'll hate malls even worse now.*

I stood frozen. Things around me didn't seem real as the feeling of water intensified. Flowing, then rushing, then flowing again, and the sound of wind and rain; the same sound I heard from time to time, the same feeling that came over me when anything important was about to happen. It came out of nowhere along with the voice and it was like I had never left. I felt as if the past four years had been a crazy dream.

And only because of the sound of her voice? *Dear God... if just hearing her voice is doing this to me, what's going to happen when I see her eyes again?* With the flowing water came a sensation of knowing that despite my pleas to her asking her to forget me, Michelle hadn't. *But does she still love me?*

Michelle

I have plenty of time to think, angel-baby. Time to ponder and reflect as I wait for you. I really have nothing else but time. Your daddy can't be with us now, but at least I have you. You and your father are my world.

My world. My world. I write the words over and over, hoping and praying that our world isn't shattered for good. Praying for you, my baby, and my husband, and what's left of our family. It's hard to make sense of what's happened even when the periods of anxiety and fear and crushing loneliness let up for a time.

I'll pray for those who are helping us: Patty and Mark and Sandy, Melanie and Brian. People I never knew existed until three weeks ago. A very kind family, but I miss my old life. Still, there's nothing to be done about it.

Since I want you to know the truth someday I've decided to write it all down for you. Just in case your daddy and I are unable to tell you ourselves.

My little basement room is cozy. There are lots of things to look at in between bouts of crying. While shuffling through shelves of old books I found a spiral notebook left over from Sandy's school days. The faded writing on the inside front cover reads: *Sandy Varachese - Grade 9 - Mount Lenni High School 1977*. Sandy must have put the notebook aside for another one though, because only a few pages had writing on them. The last entry for English was a page of notes on *Animal Farm* dated October 3, 1977. Times sure have changed. High school students no longer read *Animal Farm*. The book was banned not long ago.

Anyway, I found the notebook and Patty says I can call it my own, so I'll write down our story for you.

I love feeling your movements inside me, but sometimes I find it hard not to cry when I remember the way your daddy put his hands on my belly to feel you anytime he could. The last time I saw him he was down on his knees with his arms around me, talking to you in a whisper.

I'll try to make you understand, since I can't tell anyone else about you, not even your Uncle Brad. He's my big brother and Jason's best friend. Still we have to keep him in the dark.

I know Brad would help us if we were able to tell him the truth. Jason considered it, and came to the conclusion that it's way too risky. He's right, but it's hard. I want to talk to Brad. I want to hear his precious girls' voices and it would help me so much to talk to someone who understands. We can't tell Brad, of course, because of what might happen to the girls.

So we're alone. Both of us, without much talk about it at all, came to the same conclusion: to leave the rest of them out of it. Especially my other brother Johnny and his wife Cindy, who are suffering the same way we are, though the circumstances are different. Sometimes I feel as if what happened to them is worse than what we're enduring, as bad as our situation seems.

We have our child. We have you, safe inside me. You're safe now angel-baby, but your cousins are lost. The bureaucracy brainwashed them, and they are now a part of it. The last time I laid eyes on Jamie he was marching through town carrying a machine gun along with the rest of the MCSF. The acronym stands for Mandatory Civilian Service Force, and Junior is the leader of our town's chapter.

My tears are dripping on the page, so I'll stop for a while. I'll write more about your cousins when I can stand it.

Blessed Jesus, is all hope lost for my little nephews? They don't belong where they are, Lord. That's not your way. Please hear my prayers.

* * *

It's hard for me to trust anyone except your father. He's my rock. I pray you'll know him, and if everything goes as planned, you will. Then you'll feel safe the way I used to. I always felt safe, first with Daddy and then with Jason, but that was before the advent of the new way of doing business.

It's different now. We're safe for the moment, but only because we're hidden. *Thank You dear God, for providing this sanctuary.*

Even though Sandy and Mark are kind and Patty tries to cheer me up, I'm living in a state of such anxiety that I can hardly get through each day. I don't want to feel this way. I want to be calm. I want you to feel secure, safe and protected inside me, but I wonder how you can. The world isn't safe anymore.

I have trouble trusting anyone after the way Junior turned on us. The days seem to meld together in endless hours of anxiety, and only when I feel brave enough to walk across the yard to the cornfield do I realize how late in summer it is. You are due to arrive in late September, angel. Melanie says you'll be a good size baby. On her last visit as we listened to your heartbeat I felt you fluttering. I imagined you tossing and turning, squirming and kicking, wanting to be born quickly so you'll be safe.

Jason

Michelle had always been there. That was the truth. In hindsight I think I knew it before she was born—that maybe I knew it even before I was born. The fact was always there. It just *was*.

Michelle was my best friend's baby sister. She was literally the girl next door, and I can't remember becoming aware of the fact that we were meant to be together. It was just something I knew to be true, the same way I knew that I was a boy and she was a girl, that she had a mother and father who loved each other, and I did not. That her brother, my friend Brad, felt more like a brother to me than my own brother did. It was something I understood on instinct, the same way I knew that I needed to eat if I wanted to continue to live. The way I knew that if I wanted to grow up to be a man, and to have a happy home someday, I would have to put my father out of my mind. It was a sort of mental grasping, a knowledge taken on faith like my knowledge of God. He just *Was*.

So was Michelle. We loved each other. We didn't express our feelings in words; we never needed to back then when we were young. Both of us simply knew that we loved each other, and that we always had.

The only problem—for me anyway—was that I told myself I could never have her. Back before I left town there was absolutely no way I ever let myself start thinking the two of us might have a future. I never even saw her except when I was over at Brad's working on his '79 Trans Am, or maybe watching the game with him and his dad. Even then I paid her no more attention than hello and small talk. I kept my feelings a secret.

When I look back on my high school years it's like looking back on a little hell, a preparation for the hell on earth that awaited us twenty-five years down the road, the hell which I have survived, the story of which I'm setting down in words for anyone who might possibly be interested. To anyone on the outside looking in, my high school experience probably seemed no more hellish than the next guy's and maybe even better than most, but when I think of those years I wonder how I ever got through them.

I'm not denying the fact that there were other girls. There were, even if I do wish I could change everything about my choices between my sixteenth birthday and my return to town when I was twenty-three. The other girls were the problem; I shouldn't have done what I did. I should have waited for the one I wanted, the one I *needed,* the only one who understood anything about me. But unfortunately I let the world and all its temptations get in the way. After graduation I enlisted in the Air Force while Brad was at school down in Tennessee, studying pharmacology.

Back then I was doubtful he would pull it off. But Brad was a worker same as me, even if he did party his way through the first two years. I'd email him after twelve hours of work in the cockpit of whatever plane needed maintenance at the time, and about one Sunday morning a month he would call, hung over and cussing a blue streak, swearing solemnly that he would never touch another beer.

Brad and I kept in touch, but we never talked about his sister. He had no idea Michelle and I had feelings for each other until later. When he finally did find out he had trouble believing I was serious. I didn't blame him; the two of us had been in too many scrapes over the years—most of them with women—for Brad to believe I was serious about any girl, especially his sister. It's a good thing we were a thousand miles apart when I finally confronted him with it on the phone, otherwise he might have decked me. Then I would have been forced to beat the crap out of him. At that time Brad hadn't yet developed a sense of respect for any woman, and there was no reason for him to believe I had either. We knew each other too well.

We'd grown up together. Brad and I were like brothers, and even though his escapades with women outnumbered mine three to one, there was no real reason for him to take me seriously. After all, we spent our last two years of high school partying and raising hell and hanging out in town every weekend, chasing any chick we happened to lay eyes on as long as she was good looking.

The trouble was none of it meant anything to me.

Michelle

I prayed the Joyful Mysteries today, since it's Monday. I pray every morning for your safe arrival, angel, and that we can get you away before anyone finds out. If you're born healthy Jason thinks we can drive down to Memphis and throw ourselves on Brad's mercy. It's our only option. We can't go home. I'll never be able to go back, even though I want to in the worst way. I have a longing to visit the cemetery one last time to say goodbye to my other angel-baby.

I miss Brad. I miss everyone. I wish I could talk to Johnny. I have a suspicion he and Cindy have figured out what's happening. It's nothing I can put my finger on, but I like to imagine them knowing, and being willing to come to our aid. Telling them is out of the question of course. We can't, not after all that's happened with Junior and Jamie. But like I said, I have nothing but time now, and after thinking things through I'm almost positive both of them know. Neither of them deserves what's happened: the loss of their boys.

It hurts to remember what the boys were like when they were little. They were sweet, beautiful babies, and later ornery and cute as could be. Daddy adored them. He took them to ball games and the zoo and out for ice cream every Sunday in the summertime. Mom told me watching them reminded Daddy of Brad and Jason and the scrapes they got into when they were little. Junior and Jamie were typical, innocent little boys. We were just a typical family, like millions of others who are probably dealing with their own nightmarish realities now. *But I'll be thankful for my blessings. My baby is safe.*

* * *

I listen to Mass on the radio since I can't go to church. The signal fades in and out, but I can hear well enough, and I like this priest. The subject of yesterday's homily was Christ's teaching about how to treat others. Whatever we do to the very least, that we do unto Him. You are one of the very least, baby, and our new friends are following the gospel by hiding us.

I've gotten to know Patty over the last few weeks. We visit during the day while Mark and Sandy are working. I've agreed never to come upstairs during the day, but the laundry room is down here, and Patty and I talk while she washes and irons. This morning I mentioned the homily, and I thanked her again for everything they're doing for us. We don't talk about how they came to know about my situation, but from what I can gather we're not the only ones they're helping.

Patty likes to keep busy. I would have guessed her age at around sixty-five, and I found it hard to believe she's almost ninety. I straightened up the basement while she was ironing this morning. I try to keep the place as neat as possible, and I think Patty appreciates my efforts. I sleep on an air mattress in the corner. It's covered with a faded patchwork quilt that Patty tells me was sewn by her mother. There is stitching on the back that reads: *Adela Dorothea Davis Sheets, Ashe County, North Carolina, 1933.* Patty has kept several of her mother's quilts and told me this one was made using feed sacks. The name of the pattern is Grandmother's Fan. We laughed when we realized we're both Davises; maybe we're related in some way. It's funny in a way, but before we leave here I plan to black out any words regarding the name Davis, just in case.

Patty must sense the anxiety I'm feeling. We turned on the TV but nothing suited us.

"It's too early for soaps," Patty said. Her wrinkled face looked amused. "Let me tell you a little about my days down South. They're more entertaining than soap operas anyway." She chattered and laughed animatedly for an hour or more, and I found myself listening intently. As I folded clothes, Patty ironed and told me about her family. She was born in North Carolina and lived there until her family moved up here when she was three years old. Her grandparents owned a farm in the Blue Ridge Mountains. Patty's mother grew up on the farm.

"My Momma's name was Adela," Patty chirped from the ironing board. "She sewed that quilt by hand. She made all my clothes on an old treadle sewing machine my granny kept. I was the fourth child out of five, and the youngest girl in the family.

"Mom sewed clothes for all of us, and quilts, and everything else she could back then. My parents raised the five of us—we were poor but we didn't know it—smack dab in the middle of the Great Depression. I was born in hot summer, in a little tiny house way down deep in a hollow. It was some way down the mountain from my grandparents' farm. They grew tobacco for cash, and Daddy helped them for a while, until he decided to make the move north. His name was Calvin."

Listening to Patty took my mind off my troubles, and being told about her birth on an isolated mountain made me feel a little better about our situation. The knowledge is comforting.

Jason
20 Years Earlier

My hand was midway between the display of bracelets and the counter. I'd been trolling the damn jewelry for fifteen minutes, waiting for the sales guy to get off his cell phone. From what I could hear he was giving his girlfriend a load of bullshit.

"Jason?"

My hand stopped. I forgot all thought of rapping on the glass and barking at the sales guy. A few seconds earlier I'd just wanted to buy something and get out. Now, with the sound of her voice, everything else receded except the rush of water.

It was definitely her. There was no mistake. That voice was something I couldn't forget no matter how hard I tried. *Dear God, when I turn around and see her, if she's with someone else, keep me from beating the crap out of the guy. Please.*

"Jason?" She sounded doubtful. I knew I had to turn around then or she'd think I was crazy, so I took a deep breath and did it. And there she was. More than I'd ever dreamed.

Michelle

I'll try to write the words so you'll feel you're experiencing this place with me angel-baby.

It's evening. The sun is low, and the sky is a pink and violet mural of wispy clouds. I'm walking through the cornfield again. I need the exercise. The green blades sweep above me in the breeze, curling against the sky, softer now than I imagine they'll be when you come into this world. The corn is taller than I am now, and Mark thinks it's okay if I come out here sometimes, as long as nobody's around. It belongs to the neighboring dairy farm; the field backs right up to Mark and Sandy's yard. I go in eight or nine rows and walk along parallel to the edge of the field so I won't get lost. My arms and legs itch from the corn blades, but at least I'm able to spend a little time outside in daylight.

It's so peaceful here, like something out of a storybook. Birds sing, cows moo, and sheep bleat in the distance. I find myself near the edge of the field looking out over the countryside. It's pastoral looking in the evening glow. We seem to be very far away from things. I can't see any other houses, and even though I've been walking in a straight line for at least ten minutes, I haven't seen anything but birds and bugs. I couldn't really tell what this place was like before I started coming out to the cornfield, since it was dark when I arrived, and I haven't been told where I am. I'm not positive we're still in Pennsylvania. We may be in Delaware, or Maryland, or even New Jersey. All I know is that the drive from home lasted about an hour.

I go closer to the edge of the corn. I inch my way toward the open air, the green grass, and the spectacular purple sky. I put out my hand, wanting to feel the full breeze on one small part of myself.

Then my heart begins pounding crazily. I pull back my hand, turn around and hurry my way through the corn, feeling like a small timid mouse as I mince my way through the rows. The corn is a shadowy hiding place, but I'm back at the house now. The memories of the day the notice arrived have invaded my head again, and even the dim coolness of the corn or the pretty old house where we take shelter cannot push them out.

* * *

The day the notice arrived seems like a dream.

We were finally getting over your brother's death, angel. The pain was fading away and we knew he was in a better place. We didn't talk about it much, at least not with words. Jason said he could remember the baby's face, but my memory was beginning to fade. I can still recall his little hands, and the thick dark hair on his head—like Jason's—but the only other thing I remember about him is that he was beautiful.

What happened was horrific, but time was working its magic, until the notice arrived at three forty-five on a dark and bitter January afternoon. It was freezing cold. Afterward I wished for rain. Falling rain might have eased my pain because it would have seemed like Heaven was crying for us. I even wished for frozen tears from Heaven, but there was no rain, nor even sleet. It was dry.

It was twilight when the doorbell rang, and for me everything just stayed that way, dim and cloudy and dark. The following few months are disjointed in my memory, just one dark recall of sadness and pain until I finally started coming out of it a little in the spring. But even later when the sun was shining brightly in the summertime, our lives were dark.

The notice came by registered mail, and after I had signed for it and realized where it had come from, I thought it had to be a mistake. What could they possibly want with me? I didn't smoke and neither did Jason—he said he'd quit again. But his smoking shouldn't have mattered anyway when it came to such a thing. In matters of what they termed reproductive health the bureaucracy didn't recognize men. We were both young, too, not like Daddy and his situation. Our baby was born nine weeks before he should have been, but neither of us had been at fault.

We were feeling better. Jason was feeling better.

In all my life I had never witnessed such an agony of grief. Not even after what happened to Daddy. I'd never seen anyone suffer the way Jason did after our baby died, but finally he was starting to feel better. We had begun running together again, we were looking forward to the future, and we were beginning to consider trying for another baby. But the notice changed everything.

In conversation afterward—when he would talk to me that is— Jason told me his theory about it. He believes I was one of the first women this abomination was tried on, though we'll probably never know for sure. He thinks the three-year compliance period they gave us was engineered purposely to determine just how far they could push people, and how long it would take women to comply. That maybe they were collecting statistics on how many husbands or fathers would fight back compared to how many would just go along with it. So they could find out if there would be any resistance.

The bureaucracy was interested in resistance. They frowned on such movements. They didn't like dissidents, and they hoped not to have to take drastic action to put an end to dissent; that wasn't what they were about, or so they told us. They repeatedly stated that everything they were doing was for the common good.

They had flagged me through that damned clinic, the place where my other angel came into this world. It's supposed to be state of the art, but that's a joke. I had heard through friends that one of the teachers I worked with years ago had gone there twice. I don't think the birth side of it got much business, though. It's located less than a mile from a large university, the same school where Jason's mother works, and evidently the college kids keep the place in business. The other end of it, that is.

Supposedly the facilities for births and abortions are kept separate, and maybe that's true. If so, I ended up in the wrong section. In my opinion you put your life and your child's in danger by even setting foot in a place like that, but Jason panicked when he saw all the blood and took me there because it was closest. It wasn't his fault. He thought I was dying.

Then a few months later when the notice slammed us, Jason didn't seem to be able to deal with it. It was such an unspeakable violation that he just shut down. I think he was blaming himself, and he wasn't the same afterward, not for a full year.

Blessed Mother, please pray for us.

TWO

Jason
20 Years Earlier

She was alone. *Thank you God.* We looked at each other and smiled, and I began to lose myself in her eyes the way I used to. Time was at a standstill, and speech wasn't necessary.

How long have you been back?

You're grown up. You're beautiful.

I'm the same as always.

Yes. Beautiful.

I took a step away from the glass, wanting the guy behind the counter to know I didn't need any help, just in case he finally decided to wait on me. I wouldn't have chosen the mall as the best place to reunite with the girl I thought of as my life, but I had no control of the situation, so I decided to make the best of it.

You're grown up. She was no longer a little girl. The last four years receded like the tide. *I missed you Michelle.*

Long silky lashes framed striking blue eyes that seemed to go on forever. *I missed you too. I prayed for you. You should have called. Why didn't you write? Why didn't you email me?*

You know why.

I know, but I wish you had. I'm leaving next week.

My heart dropped. I was coming back then, from the place I could remember being lost in from time to time before I left town four years ago. I was still looking into her endless eyes, but now mine were starting to sting.

"Where are you going, honey?"

"College," she replied. "Why haven't you been to the house?"

I looked away. Of course she was going to school. She'd graduated in June, hadn't she? I should have gone to the house as soon as I got back; we would have had an extra three weeks. I knew why I hadn't done it though: I was afraid of what I might find.

But now I found that I really didn't care whether she was seeing someone else or not. I still felt the same way about her. My thoughts raced. *Look at her. No more little girl. She looks exotic, but way better than anything I laid eyes on overseas.*

She was everything I remembered and more. I wanted to finally have a relationship with her. I intended to do it unless her feelings had changed, and if anyone else happened to be involved with her, too bad for them.

"Well, I guess I'll have to give you your birthday gift early, unless you're going to school here."

"Jason, my birthday's not for another month, and I'll be back that weekend anyway. Rocky River is only a ninety minute drive."

Could be worse. At least the two of us will be living in the same state.

Michelle was still speaking. "I talked to Brad last week and he didn't mention anything about you being home. Why didn't you come by? Your motorcycle is still out back. Daddy makes sure it's covered up." She took a step backward, still smiling, but also looking a little hurt. I checked out the whole picture then.

She was beautiful all right, and not only her face, with its high cheekbones and smooth oval jaw line. Her mouth—shaped a little like a puckery bow—trembled with the realization that I hadn't been to visit. I hadn't let myself think about her much while I was gone, and when I did it was never about her body, but I checked it out now as well.

It was beautiful too. Toned and a little tan, just the way I used to dream it might eventually look. It was exceptional, actually. Her silky blonde hair was still long, thick, and full of reflecting light. I wanted to snatch the clip out of it and run my hand through it. I needed to know if she was seeing anyone. If she was I certainly wouldn't blame her, but I needed to know.

"Brad doesn't know I'm back. He knew I was being discharged this month, but not the actual day. I haven't seen anyone except my mother and Jeremy, and the guys at the garage." I hesitated; her smile was still a little wary. But then I just went ahead and asked her: "Are you doing anything tonight?"

Her face remained guarded. She didn't answer right away. I held my breath, expecting to hear her tell me she was in a relationship. I hoped it wasn't with that little punk, Joey Riley. I'd already decided that unless she told me flat out she wanted nothing to do with me, I was going to at least take her out once or twice, boyfriend be damned. *But if it's Joey she's involved with, I'll actually enjoy breaking them up.*

It wasn't a thought I was proud of, but there it was, and by the time she finally answered me I was almost convinced it was fact. But then to my utter amazement it was my dream that finally came true.

"Jason, you know I'm not." Her tone seemed a bit impatient, as if the question were a silly one. *Why would you have to ask?*

I hung back for a minute, unsure of things, maybe even a little afraid.

You're sure?

Of course I'm sure. You know there's only you.

The moment stretched far back into the distance, beyond the four years since we'd last seen each other.

Really honey?

Only you, Jason. You.

I smiled and held out my arms, and she walked into them.

I took Michelle out of the store. My mother's birthday—thoughts of which had been nagging at me like gnats for days—was no longer at the forefront of my mind. My smile was a mile wide. My face must have been an open book for anyone to read, but I couldn't have taken the idiotic grin off it to save my life.

We walked around the mall, talking. She was majoring in Elementary Education and planned to be a teacher. *That works for me.* She said she was afraid she might not get along with her room-mate and that she might run out of money.

"I saved a lot from work, but I hope I can make it last. I don't want to go back to work until next year. I want to concentrate on school. I don't want to fail any classes."

"Brad mentioned you were applying at Diesel's last year," I replied, remembering how jealous I had been at the news.

"They wouldn't hire me. They serve alcohol, and you need to be twenty-one to work there. I got a job at the diner downtown. I was a hostess at first, but after a few months I started waiting tables. The tips are okay."

I was glad. Diesel's was the sports bar on Lockhart Street, two blocks from the garage. It wasn't a dive, and the guys hung out there all the time, but I hadn't been too crazy about the idea of some of those guys being able to see Michelle and talk to her while I was stuck up the nose of a plane for twelve hours a day working on the radar systems. Especially Reese, even if he was one of my best friends. We'd both worked at the garage since we were fifteen, but he was a year ahead in school and had enlisted in the Marines right after graduation. He'd been back in town for a year. He knew nothing about my feelings for Michelle, so I was glad she hadn't been serving drinks to him and the rest of the guys.

I had a bad moment then, thinking about the fact that Michelle was almost six years younger than I was, even though she was only four years behind me in school. I was a year older than Brad. I had to repeat first grade. I had told myself for the past five years that she was too young for me, and it was a little difficult to just get that out of my mind. *But damn it! I'm doing it. It's not like I haven't had practice She's not a kid anymore. Brad will probably have something to say about it, but I'll handle him if and when the time comes.*

"Why would you be worried about failing, Michelle? Brad mentioned your grades. He wondered why he didn't get some of the brains in the family."

"Brad's as smart as anyone else. He just parties too much." She laughed. "He's doing okay though. He'll be finished in another two years."

"Isn't your Dad paying for school?"

"He's paying, but I don't want him to have to give me spending money. Since I had a lot of time on my hands, I thought I should at least earn that." She looked at me pointedly. "It's not as if I had anything else to do for the past four years. Besides, you always got good grades, and you were working, Jason."

Among other things. She was looking me right in the eye. I glanced away. I stared straight ahead and we walked along in silence until she spoke again. "But all that's in the past... Isn't it?"

My eyes stayed focused on the floor of the mall. The silence was uncomfortable until I grasped her hand and squeezed it. *I'm sorry Michelle.*

She squeezed back then and answered her own question.

"I'll take that as a yes."

She didn't refer to my past again until twenty years later.

* * *

We were back in Denfield's. Michelle helped me pick out the gift when I told her I needed it by the next day.

"Who's it for?" she asked.

"My mother."

"Well, we're in the wrong department. From what I remember of your mom, I doubt she'd appreciate a bracelet on discount."

I laughed, figuring she'd probably heard stories from Brad. Then we went over to the purse department, and Michelle picked out one she thought Mom would like.

Afterward we ended up sitting in a booth at Holiday's, the bar and grill on Route 24.

I asked about her parents and she said they were fine, and that her brother Johnny and his wife and kids had just moved back to the area. We ordered burgers and fries. I had a couple of beers, and Michelle sipped diet soda as she gave me an update on St. Bonaventure, our old high school.

"Bella just started work at that little salon on North Lockhart Street." Bella was Michelle and Brad's cousin, and also a friend of mine.

"Last I talked to Reese, he told me she and Lucio were on the outs," I replied. Lucio was another friend. He and Bella had been on again - off again for the past five years.

"They're back together now," Michelle responded in a neutral tone. "It just happened yesterday. Bella says it's for good this time, or if not, then it's over for good. She says she's done going back and forth with him."

I made no comment. Then she asked what I'd been doing since my return, and I hesitated, not knowing how to explain that I had been warring with my mother. I hadn't been back twenty-four hours before Mom started in on me about applying for school, something I was flat out refusing to do, even though I had the GI Bill.

"Well, I've been a little busy getting things together and looking for a job," I replied before telling her I was starting work the following week back at the garage, full time. It was the job I had always wanted. I'd been interested in mechanics since I was a kid, especially working on cars. The only reason I applied for work on cockpit electronics was so I could travel, figuring I'd see more of the world while working on planes than if I was stuck on some base in a motor pool. Lucky for me, I scored almost a hundred percent on the aptitude tests and my physical. They sent me to tech school for electronics. I figured it would be something I could use as a back up as well.

* * *

I started work at CJ's and told my mother in no uncertain terms that I was moving out as soon as possible. I refused to apply to any schools no matter how much she harassed me, so she finally gave up on the idea. My brother was a junior at St. Bonaventure, and he planned to go to school, so she must have decided to cut her losses with me and put her focus on him instead.

It was always a sore point between us, the fact that I had no interest in college. Mom had plans for me, and when I mentioned the military for the first time she'd almost gone crazy.

My original idea was to enlist in the Marines. Reese was a Marine, and he seemed to be enjoying what he was doing, but when I mentioned it to Mom right before my senior year of high school began, she went absolutely ballistic. I was used to dealing with my mother's controlling tendencies, but I had never witnessed her in a state such as the one she got herself into after I mentioned the Marines. It was intense. I usually didn't get into arguments with her, preferring to stay out of her way while going about my own business, but this time was different. She was in my face. She wouldn't leave me alone about it, so I suggested a compromise—joining the Air Force.

It was a good move on my part.

I made out like I thought she was worried about my safety. I knew that wasn't the real reason she didn't want me in the military, but I acted like it was the only possible problem she might have with my plans. Then I could see her calculating, wondering what she should say next.

"Jason, you need to go to school."

"No Mom, I don't."

"Everyone needs to go to college."

"Well, I'm not everyone."

"Why do you want to ruin your life in the military?"

"I don't consider the defense of this country to be ruining my life."

"Well, I do."

"Mom, please. I'm going. Just let it go."

After that I walked out of the room, thanking God that she didn't follow me.

We continued to have such conversations at least once a month during my senior year. But at least she wasn't screaming in my face anymore, even if she did spend some time saying there was no way I was getting her to sign anything. I was eighteen by the time I mentioned my plan. I didn't remind her that I no longer needed her permission, though.

I used to complain to Brad about all of this on a daily basis. That's probably how Michelle got the idea about Mom's expensive taste. She and Jeremy moved out of the neighborhood when I left for basic training after Mom got her promotion. She'd been working for the university over the state line for ten years, since right before my father walked out. She liked the idea of living in an upscale neighborhood, and even though Jeremy had never known any other home, she uprooted him anyway. My father had paid for our school tuition. He paid for everything. But he moved halfway across the country after he left, and Jeremy hardly remembered him.

* * *

By the time Michelle left for school, both of us knew we were seeing each other exclusively, even though nothing was ever mentioned about it. Like I said, there were certain things between us that didn't need to be spoken of, and this was one of them. We were together, that's all. It just *was*.

She didn't tell her parents that we were a couple until the morning of her departure. She said she wanted to spend what time she could with me, and that she didn't want her mom insisting on me eating dinner over there three times a week like she used to, or her father and I spending hours out in his garage looking my motorcycle over to make sure it was running all right. I wanted to pick her up at home the night following our reunion, but Michelle insisted that she wanted to have me to herself, just for that one week. She was adamant about it, so I went along with her, though I felt a little funny meeting her down at the diner every night. She smuggled clothes out of the house to change into because her parents thought she was working a few final shifts that week. When I mentioned that she wasn't the type to be able to deceive anyone, she laughed at me.

"If you consider this deception, what would you call the fact that I spent every day for the past five years thinking about the possibility of us getting together, and no one else knows anything about it? Not even Bella."

I could understand this. No one knew about my feelings for her, either. So I waited every night while she changed out of her work clothes in the diner bathroom before we left to go out. She had good taste in clothes and jewelry. Her clothes were formfitting but nothing too skimpy, the way some girls tended to dress, and she always wore heels.

Michelle's parents thought she was working, but what we did instead was just talk. I took her out for dinner every night. Sometimes just for pizza or a hamburger at Diesel's, but twice we went out for steak and lobster—one night in Philadelphia. I insisted. I hadn't had a good steak in four years. That was what I wanted to eat, and Michelle didn't argue; she liked steak, too. We talked for hours, just catching up. She told me about her high school years, and I recounted a few things about my Air Force service, though not everything. She asked me what I had thought about during my time away.

"Lots of things."

"Did you think about me?"

I hesitated, not wanting her to know what I'd been thinking during that first year.

"I was missing you, Michelle. You know that."

"I thought about you every day. Brad wasn't around to get information out of, so I just remembered a few things and hoped for the best. I said a Rosary for you every Friday."

"Well, I needed those prayers. Thank you, babe."

My reunion with Michelle's parents took place at church a few weeks after she left for school. I wasn't in the habit of going to Mass every week, but that Saturday night I decided to go, since I had some time to kill before meeting Reese and Lucio at Diesel's. Brad's old man nodded at me as he ambled back to his seat after Holy Communion. I nodded back, wondering what he'd have to say about Michelle and myself. The old man was a tough customer. Brad and I had never gotten away with anything under his watch.

After Mass I greeted Father Gallucio, whom I'd known since kindergarten, and then waited for Michelle's parents. The old man came down the steps of St. Catherine's with a smile on his face. I thought it was a good sign. Michelle's mother was surprised to see me. She hadn't noticed me during Mass.

"Jason, welcome home!" she exclaimed, giving me a hug. "How are you?"

It was nice to receive such a welcome after the one my own mother had given me, which was a quick hello on her way out the door to meet people from work for a drink.

"Fine thank you, Mrs. Davis. How have you been?"

The old man shook my hand before taking a pack of Lucky Strikes out of his shirt pocket and lighting one. He offered me the pack.

"Jack," Michelle's mother warned, "you're not encouraging the boys to smoke, are you?"

"He's not a boy, Marie."

I shook my head as he gestured again with the cigarettes.

"Thanks, no. I'm not smoking." *Right now, anyway.*

He knew damn well I smoked. He just wanted to see what would happen if he offered me one in front of his wife. But I hadn't smoked around Michelle before she left for school, and I didn't want her mother telling her she saw me smoking, even if it was with her dad.

"Your Harley's waiting for you," the old man said, exhaling smoke as we walked down the street. "Are you coming to pick it up?"

"Jason, come for supper tomorrow. Johnny and Cindy and the boys are coming. I'm making lasagna." My stomach growled.

"What time?" I asked. I was back in the family, just like that.

* * *

Dinner the next day was just like old times. We ate in the kitchen. They always did, unless it was a holiday. In addition to lasagna, there was roast chicken, salad, and Italian bread. It seemed the polar opposite of the way I'd been eating for the past four years.

After everyone asked about my time away, talk around the table turned to Michelle's departure for school and her conversations with her mother and Cindy about her first few weeks there.

"She likes it—she says her roommate is okay," said Cindy, Michelle's sister-in-law. "I told her not to worry about that; Michelle can get along with anyone."

Cindy looked the same as she had the last time I'd seen her. She had dark Mediterranean good looks, big brown eyes, and a low throaty voice. *Well, maybe not quite the same. She had another kid. But so what if she's a little heavier? She's still pretty. Cindy's still got it going on. She's hot for an older chick.*

Cindy scraped the tray of the high chair beside her. Her little boy, Jamie, had been picking up pieces of chicken off the tray and throwing them at five-year-old Junior.

"Michelle worries too much," said Johnny. "She'll be fine." Johnny smacked Junior's hand down on the table, as he raised it in preparation for throwing a piece of bread at his brother. Junior grinned across the table at me. He was missing his two front teeth. It gave him a mischievous look. *Cute kid. Nice family. Too bad Johnny's going bald.* I put my eyes back on my plate then, but not before I saw Brad's old man looking down the table sideways at me.

"Michelle likes her classes. She thinks she'll be able to pass all of them if the workload doesn't overwhelm her," said Mrs. Davis. "Junior, come out from under the table." She laughed, pushing her plate away and lifting her grandson onto her lap. Her dark eyes sparkled at Junior, who smiled back in an angelic fashion before making a face at his brother, who was still confined in the high chair. Mrs. Davis didn't notice, but the old man did. He threw Junior a look. *He hasn't changed a bit. Never misses a thing. And Mrs. Davis hasn't changed either.*

Michelle and Brad's mother had always seemed exactly like the mom in any number of old TV shows. Always in the house, cooking or cleaning or baking, or else down at St. Catherine's, our old grade school. And always, always smiling. The old man was the one who'd taken care of the discipline.

"Well, I hope Michelle has more of a social life at college than she did in high school," Johnny commented. "All she did was study and work and go to church for the past four years, except for the prom." I could see him shaking his head out of the corner of my eye.

I'd already seen the photo of Michelle in her prom dress. She looked like a model. Another picture sat on the sideboard next to the one of Michelle alone; a picture of her with her date, who happened to be Joey Riley. Jealousy had flared when I noticed it, but I put it out of my mind when I recalled a conversation from the previous week.

Joey's brother, Mike, had been in my class at St. Bonaventure. Mike was currently finishing up an engineering degree at Penn State. We kept in touch, and I'd given him a call to let him know I was back in town. The conversation had somehow gotten around to his brother, and what Mike had told me—that Joey had transferred to Duke—set my mind at ease. I knew Joey was interested in Michelle before I left, but the news that he was now in North Carolina made me dismiss him as any serious threat to me.

Johnny was still shaking his head. "I don't understand Michelle," he went on. "She needs to get out more. I hope she meets someone at school." *I hope this conversation doesn't end with him punching my lights out.*

"Jason, what's Michelle been telling you about her social life," said the old man.

Complete silence.

I looked up from my plate and across the table. Cindy smiled at me with a knowing look in her eye. I kept quiet.

"Dad, what are you talking about?" Johnny said.

The old man was enjoying himself. I was thinking he might have set me up. In answer to Johnny he looked down the table at me and raised an eyebrow.

"Well?" he said. I had to answer him.

"Michelle has a social life," I replied, before shoveling in another forkful of lasagna. Johnny looked at me like he thought I was insane.

"When did you talk to her?" he asked.

"An hour ago." I swallowed. "She says she's coming home next weekend for her birthday."

I had already bought her gift. It was a little silver bracelet with a prayer box attached, and it hadn't come from any discount display, either. I'd driven to Philadelphia the previous weekend and bought it on Jeweler's Row.

"You spoke to Michelle?" Johnny sounded incredulous. "I called her Wednesday, and she hasn't got back to me yet. Brad must have told her you were back. I can't believe she called you."

"She didn't," I said, reaching for another piece of bread.

"You called her?"

"I've been calling her every night since she left," I said. "Can you please pass the butter?"

"Jason, what the hell are you talking about?" Johnny shoved the butter across the table at me. "Why would you be calling Michelle?"

"So she won't have to call me."

"Well, why would she have to call you?"

I finished buttering my fifth piece of bread before looking back across the table at Johnny. Everyone else was looking at him as well. His mother was trying not to laugh. He sat for another minute before finally figuring it out. He picked up his wine glass and drained it, quickly. Then he looked at his wife.

"Did you know about this?" he demanded.

"Well, not technically. But Johnny, come on, I've been telling you this for years."

I looked at Cindy, shocked. "What? What have you been telling him?"

"Never mind, Jason. Just a private disagreement between Johnny and myself; it doesn't matter now." Cindy had a smug look on her face, and mine got a little red, thinking about what she thought she knew.

The old man was still having fun with the situation. "What does Brad have to say about it?" he asked.

"Nothing. Yet."

"Well, what do you think he'll say?"

I looked up the table at him and sighed. "I guess I'll find out tonight."

After dessert I thanked Michelle's mother for dinner and said goodbye to her and Cindy. Then the old man, Johnny and I went out back and uncovered my Harley-Davidson. As we looked over the bike I glanced across the fence at the house I had lived in for nineteen years. The red brick looked exactly the same, and the trim still needed a coat of paint. The window of my old bedroom was visible directly above the cherry tree in the side yard next to the fence. Seeing the house seemed a little strange. It had been over four years. I hadn't been in the neighborhood at all, even on the occasions when I was home on leave, and after staring at my father's garage for a minute I turned away from the house. The memories of living there weren't the best ones of my life, especially the summer after graduation.

The old man told me he'd started the bike from time to time, and had put a little gas in it for me. Johnny offered to follow me over to Mom's in my truck, saying I could bring him back after I dropped off the bike. In addition to securing employment, I had looked around for a vehicle in the three weeks between my return home and my reunion with Michelle. I was driving a four-wheel drive pick-up by the time I met up with her again, and I didn't need the Harley for transportation the way I did before I left town. All the way back to Mom's, I thought about the last time I'd taken it for a ride. I recalled the memories associated with it, and for the first time I seriously considered putting it up for sale. I parked it in the driveway next to the garage, hoping Mom wouldn't give me any shit about it. It was only going to be there until I found a place to live.

On the ride back to the old man's, I was the one who was smoking. I offered my pack to Johnny, he took one and lit it, and we rode along in silence for a while.

"That bike isn't legal," he mentioned. I smoked and kept quiet. "The tags are expired," he said, exhaling smoke. He cracked the window.

"I know."

"Well, what do you plan on doing about it?" His tone was cool. "If you take Michelle out on that motorcycle, you'd better make damn sure it's legal, and that both of you are wearing helmets." He stared pointedly across the cab of the truck at me.

I got the message.

"You don't need to worry about your sister while she's with me, Johnny," I replied.

Michelle

Last night the radio priest, Father O'Neill, preached about compassion. He said compassion seems to be in short supply these days, and that the people running things now don't have enough of it. Our situation certainly proves his point.

Father O'Neil's speech is powerful. He seems undaunted by the bureaucracy as he preaches fearlessly against the new way of doing business. You don't hear many talk the way he does these days. There used to be debate. Daddy used to like to listen to debate back before he got sick, but I never had time for it myself.

Debate is a thing of the past, anyway. Average people are too afraid to speak out, and hardly anyone protests in a media format except for a few brave souls like Father O'Neill. Even though the higher-ups still make a pretense that this is a free country, circumstances are what they are. The time for protesting has come and gone, and though there may be media figures somewhere who might finally want to speak up, they keep quiet. Most of those in media these days have only one point of view. They've been made to understand that it could be dangerous for them otherwise. After all, nobody seemed surprised when a popular radio host was found dead in her apartment in New York last winter, and she'd been in perfect health as far as anyone knew.

I miss being able to attend Mass. I'm not in a state of grace. I don't like it, even though it isn't my fault. Someday you'll be baptized, angel-baby, and I'll go to confession again. But at least we're safe. You have a chance now, and I have faith that someday when you're old enough you'll be able to read this narrative.

Sandy couldn't sleep last night and wandered down here when she heard the radio playing. She stayed with me a while and we listened. I mentioned the fact that she was overflowing with compassion for us, but she looked embarrassed and shrugged it off. Sandy isn't as talkative as her mom. But before she went back upstairs, she told me shyly that she and Mark feel as if they're doing what they're supposed to be doing right now.

I'm glad they don't mind me listening to Father O'Neill. According to the powers that be he's controversial. There are rumors to the effect that his life has been threatened, but Sandy and Mark haven't censored my listening.

I miss your daddy, angel-baby. Maybe someday, by the time you're old enough to understand, things will be different. I hope there won't be any need for you and your spouse to ever be apart, because it's hard. I miss feeling his arms around me, and his hands smoothing back my hair. There are pictures next to the bed that I brought from home, but I don't really need them; I see him in my mind's eye. The sight still makes my stomach flip flop the same way it did twenty years ago. And I wasn't the only one. Jason and I were meant to be together, but if that hadn't been the case he could have had his pick of any girl in town or the surrounding vicinity. Your father was the best looking man in that town.

In addition to what I'm writing for you, we hope to be able to tell you about the events leading up to your birth. But if we can't at least you'll be able to read about your daddy. I want you to understand the sacrifices he's made, for you and for me.

It hurts to remember the way Jason suffered. My suffering doesn't seem important now, but your daddy is still suffering. Though he never complains, I know he still suffers every day, because he's being forced to live a lie. Jason doesn't like lying.

Your daddy is my rock.

THREE

Jason
20 Years Earlier

After I dropped Johnny off at the old man's, I lit another smoke and punched Brad's number into my phone.

"Hello beautiful," he answered. I rolled my eyes.

"It's me," I said.

"Wallace? This isn't your number."

"I got a new phone."

"You're home?"

Now I knew for sure he wasn't aware of anything. "Yeah. Who's beautiful?"

"Some chick I met last night. She refused to give me her number, so I made her take mine. She's a redhead."

"What happened to the last one?"

"I lost her number."

"That's typical." I dragged smoke into my lungs.

"When did you get back?"

"A few weeks ago."

"Why didn't you call before? Come down here, we'll go out. The women are hot."

"I already started work."

"Come on. You've been gone all that time and you can't take a weekend to come down here? I'll introduce you to a couple of sorority sisters I know."

"Is your sister in a sorority?" I asked.

"Michelle...I don't know. She just started school. What's that got to do with anything?"

"What if she decides to join one?"

"What if she does? What's that got to do with you coming down here? Come on, Wallace. You can take a few days. We haven't partied in over a year. Anyway, why would you care what Michelle's doing?"

"Well, you're making it sound like a sorority house is nothing but a whorehouse, and I just wondered what your thoughts might be now that your sister left home."

"What the hell are you talking about?"

I changed the subject. "I ate at the house earlier. Your mom made lasagna."

"You bastard. I wish I could have had some. The sum total of supplies in my house right now is a fridge full of beer and half a bag of pretzels. Nobody ever restocks. We were out of TP the other day, and I didn't know it until it was too late. Nobody else was around, so I had to use my damn boxers and then toss them."

I howled with laughter. Even though I was nervous about him finding out, I couldn't let such an admission pass without ragging him a little.

"Damn, Brad. Were they the Calvin Klein ones?"

"No. They were Tommy Hilfiger. It was an old pair, but I was still pissed off about it."

I continued to howl at the image of Brad, stuck on the can without toilet paper and being forced to wipe his ass with his high end boxers.

"Shut the hell up," he snapped. "I had to do it. There was nothing else in there except Doyle's towel. It was on the floor, and he'd already used the damn thing, and I'd have wiped my ass with brand new boxers before I'd ever wipe with anything that touched Doyle."

Doyle was one of the guys who lived in Brad's dump of a house. I'd never met him, but I'd heard a lot about him, and judging from what I had heard I agreed with Brad.

"All right. But answer me this. Have you bought any underwear since?"

"No."

"Well, the next time you do are they gonna be Tommy Hilfiger, or are you gonna do what I do? Nobody sees the damn things anyway."

"Maybe nobody sees yours, but they sure as hell see mine every once in a while," he retorted. "And the next time some chick does see them, I'd prefer it if the label wasn't decorated with pictures of fruit."

"Yeah? Well I don't give a damn who sees what. And I still think it's a waste of good money. What good did it do you? They're in the dumpster now, aren't they?"

There was silence on his end, except for a little sputtering. I continued laughing. It was on the tip of my tongue to tell him that it wasn't the damn boxer shorts anyway, but the equipment underneath that mattered, and that I'd never had any complaints when it came to that. But I stopped myself.

Can't say that. Not anymore. Especially not to him. I had a feeling no one but me would have any idea about what kind of boxers I wore for a very long time. *But that's a price I'm willing to pay. What do I care? Michelle means way more than that to me.*

I changed the subject. "When are you coming up?"

"I was just up there last month," Brad replied. He still sounded a little pissed. "When are you coming down here?"

"Your sister's birthday is next weekend, so I thought you might be coming to see her."

"That's the second time you've brought up Michelle's name. Why this interest all of a sudden? And how did you know it's her birthday, anyway?"

I ignored him. "Did you buy her a gift?" I asked.

"No. I didn't buy her a gift. Not yet."

"I already got her something."

Brad was getting annoyed again. "What the hell is this? Why would you care whether or not I got something for Michelle? And why would you be buying her a birthday gift?"

I smoked and kept quiet.

"Wallace, are you there?"

"I'm here."

"Well, answer my question."

"I bought her a bracelet," I said.

"Damn it!" Brad exploded. "I don't give a flying shit what you bought her! I just want to know why."

I took a deep breath then. It was obvious he wasn't going to catch on.

"Okay. I thought you might have been able to figure it out with a couple of hints, the way Johnny did earlier, but apparently your one-track mind isn't going to allow that, so I'll just tell you straight up. Michelle and I are seeing each other."

Complete silence. Then I heard the click of his lighter as he lit a cigarette. I lit another one with the remainder of my first, and thought I could hear what was running through his mind. Brad and I had been friends for so long that sometimes we knew what the other was thinking. *Well I'll be damned. My little sister. Wallace, you son of a bitch, what the hell are you trying to pull?*

I could hear him dragging on his cigarette. By that time I was on the edge of town, driving down Main Street at the point where it turned back into Route 24, headed toward my mother's place.

"Did you hear me, Brad?"

"You're joking. Right?" He sounded incredulous.

"No, I'm not."

"You can't be serious."

"Your parents don't seem to have a problem with it."

"Is this some set up? I don't see any cameras around here, but whatever. Did Doyle put you up to this? That son of a bitch. April Fool's day is six months away."

"Brad," I said, slowly and patiently. "Listen to me. I am seeing your sister. We talk every night on the phone. I will be taking her out on the weekends when she comes home. This is a fact. Can you understand me?"

"You better watch it." Brad's voice was a little wary. Maybe even warning. "You know you don't have girlfriends. When's the last time you were ever serious about a girl?"

"I understand your misgivings," I said. "I admit I don't have the best track record with women, but Michelle is different."

"Well, if that isn't the all-time understatement of the year," he retorted. "She's different. Wallace, I don't even know what the hell you've been doing for the past four years. You never say anything. You could have been hopping from whore to whore in every country you called me from, for all I know. I know how you are."

I was determined to keep my temper. I put myself in his shoes for a minute. "You don't know as much as you think you know, if you think I'd be whore hopping."

"I didn't mean you were paying for it. I know you'd never pay for it. I'd never pay for it. But that's not the point."

That's what he knows.

He was right, except for one time. It had happened on Michelle's birthday, the October following my departure for basic training. She'd been blonde haired and blue-eyed, and I was drunk that night. I was wasted as a matter of fact, regretting my decision to leave home. A guy I was stationed with, Lawson his name was, had driven a bunch of us into town for a night out. On our way back to the base we saw her in the headlights. She was slim with long hair, wearing a short skirt and a tank top, walking along the highway about a mile from the base, almost in the middle of nowhere. Just her and the deserted two-lane road; little lights twinkling off in the distance from the Interstate on our right, the base on our left.

I could only remember a little. More lights, hanging in the sky; a cargo plane coming in for a landing. Clouds scudded across the face of the moon, sending shadows traveling. The clouds seemed to stretch far away in the sky down in Texas, not like home. *No. Not like home.*

The moon was far away. She looked sweet to me, young and innocent.

Like I said, I was drunk. When I woke up the next morning in her room in the cheap motel next to the truck stop, everything looked different. Especially her. The whole episode was a mistake. I found out I'd gotten more than I paid for a few days later, when I woke up crawling. It was the worst money I ever spent, and from that time on I stayed away from hookers, no matter how young and sweet their eyes were.

Brad's voice brought me back to the present. "Will you listen to me?"

"I am listening," I retorted. "But you shouldn't be mentioning your sister in the same breath as you mention whores. And how do I know you haven't? Paid for it, I mean. How the hell do *I* know what *you've* been doing with *yourself?*"

"Well, whatever, Wallace," he blew by me. "Makes no difference whether the two of us paid for it once or twice or not. The point is that I know damn well you go after a piece every once in a while. And I know the type you go after, too."

"Since you know all that, I guess you also know I like to keep a few things to myself from time to time." Brad had a tendency to give me too much information about his sexual escapades sometimes, but that didn't mean I had to reciprocate.

"Well if you're gonna be seeing my sister, there better be more than one thing you're keeping to yourself."

I kept quiet for a moment or two. I was driving past a few outlying houses on the very outskirts of town, and then that empty place on the right, where they were planning to build a park. *All right. I guess he thinks he needs to know every damn thing, the same as usual. Well, okay Brad. You asked for it.*

"Look," I said shortly. "I'll say it straight up, but only this once. After this, you better not ask me again." I took another drag on my smoke. "I have had feelings for your sister since before I left. Those feelings were reciprocated. I put my feelings aside because I knew she was too young. I tried to forget her. But it didn't happen, and now that she'll be eighteen in a week, I'm planning to have a relationship with her. She is interested as well, and as long as she is, we're going to be seeing each other."

"Since when? Before you left...do you mean to tell me you and Michelle have been—"

"No." I cut him off. "I said we had feelings for each other. Neither of us acted on them."

I listened to him dragging. Exhaling. Muttering and cussing under his breath. "I can't believe this shit. You? I swear... have you been in contact with her since you left?"

"I already told you. I put her out of my mind. What the hell's the matter with you? I wasn't going to let myself rob the cradle, especially with your sister, you idiot. But now things are different. She's old enough to make up her own mind now." I dragged on my Lucky Strike, before adding: "Your brother already warned me earlier."

More silence. I could imagine how Brad looked at that moment. His jaw was probably hanging down to his chest.

"The old man knows about this?" he asked, finally.

"He's known for weeks. Michelle told both your parents the day she left for school."

"And he's okay with it?"

"I don't know. I never asked him. He invited me to eat dinner at his table today, so I think he probably is, but I couldn't say for sure."

I pulled into my mother's neighborhood then. The houses all looked alike.

"All right," Brad replied, after another few minutes. "I'll go along with it. But you better keep yourself in line."

"Just give me the benefit of the doubt for a while," I said. I refrained from mentioning that I didn't care whether he went along with it or not. Instead, I decided to put him on defense for a while. "That brunette you were telling me about last time we talked," I mentioned. "You know, the one whose number you just said got lost? Was she beautiful? Like the redhead?"

"Yeah. She was."

He doesn't know who he's messing with.

"Is she as beautiful as your sister?"

Silence. I pulled into my mother's driveway, parked the truck and shut off the engine, before going on to ask innocently, "Brad... do you ever wonder if she might have a brother?" I heard him light another cigarette. He continued to keep quiet, and so did I. But finally he gave a reluctant answer.

"Yeah. I think about that kind of thing from time to time."

"Well, have you ever made the acquaintance of some chick's brother?"

"As a matter of fact I have. The redhead I met last night was out with her brother and his wife. He was a big son of a bitch."

"Is she still beautiful?"

"She may be beautiful..." His voice trailed off. "Yeah. She's definitely beautiful, especially her legs. But now that I think about it, maybe I'm too busy with school right now to really get involved with anyone."

* * *

A couple of weeks later I moved out of my mother's house. My new apartment was in an old brick building with dark creepy stairwells at the corner of Lockhart and Vine, five blocks away from the garage. It had a small bedroom, a tiny galley kitchen, a microscopic living room and a bathroom with fixtures from the 1950s. In addition to a weight set that I picked up used, it was furnished with a bed, a stereo, a broken down couch, a coffee table with three legs, and a couple of lamps. That was it. I didn't even have a television. The only thing I ever watched anyway was sports, and I could do that at Diesel's. I went to the bar almost every night to shoot pool with Reese.

The neighborhood was a little seedy, but at least I could afford to live there. Parking was free in that part of town, so I didn't need to worry about the truck, and I parked the Harley at the garage; Ceej didn't care. I could walk to work and the bars, and any place would have been a relief to me after the strain I endured while staying with Mom.

Brad did give me the benefit of the doubt—for the most part anyway —though I knew from things Michelle told me that he questioned her about me from time to time. He was keeping his eye on me, but since I treated Michelle differently than any other girl, he finally just gave up and accepted the fact that we were together.

She usually drove home once or twice a month on weekends, and we'd go out on Saturday night. I took her out to dinner or to the movies, and sometimes we'd hang out at Diesel's with Bella and Lucio, and Reese and whatever girl he happened to be running with at the time. We'd all been friends since we were kids. Lucio and Reese had played high school football together. The six of us sat around drinking beer and keeping an eye on whatever game happened to be on at the time, all except Michelle. She stuck to soda, and I always made sure she was home by one a.m.

Every once in a while, I'd drive to Rocky River, but I didn't make a habit of it.

At first Michelle wanted me to drive up every other weekend. She said she wanted to see more of me, and that she wanted her friends to get to know me. I did take a ride up on the Harley—it was legal again—for homecoming weekend. We went to the football game, which her school lost, and we went to a couple of parties. I'd already decided I wouldn't be paying her many visits at school, though. It was better for both of us if I had the safety of Michelle's family between us.

I was determined not to push her into anything. I knew she was the only woman for me, but what I didn't trust was whether or not she knew I was the one for her. I wanted her to make sure she knew what she was getting into, even though I heard a couple of things from Brad that led me to believe Michelle had known what she wanted for years, the same way I had.

Brad still got a little pissed off about the situation from time to time. He got drunk one night and decided to call me at one o'clock in the morning. In addition to forgetting it was the middle of the night, he also forgot he'd agreed to trust me with his sister, because he started in on me about Michelle and wouldn't shut up. What he said made me feel terrible.

He told me flat out that he wanted me to know that Michelle hadn't had much of a social life in high school. That she'd spent a lot of time alone, and hadn't played any sports or gone to any dances except her senior prom. And that even the prom couldn't have been too much fun for her, considering that she attended it with that little punk, Joey Riley.

"That little punk," Brad repeated, his words slurred. "I don't like that little creepy-assed jerk, but at least he took her to her prom. What the hell have you ever done for her except make her miserable for years?"

I decided to ignore his last question, hoping he would forget he had asked it. He was pretty boozed up. "What are you drinking?" I asked.

"The usual. You know damn well I only drink Jack. Why do you care?"

"I don't. I just wondered. Since you seem to be taking a page out of Joey's book, I figured you might be drinking what he used to drink. You know, wine coolers. Strawberry kiwi ones."

"Screw you, Wallace."

"Brad, did you really wake me up in the middle of the night just to tell me that Joey's a jerk?" I yawned. "Because you didn't need to. I already know he's a little stuck-up prick. I've known it for years. Can I go back to sleep now?"

"No. I can't sleep right now, so why should you be able to?"

"Well, I'd like to get some sleep right now because I just got off the phone with your sister an hour ago, and I have to work tomorrow. Is that a good enough reason for you?" He ignored my question then, and went back to his original rant.

"Michelle was one of the nicest girls in that school. She was one of the cutest too, and all she ever did was study and work, the whole four years. She could have at least played volleyball, or run cross-country, or *something*. But no. All she did was go to school, go home, do homework, and moon about you in her room."

"How do you know that?" I yawned again.

"Just because I wasn't living in the house, doesn't mean I didn't know what was going on in it."

"Don't tell me this. Tell me she at least had some friends," I said.

"Yeah, she had friends. Michelle always has friends. But she didn't run around with them all the time back then, not the way she should have. She spent way too much time around the house."

"Well, why didn't you talk to her about it?"

"I did," he admitted. "She told me to mind my own business."

"Well, I'm sorry," I retorted, "but there was no way for me to know about that."

I refrained from mentioning that I had told Michelle in no uncertain terms to forget about me before I left.

"I even brought it up in front of Mom once," Brad went on. "We were sitting at the table during Christmas break, and I asked Michelle what she was doing that week. She told me she was gonna get a head start on her senior project, and I blew up at her. I asked her what the hell she was thinking. She was only a freshman. She had three years to get the damn thing done." He paused for a minute, remembering. "I couldn't figure her out at the time, but now it all makes sense. She got up crying and ran out of the kitchen, and Mom told me to keep my opinions to myself."

I cringed inwardly. The last thing I would ever have wanted was for Michelle to have cried over me. I hated the thought.

"I had no intention of anything like that ever happening."

"And that's supposed to make it all right? What the hell were you doing that year, while my sister was crying in her bedroom?"

"Damn it Brad, I'm sorry, but I can't do anything about it now. And she got over it, right?" My voice was hopeful. "She didn't cry for the whole four years, did she?"

"No. Lucky for you she didn't. If she had I'd kick your sorry ass for you right this minute, you son of a bitch." I refrained from reminding Brad of the fact that we were on the phone, and Tennessee was five states away. "Wallace, I'm seriously pissed off at you right now," he went on. "I know damn well you weren't spending your free time crying."

I didn't answer him. He didn't need to know that he was only half right.

"Are you listening to me?" he snapped. He sounded more pissed than he had been, but by that time I'd had enough.

"All right." I snapped back. "Enough of this bullshit. I have no intention of telling you how I was spending my time that year, free or otherwise. That was four years ago. Why are you bringing it up now? Michelle's happy."

"I know Michelle's happy," he shot back.

"Then why the hell won't you let me sleep?"

"I don't freaking know, okay?" His words were still slurry. I kept quiet, hoping he was going to shut up, but after a minute he went on to say it again. "It just frosts me. It pisses me off."

"Well, you're pissing me off now. I have to be at work by eight o'clock. I need to get some sleep. So get over it. Do you hear me? Because I don't want to hear this shit again." I hung up.

Two weeks later, on Valentine's Day, I paid Michelle another visit at school. It had snowed almost every weekend since New Year's, and she hadn't been driving back and forth from school because of the road conditions.

At dinner that night I gave her a heart-shaped pendant on a silver chain. It had cost me two hundred and fifty bucks at my favorite store on Jewelers Row.

"Thank you!" Michelle beamed at me from across the table. "It's so pretty." She took the necklace from its velvet box and fastened it around her neck.

"You're welcome, honey," I said.

She'd already given me a CD I had mentioned, *Led Zeppelin III*. I had a large collection of compact discs, most of them classic rock. I spent a lot of time listening to music while I lifted weights.

After we had finished eating I asked her what she'd like to do next.

"I don't know," she smiled. "Maybe we can go sledding."

"Do you know where we can get a sled?" I asked, taking her seriously.

"No," she said, laughing. "And I don't care what we do. Or if we do anything. I'm just happy you came." Her hair shimmered in the candlelight. I wanted to reach across the table and run my hand through it, but instead I brought up what had been on my mind ever since the phone call with Brad.

"Michelle, what would you be doing right now if you weren't out with me?"

"What do you mean?"

"Just what I said."

"Why are you asking me that?"

She stared across the table with a puzzled look on her face, and I answered her question with more of my own. "Michelle, are you having fun at school? Are you doing everything everyone else is doing? Tell me the truth, honey."

"What has gotten into you?" She sounded annoyed.

"Nothing. I just want to make sure you're having a good time at school. I don't want you to miss out on things the way you did in high school."

"Who says I missed out on anything?"

"I'm not an idiot. I know the way things stood after I left, and I don't want you missing out again because of me."

"Jason, let's get out of here. We need to talk."

We were alone in her room. The whole dorm seemed deserted. Her roommate had been able to get a ride home for the weekend, and the only other person we saw in the building was some guy who had passed out in the lounge.

"Where is everyone?" I asked.

"Out partying."

"Do you want to go? Come on, I'll take you wherever you want. You should be at a party on Valentine's Day."

I reached my hand back over my shoulder. She was sitting on her bed, and I was sitting at her feet on the floor, leaning against it.

"Jason," she said, taking my hand. "I don't want to be at a party. I want to be right where I am."

"Are you sure Michelle?" I stared straight ahead at the closet door.

"Of course I'm sure."

The bed shifted as she put her arms around my neck. "I don't want to be at any party," she whispered in my ear. "I'm telling you the truth. I only want you. I've wanted to be with you since I was a little girl and you know it. Please don't do this. Why are you doing this now?"

"I don't know." My voice was a hoarse whisper. "I'm just worried that you're not getting the full experience you should. You only go to college once, and I don't want you to regret anything later."

"I'm not going to regret anything later," she whispered, kissing my cheek and hugging me. Then her tone changed. "I don't have any regrets now, either, no matter what my big-mouthed brother thinks. And don't start covering for him either. You're not the only one who isn't an idiot. Brad needs to start minding his own business. His track record hasn't been exactly stellar, you know. There are probably more girls out there who hate Brad's guts than there are in this whole building." Her hand waved to illustrate her point. The nails were long and perfectly manicured.

"You're sure?" My tone was low.

"Jason, please. I know my own mind, now stop this. We're wasting the evening talking about nothing. Brad's a jackass."

My relief was indescribable. *Thank you God.*

"Okay, baby," I said. "As long as you have no doubts. Now let's go."

"Now? We just got here."

"I know, but I think we should go for a ride before I have to leave to drive home."

"Jason, I already told you that Kim went home. You can stay here tonight."

I leaned my head back then, took her by the hand and pulled her down on the floor next to me. I put my arms around her and buried my face in her neck for a minute.

"No. Come on now. We're going for a ride." Her face was between my hands then. The blue was intense, and I don't know how long we stared at each other, but it was fine with me—I wanted to be lost for a while. I thought I could hear water flowing, very far away.

I can't stay with you tonight, baby. You know that.

You can sleep on my bed and I'll sleep on Kim's. It'll be fine.

I ran my hands through her hair as I kissed her, and she had her hands on the stubble that had grown on my face since morning. It was intense while it lasted, but after a minute or two she was looking at me again.

No Michelle. You might know it'll be fine, but I don't. And we can't. We can't have any regrets.

After a little while we took a ride in my truck. When we pulled into the mall near her school I noticed the movie playing. It was some chick-flick she'd spoken about on the phone. I knew she wanted to see it, so I bought the tickets and sat through the damn thing with her. She watched the movie, and I thought about my good luck, when I wasn't wondering how much longer I could stand staying out of her bed.

The movie ended at one o'clock. We listened my new CD on the way back. I parked the truck, and as we walked back to her building she asked me—again—if I would please quit smoking.

"I worry about your health," she said quietly.

"Honey, you know I don't smoke much. Only a pack a week."

It was true. I had cut down. I took her back inside the lobby of her dorm then, and kissed her goodbye.

FOUR

Michelle

Dear Holy Mother. Thank you for your prayers. Please continue to intercede for our family, and ask your Son, the Savior of this world, to keep us hidden if it's His will.

There are bookshelves here in the basement, and Patty says I'm welcome to read anything I want. I paw through stacks of old *National Geographics*, cookbooks, *Readers Digest* condensed books, an old copy of *Gone with the Wind*, and a *Complete Shakespeare*. There are lots of children's books that belonged to Sandy. Her favorites seem to have been the *Little House* books and *Nancy Drew* mysteries. I leaf through the Shakespeare, feeling as if our story could be considered a modern tragedy.

A tragedy, not a comedy, though our lives used to be filled with laughter. Before the advent of the new way of doing business, our family was always laughing, especially Daddy. Will someone read our tragedy someday? Years from now, will people realize that things used to be different? That families worked and played and prayed and watched fireworks together in the summertime? Will something deep inside their hearts tell them there was once another way? A better way, filled with safety, love, freedom, happiness and babies.

Will you know, angel? Will you know you were wanted? And prayed for, cried over, protected and hidden? Sometimes I feel like I'm losing my mind. The pages are blurred with my tears, and I find myself crouching against the wall, trying not to scream, wondering how this can be happening.

How can this be? How can it be that I am alone with my baby in a basement?

Jason
17 Years Earlier

It was New Years Eve of Michelle's senior year of college.

We were still together, she was still beautiful, I was still working at the garage, and we were still in love. *Love.* That's what it was, even though neither of us had actually mentioned the word.

I had kept the gap in our ages at the forefront of my mind for the past three years, since she was so much younger than me. The last thing I wanted after loving Michelle for years would have been for her to be with me and then realize she'd made a mistake.

But as the fall of that year slowly turned into winter, I had found my perspective shifting. Michelle was twenty-one years old. She wasn't too young anymore, and I decided I'd spent enough nights standing in a cold shower, telling myself to wait. *I'm ready to take it to the next level, and she's gonna know that before this night's out.*

Brad had come home for Christmas, and he decided to have a party on New Year's Eve since Michelle's parents were away on a cruise. He invited a bunch of our high school classmates.

Bella and Lucio were currently on again. They were there that night, along with Reese and his new girlfriend, Heather. Heather was two years younger than Reese. She'd been a cheerleader at Kennedy

High School, same as Bella. Heather and Michelle had been friends for years, even though they had attended different schools, and Heather hadn't gone to college. She worked as a nurse's aide in the old folks home just outside of town. Heather was cute, with reddish-blonde hair and smiling hazel eyes set off by glasses. She was short and curvy, maybe even a little chubby, but only in all the right places.

Mike Riley stopped in for a while that night. It was good to see him, but I was relieved to hear that Joey wasn't in town. He'd graduated from Duke, and was living in North Carolina, and he hadn't come home for Christmas.

Brad kept in touch with the girls in our class and he invited at least fifteen of them that evening, since he happened to be unattached at the moment. The situation seemed to annoy Michelle. She and Bella and Heather had been giving Brad the eye all evening long.

"Brad's not going to be fit to live with tomorrow," Michelle mentioned to me later. "Did you see the way they were hanging on his every word? You'd think some of them would have learned by now, especially Caroline Frangione. I can't believe she's even here. I thought she had better sense than to try to get involved with Brad again."

I made no comment.

It was twelve-thirty a.m. After everyone had toasted the New Year, I kissed Michelle under the mistletoe, and the two of us went upstairs to sit beside the fireplace in the living room next to the Christmas tree. We were alone. Michelle was wearing the gift I had given her for Christmas, another necklace. This one was a diamond eternity circle on a silver chain. She asked where I had gotten my taste in jewelry, and I shrugged. I didn't know how to tell her that I had no taste. Whenever I bought Michelle something I depended on the jeweler to point me in the right direction.

As I sat on the floor listening to Michelle's lilting voice, I decided to propose the following Christmas. *She'll be finished school by then, and I have a year to save up for the ring.* Michelle continued talking, but I was lost in my own thoughts. Suddenly she brought me back to reality.

"Jason?" She smiled and snapped her fingers in front of my face. "Where are you? You're awfully quiet tonight."

I grabbed her hand in answer and pulled her across the floor to me. Nobody else was around. They were all too busy partying it up downstairs.

Somebody turned up the music. Noise from the pool table drifted up the stairwell along with Brad's voice, sweet-talking the girls. Reese and Lucio and a few other guys had been playing beer pong for the past hour and a half and substituting shots of bourbon for the beer. Their drunken laughter reached our ears.

I hadn't joined the game. I had indulged in five shots of whiskey before deciding it was time for Michelle and I to have our own private party upstairs, though, and I was half drunk myself.

"Baby, why's your hair up tonight?" I reached behind her and removed the clip. The hair spilled over her shoulders. "It's wintertime," I said, smiling. "Can't you leave it down? I love looking at your hair." *And that's not all.*

She had no chance to answer; I was kissing her then. Her kisses were sweet. I ran my hands through her long hair the way I always did, as she put her hands on my face and rubbed her fingers back and forth over my beard. *Okay, this is it. I'm saying it.*

"Michelle, honey, I want you to know something."

The fire crackled and popped. A shower of sparks spit out on the hearth, and the light flickered over her face. The diamond circle glittered on her chest.

"I love you, Michelle."

I've loved you forever. I always have and I always will. I had never said the words before. Not to any woman. She reached her arms around me then and put her head on my shoulder, still keeping quiet. The fact that she made no answer should have clued me in, but Brad wasn't the only one with a one-track mind.

I got up off the floor, pulled her up to stand next to me, and leaned her against the wall next to the tree. I was kissing her again in the usual manner, but it wasn't enough. Not for me anyway.

"Let's go upstairs now." She stiffened in my arms. "I've never been in your room here. Come on, show it to me." Her eyes stared back, blue and clear. Maybe a little scared. *Maybe...or maybe I'm just drunk.* I gestured toward the stairs in the hallway. Christmas lights and holly had been wrapped around the banisters.

I began kissing her neck again before leaning my hands against the wall on either side of her. She shrank back as I muttered, thickly, "Come on baby, I want to see your room. Let's go while we have the chance." I took her hand and pulled her toward the hall. That was when it went the other way.

She wouldn't move. I gestured toward the stairs with a nod of my head, but she backed away.

"Come on Michelle," I said again. "Show me your bedroom."

"We can't, Jason," she choked out, before bursting into tears.

* * *

Fifteen minutes later I was no longer half drunk. I sobered up quickly while dealing with her hysterics. Well, that's an exaggeration. Not hysterics. Just tears.

"We can't do this," she sobbed, clinging to me.

"Michelle. I thought you knew how I felt about you."

"I do."

"Honey, stop crying. You know how much I want to be with you. Nothing will happen; I promise I'll be careful." She shook her head against my chest. "Baby, come on. If you're worried about getting pregnant, stop. That won't happen. I know what I'm doing."

We were still standing behind the tree, but I wasn't particularly worried about anyone overhearing us. I was on the edge. "Michelle, come on," I repeated, hugging her. "You can trust me. I can't take it anymore. Just trust me.

"I do trust you."

"Then let's go."

"Jason, no. Stop it. I thought you understood. I thought we were on the same page."

"What page," I murmured, though by that time I had figured it out. *I should have known better. Shouldn't have had that last shot.* But it was too late. My girl was crying on New Year's Eve, and I was the cause of the upset.

"Forget it Michelle," I said. "Stop crying. We'll wait a couple of weeks; you can stay at my place next time you're home. That'll be better. We just won't tell your dad."

"No. Now please listen to me." She took a breath and steadied her voice. "I know how you feel about me, and you know I feel the same about you. I love you and I always have. I've known you were the one for me since I was little. But I'm not going to sleep with you now."

Her voice was muffled against my shoulder. I was quiet then, as some of the thoughts I'd had about her, about *us,* continued running through my mind. I cussed Reese under my breath. *That son of a bitch, I know he's getting it.*

He'd mentioned a few things at work. Brad had also mentioned a few things, but only one of them had to do with Caroline Frangione, and that was his comment about her butt, which in his opinion was way too big now. Brad liked his women stick skinny, looking like those waif models, and Caroline had put on about ten pounds since high school. Michelle didn't need to be worried on that score. Brad had no interest in Caroline. He'd already had her, years ago, and she didn't mean anything to him now.

What the hell just happened? Why did I decide to try this tonight? Happy freaking New Year.

Michelle wanted to wait, but in my opinion we had waited long enough. *Damn it, she's not going to give it up. What the hell am I supposed to do now?*

I made sure her head was against my shoulder. I didn't want her to see my face as frustrated thoughts ran through my mind. *I can't frigging stand this anymore. I haven't had any in over three years. I'm going insane. Cold showers suck. Why can't she just give it up?*

For a minute I thought about breaking up with her because I didn't know how the hell I would get through another two years. But the thought was short-lived. I could never let her go.

She's the love of my life. I'll have to suck it up and wait. I guess I'm whipped. Yeah. That's it...whipped. But the hell with it—I don't care if I am.

Michelle was special. She loved me but she wanted to wait, and I should never have tried to strong-arm her. She meant everything to me. It was another fact, another certainty, something else that just *was*.

It was a conviction.

* * *

The winter passed slowly. It was a nasty one. Reese and I walked two miles down the railroad tracks in the bitter cold almost every Friday night to the pond where we played pick-up ice hockey. The games had been going on every winter for years. I went Saturdays too, if Michelle wasn't in town. I played hard. One night I took a stick in the side of the head and ended up with twelve stitches. My conviction stayed with me. I worked hard, played hard, drank hard, and took a lot of cold showers. I stayed off cigarettes. Michelle and I were happy.

* * *

Summer passed. Michelle was back home at the old man's. She'd completed her semester of student teaching and finished school, earning a Bachelor-of-Arts degree. After graduation she began applying for teaching positions, and I reconsidered my original decision and decided to take a few classes myself, though not the kind my mother had in mind. I just wanted to keep up with advancing technology, and diesel mechanics. CJ gave me flexibility at work so I could attend classes. Tech school was an hour away, but Ceej let me choose my own hours, as long as I put in forty. That was the year I started working late on Tuesday and Thursday nights and all day on Saturday.

With the arrival of September, life became busier. Bella and Lucio were married that fall, and Brad and I were both groomsmen. We treated the experience like one big party. Everyone had a great time, but later my attitude came back to haunt me. Michelle was maid of honor, and to me she outshone the bride, even though Bella looked terrific except for the fact that her dress was a little tight.

After the wedding I figured things would settle down a little, but then Ceej ended up in the hospital. The accident happened at his place. He was up on a ladder cleaning the guttering when his foot slipped. Lucky for him he grabbed the edge of the roof, and a flowerbed broke the fall. It could have been worse, but he was forced to be away from the shop for six weeks while he recovered from surgery. Danny, who was second in command at the garage, was having some personal problems at the time. He wasn't able to take charge like he would have in normal circumstances, so Reese and I, who'd been with them longer than anyone else, were given sudden promotions.

The two of us had been employed at the garage on and off since we were kids, and we knew how they ran the operation. Running the place took up almost all our time, though. The money was good, and so was the business experience, but I was glad Ceej was well by December so we could hand the reins back to him. I was a little out of shape by that time, and I was relieved when I could get back to my regular routine of lifting four nights a week, in addition to seeing Michelle when her work schedule would permit it.

Michelle was back working at the diner until her new job as a teacher began in January. I still planned to propose at Christmas, but with everything that happened I had put off getting the ring, and by the time CJ came back and my schedule opened up, it was only a week away.

My mother tried to talk me out of it. I made the mistake of thinking she might give me some advice on choosing the ring, and I regretted telling her before the words were out of my mouth. She was looking at me as if I had two heads.

"Why in the world would you want to get married now?"

"Mom, what are you talking about? Michelle and I have been together for four years. Why in the world wouldn't I?"

"But Jason, you haven't even bought a house." Mom shook her head. Her dark shiny hair was cut short. It looked good. My mother was a nice looking woman, always had been. "You're still working at the garage. How are you going to afford it?"

I sighed. *Can't she just be happy for me? Just once?*

I smiled apprehensively. "I really would like your advice. What kind of ring would you suggest? What kind did—" I stopped. The words hung in the air. *What kind of engagement ring did Dad give you?* She didn't catch it. I could read her face like a book, and she was still calculating, trying to figure a way to talk me out of it. *Mom, you'd be beautiful if you smiled. Why can't you be happy?*

"Michelle is too young to get married, and so are you. You should wait. You need a better job and a house before you get married."

"Mom. Quit it. You know I'm staying at CJ's. And we'll buy a house when we feel the time is right. We both have careers."

"Your brother is in school," she said, looking at me strangely. "He's getting an education, even if it isn't at the school where I'm employed. And you should too, before it's too late. Working in a garage is not a career. You need to go to college so you can get a decent job. I've told you that for years. You need to apply now. For God's sake Jason, you could go for free! And even if I weren't working at the university, you could go on the GI Bill. What's the matter with you?"

I kept quiet. I was still busting my ass in tech school and she knew it, but I decided not to bring it up. *Won't do any good. There's no reasoning with her.*

"Michelle has a bachelor's degree, even if it is only from that state school." Her unspoken words hovered. *That backwater state school...* Her voice rose steadily. "You need to put this nonsense about getting married out of your mind. You had high SAT scores, Jason. You had good grades! You'd probably be accepted at an Ivy League school if you tried, even with your military service on your record, and look at you! Wasting everything. How do you think I feel at work, telling people what you do for a living? How do you think it makes me feel to have to admit that you work at a garage and live in a one-bedroom apartment? You need a master's degree. Or at least a bachelor's; everyone does. Nobody can be anything without a college degree. Even Michelle, as unsophisticated as she is, has a bachelor's degree. Even your father had a degree. Never mind that it was only from Penn State—" She broke off then. The atmosphere in the room could have been cut with a knife.

Well, there's nothing new here. Same shit, different day. She always looks like she's seeing someone else—not me at all. What the hell is her problem?

"Listen, Mom." My tone was clipped. "I'm proposing to Michelle on Christmas Day. If she wants to wait a while to get married we'll wait, but as far as I'm concerned we're getting married in the spring. I have to be going now. I have things to do." She sat stiffly as I kissed her cheek. "Tell Jeremy I'll talk to him at Christmas. Goodbye." *We're getting married this spring. If I have to wait much longer I'll go crazy.*

* * *

Brad had a new girlfriend. Her name was Nicole, she was a Memphis native, and she was the one who ended up helping me pick out the ring. She and Brad had met the previous spring at the gym, and he brought her home for Christmas that year to meet the family.

I was a little surprised when he actually showed up with her. Brad had always played the field. No relationship ever lasted any longer than three months with him, so I thought the visit would probably be cancelled for some reason or other. It wasn't, though, and after I met Nicole I could understand why. Except for the fact that I considered her to be too skinny, she was almost as good looking as Michelle.

She had long, curly brown hair and big brown eyes. She looked Italian, though I found out later that she wasn't of Italian descent. Nicole was descended from French roots, with a little Cherokee thrown into the mix. She was cute and petite, with a pretty olive complexion. She had a wicked sense of humor, she spoke with a southern accent, and Brad seemed completely infatuated with her. It was an amazing thing to see; something I'd never witnessed before from Brad and never thought I would.

Looks like Brad's as whipped as I am—for the moment, anyway. I wasn't sure it would last. Brad was too fickle. But Nicole *was* cute. *She's hot, even if she is too skinny. And she has perfect teeth.* Brad had always gone after women with perfect teeth.

Sunday dinner was over. Michelle and I were on our way to pick up ice cream at the convenience store for dessert.

"I like Nicole," she said. "To me she came across as a southern belle from the toe of the boot." She was referring to southern Italy. "Did you notice the way Brad was acting?"

"Yeah." I laughed. "He was hanging on her every word. What the hell got into him?"

"Jason! Why would you say that? Don't you think he's serious?" She was annoyed at me, but I wasn't going to lie.

"Maybe." I shrugged.

"Well, I think Nicole might be the one for Brad."

"I hope she is," I replied.

I parked and went into the store for the ice cream, noticing the cigarette display and debating buying a pack. *Nah. I've been off them for too long. I'm not starting up now just because Brad happens to be smoking.*

Michelle was still annoyed when I got back to the truck, and I still had my doubts about the situation. I couldn't help remembering Brad's past attitude toward women, but from then on I kept my doubts to myself.

I was almost as bad as he was, and I changed. If I could, so can he.

* * *

Nicole and Brad agreed to accompany me to Philly the following evening, since Michelle's shift wasn't over until nine. Christmas was only three days away. I needed a woman's input before making such an important purchase, and neither Bella nor Heather was available to help me.

Nicole had great taste. I had no idea what I was doing, and probably would have made a poor choice, but Nicole gave me direction without being pushy. I finally decided on a one-carat solitaire, princess cut and set in platinum, with three tiny diamonds on either side. Nicole said the ring was beautiful. Brad and I just looked it over and shrugged, since neither of us knew any more about rings than we did about weddings.

I was a little nervous about spending so much money. The ring cost half as much as my truck. But I had enough saved for a good down payment, and I also had a back-up plan. *If I feel the need to get ahead on the payments, I'll sell the Harley. It's worth at least a few thousand bucks. It's not as if I ride it much anymore. I hope it doesn't come to that though. I hate to let it go.*

While the jeweler was taking care of the financing on the balance, I noticed Nicole and Brad standing next to the counter looking through the glass at the rings.

FIVE

Jason
16 Years Earlier

I proposed to Michelle early on Christmas morning.

It was a habit of hers to attend Midnight Mass, and she'd dragged me along for the past two years. After the service—which I have to admit was beautiful—we walked out into the cold. Snowflakes were lazily falling the way they do at the beginning of a snowstorm.

"A White Christmas!" Michelle exclaimed. "We hardly ever get snow on Christmas. Isn't it beautiful, Jason?"

I replied that it was. She smiled up at me as we walked to the truck, looking so pretty with the snow sprinkling over her hair that I decided to propose that night rather than wait for tomorrow. Instead of kissing her goodnight at her parents' backdoor, I followed her inside. It was about one forty-five in the morning, and the old man had left the kitchen light on for her. Everyone else was in bed.

"Let's go see the tree for a minute." I pulled her by the hand through the dining room and into the living room, where the

Christmas tree stood in front of the window. Michelle looked at me questioningly as I helped her out of her jacket.

"Jason, it's late. We have a big day tomorrow. Don't you think you should go home now and get some sleep?"

I put my arms around her and breathed. She smelled good. "I'll go in a minute," I said. "Just stay here with me for a while." I'd been aware of the ring inside my coat pocket all evening, but I hadn't really planned what to say, thinking I'd figure it out by the next morning. *But tonight's the night. It feels right. Here goes.*

I took the velvet box out of my pocket and suddenly found myself down on one knee holding it out to her. She took the box and opened it, and the look on her face was worth every penny I was paying for the ring.

"Will you marry me?" *I love you. Please, please say yes.*

Her eyes were starry in the glow from the tree as she smiled down at me. "Yes, Jason, I will," she whispered.

I stood up then and reached out for her. Things seemed to go gray for a while. *But this time she feels the same way. I can tell.* We'd talked more about it since New Year's Eve, and we were both still determined to wait, but it almost got away from us that night. My conviction faded into the background, and I found my hands in certain places where they shouldn't have been. *Wish we were at my place. Wish we were in my bed. Wish—*

"Jason." Michelle's gasping voice cut through the haze. She had hold of my hands. As she pushed them away from her breasts she said clearly: "Didn't I see you go up for Communion earlier?"

"Yes." I gulped.

"And I did, too." She was staring into my eyes. *We promised to wait. And even if we hadn't, it's Christmas Eve, and both of us just received Communion.*

I know, honey. I put my arms around her again. "Michelle, let's run away tonight and get married," I said. "Come on. We can be together in a few hours."

"No, Jason...I want a wedding. Don't you?"

"We'll have a wedding; just the two of us."

"I..." She trailed off uncertainly.

Yeah! She's coming around. I'll get her talked into it.

"Jason?" Michelle's muffled voice was speculative. "What do you think Mom and Aunt Rosie and Cindy and Bella will do to you if we run away and get married?"

"I don't care what they do," I said against her neck. "I'll take a chance."

"Well if you're going to be my husband I'd prefer it if you didn't take a chance. I'd like to have children someday, and I thought you would too."

"I would."

"Well, if we run away and get married there's a chance we won't. Bella would come after you. I was her maid of honor, and I promised her she'd be mine when the time comes."

"Bella can blow. She's gonna be a mom in two months, and even if she wasn't as big as a house I'm not worried. I'm faster than her. Let's go to the airport, we'll find a flight to Vegas."

"Jason, what do you think will happen if we call from Las Vegas and tell Daddy we're married, and he has to deal with Mom's crying for the next three months? What do you think Johnny's going to do if he has to deal with Cindy?"

That brought me up short, and I almost swore under my breath. I wasn't worried in the slightest about Bella and her temper, but the old man and Johnny were something else again. I knew they wouldn't really care if we ran away and that they'd probably both be happy if we did. But if I were the cause of the two of them having to listen to crying wives for three months, it would be too bad for me. The old man was still a tough customer. If I wanted to remain in his good graces, I'd better not run away with his daughter.

"All right, Michelle." I sighed. "But we need to get married as soon as possible. If you want a sane man for a husband, that is."

Of course we had to wait another year. We went back and forth over it for a while, my idea being to get married the following April, and Michelle insisting it would take at least eighteen months to plan the wedding if we wanted everything to turn out the way it should. We were still next to the Christmas tree, sitting on the floor and talking quietly.

"Jason, we have to book the church and reception hall, and I have to look for a dress. And we need to choose the flowers and a cake, and invitations, and—"

"Michelle," I said. "Stop. You're making my head hurt."

"Well I'm sorry, but that's what planning a wedding involves."

"You plan it then. I have some money saved. I'll hand it over, but I can't deal with all that stuff."

"You don't have to deal with it. I'll do it. And you don't have to pay for the wedding either. Daddy's paying for it."

"I don't want that. Why should he have to pay for the whole thing?"

"Jason, honey, don't you know anything?" She sounded a little impatient. "Daddy's not going to let you pay for his only daughter's wedding. Tradition says the bride's family pays for the wedding, and the groom's family pays for the rehearsal dinner."

"What rehearsal?"

"Jason," she replied, patiently. "Were you not in Lucio and Bella's wedding?"

"Yeah."

"Well, we had a rehearsal the night before, didn't we?"

"Just because they had one doesn't mean we have to," I maintained. "And we're not waiting another year and a half to get married, either."

"Yes, we do too have to," she said. "All weddings have rehearsals."

"Not weddings in Las Vegas," I retorted. Then neither of us spoke for a minute.

"We don't really have to wait eighteen months," Michelle mused, ignoring my comment about Vegas. "I guess it can be planned in less time than that. But we can't have the wedding next spring. If you want me to leave you out of the planning of it, then I'm going to need at least a year."

"Damn it Michelle!" I groaned and shook my head back and forth before banging it against the wall. "Another year?"

"Be quiet." Michelle clutched my arm. "You'll wake Brad, and I don't want him down here. He'll wake everyone if he finds out tonight."

I opened my mouth to tell her he already knew, but thought better about it, though at that point I really didn't care if we woke the whole house. All I could think about was how hard it would be to wait another year.

"Damn it Michelle," I repeated. "Are you sure it's going to take another year? I may be insane by then. What do you think your Dad will do to me if we elope? Do you think he'll shoot me? Because if it's anything less than that, I say let's go for it."

* * *

We set the date for December eighteenth of the following year. Michelle liked the idea of a Christmastime wedding and said we'd be able to have our honeymoon during her break from school. Even though they had been expecting it, the family was really excited, and Michelle's parents were very impressed when they saw the ring. Mrs. Davis told me I had excellent taste.

We went to my mother's after dinner to break the news and show her the ring. I was nervous during the drive, and so was Michelle. She didn't know my mother and I had argued about the engagement, but she was apprehensive nonetheless. My mother had that effect on her.

"Don't worry," I said as I pulled into the driveway. "We're not staying. Only a minute, just long enough to break the news. I want to get it over with."

We found my mother alone in the family room. Jeremy was out with some of his old gang from St. Bonaventure that night. I handed Mom the gifts Michelle had picked out and she put them under the tree, saying she and Jeremy would open them later. She pointed out our gifts and I got them. Then we sat down on the couch. The silence was uncomfortable. My mother stared pointedly at Michelle's left hand, but before I could say anything about the ring she began talking about my brother.

She spoke in glowing terms of Jeremy—how well he was doing at school, how good his grades always were, and how well the team was doing. He had a football scholarship. They'd been starting him more and more this year, and she was really proud of him, and on and on and on. There seemed to be no break in the discourse.

I knew it all anyway. I listened to the games on the radio at work every Saturday afternoon, and I was familiar with my brother's record as a quarterback.

Talking Jeremy up while ignoring Michelle on the day of her engagement was classic Mom. Her tactics never changed, and by that time I could see right through her. That didn't mean Michelle could, though. Michelle wasn't used to dealing with situations like this one, and I felt bad for her. This experience was the complete opposite of the one at her house earlier.

When we broke the news to Michelle's family there were congratulations, hugs and kisses, handshakes, tears and laughter. The old man had opened a bottle of wine he'd been saving, for a special occasion he said, and everyone drank to our future.

But there was none of that here. Only my mother and her attitude, the same one she always showed Michelle: cool, arrogant, and a little dismissive. But this time my mother was pulling no punches, and it made me mad. So I put my arm around Michelle and reached across her lap for her left hand. I squeezed it in mine for a minute then, before picking it up and holding it out toward my mother. The ring sparkled on her finger.

"Mom," I said, cutting her off in the middle of a sentence. "I asked Michelle to marry me, and she's accepted. The date is set for next December eighteenth." I stared across the coffee table at her. She hadn't offered us anything to drink. She was quiet for a minute or so, looking at us doubtfully, and making no comment on the ring. I could tell it hurt Michelle's feelings.

"Mom?" I repeated, hugging Michelle, "We're getting married next year. Aren't you going to congratulate us?"

But there were no congratulations forthcoming, only colder arrogance, and what she said next was so typical it would have been funny if Michelle hadn't been on the verge of tears.

"I'm sure I can't understand how either of you think you're in a position to take such a step," she said, looking down her nose at us. "But I know how stubborn you are, Jason, and that nothing I can say will ever talk you out of doing something when you've made up your mind to do it. So I'll just keep my opinion to myself."

Of course her words and her attitude had just given us her opinion. Michelle was getting more upset, so I decided to get her out of there. I was used to Mom's tactics, but Michelle's family was so loving, so kind and decent, that she'd probably never experienced such a scene firsthand. Even though she'd heard me complain about Mom, I don't think she realized the full force of her personality until just that minute.

"You've got that right." My voice dripped sarcasm. "The one thing you've always been able to do is keep your opinion to yourself. But it's okay. Michelle and I understand our position, and that's what matters."

Mom stared at me with the same expression I'd seen when I asked for her input on the ring—like she was seeing someone else. *Who's she think she's looking at?* I decided it was time to go; the atmosphere was getting thick.

"We have to be going now Mom," I said, getting up off the couch and pulling Michelle along. "Merry Christmas. Tell my brother I'll call him later. Have a nice evening."

"Merry Christmas, Mrs. Wallace," Michelle managed to say as I pulled her around the corner of the kitchen and out through the entry. As we ran down the sidewalk she was half laughing and half crying.

"Jason," she said as I helped her into the truck, "how often does she act that way? I feel like I'm in the twilight zone."

"I know," I agreed in a grim tone of voice. I went around to the driver's side and got in and started the engine. "Don't worry about it Michelle. Mom can do that to a person. But it'll wear off soon."

As I was backing out of the lane, I realized we'd left our presents behind. I considered going back in and maybe trying to reason with her, but I didn't want her spoiling the day any more than she already had. As we drove around the corner past the house, I could see her through the window, still sitting there.

We had a year of preparation. There were engagement parties and pre Cana classes, bridal showers and tuxedo rentals, and so many other details that sometimes I still wished we'd run away to Las Vegas. But I knew I should consider myself lucky, since almost all that was expected of me was to show up at the various events, along with getting the ring to my best man—Brad, of course.

The old man was paying for the entire wedding. He insisted. He said she was his only daughter, and that he'd been putting money by for her wedding since she was a little girl. He told me it was tradition, and said he didn't want to hear any more argument. So I shut up.

I knew he could afford it. He'd had a long and productive career as an engineer and had been employed by the same company since his return from Vietnam in the late 1960s. Mrs. Davis had been working part time since Michelle was eleven, and they were reasonably well set up. Brad had mentioned that the old man was looking forward to retirement, and that he, Brad, had suggested investing in some real estate down in Florida. But somehow I couldn't see the old man flying off to Florida every winter; he and Michelle's mom were so interested in their children that I thought they would remain where they were when they retired.

I wasn't about to ask Mom for any help with the dinner the night before the wedding, not after the episode of the previous year. Reese suggested having the dinner at Diesel's. To him it seemed the perfect solution, but I had a feeling Michelle and her mother would feel differently. The two of us argued back and forth about my problem until I wanted to scream. However all the arguing led to an inadvertent solution. CJ got tired of hearing about it and offered to have the party at his place, as a wedding gift. He had discussed it with his wife, who took care of the books at work—all of us at the garage called her Mrs. CJ—and it had been her idea. CJ had heard many tales about Mom over the years, including the story of Michelle and I telling her about the engagement. I think Mrs. CJ felt sorry for me.

I accepted the gift without question, except for an argument about the catering. I wanted to pay for it, but CJ wouldn't hear of it, so we finally compromised. He paid for the food, and I paid for all the drinks, including the liquor.

* * *

We had a great time that evening after the rehearsal at church. The groomsmen were Brad, Johnny, Jeremy, Michelle's nephews, and Reese. As promised, Bella would be matron of honor, and the remainder of the wedding party was made up of Heather, Cindy, and Michelle's college roommate, Kim. Junior, aged ten, and Jamie, who was two years younger, were going to be junior ushers.

In addition to the wedding party, Danny and his wife and a few other close friends joined us. My old Air Force buddy Jason Webb flew up from Biloxi with his wife to attend the wedding. We'd met down there, and that was where he was currently stationed. Back in those days he'd been known as Webby, to distinguish the two of us.

My mother excused herself after the rehearsal, saying she had things to do. Some distant relatives from her side of the family were in town for the wedding, and she told us she wanted to get back to them. She seemed to have forgotten that I'd invited them to the church, as well as dinner at CJ's. Jeremy stayed with us though, and so did everyone else who really cared: the old man and Michelle's mom, Aunt Rosie, Nicole, and everyone else from the garage. Lucio came, bringing his ten-month-old son Lucio Jr., nicknamed Sonny, who slept through the whole thing. After dinner we all sat around CJ's place drinking and talking, and by the time the party began winding down, I was so keyed up that I wondered if I'd be able to sleep that night. *I've taken my last cold shower. Just one more night and I'll never have to sleep alone again—*

Michelle snapped her fingers in front of my face. "Jason, where are you?" she said. "I've been calling you. It's almost midnight and I have to go—it's bad luck for the groom to see the bride on their wedding day before she walks down the aisle."

"Okay honey. You go on, unless you want me to drive you home."

"No, we wouldn't get there before midnight." Her eyes shone as she pecked my cheek. "Brad's driving Nicole and me. He said you wanted to stay and have a couple more drinks."

I gave Brad a sour look. He knew I hadn't had a drink all night. I hadn't had one for days, ever since the bachelor party at Diesels' where I'd gotten so drunk I was sick. The next day I cussed Brad until I was blue in the face, along with Reese and Lucio and everyone else who had bought a shot of whiskey for me. Brad knew my stomach still wouldn't let me drink. He'd been laughing at me all week long.

* * *

The wedding took place at St. Catherine's. Dozens of red poinsettias decorated the church, along with two huge displays of red and pink roses flanking the altar. Brad and I were in the sacristy, where I paced back and forth, waiting for Father Gallucio's signal. The voice of Michelle's cousin Angela reached us as she sang the *Ave Maria*, accompanied by the organ and flute. I glanced out at the door and saw that the church was almost full. Junior and Jamie began dragging the white carpet up the aisle.

"It's almost two o'clock," I said. "Do you have the ring?"

"Yeah, Wallace," Brad answered impatiently. "It's in my pocket. The same place it was when you asked me ten minutes ago." I continued looking out the door. Michelle's Aunt Rosie came up the aisle on Johnny's arm and was ushered into the second row where Nicole sat next to Lucio. Nicole looked gorgeous as usual. Understated but classy. Striking, actually. Brad joined me in the doorway. He must have noticed as well.

"Wallace," he said in a speculative tone, "how did you know—for sure, I mean—that you and Michelle belong together?"

"For crying out loud, can't you ask me later? Because I have to go out there now and stand in front of a church full of people, and I'm a little too nervous to remember something that happened that long ago."

"I need to know now," he shot back. "Look at Nicole. I've been thinking she's the one for a while, but I'm not sure, and I need you to tell me how you knew—"

"Oh my God," I cut him off. I closed my eyes for a second, thinking they were playing tricks on me. I opened them again...but no...there she was. My eyes weren't lying to me.

There was my mother, walking up the aisle on Jeremy's arm dressed entirely in black. And I don't mean just black; it was more than just the color. It was the accessories. She was wearing a big, ugly, black hat. The attached veil covered her face completely. And her gloves were made of hideous black lace that reminded me of a spider's web. *Damn it Mom. You had to do it, didn't you?*

Jeremy looked like he wanted to sink through the floor as he handed Mom into the front pew. The look on Nicole's face, before she hid it, was one of stunned distaste. People were shaking their heads. I elbowed Brad. His jaw dropped as he rolled his eyes, shaking his head back and forth. Even Brad, as clueless as he was about weddings, understood what an insult this was.

But then Michelle's mother—dressed tastefully in a pretty blue gown—was coming up the aisle, escorted by Junior and Jamie, one on either side. Father Gallucio came forward and beckoned, telling us to come out. The processional began as we followed him, joined by the rest of the groomsmen. We stood in a line at the altar, watching as Cindy came toward us, followed by Heather and Kim, and then Bella was floating up the aisle.

Then everyone in the church stood and looked down the aisle at Michelle and the old man. She looked like an angel as she skimmed down the aisle on her father's arm, a cascade of white roses trailing in front of her. Her strapless gown sparkled. It had a train, a long one, spread out on the white runner. Her veil shimmered around her face, glimmering and reflecting light, but as usual it was her eyes that held me spellbound. They had never looked bluer or deeper or more endless than they did at that moment in time. She smiled at me radiantly. I noticed the sparkle of tears on her lashes, but I wasn't crying. It seemed like I had been waiting for this day my whole life.

Suddenly she was next to me. The old man had tears in his eyes too, as he lifted the veil and kissed Michelle, placing her hand in mine. He gave me a nod and then went to his seat next to Michelle's mother.

All during the Mass, one word ran through my mind. *Sacrament.*

After the ceremony, before the pictures were taken, I had a private word with my mom. The hat, gloves, and veil disappeared.

* * *

Michelle and I, with Brad and Bella, traveled to the reception in style. As we opened a bottle of champagne in the back of the limousine, I reflected on the second reading, thinking about my mother in her black veil, sitting alone in the pew, her face unreadable.

"Love is patient, love is kind. It is not jealous... it does not seek its own interests... it does not brood over injury..."

Michelle hadn't mentioned Mom's get up, and I didn't want to either; thinking about it was bad enough. When Brad finally mentioned it, Bella responded smartly: "We saw her go in. We were sitting here waiting in the limo, and we saw her come around the corner." She rolled her eyes. "Michelle saw her, but I won't repeat what she said." Bella's face was comical.

I glanced sideways at my bride, who was smirking at Bella.

"Jason," said Bella, in a teasing tone, "Michelle says we're going to give your mom a new nickname."

"Oh yeah?" I answered. Brad was laughing quietly.

"Yeah. It's being changed. From Cruella Deville to the Black Widow."

I threw Michelle another look, this time one of apology, but seemed she was over her anger. Her eyes danced back at me merrily. All of a sudden the situation got the better of me, and I threw back my head and howled. The ice broke then, and the four of us laughed until we cried, before clinking our glasses in another toast—this one to my mother.

We hadn't the slightest idea of what awaited us. Fifteen years down the road everything would be different, and we wouldn't be laughing anymore.

* * *

Our wedding reception was half over. We'd been introduced as Mr. and Mrs. Jason Wallace, Father Gallucio had blessed the meal, and Brad had stood up with the microphone and toasted us. I had never seen Brad in such an emotional state; his voice was unsteady.

"To my sister and Wallace...I love you both. Best wishes to the two of you for a happy life. Michelle, I hope you have all those kids you've always wanted, and Wallace, it's been a great ride. I'm probably the only man on the planet who can honestly say that my brother married my sister." My mother-in-law dabbed at her eyes with a handkerchief as everyone in the room applauded and cheered. Brad sat back down next to me, looking satisfied with himself.

The old man had spared no expense on the reception. The inn where it was being held looked like something you'd see on TV; all lit up and decorated for Christmas, and the food was out of this world. After dinner it was time for the party to really start. The next thing on the agenda was our first dance together as husband and wife, which I had been dreading for weeks. I wasn't much of a dancer, and I was afraid I'd trip over my own feet, but when I heard the music begin after the DJ announced it, I felt much more than just nervousness.

What? Michelle? I glanced at her sharply as I held out my hand. The water was there again, and that feeling underneath, like shock. We walked to the middle of the floor. I put my arms around her and fell into her eyes for a minute, remembering. It seemed to go on forever. Then my face turned red, as Brad and every other guy in the room started whistling and shouting comments because of the music.

The song playing was *The Fever*. I recognized it from the first few bars of percussion, even though I hadn't listened to it in over ten years. Michelle was in my arms, looking at me dreamily and paying no attention whatsoever to the catcalls. The lights were dim. *Thank God.*

"Michelle, listen to them. I didn't know we'd be dancing to this."

"I like this song." She stared into my eyes. "I used to listen to it after you left. It helped me remember you." *You know what it means to us. It's our most treasured memory.*

I liked the song as well, even though I hadn't been able to bring myself to listen to it. Of all the songs in the universe it was the one that best described the way I felt about Michelle. But I wasn't sure it was the best choice for this particular dance, not with Reese's big mouth yelling out at us, and Brad and Lucio laughing it up. I didn't complain again, though. After all, I was the one who hadn't wanted to be bothered with details. The room seemed to fade into gray then. Everyone was singing the words of the refrain and hitting their champagne glasses with their knives, making a chiming sound. So I kissed Michelle and then looked in her eyes again, not caring what they thought. We danced and listened to the music.

"Is it still your most treasured memory?" Her voice was low.

"One of them."

"Mine too. I used to take it out and think about it every day. It got me through."

"I thought about it." *Sometimes...later, when I could stand it.* "But honey," my voice was rough. "We're together now. And I think that memory may have some competition after tonight."

Time seemed to crawl after Michelle and I danced. Next was her dance with the old man, to *Daddy's Little Girl,* and my dance with my mother. Mom's hair was a little flat because of the missing hat, and she cracked wise about it, blaming me. I ignored her comment, and after that she was silent, her face unreadable again.

Then came the cutting of the cake and the tossing of the bouquet. Heather elbowed everyone else out of the way in order to catch the bouquet, and Reese caught the garter; no one else had the nerve to put a garter on Heather's leg with him in the room. After that Michelle and I went around the room, visiting every table. She carried a big tray of Italian cookies that Aunt Rosie had baked, and also a white silk purse. Any gifts that hadn't already been sent to the old man's were given to us at that time.

Soon the reception was over and we were alone in the honeymoon suite at the inn. The room was part of the reception package.

Michelle's train had been removed during the reception. I watched as she stood in front of the mirror, starting to take off her veil. She chattered about the day, but I hardly heard a word she was saying, and the next thing I knew I was taking her in my arms. We looked in each other's eyes again, getting lost.

We've waited long enough.

We're done waiting now.

It was completely quiet in the room, but that was okay. We didn't need any music, not that night. I started kissing her. I finished taking off the veil and there was her hair it was in all its glory, hanging down over her shoulders. I took a lock of it and let it run through my hand. It was still as blond and smooth and thick as it had been the day of my most treasured memory. *You're beautiful baby.* I kissed her again: on her lips, her eyelids, and her cheeks.

I picked her up off the floor then, and carried her across to the bed, seeing in her eyes what I had been dreaming about for the past five years; the desire, the wanting, deep down in the blue. I laid her on the bed and stood back for a minute, just looking.

We're done waiting.

Her shoes were in my hands and I placed them on the floor. Her pink polished toenails gleamed faintly through her stockings, silky thigh high stockings with seams running up the back of each one. I found another garter then, placed higher up on her left thigh, too high for anyone to have noticed it when I took the other one off earlier. The stockings were off then as well. I backed away from the bed again, loosening my tie and taking it off, as I looked down into her eyes one final time. *We've waited long enough. Another treasured memory...it's sanctified.*

She held out her arms, and then finally it was happening. It was happening for both of us, and everything else in the world went away for a long, long time.

* * *

At three o'clock in the morning, while Michelle lay asleep with her head on my chest, the words of the second reading ran through my mind again: *"And if I have the gift of prophecy, and comprehend all mysteries and all knowledge; if I have all faith so as to move mountains, but do not have love, I am nothing."*

It's sanctified. I thought back over the previous few hours. It had taken at least ten minutes to unfasten all those buttons down her back, but she had been worth the wait.

Love...weddings...babies...happiness...future...love...I love you... My most treasured memory.

She had been worth all of it. She had been worth every last feeling of love and fear, loss and acceptance, pain and frustration and longing, hope and faith, love and prayer. *It's sanctified. It was meant to be. It was a certainty. It just* was.

SIX

Jason

I was the luckiest man on earth to have married Michelle, but to my shame I didn't act like it after the wedding. And since I have vowed to write only the truth, I guess I'll admit what I did.

15 Years Earlier

Our honeymoon was idyllic. We celebrated our first Christmas together in the Bahamas. Michelle bought a little Christmas tree at one of the resort gift shops to decorate our room. It was her first Christmas away from home, and I think she may have been a little homesick, but not me. I wanted to stay in the islands forever, and those long nights with Michelle were all I could think about. Maybe it was an obsession. I certainly don't know how else to explain my behavior.

I don't mean to say we didn't have a good time on the trip,

because we did. We laughed and swam and took long walks on the beach at sunset. I spent a day on a fishing charter, while Michelle pampered herself at the resort spa. We had a ball shopping for souvenirs and gifts for the family, but for me the best times were when the lights went out at night. The ten days passed too quickly. I didn't want the honeymoon to end, but like everything else, it did.

Then we flew home to my one bedroom apartment, and a few days later both of us went back to work. I endured the inevitable ragging from the guys at the garage, Michelle went back to school, and we settled into a routine.

I woke up to the fact that I had been acting like a pig on a Friday night in late February when we were getting ready for bed. My apartment had transformed over the years. Michelle had slowly put the stamp of her personality on the place, and it was much nicer than it had been, since Michelle had good taste and I had none.

I was happy with all the changes she had made, but my favorite room was the bedroom. The walls were painted a tasteful deep tan, and the bed was one we could keep forever. The headboard was of gleaming maple with wrought iron accents. The furniture had cost us, but we considered it worth the price. We'd discussed it before the wedding and had decided that bedroom furniture was first on the list.

I was undressing that night, getting ready to hit the bathroom, and Michelle was already wearing a cute little pair of wooly pajamas. She picked up the jeans I had carelessly tossed on the chair in the corner and stuffed them in the hamper before sitting down on the bed and staring up at a picture she'd purchased the week before. She'd been subdued all evening. *Wonder what's wrong. She doesn't seem herself.*

"Michelle," I said, going on into the bathroom, "is anything wrong?"

"Why do you ask?"

"You're too quiet," I threw out. "Did something happen at school?"

"No." Her voice sounded small and far away.

"What is it then?" I asked as I came back. She didn't reply.

"Michelle?" My tone was a little sharp. "I know something's going on. What is it?"

"Oh my God, Jason." Her shoulders were hunched. "I don't want to tell you."

That should have clued me in to the seriousness of the situation. There was nothing Michelle couldn't tell me. Half the time we knew what the other was thinking without even saying anything. I was oblivious though; still lost in whatever parallel universe I'd been living in since the wedding. *Parent-teacher conferences are coming up. That's it. She always worries beforehand.*

"Michelle, what's the matter?" I asked impatiently. "Are you worried about one of the parents again? Don't worry. You know you can handle conferences. Now tell me."

But she only sat there on the bed with her hair hiding her face. That was when I finally started thinking about another possibility... one which might upset my plans.

"Jason..." Her voice was a little shaky. She looked up at me then, half smiling, but with tears in her eyes.

No. Not that. Not yet.

I stood rigidly by the bathroom door in my boxers, staring back at her. Our eyes were locked. The nervous expression remained on her face as I walked to the bed and sat down next to her. I didn't put my arms around her. All I did was sit next to her for a minute and shake my head.

"Michelle. Tell me you're not."

We'd talked about having a family. We both wanted children, but not for at least three or four years. Especially me. I wanted Michelle all to myself for a while. I had waited for what seemed like ages, and now that I had her, I didn't want to share her, not even with a baby.

We had been using protection. Michelle—being very open minded—had listened intently to the explanation of natural family planning we'd heard about at pre-Cana. She was of the opinion that it might be a good idea to at least try it, and she had planned to find out more about it when we returned from the Bahamas. But she hadn't yet found the time, and we were still using artificial means every night. All except for one.

She was still as a statue, looking at me out of the corner of her eye. But she didn't move, so I finally turned my head her way. "Well, are you?"

"Yes," she answered, looking at the floor. I didn't say a word. I just shook my head, got up off the bed, and walked away from her.

I still can't believe I did it. I stalked out into the living room and sat down, my thoughts racing. *Not yet. It's too soon. How did it happen? It was only one night. Damn it, it was only that one night!*

I sat on the couch, thinking about the shattering of my plans, thinking of myself and only myself. That came to an end when I became aware of the retching sounds coming from the bedroom. *Is she sick?*

I got up automatically to go help her, but as I started toward the bedroom the full realization of what I'd been doing hit me like a brick. I leaned against the doorframe, listening to the agonizing sounds coming from the bathroom and looking back over the two months since the wedding.

I thought about how much I had asked of her those many nights. *Every night. Every night without a break. I...what the hell was I thinking?* I stood there in anguish reflecting on the situation, before coming to the conclusion that I had been acting like a selfish bastard.

Love is patient, love is kind. It is not jealous, is not pompous, it is not inflated, it is not rude... It does not seek its own interests... it does not brood over injury...

Michelle hadn't injured me, but I had done all of that and more. Even though my feelings were reciprocated and she wanted me, too, I was now awake to the fact that my behavior since the wedding had been wrong. I had been much more selfish than Brad had ever been way back when. *Who the hell am I to think I'm any better? At least when Brad uses a woman she isn't his wife. And now there's a baby.*

I was more to blame for that than Michelle. It had been my idea. It was me who hadn't wanted anything between us on our wedding night, and she'd gone along with me just that once.

* * *

She was sobbing on the bed with her face in the pillow when I walked through the bedroom door. The bathroom door stood ajar and the toilet was running. *How many times has she been sick? And I didn't even notice.* The remorse I felt is something I can't describe. My wife had been carrying my child for two months. She was sick and worried and upset, and I hadn't noticed a thing. *And she...she felt like she needed to keep it from me.*

That hurt. *She was afraid of me. She was afraid to tell me.*

I walked to the bed with pain in my throat because I had hurt her so badly. When I lay down next to her and put my arm around her she continued to cry.

"Michelle." I swallowed. "Honey, I'm sorry."

She lost the baby a week later.

Michelle

The morning light is beautiful as it steals into the sky. I get wet from the dew on the corn, and my belly is getting too big to fit through the rows comfortably, but I don't care. I'm glad to be out this early. The only sound is that of the birds, singing and chirping.

From the edge of the corn I look across a pasture dotted with beautiful old maple trees. It stretches down a hill to a faraway pond. Mist shimmers there, close to where the pasture meets a tree line and the woods begin. Drifts of morning mist are scattered over the low places. Dew begins to shimmer and sparkle. The reflecting light seems to be all colors as the sun creeps over the eastern edges of the fields.

You can't really see it in our time. It's just there suddenly, when it wasn't a moment ago. The eastern sky is orange-pink in color. I cast a glance up at the western sky behind me. The darkness is receding above the tall stalks of corn. It's still a little dark, a clear purple-gray against the dim green blades, but it's receding. It always does.

I turn back toward the light and beauty taking form in front of me. The mist gleams brighter as the breeze chases it away from the pond. Sunlight glitters and sparkles over the gray-green, reminding me of Jason's eyes. The pond isn't blue, like my eyes. Jason tells me my eyes are what he wants for you, baby.

I wonder what it would feel like to run out of the corn, to run down toward the pond and around it. I think it would feel cool and clean and wet. Dew would sprinkle up from my shoes, soaking them. I could skim through the mist, feeling its coolness.

I come back to myself, my hand outstretched toward the open air. A crow caws, mocking me. I haven't run in months. Maybe I never will again.

* * *

I've been revisiting the *Little House* books. It soothes me to think of simpler times. As I was reading earlier I found an old snapshot tucked away between the pages of *Little House in the Big Woods*. The moment captured was a little girl's birthday. The photo is dated September 1972. Several children are pictured sitting around a kitchen table, singing. I recognize Sandy, poised on the edge of her chair, looking at a younger girl who is blowing out the candles on her cake. Next to Sandy is another little girl, a tiny little doll of a girl, frail and delicate. She's sitting in a highchair watching the scene. It's obvious she has Down syndrome. I wonder who this is?

Jason
15 Years Earlier

After Michelle stopped crying that night, we lay in bed with the lights on. When I asked her why she hadn't told me about the baby she didn't answer me. She looked sick. Her face was white as a sheet, and tears still trickled out of the corners of her eyes. It hurt me to look at her.

After a minute she looked me in the face. "I didn't want to tell you. I knew you'd react the way you did." I flushed and looked up at the ceiling. "I knew you'd be upset, and I didn't know how to tell you."

Words can't describe how bad I felt. "Michelle, I'm so sorry. I know it's my fault. Please tell me. I want you to tell me now." Then I turned off the lamp, and in the darkness she told me what she'd been thinking since our return from the islands.

At first, everything seemed the way it should have. But then, gradually, a distance had opened between us.

"You weren't yourself. Even though we were together every night, you seemed far away. I was beginning to think I didn't really know you. That maybe we weren't right for each other after all." She put her arms around me then and rested her head on my chest.

"Baby." My voice was rough. "Honey, we are right for each other. I know that and so do you. This whole thing is my fault. I don't know what I was thinking. Tell me the rest of it."

I cringed as she told me she had spoken to Bella, and Bella's thoughts were that all men were alike no matter who they were. Bella said men were pigs when it came to sex, and not to worry about it; things would settle down in a little while. Michelle tried to explain that *something* just wasn't right, but she didn't know how to get her point across.

"Bella and Lucio are finally happy," Michelle said. "She's having another baby. I figured she knew what she was talking about, so I decided not to mention my feelings to you. But then I found out I'm pregnant myself."

She repeated that she wanted to tell me about the baby but she was worried about my reaction, and she felt too embarrassed to tell Bella or anyone else, because she knew the first question after congratulations would be: "What does Jason think?"

I lay there with her, listening to her lulling voice, deciding that in my case Bella was right. *I am a pig for sex. But that's coming to an end right now. I'm taking control of myself again.*

And it was worse than just that, anyway. I had begun taking Michelle for granted as soon as we returned home. Maybe I'd been holding onto some resentment about her decision to remain a virgin until we were married. *Was that it? But that's the reason our wedding night was the way it was.* That night was indescribable. I wouldn't have had it any other way, and waiting had been the right thing to do. I came to the conclusion then, that I was an idiot.

"Honey, I'm so sorry," I repeated shakily, glad the lights were off. I steadied my voice and went on. "I don't know why I did what I did. I wish I could take it back. I promise it'll never happen again. Will you forgive me?"

"Of course I forgive you." We lay together quietly for a time, each thinking our own thoughts. Mine were about the future, and how different things would be.

"When are you due?"

"September."

"The lease is up in April," I replied, giving her another hug. "We'll have to get a bigger place."

"Are you really okay with this?" Michelle asked.

"Yes. Things happen for a reason. We'll be sharing our happiness with a baby. What could be better?"

"Jason, I feel like we're back together again," she said.

* * *

After I got used to the idea, I found myself looking forward to next fall. With the pregnancy out in the open Michelle seemed more like herself. She said keeping it from me had been a strain. I cursed myself inwardly, but we both agreed to put it behind us.

We began making plans. Everything was getting back to normal when I got the call on my cell phone at work. It was Michelle, telling me to meet her at the doctor's office. She had started bleeding at school. After the doctor looked at her he called me in and told us the baby was gone.

I blamed myself for the miscarriage. Even though the doctor told us there was nothing we could have done differently and that we could have other babies, I still felt like it was my fault. *It was the strain she was under, or the late nights. Or maybe not...maybe it was the act of inter-course.* I couldn't stop myself from thinking that I was at fault, so I finally logged onto the Internet and looked up miscarriage. I found no evidence to suggest that anything I had done caused Michelle to lose the baby, but the night I found out about the pregnancy still weighed heavily on my mind, so I decided to do everything I could to help her through the loss. The online articles seemed to stress communication along with other aspects of coping, so while Michelle was resting the next day, I stayed with her. We talked about the future and other babies.

* * *

We were able to put the whole thing behind us, but it took some work. Even though I kept it from Michelle, I still held myself partly responsible for our loss. The thought that maybe I could have done something differently kept recurring until I finally went to confession and told Father Gallucio the whole story, including my actions after the wedding.

He didn't seem shocked, even though it was the worst thing I had ever confessed. Father seemed to take the whole thing in stride, but at the same time he lectured me sternly. He spoke of how important it was for husbands to respect their wives, making sure I understood that the culture these days was a contributing factor to the current high divorce rate. He said I should remember that fact, and that I shouldn't let any outside influences affect the sanctity of my marriage.

I didn't know what he was talking about. As far as I was concerned my own thoughts about Michelle were enough, and I didn't need any outside influences. I didn't realize until later that what he probably meant was not to let my selfish desires dictate my actions. He gave me an earful about respecting my wife, but he also gave me absolution, and after hearing the words: "God has freed you from your sins, you can go in peace," I was able to put the episode behind me.

Michelle

I can't sleep, angel-baby. I prayed the rosary and fell asleep as usual, but now it's two o'clock. I'm wide-awake again, so I'll write some more of our story.

Jason changed on the night you were conceived. He changed back into the man he used to be before the manifestation of the new way of doing business, and from that day on he was determined we would no longer allow anyone but God to run our lives.

He didn't talk about what the American way of life had slowly devolved into with me, but I knew he was discussing certain aspects of it with my brother. Brad was still unaware of our particular situation though. It was better that way. Brad had his own issues with the bureaucracy, and neither of us wanted to burden him with ours.

There was another positive change in your daddy, one that filled me with joy—Jason went back to Mass. His attendance had always been sporadic, but after the notice disrupted our lives he refused to go at all. He hadn't set foot in church for almost a year but he went back after the night you came into being.

I was working at the grocery store downtown during the time all of this was occurring. I'd been there for the previous six years, ever since I gave up teaching. I missed teaching the children who wanted to learn, but as for the rest of it I was glad to let it go. Even though I took a pay cut, Jason and I were better off.

At least I was no longer forced to deal with the disrespect and arrogance I incurred from the parents of certain disruptive kids. It was much less offensive to my sensibilities to work a cash register, since our store followed policy of a sort. If any patron or employee had ever cursed me or shoved me, no matter their age, I would have had much more chance of fair redress at the supermarket than at the public middle school. But my years at the store were without incident of this kind, at least until the MCSF began their advance of power.

Eileen was devastated, of course. She had a position to uphold, and the idea of her daughter-in-law giving up a teaching position for a job in a supermarket made her fly into a rage. Jason heard about her rants from your Uncle Jeremy, angel, but he never witnessed one himself. The one time his mom started in on him about my stupidity, he simply got up and walked out of her house after telling her how happy he was with my decision. That was his way of sticking up for me to his mother, whom he always tried to give the benefit of the doubt. Up until lately that is. Jason *was* happy with my decision. He didn't care where I worked, or even *if* I worked, as long as we could pay our bills.

We had a quiet Christmas last year, just the two of us. Because of the rise of the bureaucracy everyone in town seemed subdued. The big evergreen in the roundabout had always been decorated for Christmas, but that ended two years ago. They claimed there was no longer funding in the budget to allow for such things. Electricity was being rationed, and besides, it wouldn't have been fair to the two atheist families who had made complaints. They had to drive through town everyday on their way to work in Wilmington, and their children had asked questions about the beautiful tree with the colored lights. The parents felt uncomfortable explaining the meaning of Christmas and had been forced to make up stories about the tree. They certainly didn't want their children to feel different from others, those who were backward enough to believe in a Christ Child. Anyway such things were going out of fashion. Public displays weren't permitted under the new way of doing business.

Brad called from Memphis on Christmas Eve and Jason and I spoke to the twins. They seemed happy that night, laughing and chattering about Christmas. They lisped over the phone, informing me that they had already put out the milk and cookies for Santa. Taylor mentioned a special gift that had appeared mysteriously under the tree. Annie chirped happily, telling me that her daddy had read them the card attached. It was signed: "Your Guardian Angel."

"Aunt Michelle?" Annie whispered. "Do you think Mommy came and left that gift? Maybe we'll see her tomorrow."

When Brad got back on the phone he was almost crying. Hearing him that way surprised me. Brad was tough. Up until what happened with Mom and Daddy I had never seen him cry. As I listened to the girls chattering in the background, I started to get upset myself. Brad's voice was breaking as we said goodbye.

"Don't cry Michelle. I hope to get up there soon for a visit. Merry Christmas. Now let me talk to Wallace."

I neglected Brad after the notice came. He knew I was depressed, even though he didn't know the reason for it, but I wish my illness hadn't caused me to neglect my brother when he needed me.

After my conversation with Brad, I couldn't get my parents out of my mind, so after Midnight Mass I stopped in front of the church to look at the stars. They were faintly sparkling, far away in the frosty still night as I prayed that Mom and Daddy are together with the Infant Jesus and His Mother. Jason was standing by the Nativity on the church lawn, staring at the Holy Family.

* * *

After Michelle recovered we moved into a better neighborhood, but our new apartment was still a one bedroom. We didn't need anything bigger since it was only the two of us. When I finished tech school CJ rewarded me with another raise. I was doing well in my job, and with Michelle's teaching salary we were fine. Everything was right on track.

Michelle attended a class on NFP, the natural family planning method we'd talked about. She wanted me to go with her, but as usual I left it up to her. I was willing to do what she asked of course. I just refused to go to any more classes. When Michelle arrived home and related to me what she had learned, I was doubtful. But the information—a stack of printouts and a book—was interesting, and since she was so adamant about it, I kept my doubts to myself.

She took care of everything, taking her temperature every morning without fail, and keeping a chart. She tried explaining the rest of it, but as soon as she started talking about mucus I was grossed out. I told her I'd do anything she asked, but just not to bring that up to me again. I had a tendency to want to remain in the dark about all things related to women's issues. Back then that's what I considered anything other than condoms to be: women's issues. It was easier to just follow her lead, but I was surprised when I found things were actually going better than before, since I now had to take responsibility in a different way.

If I started making my usual overtures when Michelle was in the peak fertility period of her cycle, there was only one thing she needed to say, and that was: "Jason, myrtle's in town." Then one of two things would happen. Either I would begin cussing and Michelle would laugh at me, or I would roll my eyes and laugh with her. Either way I always backed off, because I still wanted to wait a while for a baby. Something had happened in the way I saw things since the miscarriage. I had a horror of my wife ever being hurt that way again, and since all I was required to do was to abstain for a week or so once a month, I counted myself lucky.

SEVEN

Jason
9 Years Earlier

Time passed quickly after Michelle recovered from the loss of our first child. We saved a good deal of money by staying in the apartment, and we were doing reasonably well financially. We planned to buy a house and start our family in due time.

Things went along as usual with our respective families. Brad had begun work at a pharmacy in Memphis after he graduated. He and Nicole were still a couple, but despite the fact that they'd moved in together he still hadn't made up his mind about a future with her. When I mentioned the situation to Michelle she said she hoped her parents didn't find out they were living together, since Brad didn't seem to be serious after all. She was a little miffed about it.

"Nicole should never have moved in with him. They've been together for years, and he hasn't even bought her an engagement ring! What's the matter with Brad? He should propose to her and get on with his life. It'll serve him right if she leaves him."

I'm pretty sure Michelle's mom never did find out, but I think the old man knew. He'd always been able to look right through Brad and me. Up until our senior year of high school, he caught us red-handed every time we tried to pull something.

After we came of age he tended to keep quiet. I think he must have decided to let us make our own mistakes. Unless it was a very serious matter he never gave an opinion one way or the other, but he finally told Brad what he thought about the Nicole situation on Thanksgiving, two years after the wedding. We were in the old man's garage during halftime having a couple of beers while we waited for dessert.

Johnny and I leaned back in the old kitchen chairs we were sitting in, watching Brad. He was pacing back and forth, complaining about Nicole. The old man stood at the workbench looking through the toolbox for the pack of Lucky Strikes he kept hidden in it. He seemed to be engrossed in his search, as Brad went on running his mouth about Nicole and what a pain in the ass she could be. Then all of a sudden like lightning, the old man turned around. His blue eyes flashed as he stalked across the cement and asked Brad what the hell was the matter with him.

Everything went quiet. The old man finished lighting his smoke. Then he let loose.

"Who the hell do you think you are to talk about that girl that way?" he said, pointing his cigarette at Brad. He didn't wait for an answer. "Nicole is a nice girl, and you need to stop bitching about her and figure out what the hell you're doing with yourself. I don't want to hear another word about her, unless it's to say you're getting married or you're breaking up. And you better be careful down there in Memphis. I've warned you before. You're thinking with the wrong head."

Brad didn't say a word. He just looked my way, his jaw hanging down to his chest. The old man took another drag on his smoke. "For God's sake Brad, the girl's beautiful. She's smart. She's got a job as a teacher. You think a girl like that is gonna wait around forever for you?

I felt kind of bad for Brad, being upbraided that way right in front of Johnny and me. I thought I saw tears in his eyes before he blinked and hung his head. The old man lowered his voice then. "I'm sorry son, to be so blunt. But if you're not careful Nicole might just up and leave you. And maybe that would be best, at least for her. You're thirty years old. You need to shit or get off the pot. Marry her or let her go."

The old man offered us cigarettes. I hadn't smoked since before the wedding. I had never lit a cigarette in front of Michelle, and as far as I knew she'd never seen me smoking. I wanted to keep it that way, but the episode that night unnerved me so much that I took a cigarette and lit it. Brad did likewise.

He still hadn't uttered a word. It was totally out of character for him to be so quiet. But Johnny began laughing under his breath, and after that I couldn't seem to stop myself. The two of us started howling, pointing at Brad and commenting back and forth to each other as the old man continued to stare him down.

Brad dragged on his cigarette and kept quiet, as the old man told him one more time: "You better watch yourself."

That evening I related the incident to Michelle, though I kept quiet about the smoking. Her father had recently been diagnosed with diabetes, and he wasn't supposed to smoke. As far as the women in the family were concerned he'd quit, and it would worry her if she knew.

I couldn't help laughing as I mentioned the look on Brad's face. She laughed right along with me, before commenting: "Daddy's right, and I hope Brad listens to him. It's wrong for him to lead Nicole on the way he does. If he doesn't stop it soon I'm telling him myself."

I agreed, even though I had been no better. I was lucky the old man knew nothing about the two months following our wedding. He knew about the baby of course, but not about my piggish behavior. If he ever found out he'd probably lay into me worse than he did Brad. The thought of it made me stop my laughing.

* * *

Hearing his dad light into him about Nicole must have made some impression on Brad. Nicole was with him when he came home for Christmas, and I never heard him say anything negative about her again.

He brought up Thanksgiving on a Saturday night when Michelle and Nicole were out shopping. The two of us had spent the evening at Diesel's playing pool with Reese and Lucio before returning to my place for a couple more beers. Brad lounged back on the couch and swigged from his bottle of Yuengling. He seemed lost in thought as he absently twisted the sleeve of his polo shirt back and forth. It was an old habit. He kicked his shoes off while I put a CD on the stereo. Then he came back from his reverie, jumping a little at the sound of the music. Beer sloshed onto the knee of his jeans.

"Damn it, Wallace," he snapped. "What the hell are you playing that for?" It was U2. *The Unforgettable Fire.*

I was surprised. Brad had always liked the band. "What's wrong with it?"

"I don't know..." He trailed off. I took a seat across from him. "It's the words, I guess."

"What? Brad, you know you don't give a damn about lyrics. You always said you didn't care what the words said, as long as there was good guitar playing."

"I can't explain what I mean. But I do live in Memphis now. That song doesn't exactly speak well of the place. Not that it should have..."

"Damn, Brad." I was shocked. "I never thought you'd be getting poetic this late in life. Not that there's anything wrong with that. Do you want me to play something else?"

"Nah. Forget it." We sat quietly drinking for a minute, before Brad asked, seemingly out of nowhere: "Do you remember the time the old man found us downstairs, watching *Apocalypse Now*?"

I stared, wondering just what had gotten into him. "Of course I remember. It would be kind of hard not to, wouldn't it?"

The incident he was referring to, though seemingly unimportant, had stuck with me over the years. It had made me think; given me a different perspective.

I was thirteen at the time, and my mother was gone for the day with friends. It was something she'd been in the habit of doing for the past year or so. Jeremy had slept at a buddy's. My mother would pick him up on her way home that night, around ten o'clock. I was on my own for the entire day, so of course I ended up at Brad's.

The Saturday was a cool and rainy April one. Brad and I were in his backyard, shooting the pellet gun the old man had given him for Christmas. We had set up a row of empty soda cans on the bench under the maple tree, and were proceeding to shoot them off, keeping score. All of a sudden the rain increased.

"Boys!" Brad's mother called from the back door, "Come on in now, you'll get sick. It's time for lunch."

Thank you, God. Mom had left bread in the bread drawer, and I would have gone home for a peanut butter sandwich if Mrs. Davis hadn't invited me, but she had. Brad's mother always cooked his lunch on Saturdays.

We sat in the kitchen eating macaroni and cheese and tomato soup. Brad's little sister sat across the table. She chirped to her mother about the goings-on in her second grade class, nibbling a bite or two of macaroni once in a while. Brad made faces at her. I kept my head down and listened to her voice, though I didn't pay attention to the words. I liked listening to the happiness in the old man's kitchen. I stole glances at the pretty blue eyes across the table until Mrs. Davis excused Michelle with a sigh, telling her to go back upstairs and finish cleaning her room. Michelle scampered away, and her mother shook her head as she picked up the plate of food and put it in the fridge for later.

When we were finished eating, Brad's mom told us to stay inside because of the rain. We clattered down the stairs to the family room and shot pool for a while before sitting down in front of the TV.

Brad sprawled back with the remote, flicking channels absently, before catching sight of a small spider as it crawled across the edge of the coffee table next to his foot.

"Hey—look Wallace," he exclaimed with mischievous glee. He jumped up. "I'm gonna catch it and put it under Michelle's pillow." I made no comment as he ran up the stairs, returning a minute later with a paper cup. The spider was currently on its way down the table leg. "Where'd it go?" Brad asked, looking.

"There it is." I nudged the table leg carefully with the toe of my sweat sock. The spider reached the floor and began scuttling quickly away across the rug. It had no clue.

"Let's get it!" I acted excited, and as Brad ran around the front of the table, I slid off the couch and stretched my foot toward the spider. "Hurry Brad, I'll hold it for you." Brad lunged with the cup. But the spider was no longer the perfect eight-legged instrument for terror-izing his smiling baby sister. It was only a quiet dead spider, lying there on the rug.

"Oops," I said, grinning inwardly. "My foot slipped. Sorry about that."

"Damn you, Wallace," Brad replied in disgust. He had no clue either. "You and your damned big feet. Do me a favor next time, and don't bother helping me."

I shrugged as he grabbed the remote from the couch where it had landed a minute earlier. He surfed through the Saturday cable shows, finding nothing to suit. Cooking shows, gardening shows, sob story made for TV movies, cable news and cartoons and all manner of other things.

And finally we came across the war movie. It seemed a little strange. A little crazy maybe, in an artsy kind of way. We decided to give it a try, even though neither of us understood what we were watching. We were commenting back and forth about the lunatic on the beach, when all of a sudden Brad's dad was in front of the TV.

"What the hell are you watching?" he barked. "Turn that shit off." He stooped his large frame to hit the off button before stalking back into the basement off the family room. Brad and I stared at each other again, wondering what we'd done this time. After a few minutes the old man came back and sat down. He apologized for hollering, and then told us about one of his army buddies who'd been killed in Vietnam.

The old man's tour had started in December of 1966 and finished in January of '68, just before the Tet Offensive. Brad and Michelle were late children for him. By the time Michelle was born he was in his late forties, and the year he'd spent in the jungle was long past. Up until that day I wasn't even aware he had fought, and I'm not sure Brad was either. He never spoke about the war, but that day he told us what had happened to his friend.

The old man and some of the other guys in the company had been in fighting holes, two to a hole. He was down in a hole with Paulie, one of the guys he hung around with, and his buddy Tommy was in another hole with one of the newer guys.

Everyone in the platoon had already agreed that the new guy was a total loser. Always smoking dope, never pulling his weight; always trying to get out of doing what was expected of him. And that day while they were all in the holes, there was a firefight. Brad's dad told us the asshole had done what was typical of him, even worse. He ran off and left Tommy alone in the pit, and Tommy ended up dead.

Brad and I still didn't understand what a movie about some crazy surfer who loved the smell of napalm had to do with the old man's friend. He tried to explain it to us, saying it wasn't that particular movie which upset him; he'd seen it himself years ago. What upset him was the fact that somehow, someway, people had gotten the idea that the soldiers who'd fought in that war should be ashamed. He asked us if we'd ever heard the term "baby killers." We replied that we hadn't. Then he told us he hoped we never would. When Brad asked him what the term meant he just shook his head a little, sadly. He never did explain what he meant by it. He simply went on to tell us that the war had turned into a slaughter of American boys, it had gone on way too long, that it was poorly handled and politicized. Still, none of those things meant that the GIs who fought in it should have been treated the way they were on their return. He didn't elaborate on the treatment, just told us that sometimes movies and TV portrayed the Americans as the bad guys, and he wanted us to understand that there were two sides to everything.

The last thing Brad's father told us that day was that any movie about the war reminded him of Tommy and the way he died, alone in a pit, all because of some loser who did nothing but run his mouth and smoke dope every day. The old man had been preaching to us about drugs for years, telling us to steer clear unless we wanted to end up dead or in jail. He used to bring it up at least once a month, but we never understood why until he told us about Tommy.

All of this flashed through my mind in the couple of seconds after Brad brought it up. I tipped my own bottle of Yuengling as he went on to tell me why. After everyone else had gone to bed on Thanksgiving night, the two of them began talking about the political situation. Or rather, the old man talked and Brad listened. Brad was still in shock about being lectured in front of Johnny and me, so he hadn't really done any talking himself. He just listened to the old man.

"Dad wasn't himself that night," Brad said. I could tell he was spooked. "He told me there are things going on that would scare the shit out of Kilgore no matter how much napalm he had in reserve."

"What do you mean?"

"Wallace...the old man got himself half lit after you left. He said the same kind of scum who got Tommy killed are grabbing power hand over fist. He told me to watch out. What do you think?"

I shrugged, listening to Bono's voice coming from the speaker above my head. I thought nothing. I'd never given such a thing any thought, never even considered it. "Hell, I don't know. Your sister's upset about the abortion situation." There was a new respect life group at St. Catherine's, and once in a while Michelle attended their meetings. "Some of the things she hears at church are hard to believe, but she brings home the documentation. She tells me to read it. Then I toss it. I can't stand thinking about it."

"She mentioned that on the phone. She's worried I'll dispense the morning after pill."

"Well, have you?"

"No. Dad warned me about it too, that night. I told him there are conscience laws, and he told me maybe not for long." He got up and ambled into the darkened kitchen to get each of us another beer. "The old man's worried about the Second Amendment," he went on, slouching back down.

"I thought that was settled."

"He said it might come before the court again," Brad stared into space. "Do you have any cigarettes?"

"No. I haven't smoked since Thanksgiving."

"Me either. But I wish I had a smoke right now." He stared at me across the coffee table. I could hear what he was thinking. *Do you have a gun, Wallace?*

I didn't. I'd considered buying a handgun when Michelle moved into the apartment downtown, but the new neighborhood was reasonably safe and I didn't think I needed one now. Brad changed the subject then.

"I'm asking Nicole to marry me."

"When?" I asked after I finished ragging him about it.

"Valentine's Day." He then went on to say that the old man's tongue lashing had lit a fire under him, especially considering what happened later. Brad said he wanted kids, and the old man's warning had made him start thinking about the future.

"I thought Michelle would have had a kid by now," he said idly. He was twisting his sleeve again. "She's talked about it since she was little."

I finished my beer. "Michelle's only twenty-six. We have plenty of time."

"Well, you're not twenty-six Wallace, and neither am I." Brad's voice held a teasing note. "And I'm getting the ball rolling. What the hell are you waiting for?"

He howled with laughter as I picked up a pillow and slammed it into his head. "Shut the hell up. None of your damned business what I'm waiting for."

Michelle and Nicole came in then. Brad got up off the couch and started looking in the shopping bags. "What did you get me?" he asked.

I sat back on the couch, thinking about our conversation. *What are you waiting for?*

After Michelle was asleep I thought more about Brad's revelation. His old man had retired the previous year and he had plenty of time to keep up with current events. Maybe he knew what he was talking about. As I thought back over the *Apocalypse Now* episode again, I agreed with his perception of people who looked down on members of the military.

I stared at the block of light on the ceiling cast by the streetlight shining through the window. I listened to my wife's quiet breathing, remembering an incident that occurred during my Air Force service, when I was home visiting my mother. It had been an election year, and a candidate for some office or other was on the news, making comparisons between the current conflict—the one I was serving in—and the earlier one in Vietnam. I couldn't remember the particulars, only that the politician seemed to believe that neither was justified. I probably wouldn't have given it another thought if not for my mother's comment.

She thought she was alone, but I was standing in the doorway behind her. After the candidate's sound bite she nodded her head, muttering to herself: "He's right. He's got my vote. We don't need any more baby killers."

I turned around quickly and walked back out, never letting on I'd overheard. I'd gotten over it of course, like so many other things she had said and done, but I certainly never forgot the incident.

I lay awake a while longer, thinking about my mother and how different we were. I didn't understand my mother. I never had. I wondered who I took after. I hadn't spoken to my father in years, didn't even know where he was anymore. After Jeremy turned eighteen he dropped out of our lives completely.

I wondered why he had left us. I lay there next to Michelle, remembering that spring and summer, and the sound of my little brother as he cried in his room down the hall. He had only been three years old, and he wasn't able to take in the fact that Dad was gone and wasn't coming back. Not that my mother spent any time trying to explain it, to either of us.

I rarely thought about my father. There were a few very faded memories of the year before he walked out, but it hurt so much to remember them that I'd learned never to do it. Pushing all thought of him to the back of my mind had become second nature.

As far as my mother was concerned he was dead. She never spoke about him. She refused to answer my questions, and after a while I just stopped asking. When gifts had arrived every year I wrote thank you cards and sent them to whatever return address was on the package, but the last one I'd written had been on the occasion of my high school graduation, over ten years earlier. My mother kept nothing at all in the house pertaining to their marriage. No pictures, not even of happy events like birthdays. Nothing. My father had been scrubbed from our house as soon as he left, and I didn't even remember what he looked like.

Oh? Is that the truth? I don't think so...you could remember if you wanted to.

I pushed the thought away and concentrated on my mother, ruminating again about our differences. They were all we had between us now. There were times when I thought I'd been switched at birth or dropped in a cabbage patch. To me it seemed a wonder that she could truly be my mother, because the older I got, the further away she seemed.

I brooded about it a little longer. The fact that my mother and I could look at the exact same situation and see two completely different things was a strange fact, but a fact just the same. I glanced at the clock on the nightstand, and saw that it was two a.m. I turned over and put my arms around my wife. I finally shook off the mood I'd been in since Brad and Nicole had gone, and decided that as long as Michelle was okay with it, the next time myrtle was in town I wouldn't back off.

Michelle

I'm getting drowsy baby, but I want to write a little more about what happened when I discovered you would be coming. I couldn't believe it when I realized I was pregnant. It was the last thing I expected.

My period had been irregular for months, probably because of all the stress, and I never gave it a thought when I missed it last January. Your daddy and I had gone through an extremely rough time. The intimate part of our marriage had suffered for almost a year, and I simply never considered the possibility of pregnancy.

The first morning I felt sick I tried to blame it on what I'd eaten the previous evening. Jason didn't hear me in the bathroom. I denied what I knew to be true for a week before finally taking a home pregnancy test, the results of which were positive. My prayers were almost hysterical.

Blessed Mother, what should I do? Pray for us, pray for us, what are we going to do? What about the baby?

Jason knew something was wrong as soon as he walked in through the kitchen and found me sitting in the dark. I ran to him and he hugged me. He asked me what was wrong. Did something happen at work? Did the boys come here? What happened?

I couldn't get the words out, and he got scared. He turned on the light and grabbed me by the arms, sitting me down on the couch. I collapsed against him, sobbing wildly as I put the test stick in his hand.

He stared at the blue line for a time as I sobbed on his shoulder. Then he took my face between his hands and made me look at him. His eyes showed me everything in an instant, reflecting our many memories, hopes, fears, and dreams.

Love...weddings...babies...happiness...future...love...I love you.

I don't know how long we stayed on the couch. Time meant nothing to us at such moments. He held me and told me all would be well, saying that he would take care of us. I remember him laying his head on my belly where he knew you were, and kissing you.

EIGHT

Jason

9 Years Earlier

After Christmas dinner when the three of us—Brad, the old man and me—went to the garage for our usual drink, the old man began talking about the FEDHCA, the government bureaucracy that had been implemented after reform was enacted some years earlier. He had been reading articles and hearing things on the news that had him convinced rationing of all kinds was coming.

I had forgotten all about the situation, though I remembered that protests had taken place before the legislation passed. Less than half the country had been on board with the healthcare bill, but they'd been able to muscle it through, and since the changes didn't go into effect immediately most people let it go to the back of their minds. I'm ashamed to admit I was one of them. I hadn't even paid much attention to the protests. Michelle and I had been newly married. We were both working hard, and neither of us kept up with current events.

I ought to have known better. During my time overseas I had

witnessed things that should have made me aware of the dangers of living under a tyrannical system of government, but I—like many others—had been blind to what was slowly taking place. I had thought such things could never happen in America, and that was my mistake.

Politicians and talking heads had told us that changes were necessary. People were suffering, they said, and reform was required to make sure everyone was treated equally. Along with the protests, there had been some debate in Congress about costs and quality of care, but the people in charge at the time decided to go ahead and pass it through backdoor channels. Many experts and intellectuals in all fields assured us it would pay for itself, that rationing was out of the question, and that everyone would have a better life.

For a while it seemed to be true. Nothing changed in our world. But we were unaware of what was taking place in avenues of power: changes that would eventually transform the very things we held most sacred. New bureaucracies were being built, and unelected officials were consolidating power. The funding for it all was unlimited, and by the time Brad and I figured out something wasn't right, the bureaucracy had taken on a life of its own. It had manifested itself, corrupt and out of control, and we were now seeing the results.

The old man informed us that all records—of any and every kind —were currently being entered into a government database, beginning with natural-born citizens over seventy-five years of age and working backward from there. Everyone would be issued ID cards eventually, and the database would contain medical records, social security numbers, bank account information, employment records, and DNA information, even for minor children.

A light began flickering in the corner of my eyes, making me understand that hard times were on the horizon. With this knowledge came the sound of flowing water. The lights that no one else could see always appeared during times of consequence in my life, whether good or bad.

Brad and I stared at each other. His face was sober, unlike him. Except for a few occasions, Brad was always the first to crack wise about such things, but that afternoon he only stared back at me with a stubborn look. What I read in his eyes was this: *Wallace, what the hell is going on? I'll be damned if the bastards are getting my DNA.*

Michelle and Nicole were in the house with Mrs. Davis, cleaning up after the Christmas meal. Johnny and Cindy and the boys were out of town that year, visiting Cindy's family. As I thought of Michelle and our plans for a family, I suddenly realized that I was afraid. Something was descending on us, like a ceiling with no end in any direction. Thick and solid, dark and hovering, slowly pushing us down. Descending imperceptibly, waiting for the time when we could be smothered.

After Thanksgiving dinner a month earlier when I had a couple of smokes in that very same garage, I'd been able to stay off them for a month. But now my mouth was dry. The beer in my hand wasn't helping, so I asked the old man if he had any Lucky Strikes on hand. He did of course. He hid it from the women, but he couldn't quit. As he went to the toolbox to get them, Brad asked, "Why are you limping, Dad?"

He found the pack of cigarettes, shook one out, and handed Brad the pack. "My damn foot's bothering me again," he answered, lighting up. He took a bottle of Scotch from the old cupboard above the workbench and poured us each a shot. The three of us downed them quickly, and then sat smoking in silence.

Michelle had mentioned her father's foot issues. She was worried. She said he had to be careful, because sometimes diabetics developed ulcers that could lead to complications, and that even though the old man was seeing a podiatrist he couldn't seem to get rid of the problem. Brad and I exchanged another look through the lazily rising cigarette smoke. *You ask him, Wallace.*

"Are you okay Dad?"

"Yeah. Don't worry about me Jason. I'm the least of your worries."

My mind went back to Michelle then, and her distress about the system. Michelle was a born mother. I'd come to realize it in the years since we married. She had a big heart when it came to innocent babies, and every time she heard another story about the barbarism of what some deemed "reproductive health" her heart became sicker. One thing in particular that upset her was the news that some of the existing family planning clinics were expanding their operations to include baby and child care, and even birth services. She said it made her want to cry to think of babies being born in the same facilities where others were being butchered.

I mentioned the situation to the old man. He said that funds had been allocated to some of the clinics that qualified. It was a relatively new development, but once such a thing got started, it took on a life of its own.

Brad shook his head as he got up to get another cigarette. He lit up again. The look in his eyes through the haze of smoke made me think of his question a few weeks earlier. *Do you have a gun?*

* * *

Back at home I told Michelle about the conversation in the garage. We were in bed.

"What about Daddy's diabetes?" she said.

"He didn't seem to be worried about it."

"He never worries about himself."

"Well, there's nothing we can do about the situation right now. Maybe they can get it rolled back before too much damage is done. It's going to take a while to be fully implemented, and all of it might not come to pass."

I left out the part that upset me most. After every birth a blood sample would be taken, and the DNA information on the babies would be kept on file and entered into the system. We lay quietly for a minute.

"Nicole says her school is getting out of control," Michelle said.

Nicole was a teacher too. Brad had mentioned that the middle school where she taught was going downhill. There was a lot of fighting going on, possibly gang related. Kids showed up carrying knives and even guns, and a boy had been expelled for threatening a teacher. Brad wanted her to look for another job.

"Honey, don't worry about Nicole. She's tough enough to handle anything that might come her way. Anyway, Brad's on top of the situation."

I changed the subject then. "Let's start looking for a house."

"Jason!" Michelle sounded surprised. "Really?"

"Why, you don't want to buy a house with me?" I poked her, and she laughed back, shoving me a little.

"Well I've only been hinting around about it for the last year or so."

"We're going to need a bigger place, beautiful." I smiled.

"What are you talking about?"

"Let's have a baby, baby," I said, hugging her. I kissed her and looked in her eyes, getting lost.

You're so beautiful. Let's have a baby.

Are you sure?

Yes I'm sure.

Your baby...your baby, Jason.

I turned out the light. The things of the world went away for us then, and we got down to business.

* * *

Brad proposed to Nicole on Valentine's Day. Nicole called Michelle at ten-thirty p.m., knowing she would want to hear all about it. They were on the phone forever it seemed, talking about the wedding. The date chosen was February fourteenth, exactly one year later. I lay in bed, staring up at the crucifix hanging above the headboard.

We would have to fly down to Memphis. Michelle would definitely be a bridesmaid, and Brad was trying to decide between Johnny and me for the position of best man. I lay there in silence next to Michelle, wondering where we'd be in a year.

Michelle

I'll write a little more for you, angel-baby. I want to make sure you'll know exactly how the summer before you were born unfolded. It's been hot and still here at Mark's place since the other night when I lay awake writing. It's evening now, and today was the same as the day before, and the day before that. It's pretty, peaceful, calm, and quiet. Restful, just the way your daddy said he wanted it to be for me.

Until tonight. Tonight I had a scare while waiting for Melanie. We never know when to expect her, since her schedule is subject to change at a moment's notice. But nursing positions in the few remaining private hospitals are in great demand these days, and Melanie says she will put up with almost anything to stay where the staff is concerned more with saving lives than with ending them.

I had just finished taking a shower in the beautifully renovated upstairs bathroom. There's a half bath in the basement but no tub, so I usually run up and get a shower between ten and eleven, right before bed. Tonight's weather forecast said thunderstorms are likely, though. Mark thought I should come up early, in case of a power outage. I like going upstairs in daylight. I haven't been out to the corn-field since Sunday because farm workers were close by, and Mark wanted me to stay hidden.

As I came out of the bathroom, I saw that Patty's door was open. She's usually in bed by the time I come up at night, and I've never seen her bedroom. I took in the room with a glance: wallpaper fitting the original style of the house, simple white curtains, and beautiful old-fashioned shaker furniture, nothing ostentatious. I didn't want to pry, but I couldn't stop myself from peeking inside. A wedding picture of Patty and her husband hangs on the wall, and on the bedside table sits another picture. It's a studio portrait of the little girl pictured in the birthday snapshot, the Down syndrome child. I wondered again who she might be before going on down the hall. As I started down the stairs, the front door bell rang.

I froze, clutching the banister. Mark was up like a shot, running into the entryway. He looked up at me, put a finger to his lips, and motioned for me to go back. I ran up the stairs, heart pounding, and scurried into the bathroom. I locked the door quickly and collapsed on the side of the tub, hugging you against me and praying.

After a minute Mark came upstairs and told me to go on down. It was only Melanie. She'd forgotten her key and no one heard her out back, so she'd come around front and rung the bell. I was shaking as I followed him down the stairs.

* * *

It's late. Lightning from the kitchen window flashes in the stairwell, accompanied by the sound of thunder. Melanie has gone. Everyone else is in bed. Though I'm trying to get myself under control, I'm on the verge of tears.

Why can't I have a doctor? Why can't I have an ultrasound? Why must my child be deprived and endangered? The wind whistles and howls. All of a sudden the door to the kitchen slams shut with a bang. I bury my face in the pillow to smother my sobs.

Why must I stay hidden here, scared of my own shadow, jumping at the slightest noise, afraid? How can this be happening?

I find myself wrapped in the quilt, rocking back and forth on the bed, aching for Jason's arms.

Why must we be separated at this time? The time when we should be laughing and planning and looking forward to the future? Why can't he be with me?

Jason
8 Years Earlier

Michelle and I bought our house the October before Brad and Nicole's wedding. It was a three-bedroom rancher on a shady quiet street in one of the older neighborhoods about two miles north of downtown. The house had a big back yard with plenty of room for kids to play, and the front lawn was tastefully landscaped.

When I stopped at my mother's on the way home from work to tell her we'd be moving, I had to deal with her usual bullshit. Mom looked up from the magazine she'd been perusing, ran her hand through her short brown hair, and cocked her head to the side. Her slate blue eyes were dubious, and a little scornful. I took a deep breath. *How the hell does she do it? She's only five feet two inches tall for God's sake. How does she manage to make me feel so small? Every damn time.*

"I think I know the house you're talking about," she said. "Isn't that the house where that family lived, with the father who ran away and left his wife and children? He worked at the university. He was part of the maintenance crew—a plumber I believe. If it's the place I'm thinking of, isn't it a little small? And it's old. Don't you want something more modern?"

I sighed then, passing over her comment about our new home's previous occupants. If what she said was true, Michelle and I hadn't been told of it.

"Mom, we made settlement yesterday. It's a great starter home, perfect for us. We love it. I just wanted you to know we'd be moving, and that the Davises are throwing a housewarming for us at the new house a week from Saturday. Please join us Mom."

She got out her Blackberry to look at her calendar. "Saturday the twentieth?"

"Yeah."

But Mom already had plans that day. I rolled my eyes as she explained that she couldn't make it. She was joining a group of friends from work on a ten-mile bike ride to look at the fall colors. *I give up.*

"Well, okay Mom. But if you get back any time after five o'clock and want to stop over, you're more than welcome." The party was starting around five, and it would be dark soon after. She could stop by if she wanted to, but I knew she wouldn't. I got up from my chair across the room, and finished off by asking her to invite Jeremy for me. He wasn't home at the time, and I didn't want to hang around waiting for him.

Jeremy was still living with Mom. After college his plans to play pro football had come to nothing, much to my mother's disappointment, but he had graduated with a degree in marketing. There was a new football team in New Jersey, along with a new stadium, and Jeremy had been hired as a senior sales manager. He'd done well for himself, marketing the luxury suites where groups of high-end people went to party and watch the games, and he admitted to me that he welcomed the long commute. Longer hours meant less time listening to Mom.

"Why don't you get out of there?" I had asked him.

"I plan to as soon as I get a few bills paid off. She drives me crazy."

"I'd be damned if I'd stay there with her," I told him. "She's getting worse. I can hardly talk to her anymore."

"I know. She makes me aware of that fact on a weekly basis."

I recalled this conversation as she assured me she would tell Jeremy about our housewarming party. Then, before she could start talking up Jeremy's job, how much money he was making and how many interesting people he was meeting every week, I got the hell out of there.

Michelle was kneeling on the floor of our bedroom closet when I returned to the apartment, packing up her many pairs of shoes. When I related the encounter, she paused for a moment in her work, looking at the high-heeled sandals in her hands. Then she threw me a mischievous smile. Her eyes gleamed.

"Well, don't worry about Almira."

"Who?"

"Almira. She wouldn't be good company anyway."

"What are you talking about? I was just explaining why the Black Widow can't make it to our new place. Who's Almira?"

"Jason honey, where's your mind?" she teased, getting up from the floor. She began dancing back and forth in front of me then, humming the music from the *Wizard of Oz*—the instrumental playing during the scene showing Miss Gulch furiously pedaling her bicycle toward Dorothy's farm, hell bent on removing Toto so she could take him away to have him destroyed. Michelle was using the shoes as maracas. The buckles on them clinked as she hummed and danced.

I roared laughter at her. We both lost control then, collapsing back on the bed. When we finally came back to ourselves we were lying there together. *This is our last night here. I'll miss this place. Might as well leave it with one more to remember.*

She still hadn't become pregnant. I put my arms around her, and she stared back at me.

This is the night. Tonight it'll happen. A baby... Your baby, Jason.

I stared at her for a minute longer before getting down to business.

* * *

We moved into the house. The housewarming party was fun, and as usual the food was out of this world. Neither of us missed my mother; those who cared about us were there. Michelle's whole family came: Bella and Lucio and their four kids, Aunt Rosie, and Johnny and Cindy and the boys. CJ and Mrs. CJ came, and Danny and his wife, and Reese and Heather, along with some of my buddies from the auto body shop on Route 24 and their significant others. Chippy, the owner of the place, had been a friend for years. People Michelle worked with stopped in and out all evening long as well, so we had a full house. Jeremy made a late appearance. He looked embarrassed when I answered the door, giving me a suspicious feeling that he had just that day heard about the party. It wasn't his fault. I should have called and invited him myself, instead of relying on Mom.

A shed the size of a one-car garage stood in our new backyard, and as usual the guys ended up out back, drinking and having a few smokes.

I had taken the Harley out for a ride earlier and parked it in the driveway instead of the shed, so we'd have enough room to party. I rarely rode anymore, but still I kept the bike. I hadn't been able to bring myself to sell it, even though Reese had been asking to buy it for years. He did it again that day in the shed.

"Wallace, when are you gonna sell me that Harley? You never ride the damn thing, and somebody should be able to get some use out of it." He grinned.

I grinned back, but I didn't want to discuss it. I was attached to the bike even though it was an old one; new the same year I was born.

"I took it out today. And now that I have this shed, there's plenty of room to work on it. I think I'll definitely keep it."

I gave the old man a look then, asking for help, and he didn't disappoint me. He knew how much the bike meant to me, so he started talking about another subject. He mentioned what he'd received in the mail, and his words made Reese and everyone else put all thoughts of my motorcycle out of their minds.

The old man had received his notification from the HCA a few weeks earlier, along with instructions to report—paperwork in hand—to the closest departmental building in Harrisburg to have his picture taken. The ID card would be issued that day. He'd been expecting it, but apparently it was still a shock. The paperwork stated that he had to report before January first.

"What about Mom?" said Johnny.

"She's not old enough. They're still working on the over seventy-five crowd."

It was common knowledge in the family that the old man was a lot older than Michelle's mom. They had married when Mrs. Davis was only eighteen years old, and she was pregnant with Johnny at the time.

Everyone began discussing the political situation then. Nobody was happy about it, either. Certain politicians were mentioned with cusswords attached to their names. CJ and Danny were especially pissed off. As a result of some of the policies being implemented small businesses were suffering due to high taxes. Way higher than they'd ever been.

The familiar sound of water was a backdrop as I listened to the different conversations going on around me. Johnny and Lucio stood by the door with the old man, talking about the upcoming elections, and how it didn't seem to matter who was elected anymore; no matter who you voted for, once they took office they usually did the opposite of what had been promised. The door slammed open then. Jamie and Sonny—Lucio and Bella's oldest boy—came running into the shed. They nosed around for fifteen minutes or so, getting underfoot, and then tore out the door again, leaving it open.

It was a typical October night. Cold air gusted through the doorway. I leaned against my workbench and knocked back another shot of whiskey, as Johnny got up out of the lawn chair he'd been sitting in and went to the door to shut it. The next thing I knew he was barreling outside, yelling: *"What the hell!"*

Everything went quiet. The old man started to get out of his chair, wincing as he put too much pressure on his bad foot. Michelle said he had nerve damage, and sometimes he couldn't feel pain, but every once in a while that foot gave him a reminder.

I walked to the door and looked out. The moon was full, and by its light and the glow of the streetlights, I was able to see a little. My new backyard was empty and quiet. The boys were nowhere in sight. After a minute Johnny's voice came from behind the shed: "Just what the hell do you think you're doing?"

I turned toward the sound of his voice. He stalked around the corner then, cussing and pulling Junior along by the ear. He was holding a smoking joint between his thumb and forefinger. He looked at me as he went by, eyes flashing, madder than I'd ever seen him. He let go of the ear and shoved Junior across the backyard before grabbing him by the arm and taking him around the side of the house to the driveway. A minute later he backed his truck out into the street and drove away.

Junior was grounded for the foreseeable future.

None of the women had witnessed the incident. They'd all been in the living room, sitting around talking and taking turns holding Gianna, Bella and Lucio's new little girl. When I related the incident to Michelle after everyone else was gone, she said she had no idea anything had happened. Cindy had gotten a call on her cell phone from Johnny, saying he and Junior were ready, to meet them out front.

"Jason, Cindy must be so upset," Michelle said. "She thought it was about work. I heard her conversation with Johnny. She was arguing with him, telling him to come inside and say goodbye to Mom."

Cindy had given the baby back to Michelle then, saying, "Johnny needs to go, something's going on at the plant, some emergency, and he has to get over there." She had kissed everyone, collected Jamie from the basement, and left the party.

"Did Daddy see the joint?" Michelle asked. "You know how he feels about drugs."

"Well no, he didn't actually see it, but..." Then I admitted he'd been pretty close to the door, and I thought he had probably smelled it. After I shut the door I saw the look on the old man's face. I hadn't seen that particular look since I was fifteen, when the old man caught Brad and me stealing scotch out of the bottle in the dining room cupboard.

I told Michelle that her dad had gotten up out of his chair, stalked over to the workbench and started looking through *my* toolbox.

"What for? Why would he need tools at a time like this?"

Then I realized I'd almost just let the cat out of the bag about the old man's smoking.

"Oh...uh..." I stammered, trying to think of something to say. Then I remembered my drill, which the old man had borrowed the week before. "He needed drill bits. He went over there to look for them."

"What's that got to do with Junior?" She was looking at me sideways, and I changed the subject quickly.

"Nothing. Where do you think he got that joint?"

"No idea. Cindy says he's becoming a handful." She took another tray of dirty dishes out to the kitchen. Her voice floated in at me, muffled by the kitchen wall. "She told me his grades have been poor so far this year."

When she came back into the living room, I changed the subject again. Bella had left one of Gianna's toys by mistake. I saw it sticking out from under the couch and picked it up, shaking it back and forth in front of Michelle.

"Oh, Jason," she said breathlessly, "wasn't she beautiful?"

"Yes," I answered, putting my arms around her. I turned her around in my arms and put my hand across her belly, kissing the back of her neck. "Beautiful. Like you, baby. Do you think you're pregnant?"

"We'll know soon."

* * *

After Michelle lost our second child that December, we spent Christmas quietly with her family and went home early, each in our respective world of pain.

Junior was at the old man's. He'd been grounded for the previous two months, only allowed to leave the house for school and church. When he saw Michelle he hugged her, and she cried a little. Both boys said they were sorry, and Jamie handed her a little card he'd made on the computer that read: "God is Love."

I enjoyed the meal, even though our loss seemed to affect the whole family, and the conversation around the table was stilted and uncomfortable. Michelle's mother was a phenomenal cook. She used recipes she had learned from her mother. Her parents had been Italian immigrants.

Mrs. Davis only remembered a few words of Italian. But she hadn't forgotten how to cook in Italian, thank God, and she always cooked five course meals on holidays. We'd already finished the first two courses—fruit cup, followed by wedding soup. The third course was always pasta of some sort. That day it was homemade ravioli. Michelle was hardly eating, and her mother noticed.

"Aren't you having any ravioli, Michelle?" My wife made no answer; there were tears in her eyes. She turned to me, sitting next to her, put a hand on my arm, and got up and left the room. Brad stared at me from across the table. He came by himself that year; Nicole was too busy with the wedding. He'd never witnessed such an exhibition of grief from his sister prior to that day, and I could tell it upset him.

I gave him a nod and rose from the table. *I'll handle it.*

I found Michelle in her old room face down on the bed. It had become a guest room, and Brad's stuff was scattered everywhere. I waded through the mess on the floor, went to the bed, and lay down on top of her. I covered her with my body, trying to shield her, to soothe her. Both of us cried a little as I asked the question again, the one that had come and gone over and over for the past few weeks. *Where are you, God?*

Michelle

The storm is winding down. We lost power for an hour during the worst of it, but the rain is tapering off now, and the thunder seems far away. I'm calm again angel-baby. I'm sleepy too, but I want to write a few last lines for you before I lie down.

Before she left earlier Melanie told me I have to be careful. In her estimation you are about thirty weeks old, and everything seems normal with your size. She thinks you weigh about three or four pounds. Your heartbeat is strong and my blood pressure is okay, but the urine sample showed glucose. Melanie is worried I might develop gestational diabetes. Even though it's common for glucose to be present at some point during pregnancy, she wants me to watch what I eat. I should have mentioned the fact that Daddy was diabetic. I wonder if it means anything?

Dear Lord, watch over my baby. Please let me stay healthy until she is born. Blessed Mother, did you worry during your pregnancy? How many nights did you lie awake, wondering about your Son? Did you lie awake the way I do? Or maybe you simply trusted in the Lord. I imagine you praying, and calmly trusting, relying on Joseph to take care of you.

NINE

Jason
8 Years Earlier

Brad and Nicole were married as planned on Valentine's Day. Michelle and I flew down to Memphis the Thursday before along with the rest of the family, and everyone had a great time in Tennessee. The whole family went, even Bella and Lucio and the kids. That was a good thing, since it turned out to be the last time we were all able to gather together.

Michelle looked beautiful in her bridesmaid's gown, even though it was a little big on her. She'd lost ten pounds in the weeks since the baby. She hadn't even thought about having the dress altered, and said that she hoped no one would notice. If anyone did they didn't mention it. The wedding went off without a hitch. I was Brad's best man, and I made sure to get the ring from him the night before. Nicole looked amazing, everyone had fun at the reception, and three days later Michelle and I were home again. We both went back to work, and things went on for a while.

Spring arrived, our first spring since moving. I had to get used to taking care of the yard. I hadn't had to worry about yard work back in the apartment. I got in the habit of getting up early to cut the grass on Saturday mornings before going on to work. The neighborhood was usually quiet except for a few barking dogs. Our yard was fenced on both sides, with evergreen hedges marking the back of the property and lining the sidewalk in front. The landscaping was nice.

Crocuses and daffodils danced under the front window between the sidewalk and the house. Michelle hung a wind chime from the front overhang, and it tinkled faintly and peacefully in the breeze. Out back was a huge Japanese maple tree along with lilac bushes and hydrangeas lining the fences on either side. Rose bushes grew on either side of the double doors of the shed, waiting for their time to come. All in all we were very pleased with our home, especially the yard.

But I finally had to admit to myself that Michelle was still unwell. She hadn't been the same since our child left us. She was sad and anxious and worried. Her anxiety increased in the weeks preceding parent-teacher conferences, making her ill with stress. I always listened patiently to her stories about the discipline issues she was forced to deal with, and encouraged her to be honest and straightforward with the parents. But it didn't seem to help her that year. She still dreaded the meetings, saying some of the parents just couldn't believe their little darlings would ever be guilty of the things she told them about. That year's conferences must have been bad, because afterward she brought up the idea of resigning.

It wasn't that she didn't enjoy teaching. She did, and she always said it was a very rewarding profession, but I could tell she was burning out. During conference week that spring, Michelle began suffering from insomnia, and after the conferences were behind her, the insomnia stayed. It went on for months.

When I woke up to find her side of the bed empty, I would pull on a pair of jeans and go out to her. Sometimes I found her asleep in front of the TV, but more often she was awake, and she always apologized for disturbing me.

"Honey, you're not bothering me. Come back to bed. Aren't you cold?"

"A little. But I'll just stay here for a while. You go back to sleep. It's three o'clock, and you get up earlier than I do."

The pain in her face was always evident on those nights, and I would go over to the couch, put my arms around her, and stay with her for a while.

The old man's foot was improving. He was receiving treatment for the nerve damage, and whatever they told him to do seemed to work for a while. He was limping less, and seemed to be feeling better that spring. He had also managed to get his blood sugar under control somehow, though he continued to smoke on occasion.

The endocrinologist and podiatrist accepted the coverage from the HCA. However the old man hated it. He was completely pissed off about the fact that his private insurance had been terminated. The private coverage, though it was only partial, had been part of his retirement package. But unfortunately insurance companies were being squeezed at the time, and he'd received notification that they were dropping him. Apparently the private insurers had been given a choice: Either terminate coverage for anyone older than seventy-five, or pay a one thousand dollar fine for each policy every quarter.

Brad said the old man cussed the new system for forty-five minutes over the phone to him one night, and said he'd almost rather pay the doctors with his savings. But his care was expensive. He knew it would eat everything up eventually. He wanted to leave something after he was gone, so he swallowed his pride and went along with it, and the flare-ups in his foot subsided for a while.

* * *

Junior and Jamie were growing up. After the episode with the joint, Junior seemed to straighten up for a while. His grades improved, and by the end of that school year Johnny and Cindy thought he was going to be okay.

CJ and his wife bought a beach cottage that summer. It was down on Delaware Bay at a little place called Broadkill Beach. CJ liked to go fishing. He'd had a boat for years, since before I started working at the garage. It was common for Reese and me to spend days fishing with Ceej on the bay or out in the Atlantic, but we always had to get up at three o'clock in the morning to drive the two hours, pulling the boat with his truck.

Now things were better. We could sleep at the cottage the night before, and once in a while we could even sleep a little later if high tide cooperated. CJ was a drill sergeant when it came to getting ahead of the tide, and he would drag us out of bed at two o'clock in the morning sometimes. Fishing was CJ's passion, same as mine. In those days he paid for the whole garage to go out on a charter every year as a Christmas gift, usually tuna fishing. We'd go every summer, and Ceej always paid for each of us to bring a guest. I usually took Junior with me, or Brad, if he happened to be visiting from Memphis. CJ called these fishing excursions "Christmas in July."

Like I said, many things about the American way of life were in the process of change, and I knew that CJ hadn't made the decision to purchase the fishing cottage lightly. But even though the high taxes were pinching him, business was still okay at that point, so he decided to invest in the cottage before he'd be too old to enjoy it. I think he did the right thing, and not only because he'd worked like a dog all his life, and deserved to have a fishing shack as long as he could afford it. There are other reasons I thank God for CJ's shack that will become apparent later in this narrative.

Michelle and I spent a weekend alone at the cottage early that summer. She rested in the sun on Broadkill Beach while I spent time surf fishing. She enjoyed that weekend. Michelle always felt better after lying in the sun.

Junior also accompanied us guys on a different fishing trip. CJ took us out on the boat all day, both Saturday and Sunday, and Junior seemed to enjoy it. He caught a couple of flounder and was disappointed they were too small to keep. In my opinion he had come out of the troubled period of the previous fall. Junior never mentioned anything to me about the incident at the housewarming, and I never even considered bringing it up to him. Junior was Johnny's son, and I assumed Johnny had handled it.

* * *

7 Years Earlier

Another year had passed.

Michelle's insomnia increased during the course of the school year, especially at conference times. Even though she didn't complain about work, it was plain to me that it was getting more and more difficult for her to get up and go each day. I had my own ideas about the reasons, and to me it seemed more than just the conferences twice a year. I was of the mind that it was hard for Michelle to be around so many kids now, because we still didn't have a baby of our own.

After the New Year her stress increased again. It upset me. I didn't want Michelle to suffer anymore, so I urged her to resign.

Though she had already looked into finding a position at a parochial school, nothing worked out, so we finally decided it would be best if she resigned from teaching effective the end of the school year. Since we had a reasonable amount saved for a rainy day, I told her not to worry about finances. The current situation qualified as a rainy day in my book. Her health was what was important, and I assured her she'd be able to find another job when she felt better. Her relief was palpable.

My mother sniffed at this news, before starting in on Michelle and what a mistake she was making. So I got up from the chair I'd been sitting in and told Mom I had to be going, and to tell Jeremy I'd call him.

Summer arrived, and with it Michelle's last day as a teacher. Some of her friends threw a goodbye party for her, and many of her students presented her with going away gifts and cards, artwork and pictures and letters, all saying how much they would miss her, and that they loved her. She was sad to say goodbye, but it was also a relief, for both of us.

She'll put that weight back on now. She'll be healthy again. She'll get better, and then we'll have a baby. God? These were my thoughts and prayers as June passed into July.

Michelle

Patty is a terrific cook, angel-baby. She has a garden out back behind the barn, and says the green beans are taking over her life. She's been bending over backward to feed me well, after what Melanie told us. I've been able to see her in action as she puts up food from the garden, because there's an old stove down here in the laundry room, and this is where Patty does her canning.

Yesterday she made bread-and-butter pickles. I offered to help with the preparation, so Patty put me in charge of measuring out the spices and the sugar and vinegar, while she put the cucumbers and onions through the food processor. After a while I realized that the old kitchen table we were working on looked like the same one in the photo of the birthday party, and before I could stop myself, I mentioned the picture to Patty. She wanted to see it, so I got the book. Patty took the picture out and stared at it for a while in silence, before telling me it had been taken on Liz's fourth birthday, and that the little girl in the high chair was her third daughter, Lori Ann. Lori had passed away the following year.

"Sandy must have kept this picture of Lori Ann to remember her by," Patty said sadly.

I mentioned to Patty that she and I had something in common, angel-baby. Patty and I had both lost children, even though your brother was born two months early and he died before we could take him home with us. Then Patty told me a little about Lori.

"Lori Ann was born prematurely too," Patty said as she continued staring at the snapshot. "She was born with Down syndrome and she was always sickly. She never learned to walk, and only weighed eighteen pounds when she finally left us. She was three years old when she died."

Patty's voice was unsteady as she related that the family was devastated by what happened to Lori, and that her husband in particular was never the same.

"Still," Patty said, wiping tears from her eyes, "we were blessed to have had her in our lives, even for a little while. She taught everyone. It's amazing really, how much all of us learned from that little girl during her short time on earth."

Jason
7 Years Earlier

We spent the July Fourth holiday at the old man's that year, grilling steaks and hamburgers in his backyard. Brad and Nicole were home. She was on break from her school in Tennessee, and he'd taken a couple of weeks off.

After the food was all finished, the boys lighted sparklers and ran around waving them in the dark. Then they started tossing firecrackers. Little Gianna was the only girl among the cousins. She seemed fascinated by the sparkling lights, but she screamed herself sick at the sound of the firecrackers, forcing Bella and Lucio and their brood to go home early.

After the women went inside to begin the cleanup and Junior and Jamie ran out front with more firecrackers, the four of us went inside the old man's garage. There we proceeded to drink a couple of shots and indulge in a smoke or two.

The old man was still worried about the Second Amendment. He mentioned a case that had worked its way through the courts. According to news reports the Supreme Court was considering it, and there was a good chance it would be on the docket that fall. He leaned back in his decrepit old office chair, knocking back shots of Dewar's and informing us of possible consequences if the decision went the wrong way. Nothing he said was positive.

I leaned back against the wall next to the old man's refrigerator. A breeze blew through the open garage doors. Moths fluttered around the naked light bulb hanging from the ceiling, and crickets cheeped monotonously. Shouts came from the back yard along with more crackling sounds, as the boys lit off their final firecrackers of the night. Brad and Johnny sat smoking, alternately cussing and slamming their shot glasses down on the workbench as the old man went on talking. I smoked along with them, but I wasn't cussing. Not right then.

I was feeling the water as the lights flickered in the corners of my eyes. The old man's voice was crystal clear, cutting through a sensation of shock. It seemed somehow like I'd been there before. It seemed to me that I just *knew*. *It just is.* I saw Michelle and our future children in my mind's eye as the water rushed through my brain, and realized I was praying again as the old man's voice went on, calmly telling us what could (*would*) happen. *God? Please. What about our children?*

I became aware of something else then, which may or may not have been with me during previous experiences of this sort but which I perceived to be there that night. *Are you my Guardian?*

It was a presence of some kind or other. I can't explain it any better than that. After a minute it was gone, and I came back to myself. The old man was still talking as he stumped to the toolbox to look for more cigarettes.

"Dad, you better not smoke," Brad interrupted. "Your foot's been better since you cut back."

"I'm only having one, boy," he growled. "Don't worry about it."

Then he handed his pack around and we all lit up again. *Water... a storm.* I gave Brad a look. Smoke curled lazily. *Wallace, you better get a gun. You might need one.*

The old man changed the subject then, and told us that Michelle's mom and Aunt Rosie had received notification from the HCA. I knew that CJ and Mrs. CJ had as well, along with Danny and his wife. All of them had been ordered to report to Harrisburg no later than September first.

"Things will probably move along faster now," the old man said. "Now that most people over fifty-five are in the system, it'll probably take less time. Families, younger people, they can probably be entered more easily. They're not in Medicare, and family IDs are usually the employee social security number."

"Was Mom on Medicare?"

"Nah." The old man took a drag on his smoke. "She just retired and went on this bullshit." I asked him if he'd tried getting coverage under Brad's mothers insurance, but he told us it was out of the question. "I looked into it a few years ago," he said. "They laughed at me." The four of us were quiet for a minute.

"Why didn't they just use the social security numbers," I mused. "They could have done it all with a few keystrokes."

The old man said he didn't know. His theory was that it was being done gradually so as not to worry people. Most people were so busy working that they didn't have a lot of time to research the situation, and maybe they believed what we'd all been told: That we'd be able to decide for ourselves when or whether we'd opt for it.

"And you know why they started with senior citizens," he continued. He was right. We did. They'd been making noise for years about end of life issues, even while stating the opposite, and the first thing on the list after reform had passed was to get control of the old people.

"Doctor's offices are getting overcrowded," Brad remarked. "We get an order, people come in to pick it up, bitching and complaining about the wait."

"Apparently doctors are quitting right and left," the old man spat. He sounded disgusted. "I ran across an article online. Some doctor who quit practicing. Whoever he was, it was published as an anonymous exposé—had so much debt from student loans that it would have taken him twenty years to pay it off even with the way things used to be. But now it's impossible for him to make any kind of profit, let alone pay off loans, so rather than work sixty hours a week for nothing he closed his practice."

The old man sat in his creaky desk chair, smoking his Lucky Strike. "And what do you know. The website where I found the article is no longer there. The other day I tried to log onto it, and I couldn't find the damn thing." He spat on the floor of the garage. "Wonder what happened to it?" he asked. "And that doctor. Those bastards almost have us."

Brad glared at me through hazily wafting smoke. I knew exactly what was going through his mind. *Those sons of bitches, they're not getting me under their thumbs. No damn way. Those bastards aren't running me...no way they're running me... no way in hell.*

I had an image in my mind of a giant hive. A few queens based in Washington. Others swarming out, looking to start new hives. And then the worker bees, working busily. Some tapping computer keys, some nosing into families, some teaching college kids, and others protecting the hives. Some kind of media drones, hovering until the time to mate. They would fertilize the queens and then live on; not disemboweling themselves as true drones do after mating but continuing to disseminate poison through the airwaves. *Poison... Lies... It just is. And soon we'll be feeling the stinging.*

"I might have to go to the VA," I said, staring down at the cement. I took a drag on my cigarette.

"What about Michelle?" the old man asked.

Michelle had applied for work at the supermarket downtown, and received word a few days earlier that she'd been hired as a cashier. We'd informed the family of this new development earlier that day.

"They don't need her till after Labor Day," I replied. "And even then I think we have to wait awhile before she's covered. I don't even know if there'll be private coverage offered by then. CJ's letting one of the newer guys go. They raised his taxes again. He's feeling the pinch—he has to do it." I went on to tell them that CJ was feeling pressure to dump us into the new system, mentioning that he'd probably be fined soon if he didn't, and that he'd received a government notice, full of legalese, to the effect that they could freeze his bank accounts.

That was all I said about the situation that night, but my worry was worse than they knew. I didn't want to say anything about it, but I'd been dealing with a toothache on and off for the past three months. It may or may not have been a wisdom tooth. The whole left side of my face throbbed, and the pain made it hard to think sometimes. I didn't have the funds to cover a root canal—not with Michelle off work—and I didn't know what I was going to do about it. I worried about what might happen to Ceej if I put in for it under the garage coverage.

The image of the hive came to mind again. I pictured the worker bees tapping away, thinking about what might happen to someone's bank account if the wrong key was hit, mistakenly or otherwise. In that moment right there in the old man's garage a sense of anger and helplessness overcame me for the first time but not the last. We looked at each other again, the four of us, dragging on our cigarettes as the old man repeated: "They almost have us."

* * *

After Johnny and his family went home, the old man stumped back to the house to go to bed. Brad and I stayed in the garage a little longer though, talking and smoking a last cigarette each.

"The older he gets the more stubborn he seems," said Brad. "Do you have any more cigarettes?"

"Yeah," I answered. I had another half-pack in the truck. I went out and got them and handed the pack to Brad. He handed it back and lit up.

"Aren't you smoking?" he asked.

"I guess so." I sighed, shaking my head. "But up until tonight I've been off the damn things since Easter. Michelle's not gonna be happy with me." I lit up again myself, and we smoked in silence for a few minutes, quiet with our own thoughts.

Brad and Nicole had moved into their house. He said it was a money pit, and that Nicole was driving him crazy with the renovations. But he wasn't really complaining. Not about Nicole—not the way he had in the past. Brad was a changed man. Sometimes it was hard for me to get my mind around his transformation, and if anyone had told me ten years earlier that he would have turned out to be such a devoted husband, I would have said they were crazy.

I found myself telling him about Michelle's slow recovery from the miscarriage two years earlier. He knew a little already, from Nicole, who spoke to Michelle regularly.

"Do you think she's depressed?" he asked.

"It's possible."

"Is she eating?"

"She eats, but not a lot," I said.

"Take her to the doctor."

"She doesn't want to go."

"She might need antidepressants."

"I know, but the last time I brought it up, she told me no. She said she's feeling better, and I didn't push it. She does seem a little better now that school is over."

"Well, you better be keeping an eye on her Wallace. Depression is nothing to fool around with."

"I have been. Don't worry about it."

Brad changed the subject. "The conscience laws are being overturned."

"I heard they were. Has anyone said anything to you?"

"Not yet. But things are getting hairy for me. I hope I can get around this shit." He stared into space.

"What happened?"

"Some little tramp came into the store last week looking for the one-frigging-day-later pill. I was the only one around, thank God."

"Well, what did you do about it?"

"I told her we were currently out. I sent her to the pharmacy in the grocery store down the street."

"What good did that do?" I cocked an eyebrow at him. "She got it anyway."

"I know. But at least she didn't get it from me."

"What are you gonna to do next time?" I asked, and his reply gave me a glimpse of the old Brad.

"I'll do the same damn thing I did that day," he said, laughing. "There's a display of condoms right under the counter. Before she left I pointed them out to her and said that if she cared to purchase a pack she could pay for them at my register."

"Brad, you better watch your mouth. How do you know she needs condoms? You don't know what her life's like. Maybe she couldn't help it." I finished my smoke.

"You don't know what the hell you're talking about," he retorted. "I know where she lives, unless she gave us a phony address, which I doubt. It's not that far from my new place, but the neighborhood's a lot ritzier. The houses are all in the eight hundred thousand dollar range. It's at least thirty minutes away from the store. She came in because she knew nobody from her end of town would see her. You should have seen the size of the rock on her hand. It had to be at least three carats, and she's been in at least three times for the same thing since January."

I kept quiet. Brad went on speaking.

"She's a tramp," he repeated, as he dropped his smoke on the floor and ground it out. Then he lit another one. "She's probably sleeping around on her rich old man. She knows exactly what she's doing. She uses it as birth control." Cigarette smoke curled, as Brad stared moodily off into space.

Okay. There's more to this. Wonder what it is.

"What aren't you telling me?"

"Nothing," he replied, glaring sideways at me. I kept quiet. I knew there was more to it than what he'd told me. Brad picked up the cigarette butts from the floor and put them in his pocket. "Don't let me forget to get rid of these before we go inside," he said.

I said nothing, continuing to wait him out. The silence stretched for a time. But then, finally, Brad let loose. "Damn it Wallace!" he snapped. "All right! I'll tell you. After I pointed out the condoms to her, she came on to *me*, okay? Right in the store."

I remained quiet. "She's hot," Brad went on. "If you like whores, that is." He paused a minute then, before remarking in a speculative tone, "If I wasn't married and I didn't know what she was, I might have taken her up on it."

Still I made no comment. "Damn you," he sputtered. "What the hell is wrong with you? Can't you have a normal conversation? Ever?"

"Brad, you fool," I said harshly. My jaw throbbed crazily, and I wanted to smack him on the side of the head. "Tell me you didn't take her up on it."

"Of course I didn't. Do you think I'm an idiot? I don't know

136   DANIELLA BOVA

where the hell she's been. Anyway, she's not my type. She's more like the type you used to go after. She reminded me a little of that girl from the university, the one you used to—"

"Well," I cut him off. "It's a good thing you didn't take her up on it. Michelle told me Nicole's fixing up the second bedroom at your place. For a baby's room." I was looking him right in the eye. He held my gaze for a minute.

"Damn you," he repeated, quietly this time. "You know better than that. I'm not going to mess around on my wife. I married her, didn't I? I wouldn't have married her if I was gonna mess around. And yeah, we're fixing up the room a little. Next winter we're gonna start trying. But damn it, Wallace, I'll tell you something, and you can take it any way you want to. She looked like something right out of Hollywood, and if I wasn't married, and if I wasn't afraid of what I might catch, I'd—"

Then he said what he would do. It shocked even me, after everything I had heard from him over the years, and my jaw dropped.

"Yeah, that's right." Brad laughed. "What are you, shocked or something? It's nothing you haven't done, and you know it."

I had nothing to say.

"That tramp isn't why we're on this subject anyway," Brad went on. "We're on this subject because I'm going to be backed into a corner sooner or later at work, and I'll be damned if I know how I'm gonna get around it. But those government bastards aren't making me do anything. I'll figure something out."

A few weeks later I went out and bought a shotgun. It had been in my head since the evening of the Fourth. I went into the store and bought it, a twelve-gauge slugger along with four boxes of shells. When I got home I took it out to the shed, and locked it in the metal cabinet where I kept my fishing tackle.

TEN

Michelle

Things went on as normally as possible after Jason found out I was pregnant.

I found it hard to be on my feet for hours, and on the nights I worked late I came home exhausted. I seemed to feel nauseated all day long, and I could hardly keep anything down. I could tell it upset Jason, and he worried about me. The morning sickness was worse because I was weaning myself off the antidepressants. I started decreasing them the day after I took the pregnancy test.

I kept this from Jason. The two episodes of depression I had suffered scared him, and he didn't need to know what I was doing. He said the medication was safe. That might have been true; the previous pills were safe but these latest were different, and I didn't want to ask Brad any questions.

I'm determined that you will be breast-fed, baby-angel. According to online sources nursing isn't possible if the mother is taking certain antidepressants, so I felt I should at least try to get off them, and I seem to be okay without them so far. The crying jags and episodes of paralyzing fear that come over me each day are a little worse now than they were before, but you're worth it.

Jason wasn't the only one who was worried in the months following our discovery that you were coming, baby. I was worried about him, too. He'd taken to coming home late on weeknights and going out at night on Fridays, something totally out of character for your father. He had his pastimes, but usually it was fishing with CJ for a weekend or getting together with some of the guys to play ice hockey at the pond. Sometimes he played pool at Diesels' after work, but he'd never been one to stay out really late at night. Now he was doing it on a regular basis.

He checked the windows, reinforced locks, installed deadbolts, and made me promise to lock myself in our room and then call him immediately if I heard anything suspicious. The guns were in there. Sometimes a gang of kids hung out in our neighborhood. Jason was worried about one in particular, whom he referred to as "that little bastard" when he wasn't calling him something worse under his breath.

When I asked him where he was spending so much time, he said that Reese and Lucio and the rest of the guys had taken to getting together at the garage after work to play cards. He worked late on Tuesdays and Thursdays anyway, but still, he was a little evasive when I asked. He simply addressed Friday evenings. He reminded me that I was at the store until at least ten o'clock on Fridays, and he thought I would be okay with him staying out. He mentioned nothing about the other nights, and I decided not to push him.

It upset me that he seemed so uncomfortable talking about it, and I started to worry, thinking something else was going on. In daylight the very idea that Jason would be running around on me was laughable, especially with a baby on the way. But sometimes at night while I was lying in bed, watching the clock and waiting for him to come home, my mind would start racing and I'd get upset, thinking he might never come back. Then, just when I thought I couldn't stand waiting another minute, I'd hear the truck in the driveway and his key in the door. I always acted like I was asleep so he wouldn't know I'd been crying. Again, I didn't want to make waves. Jason had never lied to me before so I let things go on that way, but the stress must have affected me more than I realized.

One night before bed as I was coming out of the bathroom, I started getting dizzy. I grabbed onto the doorknob to steady myself, but everything was going gray. The last thing I remembered before everything went black was lurching across the hall as I called out to Jason.

I woke up to Jason's voice. He was calling my name and patting my cheeks, pleading for me to wake up. Then my eyes fluttered open to the sight of his agonized face as he crouched over me, frantically begging God to keep me with him. I was sprawled out in the hallway with my head knocked against the baseboard and my left arm twisted beneath me.

"Michelle, are you okay? Does anything hurt?"

As I started to rise the pain shot through my arm. I held it against me, crying weakly that I must have hurt it somehow as I went down. He helped me get up, took me to our room, and made me lie down. I winced as he looked at my arm. It was starting to swell, but he said he didn't think it was broken, could I move it? I moved it up and down, and we decided it was probably only sprained.

What happened next shocked me more than I can describe.

Jason went out to the kitchen to get some ice. I lay quietly, feeling utterly sick and wasted as I listened to the sounds from the kitchen. I heard him looking through the cupboard for a plastic bag, and the clink of the ice as he filled it. And then it went bad.

The cupboard door slammed shut with an oath. Ice shattered. Jason was cursing and swearing and screaming. Then came what sounded like furniture being thrown, chairs shoved and walls kicked. The profanity went on, punctuated with threats that he was going to kill that little bastard.

Understand that he didn't have a temper, angel, at least not in front of me. He was always so laid back around me, especially when I was pregnant. He treated me—and you—like gold, and ever since he'd come back to himself two months earlier, he'd been my rock—the one who was always there for me.

But he wasn't himself right then. He continued swearing, saying he would kill him, saying he wished he could kill them all, and that he wanted to tear them apart with his bare hands for making it impossible for him to even take me to a doctor because we might be arrested.

He came back into the bedroom then, still in a rage. His face was flushed and his green-gray eyes flashed at something only he could see as he stalked past the bed to yank open his dresser drawer. He fumbled in the drawer and all of a sudden there was the lock box. The latch popped and then Daddy's revolver was in Jason's hand. I shrieked when I saw it, but he paid me no mind. He turned and went toward the door.

"What are you doing?" I screamed.

He looked toward me with a wild look in his eye.

"I'm going. That little bastard isn't getting away with this."

"Who? Stop, Jason! That kid hasn't been around here for days! What are you talking about?"

But he started out the door anyway. I wailed, knowing that if he walked out that door I would never see him again. I started getting up from the bed, and the pain shot through my arm. Then I fell back with a cry.

Maybe seeing my pain was what got through to him. He froze.

"Jason! Please!"

He stood rigidly, sweat pouring down his face in rivers. It soaked his shirt and dripped onto the floor, even though the temperature in the house was only sixty-two degrees. Energy was being rationed by that time, and in order to keep the heat on for the full month we needed to keep the thermostat low.

Your daddy looked like some sort of ancient statue, frozen in time. The moment stretched. Then he looked my way. Tears and sweat fell.

"Oh my God... I'm sorry."

He sagged down on the bed, set the gun on the nightstand, and reached for me.

"I'm sorry," he repeated, half-crying. "I don't know what came over me. But it's over. I'll never take that gun out of this house in anger again."

We weren't even supposed to have the gun. With the exception of farmers in rural areas it was now against the law for any civilian to possess a firearm, and even the farmers were prohibited from owning handguns. They were only permitted to own one shotgun per farm.

As of that time there had been no real effort to collect guns. They only did it on occasion, when authorities happened to be called and questioning revealed there was a gun in the house.

But Jason and Brad and Johnny pay no attention to the gun ban. They term the loss of freedom in America the "New Way of doing Business". They don't follow the new rules, though they don't trust anyone in authority either. After Daddy's funeral they divided up his guns. Jason has the Colt .45 revolver.

It's getting late angel, but I want to write about one more thing while the memory is fresh in my mind.

Later that night, the night I fainted, Jason told me what had happened at work that day, and after he related how far Junior had gone I understood why my fainting episode set him off the way it did.

After icing my arm for twenty minutes, the swelling stopped. Though it looked like it was going to bruise I could move it, and it didn't seem as bad as it had at first. Your daddy had put the gun back in the drawer with the promise that it would stay there unless my life was in danger. He assured me I had no need to worry about him ever losing control that way again. And for the record, he hasn't, even though he's taken much more abuse from the bureaucrats than lesser men would have.

We were lying in bed together. I had crawled into his arms, somehow managing to find a comfortable position even with my swollen arm. My head was pillowed on his chest as I listened to the beating of his heart, a sound that had always soothed me. He lay quietly with his arms encircling me. I thought he had finally fallen asleep when I heard him whisper my name.

"Michelle." The whisper was urgent. "What have you noticed around town lately? What's been different?"

I thought about it for a time, knowing something must have changed or he wouldn't be asking, but unable to pinpoint it. And then Junior and Jamie came to mind.

My nephews had been drawn slowly into the ranks of the bureaucracy. The organization they were a part of was touted as a way to serve America, but in truth it was nothing more than a legal gang. In our area of the country the "service" was optional, however the name of the group, "Mandatory Civilian Service Force" led Jason to believe that it would soon be compulsory. Johnny and Cindy had been devastated when their sons joined the MCSF, but they could do nothing to change things.

I haven't written much about the MCSF for the simple reason that thinking about my nephews and their involvement in it almost makes me ill. But when I wrote that the group had marched through town with machine guns, I wasn't kidding.

It happened shortly before Christmas. Jason and I saw them, Jamie was with them, and Johnny and Cindy were almost out of their minds with grief and fear afterward. It only happened once, but the march had a chilling effect on our town. On that day, people learned to fear their own children. That's all I'm going to say right now, because my heart is hurting.

Up until that day the MCSF had stayed on the streets, and since I had little to no contact with my nephews I tended to gloss over their presence in town. But as I pondered Jason's question I realized that they had begun encroaching into businesses. Lately groups of them had taken to coming into the store, hanging around the cash registers, and talking to the younger employees. None had spoken to me though, and I guess I'd been feeling so sick for so long that I just hadn't paid much attention.

I related all this to Jason, and finished by saying, "But I haven't seen Junior or Jamie. Nobody's bothered me. Did something happen? Is that why you got so upset?" He kissed the top of my head then before finally telling me what had happened that day.

He said that your cousin Junior had come into the garage that afternoon while he was doing a brake job. Jason was alone. He had a feeling something wasn't right, so he turned away from the car on the lift and there was Junior, staring at him. Jason could tell something was wrong. He asked Junior if everything was okay.

Understand, baby, that your father and Junior had always been close. Jason used to take him fishing every summer, and also to the pond to play ice hockey. Your daddy treated Junior like a younger brother, but after Junior defied his own father and joined the MCSF, a rift opened between them. I could see it happening and I hated it, but there was nothing to be done. The rift could be blamed on no one but Junior. His many poor choices had caused the separation. There were numerous incidences of harsh words and arguments that Jason, not wanting to give up on Junior, managed to smooth over. But that day in the garage the cord was severed for good.

"Michelle, we need to get you away from here. It's not safe anymore. I'm going to tell you what happened, and I want you to stay calm. Just understand, honey. We have to get you away. Soon."

Then Jason finished his story.

Junior started in on your daddy about Christmas, asking why hadn't we come to the house? Jason hardly knew what to say to him.

Was Junior actually thinking we would care to eat Christmas dinner with him after he turned on the family by joining the bureaucracy? So he told Junior to lighten up.

"I mentioned those punks goose stepping down Main Street and asked him what the hell they thought they were doing. Then I told him we would be staying away until he and Jamie leave that damned cult. That's what it is and we both know it." He hugged me before going on.

"But he went too far today. This is what he said in a nutshell: He stood there and looked me right in the eye and told me I better watch myself. Honey, he says he knows about our situation. His words, and I quote, were: Aunt Michelle better not think she's exempt from anything. You two better not expect any special treatment. I know exactly what happened. You two are idiots, following the Church. The Church is over you old-fashioned freaks—don't you know that? You're hanging onto stupid, religious bullshit. You're not getting away with it, though. You tell Aunt Michelle she better not try anything, because she's expected to do her part." Jason breathed heavily. "Baby... That's what he told me today."

I stiffened in horror as he finished his story. He whispered that when Junior mentioned my name he grabbed him and threw him up against the wall. He shoved Junior against the toolbox and told him he'd better never speak my name in that tone again, and to get his little punk bastard friends out of our neighborhood unless they wanted to feel a load of birdshot on their asses. By that time CJ and Reese had come in, and Junior clammed up. Then your daddy told Junior to get the hell out of the garage and not to come back until he was ready to apologize to his aunt.

Dear God in Heaven, how did he find out? He can't know. I haven't told anyone! Dear God, Dear Holy Mother what does he know? Holy Mother pray for us, help us, what are we going to do?

* * *

Jason went back to the kitchen to get me some ginger ale. After his admission about Junior I got sick again. I felt dizzy and wasted and hopeless. He soothed me as best he could, supporting my head as I vomited into the trash basket.

"Jason," I cried, "what aren't you telling me? I know you're keeping something back. What is it?" My stomach was churning so hard I could barely stand it.

"Baby," he murmured. "Stop. You need to rest. I've told you everything you need to know right now. Someday I'll tell you the rest of it, but believe me you don't want to find out now. Junior doesn't know about our baby. There's no way he could, because neither of us has told a soul. And he'll never find out, honey. Have no fear about that."

His words were a further illustration that there was more to it than he was willing to admit. But I knew he was right. I didn't need to know the full extent of it. Jason managed to convince me there was no way Junior could know about you, angel-baby. At that point nobody knew except us. Junior was a smart boy though, even if he was using his brains for evil purposes, and somehow he had managed to find out about the notice.

Jason
7 Years Earlier

After Michelle started work at the supermarket she seemed to shake off the sadness of the previous two years. She liked working there, she was making friends, and she loved the fact that the garage was only a few blocks away, so we could see each other during the day.

Her appetite was coming back. The fact that she was actually eating and not just pushing food around with her fork gave me the hope that she was finally getting better. But it was going to take more time. I should have been more careful in my comment. I was so relieved to see her eating again that I brought it up one night after dinner. She had actually finished what was on her plate before getting up to do the dishes.

"Honey, you're looking good," I mentioned as I scraped plates into the garbage. "You're getting some meat on your bones."

She smiled back at me from the sink. She was well aware of the fact that I liked her looking healthy and not as if the next wind would blow her away, though it wasn't her fault she had lost twenty pounds.

I knew the exact amount because after arguing with her about it for a week or so back in July, I'd finally given up and forced her onto the bathroom scale. I hated doing it, but she had me scared, and once I knew it was easier to decide where to go from there. Michelle was 5'7" tall, and at that point she weighed a total of a hundred and eight pounds, fully clothed. But she'd gained about half of it back. *Thank God.*

I put the ketchup in the fridge, walked to the sink and grabbed her backside. There wasn't much there to grab, not like before, but at least there was something. "You're looking good," I repeated. Then it happened. She put her arms around my waist and looked up at me.

"Jason, let's have a baby." She was looking into my eyes with an unfathomable longing, and I was getting lost again in the sad, clear blue. But she knew what my answer would be.

"Honey, we can't."

"Please."

I murmured into her hair as I ran my hands through it.

"It's too soon. We can't, not yet."

"It's not too soon. I want a baby. I'm getting older."

"Michelle, honey, you know that's the thing I want most. Are you sure you're okay?"

"It could happen tonight. *Tonight.*" Her voice was muffled against my chest.

I knew she was right. You got the sense of these things after a while. She had never stopped the charting and the monitoring.

"Let's wait another month."

"Jason no, now, tonight."

"Honey we will, but not yet." My voice was breaking a little; I hated to see her suffer. But there was no way she was ready for a baby. I continued hugging her, soothing her with words and my hands, feeling her bones through her skin.

"One more month," I said. I took her down the hall to our room then. We went in and lay on the bed, and after a while she fell asleep.

She knew it was too soon. She admitted it after she woke up; we were still in the bed together. She told me I was right, but that she was feeling better, and soon we'd have our baby.

"She's coming out of it," I told Brad later on the phone. Michelle was sleeping. He asked me what happened.

"Nothing happened. She's eating more, she's gaining weight."

"The old man's worried—him and Mom." Brad remarked.

"I know they are." I'd already confided my worries to the old man. He knew I was keeping an eye on the situation. "We'll go over there this Sunday," I said. "She's eating again."

I finally got around to the dentist in November when I couldn't stand the pain anymore. I called the office and they were able to fit me in five weeks later. The situation was worse by that time, almost unbearable really. The dental assistant took an X-ray and told me my top left wisdom tooth was bad. When the doctor came in he said I could go to the oral surgeon or let him take care of it.

"Can you do it now?" I asked, hoping and praying he'd say yes.

"You need antibiotics first."

"Doctor," I said from between clenched teeth. "This thing's killing me. I've lived with it for six months already without antibiotics, and nothing's happened other than me questioning my sanity. Is there any way you can just get rid of it today?"

"Yes. I had a no-show, so I can fit you in. But it's going to be painful."

"I don't care," I replied. "Let's just get it over with."

Again, I wasn't able to think clearly. I didn't know the various costs of pain relief during dental procedures, so I said I didn't want nitrous oxide, thinking it might be more costly. I told him I wanted Novocain.

"I'll give you Novocain," he said. "But let me give you the nitrous along with it. You're going to need it."

"No," I argued, summoning my last vestige of civility. "I don't want it. Just give me the needle."

"All right." He administered it, and forty-five minutes later the procedure was finished. I staggered out to the desk then, and asked how much I owed.

"Mr. Wallace," said the receptionist. "We're required to do paperwork. Give me your card."

I informed her that I'd had this conversation on the way in, and had told the front desk I'd be paying cash. She had the computer screen up with my information—nothing there about single payer.

"Give me your private insurance card."

"No. I already discussed this out front. I'm paying you now. How much is it?" My jaw throbbed crazily.

"Mr. Wallace, this is out of the question. The front desk should never have let you back. We need verification." She was holding out her hand for the card. "Give me your private insurance information, please."

I took a deep breath, trying to keep my temper. My jaw was killing me. The Novocain didn't take, and it had felt like he was pulling off my head.

"Ma'am, with all due respect, I already showed the front desk my driver's license and the cash I have in hand. They seemed satisfied, and gave me permission to bypass all this red tape. Now please. Do you people want to be paid?" I was looking her in the eye.

"Mr. Wallace, I—"

"How much do I owe you?"

I continued staring her down until she clicked the printer and handed me the bill. Then I took the cash out of my wallet and paid her.

* * *

I complained about it later to Brad. I went out back for a drink and a smoke after Michelle fell asleep, and called him on my cell.

"They'd rather do all that paperwork than take the money," I mumbled through my swollen jaw. "What are they, crazy?"

"They're probably feeling pressure to do it."

"I know. I feel bad about it now, but my jaw felt like someone was using a jackhammer on it. I could hardly see her. I just wanted to pay and get out."

"How much was it?" Brad's tone seemed a little cool.

"More than we can afford right now." I searched through the toolbox for my pack of Lucky Strikes, as I told him what was going on at work.

CJ had been forced to lay off another employee, the third since January. The high taxes were killing him, and the bureaucracy was squeezing him. He had received another notice about insurance. They were fining him again and threatening to freeze his accounts. He'd taken Reese and me aside the day before, and related sorrowfully that he was probably going to have to dump us. He was already on single payer himself. He didn't like it any more than the old man, but he didn't think there was any other option at this point.

"Nicole's brother and his wife are on it," Brad remarked. I remembered her brother from the wedding.

"How old is he?"

"Forty-two."

I lit a cigarette. "You're smoking?" He sounded surprised.

"Yeah, I'm out back. Michelle's put on fifteen pounds."

"I talked to her the other night," he replied. "She sounded more like herself."

"Things are back to normal around here."

He didn't answer me. *Okay. What the hell is his problem?* I knew from experience there was something. I waited, listening to the clicking sound of his lighter, and the sharp draw on the cigarette.

"All right," I said. "What the hell is wrong with you?"

"Nothing," he answered, but I could tell he was pissed off at me for some reason or other. I waited. "Nothing's wrong with me."

I kept quiet. So did he, until he figured out I wasn't going to ask him again. Then he exploded, yelling in my ear: "But what the hell's wrong with you Wallace? Why didn't you take Michelle to the doctor?"

Okay. So that's it. I dragged on my cigarette, thinking.

"Brad," I replied in an even tone. "Are you sure you want to open this can of worms with me? Michelle's fine now. Like I said, things are good here."

"She's fine? Well if she is, it's no thanks to you," he retorted. "But you took care of your damn tooth, didn't you?"

"Stop. You don't know what you're saying."

"You're lucky she came out of it." *Lucky I didn't come up there... Wallace you son of a ...*

"I did take her. I took her to DeLuca back in August."

"What?" Brad's voice was rising. "Why didn't you tell me?"

"I'm telling you now."

"Why are you so freaking closemouthed, Wallace? You piss me the hell off. What happened?"

"All right," I said, and went on to fill him in on what happened after he'd gone back to Tennessee. A few weeks after I figured out that Michelle wasn't getting any better, I got so scared that I finally made an appointment with the family practice we belonged to.

"We argued about it for weeks before I went ahead and made the decision to call them myself. She seemed better for a while after school ended. You know that—you saw her on the Fourth of July." I stalked over to the workbench to look for the bottle of Jack Daniel's.

"Yeah," he admitted. "But you knew I was worried about her."

"Yeah? Well you went home without mentioning it again. Things were okay until the end of the month. The old man knew; I talked to him about it."

I poured myself a shot and drank it down, before going on to tell him the rest of it. The office staff had started in on the phone asking for ID cards—HCA or otherwise—even before they asked what ailed her. Telling Brad about it upset me. Michelle and I were trying to forget that day.

"But they finally agreed to fit her in, so I got her in the truck and drove her over there." I paused for a minute then, before adding: "She didn't want to be there, and I don't really blame her. It was messed up. The damn place was so crowded that we were in the waiting room for almost three hours. Then your sister got up out of the chair and walked out the door."

Silence from his end.

"She wanted to go home," I said roughly, lighting another smoke. "But it all worked out. She's okay now. She's better."

"You should have made her go," he replied. That was when I finally lost my temper.

"*Brad!*" I yelled into the phone, exhaling smoke from my Lucky Strike. "Do you have any idea what the hell I've been dealing with up here?" He started to speak and I cut him off. "Your sister has been crying her life away right in front of me. She couldn't sleep, she could hardly eat, she's begging me for a baby, and I'm dealing with it. She gets up and walks out of the damn place, goes out to the truck and won't go back in. She started having dry heaves right there in the parking lot. What the hell did you expect me to do? Why do you feel the need to make me tell you all this?"

Silence.

"I finally convinced her to go back in. The doctor prescribed something for her and she's better now. Nicole is healthy." My voice shook. "You don't know what the hell's been going on up here." My jaw was throbbing wildly. "You're down there in Memphis, so shut your freaking mouth right now if you can't be of some help to me."

Then neither of us spoke for a time, until Brad finally ventured a comment.

"I don't know what to say..." He trailed off, sounding completely floored.

"I'm handling it. But she's begging me every month to get her pregnant again. It's too soon, and I know it. What the hell do you suggest I do?"

Silence on the other end of the phone, and then finally: "Wallace, I'm sorry."

I dragged smoke into my lungs. They had warned me not to smoke at the dentist. I did it anyway, hoping I wouldn't end up with a dry socket.

"Brad, you don't know what it's been like up here. But she's fine now, back to normal."

"I'm sorry," he repeated.

"Okay. Forget it."

I repeated that CJ was dumping me into the HCA healthcare system.

"It's not his fault—he got another notice. They have his account information on the business and he has to do it. I'm paying for this out of our savings until I get the freaking ID cards. Not that I'm complaining about it. But making sure you were told about each and every last thing I do wasn't a priority for me."

I heard him take another drag.

"You don't need to be informed every time I wipe my ass," I said. Then I went on about events at work. "There's only the four of us left over there now. Ceej, me, Danny and Reese. Business is slowing down."

"Down here, too," he replied. "Wallace, I really am sorry. I didn't know all that."

"Well what good would it have done if you had known?" I wiped my eyes. "It was a bad situation. Now that you do know, I don't mind telling you that." I was still crying a little. *I hope he doesn't know. I freaking hate to cry.*

"And quit apologizing. Just forget it. It wasn't exactly something I wanted to worry you with. She's my wife. I would have told you if things got any worse, but she came around, and afterward she was so embarrassed that she told me to keep quiet."

We smoked in silence for a while.

"I could tell she felt better on the phone," he finally said.

"She's back to normal," I repeated. My hand shook as I poured another shot of whiskey.

"You waited till now, today, to take care of that tooth." Brad sounded ashamed. "Wallace—"

"Don't say it again," I warned. I didn't want to hear another apology. "I mean it. Neither of us is perfect. If I did the wrong thing in keeping it from you, I'm sorry too, but it's over."

"All right." Brad's voice sounded strangled. I realized then that he was crying too. It surprised me; I hadn't heard Brad cry since we were kids. "We'll be up for Thanksgiving. I'll see you in a couple of weeks." He hung up.

I glanced at the locked metal cabinet. Then I finished my cigarette and went back to the house.

ELEVEN

Michelle

Dear Lord. Thank you for our sanctuary. Please be with my husband. He's doing his best for us.

I've taken to venturing upstairs for dinner with the family, now that I've gotten used to being here. Mark says there's no harm in me coming up sometimes, as long as we keep an eye open for any strangers.

Talk around the table had to do with worries stemming from the new way of doing business. In addition to hiding an illegally pregnant woman in their home, Mark and his family have other new fears. People in the neighborhood have noticed a change in the wildlife inhabiting the area. One of the men at the store in the village saw a raccoon stalking back and forth in his yard in broad daylight, and lately there's been concern about an upsurge in rabies. The consensus is that there's an outbreak in the abandoned park nearby, but there's nothing to be done about it except be on guard.

Jason
6 Years Earlier

I hadn't seen my mother in over a year though we had spoken on the phone a few times. The one time I brought up Michelle's illness, Mom suddenly had to take an important call. She said she would call me back, but the call never came. That's how I knew that my mother had no interest in my wife's health. So I never brought it up to her again.

Jeremy and I got in the habit of meeting once a month for a beer after work, and he kept me updated on Mom.

"I'm moving out," he told me. We were sitting at the bar in Diesel's on a late spring evening. "Does Mom know?"

"Not yet. I'm moving in with Lauren. Her roommate's leaving."

"You'll be closer to work," I remarked, lighting a cigarette. Lauren lived in an apartment high-rise in Philadelphia.

"Yeah, and further from Mom."

"Michelle wants to meet Lauren," I mentioned.

"She's planning a party for New Year's Eve; you'll be getting an invitation."

"Mom told me about Lauren's work." I said. In fact, my mother had gone on over the phone for thirty minutes without a break, raving about Lauren: her job as a model, how gorgeous she was, her upscale neighborhood, and the catalogues in which she'd been featured. Jeremy took a picture out of his wallet and handed it to me. I looked at it and whistled. "What's she doing with you?"

He laughed as he took the picture back.

"How's Michelle?" His tone was guarded.

"Fine now. Did Mom know Michelle was ill?"

"Yes. I told her. I bring it up to her every time I talk to you."

"She never asks me about her." I stared down at the ashtray as I ground out my smoke. I could see Jeremy out of the corner of my eye.

He was shaking his head but he made no comment. There was really nothing to say. We both knew what our mother was.

"I hope I can get out of there with my scalp," he said.

* * *

CJ called Reese and me into the office the day before Thanksgiving. He said he'd canceled his private insurance carrier. This meant that we'd have to go on single payer, unless we wanted to chance going without healthcare insurance and paying the fine for the privilege. CJ said it sucked, but there was no way he could continue to carry us on private insurance. They'd already threatened to fine him and to freeze his accounts. He said it would cost too much to fight, and that if he wanted to keep the place running he had to do it.

He told us this straight up. We had known it was coming. We knew there was nothing else to be done, and that private insurers were going out of business right and left anyway. It was more or less over.

Ceej invited us down to the cottage on Saturday to go fishing. It would be cold, he said, but maybe we'd catch something. I told him no, not this time, but to keep me in mind for next time.

* * *

Michelle was back to her old self on Thanksgiving at the old man's. The meal was a typical one. Noisy. It took a while to get through all those courses, and Brad and the old man always got a little loud after a couple of glasses of wine.

After we finished the appetizer and set about eating the soup, the old man started complaining about rolling meatballs. Michelle's mom always made wedding soup for Thanksgiving—Christmas, too—and she always made my father-in-law help her roll the meatballs. He told us he was so sick of doing it by the time they were finished that he wanted to throw them all right out the door.

Mrs. Davis argued back at him, saying his meatballs were too big, and that they needed to be much smaller than the way he rolled them if the soup was to turn out the way her mother's would have. The old man looked pissed at her words. All of us at the table tried not to laugh as he glared at her, saying: "Well then, I guess I'm not helping you at Christmas. And if I do, I'll make them as big as my fist." Everyone laughed under his or her breath, knowing the old man would do nothing of the kind.

After the soup we had manicotti, and about fifteen minutes later, right after they'd finished loading the table with more food, the women sat back down and started eating again. My plate was over-flowing as usual, and I didn't look up from it when Brad remarked: "Something's burning."

I could tell he was looking at me. I smelled the smoke, but I was on the other side of the table; Brad was closer to the kitchen door.

"You get it," I told him dismissively.

Nicole was finally eating something. She didn't move. Junior and Jamie were wolfing food, and Cindy wasn't about to get up; she had baked all the pies we were going to eat later, and she looked tired.

Brad looked at me pointedly, but I didn't get up either. All I did was give him a stare back before taking another forkful of turkey. Finally he jumped out of his chair and ran through the door to the kitchen. He began to cuss, yelling that he'd burned himself. Then came the sound of the back door opening followed by a clattering noise. A draft of cold air made its way into the dining room. I could still smell whatever it was that burned when Brad came back to the table, holding a couple of ice cubes in his hand.

"You women!" he barked, shaking his head. "There were four of you in that kitchen, and not one of you could remember to turn off the stove?" He went on to tell us the pot that had held mashed pota-toes had been emptied and put back on the stove with the burner lit.

It was just getting ready to catch fire when Brad got to it. He was so mad when he burned himself that he threw the damn thing out the door. I guess the old man had given him the idea when he complained during the soup course.

"Michelle," said my mother-in-law in an exasperated tone, "I told you to fill it with water and leave it in the sink."

"Well, I'm not the one who left the stove on." Michelle raised an eyebrow at her mother.

"That stove's left on every other night around here," the old man growled. "I tell your mother but she keeps doing it."

"Jack," my mother-in-law warned, "I do not."

Nicole asked for more potatoes, saying she liked them. Brad was still mad about the burn on his hand, and as he passed them along, he told her: "Well, they don't like you."

"Brad, sugar," Nicole drawled poisonously, "are you saying you think I'm fat?"

Nicole had put on a little weight since the wedding. Only about five pounds according to Brad, and no one could even tell, but he said she drove him crazy, asking him every morning how she looked before work. I could tell he was kicking himself for the remark he'd just made. He looked at Nicole sideways, trying to decide whether or not she was kidding, before rolling his eyes back at her.

"Yeah, Nicole," he shot back. "Look at you; you're really fat."

Everyone around the table cracked up. Nicole looked like she weighed a total of one hundred pounds soaking wet, way too skinny for my taste. I thought in passing that I was glad Michelle didn't ask me about her weight all the time. I laughed right along with everybody else, but then I thanked God again that Michelle had gained back that twenty pounds.

* * *

Afterward, the four of us ended up in the garage as usual. We discussed the current state of the economy. I mentioned that CJ was being forced to dump us into the HCA. "I figure Michelle and I'll be receiving notification by Christmas."

Johnny said the same thing was going on with him; his boss had started talking about it and it was only a matter of time.

"The firehouse in town is closing," I said.

"That's the end result of those budget cuts," the old man threw back over his shoulder as he searched through his toolbox for Lucky Strikes. He stumped back to his chair and passed the pack. "We're gonna have to depend on neighboring fire departments from now on," he said, lighting up.

"Business is slow at the garage."

"The store laid off two people in the pharmacy," Brad commented, flicking his Zippo. "The guy under me, and a tech."

Johnny was worried about Cindy's job. She'd heard rumors of coming layoffs, and they depended on her salary to pay the boys' school tuition. "We need her salary," he finished. But there seemed nothing more to say right then, so we sat in silence, smoking, until the old man told us he wanted us to take his guns.

He said the Supreme Court had decided. They were taking the gun control case. It was definitely on the docket, and he was afraid our Second Amendment rights would be overturned. He wanted us to take his guns and hide them. He had a Colt .45 revolver, a .38, a standard C17 and a C27 subcompact.

"I already bought a twelve gauge," I said, as the old man lit another Lucky Strike and handed me the pack. I took one and handed it to Brad. "I got it last summer, after the Fourth of July."

"Dad, I'm not taking your guns; we don't even know what the decision's going to be," Johnny said.

He and Brad lit their cigarettes, and we sat in silence for a minute.

"I think I know what it's going to be," the old man stated with finality. "I want you each to have one. I'll keep the .38."

"No," Johnny replied. "Keep them here; what difference does it make where they are?"

"Brad, you take the C17. That's your gun of choice, isn't it?

"No Dad, I'm not taking it."

"Why the hell not? Take the damn thing, you may need it."

Brad dragged on his cigarette. "I don't need it," he said, blowing smoke out of his mouth. Something about his tone gave me pause.

Brad, what's going on? What did you do? He was leaning back against the workbench with a moody look on his face. Smoke curled in a blue haze. I caught his eye.

What happened?

Wallace if you only knew...I thought I was dead.

"Jason, where's the shotgun?" the old man asked.

"Locked in the metal cabinet out back." I finished my cigarette, ground it out under my heel and picked up the butt. The old man didn't keep ashtrays out there. We used our empty beer bottles, but I'd eaten too much at dinner to drink a beer.

"What good is it going to do you locked out there? It'll rust."

"I know. I'm keeping it oiled. But I guess I'll take it in the house. Michelle doesn't even know I bought the damn thing, and now I have to explain why." I was starting to lose my temper. "I don't have time for this HCA bullshit. How the hell did we end up where we are right now?"

"Calm down," the old man said. He went to the cabinet over the workbench and took out a bottle of scotch. He gestured to the rest of us, but I was the only one who took him up on it. I got a glass from the shelf, poured a shot and drank it down.

"I can't believe where we are either," the old man said. "They seem to have us where they want us now. But the four of us are going to keep our heads. Do you boys hear me? We're not doing anything stupid, but they're not getting our guns, either. No matter what decision comes down. They're not taking anything from us."

He poured himself another scotch and drank it down. "I'll be damned if they're taking one more thing. I didn't spend a year of my life crawling through that Vietnamese shithole to let it come down to this. I know what I was supposed to have fought for. This latest bullshit reminds me of what I was fighting against, and I'll be damned if I'm putting up with it. Just because they've gotten used to pissing on the Constitution doesn't mean we have to go along with it."

Just then Jamie came in. When he noticed the cloud of cigarette smoke he bent over and began coughing and hacking theatrically, acting like the smoke was choking him.

"Dad," he coughed, "wait till I tell Mom you were smoking. She's gonna *kill* you!"

But the atmosphere in the old man's garage was still tense, and Johnny didn't appreciate the joke.

"Don't you dare go back in there and mention this smoke. None of us are in the mood right now."

"Well," Jamie said, grinning, "unless they all have colds they're gonna smell it on you. Look at this place."

"I can see the damn smoke, boy. But you just open the windows out here and get your ass back inside. We're taking a walk around the block in the wind before we go back in. Tell them we'll be there soon, and keep your mouth shut about us smoking."

"Okay." Jamie shrugged. He looked at me sideways. I grinned back at him, gesturing toward the windows, and he opened them. Then he walked out the door.

"Come on," the old man said. "I'm getting outta here for ten minutes. Johnny, go take your walk and cool down. Jason, run down to the store and get me another pack of cigarettes before you come in. I only have one left." He was handing me the money, and before I thought, I mentioned that I'd finished my last pack the week before and that I could no longer afford to keep a pack in the shed the way I had been. Then he handed me twenty-five dollars.

"Get two packs. You can take some home."

"No. Maybe all of us should give them up; they're too expensive now."

"I already said I'm not giving up anything else. I'm getting a couple of cartons tomorrow. We're going to have to cut back, but as long as I have some money and the tobacco companies are still operating, we'll continue to indulge ourselves."

The four of us exited the garage. Johnny went down the driveway, and Brad followed me to the truck. We headed toward town, opposite of the way Johnny was walking as he tried to get his temper under control.

"Brad, what's going on down at your place? What did you do?"

He looked at me from the passenger seat, and asked me what I was talking about.

"Why did you refuse to take the gun?"

"You know I can't take it on the plane."

"Come on Brad. Give me a break."

He stared straight ahead for a minute. "I don't need the old man's gun, Wallace. You know that."

"I know you have a gun. What I don't know is what you're hiding."

I was a little surprised at Brad. Usually he couldn't wait to tell me about anything and everything that happened in his life. That's the way the two of us operated. I seemed to say too little, and he always said too much. But not this time. It made me suspicious.

"I know something happened," I repeated. Silence from the shotgun seat. The windows were open. Cold air gusted in.

"Brad," I ventured again. No answer. "All right then," I went on. "I've been meaning to ask you something anyway. What are you giving Nicole for Christmas? Are you giving jewelry again? I've been giving Michelle jewelry every year since we got together, and I was thinking I might make a change this year. Do you have any ideas?"

"Damn it, Wallace," he snapped. "This is no time to discuss jewelry."

"Why not? Discuss jewelry, I mean. It's not like there's anything else going on," I shot back. Brad stared moodily out through the windshield. I noticed that his fists were clenched. "I know something's going on," I said. "If you're gonna tell me then tell me, but if not I really could use some help with Christmas ideas."

We drove through town. The big evergreen in the middle of the roundabout had been lighted for the first time that day. I kept quiet, while Brad considered the pros and cons of telling me what he had done. Finally the pros won out. He took a deep breath, looked across the cab at me.

"Wallace...they...they came and got my gun."

Lights began flickering in the corners of my eyes and that feeling came over me then, that shock feeling. *I knew it.* Water that only I could hear rushed through my head. *The sons of bitches couldn't even wait for the court.*

"What? Who did?"

"The cops." Brad's voice shook.

"The Tennessee State Police took your gun?" It sounded incredible. "Where?"

"No, it was local. They came to the house."

"What the hell are you talking about?" I asked. Then he told me what had happened.

It had to do with the unrest going on around the country in general, but Memphis in particular. The whole country was enduring a period of inflation, but the South had been hardest hit, and people were feeling the pinch. Everything cost too much, and it had led to some ugliness in certain areas of Memphis. Brad explained that there had been instances of looting down there and a few food riots. Arrests had been made.

"That's the excuse they used," Brad said. "Looting and food riots in certain areas of town."

We pulled into the parking lot and I parked and shut off the engine.

"But you don't live in that part of town. Why did they come to your house?"

"Safety reasons they said. They wanted to make sure there wouldn't be any trouble."

"That makes no sense. If something happened in your neighborhood, you'd need your gun, wouldn't you?"

"None of this makes sense to me anymore."

Brad went on to tell me that he'd argued with them. Said no, they weren't taking it, and to get the hell off his front porch. But they had a copy of the bill of sale from when he purchased the gun, and they told him he had to hand it over.

"How the hell did they get the bill of sale?" I was floored.

"I don't know," he replied. "I bought the damned thing twelve years ago. I barely remember the shop." We sat in silence for a minute.

"I made the controlling SOBs wait outside while I went back to the office and got it out of the safe. They gave me a receipt, told me I could apply to get it back after things settle down."

"I can't believe this," I said.

"It happened twenty years ago during that hurricane in New Orleans, remember?"

I got out of the truck then and went into the store to get the old man his cigarettes, thinking all the while about how crazy everything seemed. We continued the conversation on the ride back to the house.

"If they took your gun, why won't you take the old man's?"

"I don't need it."

"You're not making any sense."

"I got another one."

"Yeah Brad. They just came to your door and collected your legally owned firearm. And now you're telling me you went right out and bought another one?" He kept quiet. "You expect me to believe that?" I shook my head. "No way. Tell me, damn it—what did you do?"

"Okay Wallace," he answered. "I'll tell you. I went down to the neighborhood south of work the other day and bought one off the street."

I was too shocked for words. I kept my mouth shut for a minute, and for once so did he. But finally I had to speak up. I could hardly believe what he'd told me, but I knew damn well it was the truth. "Are you crazy?"

"Maybe. I don't give a shit if I am. His tone was quiet. "I'm not letting them run me."

"They're not going to be able to run you if you're dead!"

"I'm not dead. And they pissed me right the hell off. Do you want to hear the rest of it, or not?"

He began speaking in that same quiet tone, telling me about the aftermath of the removal of his gun from his home. After the cops went on their merry way he had started asking around. There was a guy at Brad's store who'd always come across as being a little shady. Brad mentioned a couple of things to him, and he, in turn, introduced Brad to a few other shady characters. To make a long story short, Brad had been able to find someone to help him obtain a replacement. The guy needed a ride, so Brad met him at the drugstore and drove him to a bad part of town.

"You're freaking insane." I gripped the steering wheel as visions of what might have happened shot through my skull at lightning speed. "Crazy. What if something happened? You could be dead right now."

He was quiet for a minute, before answering me in that same detached tone. "I know it, okay? It was a stupid thing to do, and I was scared the whole time, but I'm telling you right now that I'd damn well rather take a chance like that than to let the sons of bitches run me. Anyway, nothing happened."

His fists were still clenched on his knees, and I knew he meant every word. Brad had always been his own man. He played by the rules, but the rules had been broken, and not by him. I couldn't really blame him. For all I knew I might have done the same thing. I did have a couple more questions, however.

"How much did you pay for it?" He hesitated again. Cold air whipped through the windows. "Brad, how much?"

"Fifteen hundred."

"Holy shit. What's it made of, gold?"

We pulled into the driveway and I shut off the engine.

"I don't give a damn. It's a .357 Magnum, way better than the one they took from me."

"What about the serial number?"

"Filed."

"How do you know it's safe?"

"It's safe."

"How do you know?"

"I already shot it, okay? I tried it out before I paid the guy."

"Where the hell were you?"

"I don't know, Wallace," he snapped. "Some vacant lot somewhere down there. I had no idea where I was. I just followed the guy's directions when we were driving. But you know I wouldn't have handed over that much money without trying the damn thing out first."

"You're frigging crazy," I repeated, shaking my head.

TWELVE

Michelle

Time seemed to slow to a crawl angel-baby, after your father told me about Junior.

The following morning I woke up with a sense of dread. My heart lurched when I remembered the night before. I worried about it all day long at work, and for the second time in two months my cash register came up short. Currency was going out of fashion anyway, and it was only seven dollars and change, but my supervisor mentioned it offhand, and the way she was staring at my arm in the sling made me wonder what she was thinking.

Weeks passed. Junior seemed to have backed off for the time being. Jason continued his Friday nights out, although he stopped coming home late on weeknights. He was home every evening for dinner, even on Tuesdays and Thursdays. He came home for an hour and fixed supper as best he could. Then we'd eat together before he went back to work.

I found that I couldn't cook much anymore. Besides being unable to stand the smell of cooking, I was wiped out after being on my feet all day at work. I still managed to shop for food since I was right at the store, but I couldn't get near the meat case. Jason went out looking for whatever meat he could find. Supplies of any and all meat and poultry were sparse by that time anyway, but he managed to find enough for me to at least have a little when I could stand it. Meat is still sparse, little angel.

I questioned him again about Fridays one morning while we were getting ready for work. He repeated what he'd already told me: he was playing cards with the guys. I started to ask him how he thought we could get away, but he cut off my words. He took me in his arms and said he didn't want me stressed in any way; it was bad for the baby.

"I'll never let anything happen to you. I'm working on a solution to our problem. And stop worrying about Friday nights; there's nothing going on."

I believed him until that Friday night when Jamie came into the store.

It was early June by that time angel-baby, and you were growing steadily inside me. I was feeling better physically. The morning sickness had abated and my arm had healed, but it was getting harder and harder to hide the fact that you were there.

During the winter it was easy. I had a big puffy coat that covered my stomach and I always wore it to the store and church. Almost everyone at work kept his or her long sleeved polo shirts untucked, so I had no trouble hiding you in the early months. But by the beginning of May my pants were getting tight, and I was wearing them unzipped, held closed with a big safety pin. My shirt was long enough to cover the opening. I also started wearing a cardigan sweater to help hide my stomach. You were starting to show, baby.

Jason wanted me to stop working. He worried about my illness, and he didn't like me being on my feet for hours when I was having such a rough pregnancy. I wanted to quit as well, but I was afraid if I quit it might raise suspicions. Even though no one but Jason knew I was pregnant, something was telling us to keep quiet, and we did.

We didn't even tell Brad. We knew it would upset him, and Jason worried that if Brad found out he might get Johnny involved. Brad still wasn't aware of the distressing fact that both boys were now deeply entwined in the MCSF. We hadn't mentioned the march down Main Street to him, and neither had Johnny; even though similar things were going on in Tennessee.

So we were alone. I wished for my mother with everything in me during those months. I woke up half crying almost every morning, with the remnants of a dream of her fading from my mind. Then I would drag myself out of bed for another day at the store.

In addition to keeping anyone from getting suspicious, I needed to work for my paycheck. We had to pay the mortgage, and Jason was saving every penny he could to prepare the way financially for what he was planning to do. So when the morning sickness finally stopped, we decided to go on as we were for a while longer.

I continued working until the night Jamie came in to the store around ten-fifteen p.m. on a Friday night in June. He walked in right before closing accompanied by two other boys. All three were dressed in the khaki pants and black three button shirts of the MCSF, and each carried a stack of leaflets.

My heart lurched. Though Jamie seemed to pay me no mind, I could tell he knew I was there. He looked around in an arrogant manner, seeming to size up the place. He was so different—unlike the little nephew I had loved to laugh with such a short time ago. Tears came to my eyes as he and his friends stopped at the register next to mine and began speaking to one of the younger employees, talking up their organization. Jamie tried to convince the girl working the register to stop at the firehouse after work to get a little more information. He was telling her a lot of manure about helping people in need. Then he handed her a leaflet and moved on.

The three of them separated then. The two other MCSF went

toward the back of the store, evangelizing all the while; some of the younger employees accepted the leaflets. Jamie ignored me as he walked past my register toward the customer service counter where one of the girls I had taught in fifth grade was working. Kristin wasn't the type to fall for Jamie's line. Evidently she said something that rubbed him the wrong way, because a minute later he stalked away from her counter and came back to the register next to mine, where a sweet young guy who was mentally disabled stood. The young man's name was Nicky, and he worked part time at the store. He loved his job. He was always smiling as he bagged the groceries for the customers.

Jamie didn't even looked my way, but he made sure I knew he was there. I clutched the counter before glancing over at him. Jamie was standing next to Nicky, talking to him under his breath. Whatever he said seemed to upset Nicky, who turned away and continued putting groceries into a bag.

Oh Jamie... Why would you do such a thing? Especially right in front of me?

Nicky may have turned away, but Jamie wasn't satisfied with his harassment. He started to go around the back of Nicky, squeezing behind the counter and whispering again. Nicky reached out and pushed Jamie away as the checker at the register spoke up, telling Jamie that customers weren't allowed behind the counters. She ordered him out of the store.

I was surprised anyone would stand up to him. Everyone knew that our town's chapter of the MCSF had been armed, and most people were scared of them. I certainly was. I was so afraid at that moment I thought I was going to pass out again, and I grabbed onto the counter to steady myself as my co-worker again told Jamie to go.

Jamie didn't push it; he went ahead and walked back out into the aisle. I glanced up again to see that Nicky was crying. I tried to catch my nephew's eye, but he seemed to look right through me and he turned away.

Jamie. He must know...he has to know how much that would hurt.

I looked back down, my eyes swimming with tears, knowing Jamie had done what he did just to hurt me...because of your brother little angel. Jamie knew my child had been born with Down syndrome. After the baby died, I told Brad about him and asked him to make sure the rest of the family was aware. I was devastated, but it only got worse.

A few minutes later as he and his friends were leaving, Jamie stopped right in front of me. I almost sobbed as I clutched the counter, afraid to look up at him. He didn't move a muscle or say a word. He just stood. When I finally raised my eyes, I saw where he was looking. Jamie's eyes were on my stomach. After a minute he looked up at my face. Our eyes met then. I smiled automatically, but it wasn't my sweet nephew with my brother's eyes standing in front of me, not anymore. Jami's eyes were different now. He looked down once more at my growing belly, and as he walked away, he lifted his shirt to make sure I saw the gun sticking out of his pocket.

After they were gone I swallowed my tears and went to give Nicky a hug. He'd already stopped crying, but I felt awful, and hugging him made me feel a little better. I managed to keep control until I got out to the car. Kristin was leaving as well. We walked to the parking lot together. Even though she was half-crying about what had just happened, I knew she hadn't noticed the gun. She never would have let me leave there alone if she knew Jamie had threatened me.

Kristin said there were rumors about some sort of draft. She'd heard through back channels that all kids were going to be required to serve for at least one year. It would be a requirement for admission to college, and proof of membership would be part of the application process. Kristin was scared. She asked if I knew anything. Unfortunately, I did. I had overheard Jason on the phone with Brad, saying the HCA had taken control of all student loans, and that new regulations would be implemented.

I didn't tell Kristin what I knew. I don't even remember how I answered her. All I could think about was the fact that my nephew—a baby whose diapers I had changed—had just threatened to kill my own child. After Kristin drove off I got behind the wheel, tore out of the parking lot, and drove to the garage to get Jason. Even though the garage was only four blocks from the store, I never went by on Friday nights. Our house was in the other direction, and I refused to drive by to check up on him. He told me where he was spending his time, and I trusted him.

But that night the garage was dark. There was nobody there, and I had no idea where to find your father. I sat behind the wheel of my car, wondering where he could be at eleven o'clock at night when he was supposed to be playing cards. I was on the verge of losing it as I put the car in reverse and backed wildly out onto Pine Street, heading for home since that was the only place that could possibly be safe now.

I turned into a street running parallel to ours and drove slowly toward the intersection to see if the gang was hanging around on the corner. *Of course they're there... Dear God!* I kept on straight for two more blocks and then turned left so I could enter our street from the opposite direction.

When I finally turned into our driveway and found it empty as well I didn't know what to do. I sat looking over my shoulder to make sure that that little bastard wasn't coming up behind me from the corner. I was afraid to get out of the car, thinking Jamie might be in the house waiting for me.

Just as I took out my phone to call Jason, headlights turned in behind me, and he pulled up in the truck. I got out of my car and jumped in next to him, crying hysterically that Jamie knew about you.

Jason
5 Years Earlier

Michelle wasn't overly excited about the New Year's Eve party. Though she wanted to meet Lauren, the fact that my mother would be there was a bit of a downer for both of us. Around three o'clock that afternoon, we were almost ready to go. We were driving to Philadelphia early, to meet Lauren and help out with last minute party details.

"Jason, how do I look?" Michelle asked.

"Good enough to eat."

"Is this dress okay? Is it too short?"

She looked terrific in a little black dress and lacy sweater. "Michelle, you know you look good," I replied.

I wasn't lying, either. The sweater barely covered her chest, and she was no longer too skinny, especially in that area. Her body looked better than ever. She'd started running back in October when she turned thirty-two, after reading that exercise helped with stress.

"Are you sure?"

"Honey, yes," I said, giving her the eye. The running had really gotten her into shape. "You've got nothing to worry about," I assured her.

* * *

Jeremy had succeeded in moving out of Mom's, but it took longer than he thought it would. According to him, the two of them fought back and forth about it for weeks.

"She was driving me nuts," he said. We were in the elevator on the way to the fifteenth floor with bottles of hard liquor and three cases of beer.

"I know the feeling. Is this beer going to have time to get cold?"

"It will by the time we need it. I already have four cases on ice. I finally lost it on Mom. The last time she told me I was too young to move out, I blew up. For crying out loud, I'm thirty years old."

"She's definitely coming tonight?"

"Yeah. I think she wants to see you."

"That's news to me."

"It might be because of something I said."

"What?" I was surprised. Jeremy tended to stay out of my mother's disagreements with me. He had to deal with enough of his own.

"She didn't know when to quit. When she brought up my age I told her she better watch herself. I mentioned the fact that you hardly speak to her, and told her I was going to follow your lead if she didn't get off my back."

He has a set after all.

"What did she say to that?"

"Nothing. She shut up."

"Have you spoken to her since you left?"

"No. But she left me a voicemail yesterday, saying she'd see us tonight."

Michelle

Dear Holy Mother. I like to imagine you in the middle months of your pregnancy, after the angel had appeared to Joseph in a dream and he decided to take you into his home. I wonder what your life was like in those months when your Child was growing inside you. I like to think of you living quietly in the village of Nazareth, safe in Joseph's house. Working, reflecting, pondering, and waiting.

Father O'Neill denounced the HCA last night during his homily. He mentioned them by name, and preached against them so fervently that it gave me a funny feeling. I wonder how he has the courage. Lately I've had to search the AM dial to find his broadcasts.

Sometimes I can't find him at all, but that's no surprise. I just hope there won't be anything worse than his show disappearing.

After the Mass, as I lay down to turn off the light, I glanced at the pictures of Jason on the bedside table. My favorite was taken during his Air Force service. He's dressed in camouflage, young and tough looking, standing on an airstrip in Kenya. In the background are helicopters and a huge cargo plane. I love that picture. When I look at it I feel the way I used to when I was a little girl.

I rarely let myself think this way. It hurts too much and I have to be strong now. But I can't help writing a few details about your father. If the worst happens and we don't make it out of this maybe someone will read this journal. I want someone, anyone, to know about him.

I once went out to Daddy's garage and peeked around the door. Jason was looking under the hood of Brad's Trans Am. He was bent over in his faded grease-stained Levi's and worn out T-shirt with the knobs of his spine showing through. He always wore what I thought of as motorcycle boots, scuffed and worn and dusty. There's a faded memory of hearing Brad talking about those boots—some tale of Jason being disciplined by one of the priests for wearing them against dress code. And always in the background of these memories is an association with the music of Bruce Springsteen.

On the day we reunited at the mall I wanted to reach up and run my hands over the stubble on his face. I wanted to touch the tattoo around his heavily muscled left arm, as he reached for my door handle in the parking lot of Holiday's.

Angel, my tears are dripping on the page. Will I ever see your daddy again? Will you?

Jason
5 Years Earlier

My mother showed up at Lauren's around nine o'clock. Apparently she had decided to cut her losses with Jeremy, because she treated him the same as ever at the party, and Lauren seemed to meet her expectations as well. But after the stunt she pulled later, I found that Jeremy was mistaken in thinking Mom was interested in seeing me. Or Michelle. It was always a different story with the two of us, and I shouldn't have had any hopes to the contrary.

I was right in my earlier assessment of my wife. She looked as good as any of the women there that night and better than most, even Lauren and some of her model coworkers. Lauren was gorgeous, better looking in person than the picture, and she seemed happy to finally meet us. She said she hoped we wouldn't be strangers, and suggested a trip to Atlantic City to play the slots later that year. This exchange occurred before my mother entered the apartment, of course. The atmosphere changed with her arrival.

Yet even before Mom made her grand entrance I started feeling a little strange. Michelle and I exchanged looks throughout the evening. It really wasn't our kind of crowd. Most of the guests seemed nice enough, at least until they started getting drunk, but something about the situation bothered me.

I didn't understand it. I wasn't in the old man's garage discussing possible scenarios to the current troubles in the world in general and America in particular. I was at a New Year's Eve party at my brother's new place, a very nice place indeed. I should have been having a good time the way everyone else seemed to be. None of the people there seemed worried about anything at all. Most of the women were beautiful. *Maybe. But maybe not. Maybe not inside.*

As you may have noticed from some of my comments throughout this narrative, I've always taken note of any woman's looks. I'd done it for years—since I was a thirteen-year-old kid. Not that anyone else would be aware of the fact. I kept my thoughts to myself. Anyway, I appreciated my wife. She was one of the best looking women in the place that night, but the whole thing went deeper than just good looks. *Michelle...she has heart. She's got something else, something none of these chicks have. Michelle's got it going on inside.*

The contrast was amazing, actually, but nobody noticed except me. Everyone else in the room that evening seemed to see only the surface. It was different than any other New Year's Eve that I could remember.

Jeremy introduced us to everyone. My mother had been flitting around like the queen of the party since her arrival. She was standing with us when one of Lauren's coworkers asked Michelle and I what we did for a living. We were making small talk, and we hadn't yet been introduced. I was working on my third Jack and Coke—my limit for the night since I was driving.

"I'm Jason Wallace. This is my wife, Michelle, and my mother, Eileen."

"Nice to meet you. My name is Stacy. Lauren and I work together."

"In answer to your question, I'm an auto mechanic." I gestured to Michelle, next to me. She smiled and started to speak: "I work—"

"Michelle's a teacher," my mother interrupted, her tone cool. "She's taking some time off right now for health reasons."

I glanced at my wife, who stood open-mouthed. What I saw in her eyes sent a wrench of pain and humiliation through my person. I grabbed Michelle's hand and stood looking into her eyes.

She...Jason, it's okay. We'll go soon. But what are we even doing here?

Her blue eyes flashed. My mother was deeply engrossed in conversation with Stacy during the pain she inflicted on Michelle. I shouldn't have been surprised in the least, but this blow seemed too low even for her.

Mom hadn't shown the slightest interest in Michelle's health since she found out about the miscarriage. On the couple of occasions we'd spoken she had brushed our loss aside like it was nothing but a piece of lint on her shoulder, and here she was bringing it up now? *What a piece of work she is.* My face turned red. Anger rushed. *That shallow, hateful, nasty b—*

I stopped myself before the word fully formed in my mind. I had promised myself long ago that I would never use that word in connection with my mother. But the word was there, right under the surface of my consciousness. My mother was ashamed of my wife and myself. She was embarrassed that Michelle now worked at a store, and she didn't want anyone at the party to know.

Why should we care what Stacy thinks? She's nothing to us. After tonight we'll never see her again. What's wrong with my mother?

Every time I thought I'd seen it all with her, she dropped down one notch lower.

Michelle and I continued our eye lock. The room was oblivious to us and vice versa. Mom and Stacy were chatting with a few other people by that time. Certain phrases in the buzz of conversation filtered in and out of my head. *Red carpet... What the hell is that?* I turned my gaze toward Mom, opened my mouth, and then shut it again. I had ceased to exist for her, so we excused ourselves, telling Stacy it had been nice meeting her. Then we got as far away from my mother as we could.

"I'm so sorry," I whispered. My face was still flushed; I couldn't believe my mother's gall.

"Jason honey, don't you worry about her. She doesn't know what she's talking about."

Michelle found her way through the crowd at the bar and poured herself a glass of red wine. The fact that she called me honey was telling. She rarely did it. I was the one who called her honey. And baby, and sweetie, and every other term of endearment that fit. I'd done it forever, but she only did it when she knew something was upsetting me. That was when I figured it out. Michelle was

completely pissed off at my mother, not for herself but for me. I gave
her a hug.

"Let's put it out of our minds then, sweetie. Okay?" I smiled
down at her.

But she didn't see my smile. She was looking at the floor. She
wiped her hand across her eyes before answering. "Okay."

We circulated a little longer, talking. There was a big crowd at
my brother's that night. The place was packed. And no matter what
my mother's opinion of Michelle happened to be, she was certainly
turning heads in that room. Most of the guests were drunk, and something about the way certain men were ogling my wife made me want
to slam them into the wall. Brad in his worst days had never acted the
way they did, even the ones old enough to be Michelle's father. *This
is one strange-assed situation.*

I couldn't really put my finger on it. But as time crawled on
toward midnight, I got the idea that underneath everything else the
party was nothing but a giant meat market. It was the opposite of the
parties we attended with our friends. Those were good times. This
was not. *I wished we'd just stayed around town. We could have been
partying at Reese and Heather's instead of standing around with this
bunch.*

After Michelle and I kissed at midnight, we decided we'd had
enough. She went to Lauren's bedroom to use the bathroom and get
our coats, and I stepped out on the balcony to have a cigarette while I
waited for her. Cold air slapped me in the face. The balcony was dark
except for the silvery light of the moon. Shouts came from the streets.
I listened to the revelry going on around me, thinking about my
mother. *Why can't she accept me?*

I brooded about it for a few minutes, standing there in my shirt-
sleeves, not feeling the wind as I finished my cigarette and lit another.
The hell with it. Michelle loves me. The old man loves me. I felt an
ache in my throat, and tears just below the surface of my eyes. *I don't
need her. Her, or my father.* I heard the door open then and turned

around, thinking Michelle had come to fetch me. Unfortunately, it wasn't Michelle.

It was Stacy. She shut the door behind her quietly and stood next to it looking around. She probably couldn't see me; I was standing in the shadows where the moonlight didn't reach.

"What are you doing out here?" My voice was a little harsh. She jumped. Then she caught sight of the end of my cigarette as I dragged on it.

"I saw you go out a few minutes ago," she said, walking toward me.

"I needed a smoke for the road. We're getting ready to go." I stared past her, wishing I were still by myself. I wondered why she'd come out.

"Can you spare a cigarette?" Her voice was a little breathy. I couldn't see her face very well. Only a little light reached us from the street and the neighboring buildings. The door to the apartment was heavily curtained. I shook a cigarette out of the pack and handed it to her.

"I doubt this is your brand." I flicked my lighter. "You didn't need to come out here. I saw you smoking earlier. Inside."

"I came out to ask you about mechanics." I held the lighter for her. She took a drag on her Lucky Strike, coughing a little.

Well I'll be damned. This is the last thing I need.

"What does a model need to know about mechanics?" I leaned back against the railing, dragging on my smoke.

"I wanted to know what kind of hours a mechanic keeps." Her voice was soft. It held a certain tone. *Damn it, why now? I don't need this.*

"And why would you want to know that?" I asked resignedly. I already knew the answer. It was ironic. *Son of a bitch. One of the women my mother admires so much is looking to get in the sack with me.*

"Just curiosity. My hours are flexible. I travel a lot. I was wondering what it would be like to spend time with someone who works steady hours. Like a mechanic."

She was something in the looks department. I had checked her out earlier during one of Michelle's trips to the bathroom. I enjoyed looking at women. I could appreciate beauty. I just did it in a different way than those lowlifes inside. She was a model, so of course she was thin, but not too thin, and her legs were as good as Michelle's. Her skimpy dress ended about ten inches above the knee, with a neckline so low that half her rack showed plainly. I wondered how she could stand being out there in the cold.

"What kind of car do you drive?"

She mentioned a popular sports car before coming over to the railing. She leaned back next to me, letting her cigarette burn down. I glanced at her sideways. She was looking up at my face, but I didn't make eye contact. Instead I cast my eyes downward and looked right inside her dress. She had a set, all right. I stared for a minute, wondering whether or not they were real. I suspected they weren't.

I should have gone inside. It wasn't like this was the first such situation in which I'd ever found myself. Brad wasn't the only one women came on to. It had happened to me many times over the years. I knew how to handle myself. I never had any trouble extricating myself, and I always kept the upper hand.

She edged closer to me then. I raised my left hand in front of me, hoping she would take the hint and get out of my space. Apparently I didn't get my point across though, because the next thing I knew the right side of her rack was under my hand. I could feel her hand, too. It was on the inside of my leg. *Well no shit. She wants to know what it would be like to get laid by a mechanic, and she thinks I want to know what it would be like to screw a model. Maybe she's right.*

The tears were still there, right below the surface of my eyes. *What the hell is wrong with me? Damn it, I must be crazy!* But before I took my hand away, I gave what was under it a good grope. *I was right. She has implants.* I knew it was the wrong thing to do before I did it, but she put it right in my hand. Then her hand was moving upward.

This is one messed up situation. What the hell do I think I'm doing? Before she could grab onto me I let go of her and edged around the corner of the railing. I dropped my cigarette on the floor and ground it out before telling her I wasn't interested.

"I can't help you with your car. Take it to the dealership. I don't have any extra time these days."

She stood quietly for a moment. "I never said I needed any help with my car.

The sweet smell of her perfume was in the air. She smelled good. My hands clutched the railing as I looked down at the street full of people celebrating. Then she took one of my hands, disengaging it from the railing before placing what felt like a business card in my palm. "Take this," she said, "and if you ever do find yourself with some extra time on your hands, call me. Like I said, my hours are flexible. I'm interested in mechanics. Maybe you could show me a few things."

"Like I said, I'm pretty busy. I make it a point to spend any extra time I do have with my wife."

"Your wife can't show you anything you haven't already seen, can she? And I doubt I'll ever find another mechanic who could show me the things you could."

Her mention of my wife sent another wrench of pain and love through my person. Along with contempt for her, and my mother, and the rest of the shallow beings with whom I'd just wasted the evening. I stared off into space, holding my hand back and hoping she'd take the damned card. She didn't. *Well son of a bitch. I've had enough of this bullshit.*

"I'm going now," I said, edging away from her and walking toward the door.

"If you change your mind, let me know," came her voice, sounding like she thought it was only a matter of time. *What a whore.*

"Happy New Year."

I went inside. The bathroom off the hall was empty. I went in and looked at her card, wondering why I was so upset. I asked myself how she'd managed to get the upper hand. I almost tossed the card in the trash, but instead I took out my wallet and slipped it in the back behind my credit card. I did it quickly and against my better judgment, refusing to ask myself why I might be saving it. Then I washed water over my face and looked at myself in the mirror. *You cheating bastard.*

I took a deep breath. I had to get myself together before Michelle figured out something was wrong. *Nothing happened. And nothing will. There's only Michelle. She loves me.* Michelle was back in the living room.

"Are you ready, baby?" I helped her into her coat.

"Let's go," she said.

We found Jeremy and Lauren in the middle of a group of party-goers, my mother among them. After we thanked them for inviting us, Michelle managed to get one back at Mom. As we were saying our goodbyes Michelle looked straight at my mother and said in a sweet tone of voice: "We have an hour's drive, and I have to be at work at the supermarket early tomorrow."

The ride home was quiet, except for the sound of the Eagles coming from the stereo speakers. The CD had been Michelle's choice. She was sleeping next to me. I listened for a while as I drove along the interstate, thinking about the business card in my wallet.

THIRTEEN

Michelle

The heat is oppressive tonight, angel-baby. Since I can't sleep, I'll write down more memories.

I've kept many memories of Jason over the years. I had always known he was mine. After he left town I did nothing but mark time until he returned. Though I dated a few guys in high school, it was only to keep up the appearance of being a normal teenage girl. With Jason in mind my schoolmates were all little boys to me, and I wasn't interested.

My memories of him will never leave me, not if I live to be a hundred. There was always the knowledge that I could depend on him, ever since I was a little girl. There were images of his gray-green eyes...and his smile, the one the other girls never saw. My favorite memory is of standing at the window of daddy's garage and watching him work as he lay on his back under the Trans Am. He never knew I was there. He muttered and cussed under his breath while I stood outside. I stared at his six-pack stomach disappearing into his faded jeans.

This leads to still another memory, of a trip to the beach with Aunt Rosie and Bella the summer before I turned thirteen. Bella and her friends were four years older than me, but Mom still allowed me to go to the beach with them every summer; it was a tradition. On that particular night I overheard a conversation between Bella and the others after their return from the boardwalk.

I would be starting eighth grade at St. Catherine's the following September and the three of them would be seniors, the same as Brad and Jason. Mom had rules for me when I was at the beach. One of them was that I had to be in by ten o'clock. I would go to bed and read. Sometimes I would fall asleep, but when the older girls came in that night I was lying half awake on the cot under the window, breathing in the scent of sea salt.

I dozed as the girls snuck past my sleeping aunt and came down the little hallway. They all assumed I was sound asleep. Bella warned Jen and Emily to keep quiet as they undressed in the light from the bathroom. Then they began talking in whispers.

Jen and Emily teased Bella about her cousin, who was also my brother. They considered him hot, even if he was a total player. They went on to talk a little about Emily's cousin, Caroline, and her perpetual wish that she and Brad might get together after school resumed.

"Caroline never stops hoping," Emily said. "She's been in love with Brad since eighth grade. What do you think, Bella? Maybe Brad's grown up enough now. Caroline's beautiful."

"I know she's beautiful, but she better not get her hopes up," came Bella's hushed voice from the bed. "Brad's way too much of a player. The word in the dictionary probably has his picture right next to it."

I was still half asleep, agreeing with Bella. *Brad's stupid. Caroline's pretty. And nice. What's wrong with him?*

They chatted and laughed about Brad for time. Then Jen started talking about Brad's friend. She and Emily both agreed he was the best thing they'd ever laid eyes on.

"Even if he does tend to sleep around from time to time," said Jen. She sounded hurt and wistful at the same time.

My eyes popped open.

I knew who they were talking about right away. I didn't move, but I was no longer half asleep on the cot in the corner, either. I was awake and listening. They went on with their conversation, talking in low voices about Jason and their classmate from Kennedy. The two had had a one-night stand back in June, right before school let out.

"That slut," came Bella's voice. "Nobody would ever have known. But since she told the whole school, I decided to see what Brad had to say."

"And?" Jen sounded sad.

"He didn't know anything about it!" Bella sounded amazed. "Apparently Jason never talks about his private life. Never says a thing, not even to my cousin. Or if Brad does know, he's not telling. They're like brothers. Brad says he's an enigma."

He is an enigma. My enigma. I lay stiffly on the cot, not moving a muscle as they continued their gossip.

"Brad's right," Emily said, laughing. "Jason Wallace is an enigma. He always has been. But her... She's nothing but a slut. She should have kept her big mouth shut."

The three of them agreed, continuing to refer to her as a slut and saying she'd told everyone whether they wanted to hear it or not. Then Jen remarked that she wouldn't mind being a slut for a night or two if it meant she could get her some of *that*.

She's lucky I want to keep eavesdropping. Otherwise I'd get up off this cot and whack her on the side of the head.

They whispered more about the slut and something else she had said. She hadn't known when to shut up, and word had gotten around the school. They giggled in their agreement that the slut probably knew what she was talking about in that regard. *I better never catch that slut around our neighborhood.*

Then the talk went back to Jason and how good-looking he was. They said he was hot, tall, had sexy eyes, and that he might as well be on a poster hanging in the mall. Emily wondered why he wasn't on the football team, remarking that he looked like he could run rings around the quarterback at Kennedy.

"Shut the hell up, you biotch," Bella whispered. "Lucio's the quarterback."

"Yeah, Bella, whatever." Laughing. "Did he call you?"

"No." Bella whispered fiercely. "Not yet. But that makes no difference. He paid me plenty of attention before school let out. It'll happen again in September."

"Okay." Emily sounded abashed. "Whatever you say, Bella. Now back to Jason Wallace."

I still hadn't moved a muscle, and they had no idea I was listening to their comments. Here's a sampling: They couldn't have helped noticing that he didn't smile often and they wondered why, but they all agreed that he had great teeth. They loved his beard. He always seemed to look like he needed a shave; that was sexy. He had the broadest shoulders, and he must work out every night to keep his arms the way they were. Not to mention that he actually had a few brains in his head. Was it true that he almost always got straight A marks? And that he'd be taking college level courses next year, even calculus?

Finally, right before they shut up and went to sleep, the talk returned to the slut and her big mouth.

"She should never have brought up that part," said Bella. "What the hell is wrong with her?"

"She may be a stupid tramp with a big mouth, but she probably knows what she's talking about," Jen repeated mournfully. Then the three of them giggled as they came to a final conclusion: Jason had everything going for him, and even *that* was bigger than anyone else's.

The hushed giggling went on for a bit longer before finally tapering off into quiet regular breathing, as they slept and dreamed their dreams.

I dreamed as well, but I didn't sleep that night. What I had heard raced through my head, keeping sleep at bay. Just like tonight. I might as well keep writing since I'm still wide-awake, even though I'll probably have to censor some of it. I may never be able to let you read parts of this, my angel-baby. I'll write it down anyway though, for myself.

Years later I learned for myself that the slut *had* known what she was talking about. I found out on a night in Jason's apartment the summer before we were married. It was the one time I had almost given in and let him make love to me. I was scared and unsure, but also helpless on his bed, wanting him so badly I could hardly think. He lay on the bed with me, holding onto my hands, telling me with his sexy green eyes how much he loved me. How much he wanted me. That he was burning. That he would walk through fire for me. But it was my choice now.

I wanted him, too. My body cried out for him. But we had promised to wait for our wedding night and that's what we ended up doing. If Jason was angry about it he never let on to me.

Now back to the night at the beach. I was twelve years old, but only in the limiting time of humanity. Not in the time of destiny. I seemed to grow up then in my mind and my heart, as I lay with sea-scented air blowing over me. Images of weddings and babies ran through my head. They rushed through my brain like waves, crashing over the past and the future. Jason and I belonged together. I had loved him forever and he was a part of me. That night at the beach brought what I already knew to the forefront of my mind.

However I refused to be stupid about it. I knew he could be mine someday, but even at age twelve I was under no illusions. Jason ran around with my brother after all. *He's an enigma. Mine. But I'm never going to do what that slut did. Never—no matter what. I'm making a plan now. A vow.*

I decided that night not to worry about the other women. I understood that the slut hadn't been the first, and that she also wouldn't be the last. My plan was simply a promise to myself that I was never going to do what that slut had done.

The years passed. I went to Mass on Sunday, looked at the statue of the Virgin, and told myself I would wait. I wanted him to be my husband, and I vowed not to let anything stop me from marrying him as long as I could be sure he would stay true to me. And he came back to me. He stayed true to me and he came through for me. For me, angel-baby, and for you.

I miss him so much right this minute I can hardly stand it. It's a physical ache. I'm putting the pen down now. I'll lie back and listen to what I've been hearing for the past hour. The sound comes in through the open kitchen windows and filters down the basement stairs. It's a pack of dogs, barking and howling in the distance. It makes me shiver as I write these last few words, hugging the camouflage picture against me.

Jason
5 Years Earlier

Michelle brought up my mother and her nonsense when we got home on New Year's Eve.

"I don't understand that woman."

"Neither do I."

"What do you think her problem is?"

"Michelle, I don't know. She's always been that way. I've given up trying to figure out why."

I finished taking off my tie, thanking God I didn't have to wear one everyday like Brad did. My work uniform was jeans and a T-shirt, and maybe coveralls once in a while if the job was especially greasy. CJ didn't care what we wore as long as it was clean.

Michelle was undressing on her side of the bed. She took off her sweater and her dress.

"You were the belle of the ball." I said, giving her the eye.

"I wish I'd worn something a little less skimpy," she mentioned. She'd been the most conservatively dressed woman there.

"No way baby. You put them all to shame."

It was the truth. I found myself next to her then. It happened that way a lot lately. One minute we were talking, and the next we were all over each other. I took the clip out of the back of her hair and started running my hands through it. She traced the tattoo around my upper arm back and forth as she murmured under her breath: "Those women up there wanted to eat you alive." She put her head against my chest, continuing to rub my arm. She'd always loved that tattoo.

"I heard a couple of them talking when I came out of the bathroom," she went on. "They didn't know who I was. One mentioned Jeremy's brother and wondered whether or not he was single. Then the other one answered that she didn't care if he was married with five kids. She said she was going out there to see what she could do about it."

I had her on the bed by then. "I don't know who you're talking about, but she didn't approach me." I wasn't lying. Michelle had met Stacy. *Whoever it was, it couldn't have been Stacy. She might be a tramp, but she can't be that stupid.*

"That whole place was nothing but a giant meat market," I remarked. "Did you notice the way those old men next to the bar were eyeing you up?"

"Yes. They were pigs."

"Don't worry." My voice was muffled. I was kissing her neck, pulling off her bikinis. Then things were happening for me.

"Jason, are you happy?" Michelle's voice sounded far away.

What's wrong? She sounds upset. I was on top of her. I paused, suspended there, my arms stiff on either side of her, my hands flat on the bed. I opened my eyes to the sight of hers, staring up at me. She reached up to feel my beard with her hands.

"Michelle, where's this coming from?" I asked. But I already knew. She hugged me. I rolled off her then, took her in my arms, and waited for her answer.

"Those women up there. I'm not like them."

Thank God for that. "Honey, why are you bringing them up?" There was no way she could be aware of what happened on the balcony. I'd been out there less than fifteen minutes.

"I don't know." Her voice shook. I felt a sudden sense of shame.

"Honey, why are you so upset? Why would you even want to be like them?"

"I don't want to be like them. But..." she laid her head on my shoulder.

As we lay together quietly I was wishing we had never gone to that damned party. I could feel her breasts against my chest. She was the real thing; there was nothing fake about Michelle.

"I didn't belong there," she said.

"Well, neither did I. I was thinking all night about how much more fun we would have had at Reese's."

"Are you happy?"

"Baby." I hugged her. "Honey, you know I'm happy. Why are you upsetting yourself?"

"But your mother..."

"Is a freak. You're everything to me."

"But they were all so beautiful, those women."

"Beautiful," I repeated harshly. "They weren't beautiful to me." *Especially Stacy.* "They're a bunch of fakes. Did you hear the stupid shit they were talking?"

"Well I never said I thought they had brains." She laughed a little. "And not all of them were fakes. Lauren seems nice."

"She's okay." I kissed the top of her head. "But she's nothing compared to you. So forget about the damn party. I don't want you thinking you're inferior to that bunch of skanks."

"All right."

"You're just as good looking as any of them and I'd be upset if you were anything other than what you are. I love you. We have everything. I know things have been hard for us lately, especially for you. But they'll get better." I breathed in the fresh scent of her hair. "If that's Jeremy's choice, that kind of life, so be it. My mother, too."

I could feel her sense of relief, as I contemplated the business card in my wallet. I wished it wasn't there, lurking. *Why didn't I just throw the damn thing away? Why didn't I toss it down right in front of her?* Then I put it out of my mind. *I'll get rid of it tomorrow.*

"Michelle," I questioned, "when's myrtle coming to town?"

"Next week."

"How are you feeling?"

"Like I'm ready to be a mother."

"Are you sure?"

"Jason, you've seen me over the past couple of months. You know I'm fine now."

"Okay baby. Let's have a baby." My hands ran through her hair. It was silky and soft in the glow of the bedside lamp.

"I'm going to the doctor," she said. "I'm discontinuing the meds."

"You do what he tells you," I answered sharply. I had her underneath me again. I stared into her eyes. "Do you hear me?"

"Okay."

Things began to go away again then, the things of the world, the things we'd seen earlier. I was losing myself in Michelle's blue eyes. I could see all the years we had shared in their depths. I felt the shock again, a sort of longing. *This is what it's all about. It's what's right.*

I thought back over the party one final time. The faces of the women there reminded me of masks. I had an idea that the people were asleep. Sleepwalking through another night, the same way they probably had at countless other parties on countless other nights. Then the thoughts broke up, and as they faded away I had another brief flash of memory. It was a remembrance of Brad and me, way back.

I couldn't consciously remember the first time Brad and I met. He'd always been there, from my earliest memories. But that New Year's morning I remembered being out in the old man's backyard. Brad and I were playing in a sandbox with Tonka bulldozers and dump trucks. Then someone came crawling up to the sandbox. She pulled herself up and stood there swaying. I remembered bright blonde hair and those same blue eyes, immense and liquid, ringed in dark lashes. Time meant nothing as we gazed at each other.

Where did you come from? You're pretty.

Then Brad spoiled the moment, and she wailed as he shoved her away. I stood up. She was lying flat on her back, her beautiful eyes filled with tears. She struggled to her feet and ran toward Brad, but I got to him first.

"*I told you not to hurt your baby sister!*" came Brad's mom's voice. *Now look at you! Your nose is bleeding!*"

Her eyes were the same all these years later. The last thing I remember about that New Year's morning was murmuring over and over: "Michelle, you're beautiful." I was kissing her neck. I reached over and turned out the light.

* * *

The New Year's Eve at Jeremy's marked the beginning of the end of something. After that night things began happening faster. My eyes opened a little more, and to me the years before that night became a sort of Gethsemane, leading up to our own agony.

I don't pretend to understand the mind of God. Maybe His agony in the Garden of Gethsemane was years long as well. It may be so, even though to us it appears to have taken place during the early morning hours of that first Good Friday. Our time and God's time are not the same thing.

The years of our Gethsemane contained periods of sleep, wakefulness, and watchfulness. There were tears, laughter, and feelings of helplessness. Times of sorrow and distress would be followed by intervals of calm, when it was almost possible to believe that none of what was happening was real. Sometimes we almost believed we were crazy. Crazy, fringe, stupid, uneducated religious fanatics—all the things we were told, and that people believed about us.

Some of us were in denial. Some went to sleep under trees. Some took crazy chances, the way Brad did when he found a way to get hold of that Saturday night special. Some of us ran away, and some tried to give strength to others the way the Angel gave strength to Him in the Garden. Some even took up swords, raised them, and slashed off ears.

Some of us were able to realize the futility of doing such a thing. We remembered what He had said: "Those who live by the sword shall also die by it." We kept His words in mind during periods of anger and rage when all sense seemed to leave us, and somehow we managed never to heft the sword.

We made our choices. Others chose a different way, figuring out too late that the bureaucratic sharks had enslaved them. People have free will, but not all of them seem to know it.

America was toppled from within. I have no way of knowing who was behind it. No one does; the traitors are nameless and faceless. Not all of them are politicians. Some of the politicians were deceived themselves. The traitors work behind the scenes. They are calculating, cold, manipulative, unknowable, and untouchable.

There are others whom I consider traitors of a sort, my own mother among them, but the ultimate betrayers were those who knew what the results would be. They set their wheels in motion lifetimes earlier. Ideologies were formed, honed and disseminated, becoming truth to many. They turned our world upside down by pulling strings in low places to manipulate our average ordinary lives. They glory in the destruction of our country.

Though my writing is impassioned, I'm not vengeful. I don't want revenge. Nothing I could do can compare anyway to what awaits the ones who don't repent. They will be brought to justice, if not in this life then in the next. No one can escape that Ultimate Justice.

The first time I considered that America might fall was on the morning of September 11, 2001. Brad was sitting across the aisle from me when the intercom interrupted honors calculus with news of the attack. The two of us looked at each other the way we always did when anything out of the ordinary happened, but on that day there was something else for me. It was the first time I remember experiencing the lights no one else could see, accompanied by the feeling of water. *America is over. Another fifty years if we're lucky.* The thought came out of nowhere as the water rushed through my head.

We went to the next classroom where there was a TV. Brad and I leaned against the wall watching the towers come down. I wanted a cigarette, and I almost pulled the pack out of my pocket. Brad's blue eyes were narrow.

Damn it Wallace, is that true? What we just saw? Did that just happen?

Yeah it happened, look at it. I need a smoke. Let's get the hell outta here, nobody'll notice.

We exited the science lab and walked out of school. I checked my cell phone as I folded myself into the shotgun seat of the Trans Am, wondering if there might be a message from Mom checking on me, but there was no evidence that anyone had called. *Dad? Are you gonna call? Where are you?* Then the phone rang and I answered. It was Brad's dad, calling to see if we were okay, and telling us to go home. Brad didn't have a cell phone. We lit up our cigarettes then. I remember it like it was yesterday. The smoke, the air blowing through, the bright blue sky.

And the strange perception that I wasn't alone. It was out of the ordinary, but not alien, comforting in a way. The flowing, rushing feeling made what my eyes saw seem only one small part of something more, something huge, bigger than anything I might perceive with my human limitations. It dissipated as Brad squealed around the corner of Aster and Harrison and pulled into the old man's driveway. It would be back, though. The lights and the feeling of water would return to me at intervals over the years.

It (*He*) was trying to tell me something. He'd always been there and always would be. I may have turned away at times but He remained, always waiting patiently. *He just is.* He stayed with me through all that happened, until I finally ended up on my knees in the chapel at St. Michael's, trying to find an answer for Michelle's loss of our children. It was then that I began to listen. To listen, to hear, and to find answers. Answers I didn't always accept, but answers just the same.

FOURTEEN

Jason
5 Years Earlier

"Nicole is pregnant," Brad said in my ear. We were on the phone.

I got a glass from the workbench in the shed and poured myself a shot. Michelle and I had been at it every night, trying to make a baby. *If it happens soon, she and Nicole will give birth within a few months of each other.*

"Did you hear me?" Brad said.

"Yeah, sorry. Congratulations." I drank down my whiskey.

"Thanks."

"What do you think about it?"

I knew there was no telling what Brad might have thought about it but he outdid himself that night. When I heard his answer I thought he might be going off the deep end.

"What do I think?" He sounded a little irritated. "It's your fault—that's what I think."

"My fault?" I thought I had misunderstood.

"Yeah."

"My fault," I repeated. "Well...all right Brad. I'll bite. You and your wife live in Tennessee. I live in Pennsylvania. I haven't seen either of you since last July. Your wife is now pregnant, and I assume you were the one who knocked her up. And it's my fault how?"

"Because it happened the night we argued, that's how." I heard him light a cigarette. I thought I heard him laughing.

"What are you talking about? You and Nicole are always arguing."

"Not Nicole. You."

"Me," I repeated, feeling like a parrot. "Brad, you're pissing me off now. What are you talking about?"

"The night I accused you of neglecting Michelle, back in November. That's the night it happened, and it's all your fault."

"Are you insane?"

"No. But I wasn't planning to get laid that night, and if I hadn't argued with you I wouldn't have." He laughed under his breath. "I felt so bad about what I was thinking that I went upstairs and got laid. And let's just say it may or may not have been the right time. So now I'm gonna be a daddy. And it's *all—your—fault!*" He busted out laughing.

I sat in stupefied silence as what he had said sunk in. "You asshole." I shook my head before starting to laugh myself. We laughed together then.

"I'm not the asshole Wallace; you're the one who fell for it."

"Brad," I said, laughing, "You are seriously messed up."

"Yeah," he agreed. "But you fell for it. I wish I could have seen your face."

"Yeah, I guess I did. Do you have any whiskey? Let's drink to it."

I poured another shot, listening to Brad banging cupboard doors over the phone.

"You ready?"

"Yeah. To Nicole and Brad, and their impending arrival." I knocked back my shot, and I assumed he did as well.

"Thanks Wallace."

"Okay. So what do you really think about it?"

"We're both happy, even though it's a little sooner than we planned."

"Well count your blessings."

"I know, I am. But you have no idea how bad I felt that night."

"Well you're getting a baby out of it aren't you?"

"Yeah."

"Good."

I lit a cigarette. The old man had given me a carton for Christmas on the sly. I took a drag, remembering his words as he presented me with the carton: "Make them last, boy." This was the first one I smoked. *The old man might have two more grandchildren by this time next year. Wonder what Brad'll say about that.*

"Your child might have a cousin a few months younger," I mentioned.

"Michelle's pregnant, too?"

"Not yet. But maybe soon." I dragged on my Lucky Strike. The two of us smoked quietly for a few minutes. That was all I said to Brad about Michelle and myself that night. He didn't need to know the details. Though I had, on occasion, mentioned certain things to Brad, it had always been in the context of my concern for Michelle. Never anything like what he would tell me, and had told me in the past about his sexual exploits.

It wasn't only because Michelle was Brad's sister. I never said anything about our private life to anyone. Not down at the garage, not when the guys were out fishing, never. I considered my marriage a sacrament even back before I came to faith more deeply. The thought of talking about Michelle the way some men talked about their wives made my stomach churn. On one occasion I even lost my temper over such a thing.

One of the guys who used to work at the garage—the first one Ceej had been forced to lay off—made a couple of comments about

Michelle once. He'd met Michelle the previous week when she stopped in for some reason or other, and he must have thought he could get away with talking about her the same way he talked about his girlfriend. I went into the break room to get a soda one afternoon while the guy—he went by the nickname Kippy—was in there with Reese and Danny. They were sitting around the table shooting the shit and drinking the brew that CJ tried to pass off as coffee. As I squeezed past the break table, he said something crude in an aside to them, before looking up at me and mentioning the size of two certain portions of my wife's anatomy. He finished off with a comment about how great it must be to have her in the sack. That was when the atmosphere changed.

Everything went quiet. Danny and Reese knew Kippy was screwed. Reese told me later he could tell I wasn't going to let it go.

I slammed the Pepsi can down on the table, and it exploded. Then I hauled Kippy out of his chair and shoved him against the wall.

"My wife is off limits as a topic of conversation around here," I said through clenched teeth. "Do you understand?"

Kippy was shocked. He muttered something about there being no offense meant.

"None taken," I replied, staring at him. "As long as it doesn't happen again." I shoved him back down in his chair and stalked out of the room. Half an hour later I went back to clean up the mess I had made with the Pepsi.

Thinking back on the incident I felt bad about scaring the crap out of Kippy, even though I hadn't at the time. The poor guy was only a product of the environment. Kippy was no different than the snobs at Jeremy's New Year's Eve party in that regard, even though those people would never have given him the time of day. That's the way the way most people acted back then. It was people like Michelle and me who were considered the strange ones.

I came back when I heard Brad's voice, talking in my ear again.

"Have you told anyone else?" I asked.

"No. We're calling tomorrow. I wanted to tell you first."

"I'm telling Michelle," I said.

"All right, but tell her to act surprised tomorrow in front of Mom and Dad." It was a Saturday night. He knew we'd be there for dinner the next day.

I changed the subject then. "What about single payer?"

Michelle and I had received our notification two weeks earlier, and so had Johnny and his family. It had almost been a relief, strange as that might sound. After all, we'd all known it was coming, and the waiting was stressful.

"We're on it." Brad said.

"Same here."

"I'm hoping things will go along okay. Nicole had a blood test, and she has her first appointment next month."

"When's the baby due?"

"Nicole says August."

We talked another few minutes. Then I congratulated him again before telling him I'd talk to him later. I hung up, lit another cigarette, and sat there in the tool shed, smoking. I poured myself another shot of whiskey and drank it down before going through the frosty back-yard to the house.

Michelle was waiting for me. She smiled and held out her arms as I went to the bed. Then everything else went away.

* * *

A while later, things came back. The weight of having to tell Michelle about her brother's wife's pregnancy descended on me with a thud.

"Jason, I thought you were going to quit smoking," she said from underneath me. "I was really hoping you were serious this time, but I guess I was wrong." She sounded disappointed.

I groaned and rolled onto my back. Moonlight shone through our window, casting silvery shadows over the bed. *Not now... Love is patient, love is kind.* "Why are you bringing this up now?"

"Because I know I have your full attention." She put her head on my shoulder.

"You're right. I put my arms around her. "But tonight's not the time for this conversation."

"Well, you're smoking again, aren't you?"

"You know I am."

"I don't like it." She poked me in the ribs.

"Well, I do."

"Is Daddy smoking?"

"Michelle, please." I sighed.

"Has my diabetic father been smoking? Because I suspect he has."

"Honey, let's get some sleep, it's late."

"Answer me," she said, ignoring my request.

I sighed again. "Yeah. He smokes sometimes."

"Jason! You know Daddy's not supposed to smoke. His foot's started bothering him again. I can't believe you and Brad go along with him."

"I can't control your father. You know how he is."

"You can control yourself."

"I know I can control myself. I've been doing it every month for years now." I put my hand on her belly. "Let's not argue about this. Maybe there's a baby here."

"You're going to drive me crazy someday." She laughed a little. "No one can tell Daddy what to do," she admitted. "But you should quit."

"You got that right," I replied. "About your father, I mean. And I'll let you know when I decide to quit. Now I have something to tell you. Brad called earlier. He says Nicole is pregnant."

She stiffened in my arms, saying nothing.

"Now don't feel bad about it. You'll be pregnant soon."

"Sometimes I wonder if we'll ever have a child who lives," she said, her voice shaking.

"Our babies are in heaven, honey. And you're probably pregnant yourself."

"I hope so," she said.

* * *

By the next morning Michelle was feeling better about the prospect of being an aunt again. She mentioned it after Mass. We were in my truck on our way over to the old man's house.

"I have a feeling Brad's baby might have a cousin around the same age." She smiled at me from the passenger seat.

"I told you you'd feel better after sleeping on it," I said. "What's for dinner today?"

"Spaghetti and bracciole," she replied. Oh, I almost forgot! I have to pick up a bunch of parsley for mom. Can you run me over to the store?"

"Sure," I said. "I'll do anything for bracciole."

* * *

On Sundays we always ate early, around three o'clock. Johnny and his family came that day too.

The bracciole—thin slices of steak wrapped around chopped parsley and garlic, held together with toothpicks, and cooked in tomato sauce—was delicious. I was pigging out as usual, until Johnny broke the news that Cindy had been laid off on Friday. Then I saw that Cindy hadn't touched the food on her plate, and I felt bad all of a sudden about my appetite. She blinked back tears as we all told her how sorry we were.

"Any chance you'll be called back?" The old man's voice was hopeful.

"No," Cindy replied. "My whole department was cut." She wiped her eyes.

Junior sat across the table from me, glaring at his mother. "You better find another job quick," he said.

Who the hell does he think he is? "Be quiet, Junior," I snapped. At that moment I didn't care whose son he was. Nobody talked like that at the old man's table. But Junior didn't know when to quit.

"Just because she lost her job, doesn't mean I'm changing schools." His nostrils flared as he looked at me, his chin jutting.

Everything went quiet. Cindy burst into tears and left the table, and Johnny followed her out of the room. My answer was to kick Junior in the leg, hard. Though I was wearing boots, he acted like he didn't even feel it.

"Junior?" I stared with narrowed eyes. "You better apologize to your mom."

"I don't give a shit, Jason. I'm not switching."

Well I'll be damned. Did I just hear that? My response was automatic. I got up immediately, went around the table and hauled him up out of his chair.

"Junior!" The old man roared. "What the hell is wrong with you?"

I had him by the arm. "Apologize to your grandmother and your aunt for that language. Now!" I gave him a little shove.

"Sorry." It sounded insincere.

"There are people other than you in this, Junior." The old man's face was bright red. A vein in his temple throbbed. "Think about your mother."

Mrs. Davis seemed too shocked for words. Jamie sat still as a mouse, and Michelle had tears in her eyes. "Junior," she said softly. "Wait and see what happens. You don't know for sure that you're going to have to change schools."

Junior responded by storming out of the kitchen. He slammed the door on his way out with a curse.

* * *

Half an hour later Brad called to give his parents the news about the baby. Cindy and Johnny had come back to the table, and they were there at the time of the call. It broke the ice. After everyone congratulated Nicole and Brad, I excused myself and went out to the garage.

Junior was leaning back against the old man's workbench, sulking in the cold and dark. I hit the light switch.

"Can I talk to you for a minute?" I said, keeping my tone moderate. But Junior didn't answer me. He turned his head and looked pointedly at the garage doors.

"Junior," I said in the same mild tone. "Grow up. Please."

He'd be eighteen in August. I knew it wasn't my place to speak to him that way, but what happened at the table had made me so angry that I wanted him to know what I thought.

"Why don't you look for a job?" I went around the old man's car to the workbench and leaned back next to him.

"There's nothing out there."

"Maybe you'll get lucky."

"Come on Jason," he said. "You know that's a load of horseshit." He was probably right on that score. Most businesses were either downsizing or shutting down outright.

"You have to think positive. You should apply in food service. Somebody might quit, and maybe you'd have a chance."

"I went to Holiday's before Christmas. I never heard anything back. Jimmy McGill—he works there—he said last week they might go out of business."

"Okay, but that's only one application. Try some other places."

"Don't tell me what to do," he snapped. "You had it easy. You had a job handed to you when you were my age."

I took a deep breath. Junior had no idea what he was talking about.

"That's not true, and what we need to do right now is solve your problem. Don't worry about what you think you know about me when I was your age."

"Whatever." He took a pack of Lucky Strikes out of his St. Bonaventure jacket and lit one, arrogance in his tone and demeanor. I could hardly believe my eyes. I asked him where the cigarettes had come from, and he ignored me.

"Put that out." I said.

"No."

"Junior, you're on thin ice. You're out of control, and if you don't want me to either call your father or knock the living shit right out of you, you'll put that damn thing out."

He ground it out under his shoe then, before kicking the butt across the floor. It ended up under the window. "I only have the rest of this year and next," he said stubbornly, "and I'm not switching."

You little shit. I agreed with the old man. Junior was thinking about no one but himself. He almost reminded me of my mother.

"Just give it some time. You don't know what's going to happen, so stop acting like a spoiled little punk before you regret it." I gave him a stare. "Now get your ass back in that house and apologize to your mother. This is not her fault, and you have no business blaming her." I gave him a shove to get him going.

"Okay," he said. I followed him around the car to the door. Before opening it he bent and rubbed his shin where my boot had connected.

"That hurt."

"You deserved it," I replied. He didn't answer me.

* * *

The episode with Junior was so unnerving that I went out to the shed again that night and called Brad to tell him about it.

"He's stealing Johnny's cigarettes," I said, lighting one myself.

"You remember how we were at that age."

"This is different."

That was an understatement. Brad and I had been a little wild, but neither of us would ever have acted the way Junior did that afternoon. We were too afraid of the old man to ever even think about it, but it wasn't even that. Something else was going on with Junior. Unless there was a side of him I'd never seen, what had happened was out of character for him. Even witnessing the episode with the joint hadn't disturbed me the way I was now.

"Something's wrong," I went on. "If you'd been at the table you'd know what I mean."

"How'd it end?"

"We were back on good terms when they left."

"Well maybe you got through to him." Brad was getting impatient. He told me we'd talk about it later. It had been a long day, and he and Nicole had just returned from his in-laws' place. "Don't worry about Junior, Wallace. Johnny'll kick his scrawny little ass if he pulls anything else. I'm going to bed."

Brad hung up. I leaned back against my own workbench for another few minutes, thinking. Then I poured myself a shot, drank it down, and went in to Michelle.

Michelle

It's hot, angel-baby. I can barely stand the humidity, but I'll try to write for you. It gives me hope that you'll be able to read my words someday.

All night long the faint sound of crickets comes through the open windows upstairs. I lie awake without any covers, the fan humming as it sends air across my swollen body. I doze off for a while, until I need to go to the bathroom again.

I struggle off the air mattress and stand up, feeling pressure at the top of my legs. It's you, angel, pressing down in your eagerness to enter this world. I use the bathroom and lie down again, sweat trickling down my neck. As the night progresses there are contractions on and off—what Melanie terms Braxton-Hicks. Finally the closeness of my room overwhelms me, and in the early dawn I venture outside.

The air doesn't move as I push my way through the rows of corn. It's so humid that I find it hard to breathe. My body is covered in sweat. The sun is just coming up, but already the buzzing of a cicada reaches my ears. The low chirping reaches a crescendo and then winds down again.

It's mid-August, and I find myself in the cornfield less and less because of the heat. I'm tired, and glad you'll arrive in another month. Mark walks behind me. He carries a rifle to protect me from anything that might come out of the corn.

FIFTEEN

Jason
5 Years Earlier

We were overjoyed when we found out Michelle was pregnant. After the little blue line appeared on the home pregnancy test, Michelle calculated that the baby would be born in November, three months after Nicole and Brad's child. We both agreed that it would be fun for the cousins to grow up together, especially if they were the same sex.

But our plans for the future ended on a Saturday morning three weeks later.

I slept late in winter since I didn't have to cut the grass, and I didn't go in to work until ten o'clock. I was deeply sleeping when a voice cried out *no,* interrupting an unremembered dream. I came to awareness when Michelle shrieked my name from the bathroom.

I jumped out of the bed and ran around it. Michelle was bent over in pain, clutching the vanity. I took her in my arms.

"It'll be okay, honey," I lied. "We'll get you to the doctor right away."

She sagged against me. Blood trickled down her leg. Her pajamas were spotted red.

"It won't be okay!" she cried.

"Baby, let's get you into the shower." I helped her get cleaned up. We cried together as the blood washed off and swirled down the drain. We both knew there was no way the baby could have survived.

After she was dressed I got her some ibuprofen and called the OB. They told me to bring her in tomorrow.

"Tomorrow...she's still bleeding. You need to get her in today, now."

"Mr. Wallace, take her to the emergency room. We can't fit her in today."

"She's scheduled to see someone from your office on Tuesday anyway. You have Saturday hours—can you please fit her in?"

"I'm sorry, but there's no way we can see her today. Please take her to the emergency room right away. The doctor will see her on Tuesday."

I hung up. *There's no way I'm taking her to the frigging emergency room. If I do we'll probably be in the waiting room till Tuesday anyway.*

I called the family practice and was placed on hold. After ten minutes the receptionist said they could fit her in around four o'clock.

"Don't you have anything earlier?"

"Mr. Wallace, just keep an eye on her. Call us if the bleeding gets worse, and bring her in at four."

I thanked her and hung up. Then I called CJ to tell him I wouldn't be in that day. He knew there was something wrong, and he asked what it was. I think he could hear Michelle crying.

"I'll fill you in later, Ceej. Michelle's sick."

"Is there anything I can do?"

"No, but thank you. I'll call you tonight." I hung up the phone.

The bleeding was slowing down. Michelle soon stopped crying and fell asleep for a while.

"How are you feeling?" I asked when she woke up.

"Like this is a bad dream."

Her eyes were full of pain. I squatted down next to the bed and put my hand on her face. "Honey, I'm so sorry. Cry if you want to."

Both of us cried on and off all day.

* * *

Around three-thirty I got her into my truck and drove her to the doctor. They knew as soon as they saw us that she was in no condition to sit in the waiting room, and a nurse took us right back. After a few minutes Dr. DeLuca came in and examined her. He said she would be okay, and that as long as the bleeding stayed steady it was almost like a really late period.

The doctor mentioned that he'd spoken to Michelle on the phone on January fourth about decreasing her antidepressant dosage and gradually stopping them.

"She's off them," I replied. She had taken the last dose a week earlier.

"Okay. She should start on them again right away." He told me he was prescribing a different type this time along with pain meds. He sent the order to the drugstore and said to get her started on them that night.

Michelle was listening and nodding her head, but she didn't speak. I did the talking the whole time. The doctor said to come back in a month, and to call if the bleeding became heavy again or if I noticed her acting depressed. He also said to come in immediately if she began running a fever.

Back at home I fixed her some chicken noodle soup and toast, thanking God that she didn't push it away. She ate half of it. When she was finished she went back to bed, and I went out to the kitchen to call Brad. I asked him about the new prescription.

"That's a common one," he replied. "Have you gotten it?"

"DeLuca sent it to the drugstore, but I don't want to leave Michelle."

"Get them to bring it over."

"They don't deliver anymore."

"She needs to start taking it tonight."

"I'll call Ceej. He already knows something's going on anyway. He'll pick it up."

"Okay. Is she having a D&C?"

"DeLuca didn't mention anything about that. He said to come back in a month."

"Why didn't he order one, do you think?"

"You know why." *The HCA doesn't think its necessary anymore, the bastards.*

"Those fucking sharks," Brad said. Then the subject was dropped. We both knew why Michelle wouldn't be having such a costly procedure.

"Wallace, I'm sorry. Poor Michelle... And you, too."

"I can't believe it happened again. I thought for sure our kids would grow up together like we did."

"I was thinking the same."

"All right... I better get back to Michelle now." I wanted to get off the phone. My throat hurt from holding back tears.

"Do you want me to call the old man?"

"No, don't. They'll just get upset, and Michelle's already asleep. We weren't planning to go over for dinner tomorrow anyway. If Michelle doesn't call your mom tomorrow I'll call on Monday.

"All right. Get some sleep Wallace. I'll check in tomorrow night." Brad hung up.

I called CJ and told him what had happened. He drove over and picked up the ID card, went to the drugstore and got the prescription, and brought it back. Before he left he told me not to worry about coming in until things were under control.

"Thanks, Ceej. I'll update you Monday."

I shut the door behind him and locked it. Then I went back to the bedroom, and we started putting our lives back together.

* * *

Michelle didn't call her mom on Sunday, and I was still too upset to do it. But on Monday morning I knew I had to break the news to the family. I called Michelle's supervisor first and explained what had happened. By law they were required to give her six weeks with full pay, and the supervisor—Janet was her name—said the job would be there at the end of that time.

"I don't know if she'll need six weeks," I replied. I was still worried about depression, and hoping she could go back earlier to get in a routine. Janet said to have Michelle call her when she felt up to it, and I thanked her and hung up. Then I hit the old man's number on speed dial.

My mother-in-law said he was giving himself his shot, and to hold on. A few minutes later he came to the phone. He must have seen the number on the caller ID. He knew I was usually at work by that time, and he asked right away if something was wrong.

"It's Michelle," I said. "Is Mom in the room now?"

"No, she's making the bed."

"Dad..." My voice broke. Telling him was harder than telling Brad had been. "Michelle..." I trailed off, crying.

"Jason," he said sharply. 'What's the matter boy? Is she okay?"

"She had another miscarriage." I could hardly get the words out. "Saturday morning."

"Oh, no. I'm sorry son. Is Michelle all right?"

"She's okay." I took a deep breath and went on to tell him what the doctor had said.

"Are you okay?" He could tell I wasn't. "What do you need? Do you want us to come?"

"No, don't come now. Michelle's asleep. I'm staying with her today."

"Can I call anyone for you?"

"Brad already knows. I called him the other night to ask about a new prescription. I'll call my mother myself. Later." The thought of it made me shudder. "Just let Johnny know."

"I'll call over there now. You go get some rest, you sound terrible."

"Yeah, okay. But I need to go back to work, probably Thursday. Can you come stay with her?" He told me of course, whatever we wanted, and asked was I sure I didn't want Michelle's mother to come now?

"Dad, she's sleeping. I'll just go stay with her for a while. She wants me."

"Well, we'll be over tomorrow then. I'll call you later for an update."

Michelle

Melanie visited this morning. Patty made us go upstairs for the examination. It was only seven-thirty, Mark had already gone to work, and she said the air and the light were better up there. I argued but Patty insisted, so I lay on my back looking around at Patty's pretty bedroom while Melanie checked me.

My blood sugar is normal now. *Thank you, dear Jesus.* Melanie says the baby has descended and I'm partially effaced. She won't examine me vaginally again because it might bring on labor, but she'll continue to monitor my blood pressure and blood sugar. Your heartbeat is strong, little angel.

I'm a little worried about the weight I've gained, in more places than one. My breasts are much bigger now. I wonder what Jason will think when we finally see each other again. I haven't seen him since the night we said goodbye in the deserted parking lot of Holiday's, and I know now that I won't until you come into the world.

He says nothing will keep him from being here when you enter this world, and I trust that this is God's plan for us. I believe I'm finally going to be a mother, and that Jason will be able to be your father. I feel more certain of this every day. I thank Our Lord for this blessing, and for His protection of us.

Jason
5 Years Earlier

Michelle never got depressed the way she did with the loss of our second child. This time I was on top of it, and after the first few days, so was she. I stayed home until Thursday, when I went back to work at the garage. After that one or the other of her parents stayed with her while I was working. She said she was sleeping all right, and after the medication kicked in her appetite returned. Things never got as bad as they did before, and by the time I took her to the doctor for the follow up she was pretty much back to normal.

She had gone back to work right before the doctor's appointment. He instructed her to stay on the meds, to eat healthy, and to get back to running. He always stressed fresh air and exercise to help with anxiety. So when Michelle began going out for short runs, I went with her. I was in reasonably good shape. In addition to lifting weights with the guys down at the garage, there was an old elliptical trainer in the shed. My mother had upgraded hers a couple of years earlier, and her old one was fine for me. I used it regularly, along with Brad's old punching bag hanging in the corner.

The old man had bought the punching bag the week after he caught us drinking, back in eighth grade. Brad and I were both grounded, but when our punishments were over the old man hung the bag in his garage, saying to use it to get out our frustrations or if we were bored. He told us to do something constructive instead of acting like a couple of idiots, drinking his scotch. Brad didn't want the thing; he belonged to a gym in Memphis, and when Michelle and I moved into the house, the old man told me to take it if I wanted it.

Like I said, I was in okay shape, so I decided to try running. That way Michelle wouldn't be alone when she ran. Running helped both of us. We usually ran in the streets of our neighborhood or the park on the outskirts of town. Once in a while we'd drive across town to the track at Kennedy High School and run there. Jamie would be attending Kennedy next year.

The old man told me that Junior would be finishing high school at St. Bonaventure. I was on the verge of asking how Johnny was going to pay for it. I had a notion the old man might be paying next year's tuition, but I kept my mouth shut about it. He would probably have told me it was none of my business, and he would have been right.

The episode back in January continued to bother me. I'd seen Junior twice since, and he'd done nothing to make me change my current opinion of him. He was still acting like a selfish, spoiled little creep. I wondered where Johnny would find fifteen thousand dollars for his tuition, since Cindy had been unable to find another job. *Shame, that. Hope she gets something, but I doubt it.* Poor Cindy. She hadn't been the same since she lost her job. Finding another one wasn't easy, though. As a matter of fact, it was nearly impossible.

But bad as I felt about Cindy's unemployment, it wasn't my problem. *We have enough of our own.* And Jamie didn't seem to be following in his brother's footsteps, thank God. The old man reported that he hadn't made any waves about Kennedy. There was nothing wrong with the school anyway. Reese and Lucio had both gone there. Jamie would be okay.

I thought about these things and others while running with Michelle. It was a good thing—something we could do together, though we didn't talk during the runs. I always listened to music, and

Michelle prayed the Rosary. We got in the habit of going every Tuesday and Thursday morning, just as it was getting light. Michelle liked running in the early morning light of spring. The sight of the rising sun shining on the snowdrops and crocuses made her feel better about the future. We ran on Saturdays too, until the grass started to need cutting again. After that, Michelle ran on Saturdays without me.

One Saturday afternoon in late in April I went to see Father Gallucio. I only worked six hours on Saturdays, from ten till four, so I walked across town to St. Catherine's when I left the garage to talk to him during his scheduled time for hearing confessions.

When I entered the church I saw my mother-in-law kneeling next to the tabernacle, praying, and I hurried to the sacristy before she noticed me. The door was ajar, and I knew Father was alone inside waiting for the next person who wanted reconciliation. He was silent while I told him about Michelle's loss of our child. I was almost in tears as I told him the latest development—that Brad had called the previous evening with the news that Nicole was expecting twins.

"Father." I looked down at my hands. "How am I supposed to tell Michelle about this?"

He was sitting in a chair across from me. "I think you need to pray about it before you do it."

"I don't know what to say to her."

"Jason, you have to pray. It's something Our Lord can help you figure out.

I stood up and went to the window. The shade was closed of course, but I could see outside by moving it a little. Daffodils bloomed behind the church, surrounding a weeping cherry tree. The blossoms blew gently in the breeze.

"Father, my wife lost our third child two months ago. She suffers about this every day. Now I have to go home and tell her that her brother's wife is having twins. I don't know what to say to her. Please tell me what to say." I turned to look at him as he got up from his chair and picked up a Bible. He leafed through it, found what he was looking for, and held it out to me, pointing to a verse.

"Read this. Verses one through three."

I took it and read silently: *As he passed by he saw a man blind from birth. His disciples asked him, "Rabbi, who sinned, this man or his parents, that he was born blind?" Jesus answered, "Neither he nor his parents sinned; it is so that the works of God might be made visible through him."*

"Father, I need to know what to do. This is not helping me."

"What do you think that passage means?"

"I don't know." I stood next to the window, holding the Bible. "What's that got to do with my problem tonight?"

"Jason, I want you to do something before you go home today."

"Father, please tell me what to say to her. Just give me the words I should use. I'm at the end of my rope with this thing."

"Jason, I could tell you what words to parrot, but Michelle would know they weren't yours. Now listen to me. You're going to make your confession, and I'm going to give you absolution. Then I want you to drive over to St Michael's chapel. Go inside and pray in front of the exposed Blessed Sacrament."

"Father Gallucio." I shook my head as I handed him the Bible. "What are you talking about?"

"Didn't you kids learn anything when I was teaching you?" He'd been our grade school religion teacher at St. Catherine's, before high school at St. Bonaventure. "Michelle knows about praying in adoration. I've seen her do it here when we sometimes have exposition. "

"Well, I've never seen her do it," I said shortly. "Her devotion is the Rosary."

"All right Jason. Stop arguing. If you attended Mass regularly you would have seen your wife praying. Do you have a devotion?"

He knew I didn't. He'd been absolving me for years while continuing to stress the fact that it was a mortal sin to miss Mass, unless you had a really good reason.

"I'll just pray here." I gestured out to the church.

"No," he replied, looking at his watch. "Mass starts in fifteen minutes. People are already out there. I want you to have quiet. I have to go get ready, now get over here on the kneeler and confess your sins. Don't give me any more lip."

I went around the divider he had in there for people who didn't want to talk face-to-face and knelt down. I confessed my sins and followed with the Act of Contrition. Father Gallucio gave me absolution then. I felt better immediately, just like always. He gave me back the Bible, an old paperback with the cover falling off. "Take this with you." He folded down the page corner he'd shown me. "Read it again before you go in. Now get going. Pray in front of the monstrance, and ask Our Lord what to say."

He followed me out of the confessional, and there was the old man waiting outside the door, looking annoyed.

"Father, can you hear my confession?" he asked.

"Jack, I'll hear it after Mass; Jason and I ran over." Father Gallucio hurried away.

"I'm sorry. You know about the twins, don't you?"

He nodded. "Do you want us there when you tell her?"

"I don't want to tell her at all."

The old man made no reply to that. Michelle had to be told, and it was my responsibility to tell her.

"I'm gonna tell her tonight," I went on. "Father's making me go to St. Michael's chapel to pray about it. I don't see why." My tone was stubborn.

"You don't need to see why," the old man said. His tone was stern. "Just do what he says."

"I dread telling her this worse than anything I've ever had to do."

"Where is she?"

"Picked up an extra shift at the store—someone needed off."

The church was filling up. I wanted to get out before Mass

started, so I told the old man I'd better go. He put his hand on my shoulder. "Call if you need us," he said.

I walked the four blocks back to the garage, got in the truck and drove out Route 24 toward the state line. Music played as I drove for fifteen minutes or so before turning down the back road to St. Michael's church.

My eyes started to sting when *The River* began playing. I pulled into the parking lot with the wheels squealing, ejecting the CD and stopping the truck with a lurch, but not before I heard the words about memories and how they could sometimes become curses that haunted.

The old man had told me to do what Father Gallucio said, so I picked up the Bible and read the passage again. *Born blind... At least he was born.*

I sat for a moment to collect myself before getting out of the truck and going into the chapel. The sound of water came to me as I opened the door. I went quietly through the vestibule and into the chapel proper, and saw that the sound was issuing from a small fountain of holy water streaming down into a little pool set against the wall. I stood frozen, feeling a sense of shock. *What's going on? Have I been here before?*

I went to the fountain and dipped my fingers, making the Sign of the Cross. Then I looked around. St. Michael's parish had built a new modern church about fifteen years earlier. I had been inside the newer church; Bella and Lucio were married in it. It was located about a quarter of a mile away, down a little road to the right. But I'd never been here inside the chapel. It was a little place.

Up in front on the altar stood the monstrance. It was golden, looking like a sort of starburst resting on white linen. An old lady knelt in the front row, head bowed. She was the only other person in the place.

On either side of the altar stood statues of the Blessed Mother and St. Joseph, along with a statue of St. Michael the Archangel standing in an alcove off to the left. Beautiful old stained glass windows depicting saints lined the walls. The sun shone through St. Patrick, St. Mark, St. Joan of Arc, St. Elizabeth, and many others. High up behind the altar was an old-style round window, the center of which resembled flames. Other colors fanned out around the center, melding one into the other—all the colors of the rainbow.

The flowing of the fountain was loud in my ears as I started up the aisle, feeling a sense of déjà vu...like I'd been there before, even though I knew I had never set foot in that chapel. I genuflected and knelt in the front row across from the old lady, feeling unnerved.

But for the water the chapel was silent as I put my eyes on the Host in the center of the monstrance. *Why do I feel like I've been here before?* The Bible verses ran through my mind. *At least he was born...*

I bowed my head, blinking back tears. I glanced over at the lady, but she was paying me no mind at all. She was still and silent.

Silence and flowing water... I came to the realization that a powerful Presence was with me. *Have I been here before?* I knew I had felt it before, on and off at different times. *What should I think?*

It was similar to what happened to me in the old man's garage, yet different. *What's going on?* I didn't know what to do next, so I continued to bow my head and listen to the water. *What do you think that passage means?*

Did I just ask that question?

I shook my head, glancing over to see that the old lady was getting up. Someone else had come in—a guy about ten years older than me. The lady in black genuflected and made her way down the aisle, and he sat down further back. *Born blind... At least he was born... Neither he nor his parents sinned.*

Why must my children die? Why must my wife suffer?

I raised my head. I looked up at Him, there in the monstrance. *What am I supposed to think?*

Understand that I never heard any words. Never. That's not the way He operated when I was watching. I just felt things in my heart as I stared at Him. *Suffering. Born blind... But at least he was born.*

I bowed my head again. I waited and watched, asking the same questions over and over and over again. *Why? Why us? What are You telling me?* The water flowed on and on, and by the time I was ready to get up off my knees I felt as if I had an answer. *Neither he nor his parents sinned. But he was born.*

The answer, it seemed, was that Michelle and I had three children living in paradise with God, instead of on earth with us. It wasn't because of anything we'd done...it just *was.* That's what I took to be His answer. I didn't understand why and I probably wouldn't, at least not for a while. Maybe not until I passed from this world. The answer was hard to accept, but I resolved to try. I looked up at the crucifix where hung Our Lord, knowing I'd be able to find more answers there where everything that meant anything intersected.

I was crying again as I bowed my head and listened to the soothing water. Tears dripped down on my folded hands. When finally I raised my head, the sun was streaming through the giant round window above the crucifix. It blazed through the center, casting the colors of flames across the church, covering me.

SIXTEEN

Michelle

Dear Holy Mother. What was it like during the last weeks of your pregnancy? I see you waiting quietly in my mind's eye. Maybe visiting your parents' home during the day and then going back to Joseph's house to sleep safely at night.

How did you feel when you found yourself on the back of a donkey, heading toward Bethlehem? How did your heart ponder this latest development; that you were forced to travel so far on the eve of your Child's birth just because the man who considered himself the ruler of the world decided he needed more tax revenue?

Jason
5 Years Earlier

I pulled into the parking lot behind the grocery store around six forty-five. Michelle's shift ended at seven, so I decided to wait for her there.

I recalled my visit to St. Michael's while I waited, still in a bit of a daze. *What just happened in that chapel?*

Something had. I just wasn't sure what it was. I sat mulling it over until Michelle came out of the store and began walking toward her Civic. Then I got out of the truck. She seemed surprised to see me.

"What are you doing here?" She smiled.

"Just felt like taking a ride. Come with me." I grabbed her hand and pulled her back to the truck.

I said nothing as we passed our neighborhood near the town boundary. It was beginning to get dark. *Darkness... On the edge of town...* I shook my head. *Why am I thinking of Dad? What's wrong with me?*

"Where are we going?" Michelle asked.

"Let's go to the park for a minute. I want to talk to you."

I pulled into the parking lot, parked the truck, and shut off the engine. The place was deserted. Though the sky was beginning to cloud up, a little light still shone in the western sky, pinkish and glowing eerily through dark silhouettes of trees. It was completely quiet except for the chirping of one lone bird.

"Are we getting out?" asked Michelle. "It's almost dark."

"No, honey." I swallowed.

"Jason, what's going on?" Her eyes were wary. I could just make out her face in the dim light.

"Michelle... honey..." I trailed off. *I don't want to break your heart, but I have no choice.*

"Is it Daddy?" she whispered, grabbing my hand. His blood sugar was out of control again and his foot was getting worse; he had an appointment scheduled with the endocrinologist in June.

"Nicole is..." I took her hand.

"Is she okay? Is it the baby? What's wrong, tell me!" Her eyes widened.

"Nicole is having twins," I said, my voice breaking. "Brad called last night. I wanted to tell you before the family finds out."

Her face crumpled. Tears overflowed and ran down her cheeks.

"Baby, I'm sorry. But don't get upset—it'll be okay." I reached for her, meaning to put my arms around her, but she jerked away. "Michelle honey, please—"

She opened the door and got out before bending over and throwing up. I jumped out, ran around the truck and grabbed her around the middle. She whipped her head back and forth, crying that it would never be okay.

"Why? Why did God take our child and give Brad two?"

I put my arms around her, my own heart breaking as I felt what she felt. *Why did I bring her here?*

At least nobody else was around. No one but me witnessed Michelle's grief as she sat down on the curb and lost it. I sat with my arms around her, rocking her as she cried. *This was a mistake. I should have taken her home.*

But that would have been another bad memory in our house. We stayed for a time. When it got cold I took off my work jacket and put it around her. Tree frogs sounded in the distance as the sun sank behind the trees to the west. Then it was full dark. *It's on the edge... The edge of town.*

"Michelle," I whispered, taking her hand and standing. "Come on, we're going home."

I helped her into the truck. As I turned to go around to the driver's side she gagged, pointing to the splattered vomit she'd left on the pavement. I got a bottle of water from behind the seat and poured it over the mess.

"Don't worry about it baby. It's supposed to rain tonight."

Michelle was still crying quietly as I followed her down the hall to our room. She picked up her rosary from the nightstand and lay back against the pillows. After asking if she'd be all right for a little while, I changed into sweats and my running shoes, got the keys from her purse, and ran downtown to pick up her car. It was only two miles away. I was back in twenty-five minutes, right before the rain began. I took a quick shower and got into bed with her.

Raindrops hit the roof and the windows, starting out slow before becoming a torrent. The streetlight shone into our room, moving with the raindrops running down the glass. It flickered over the bottom of our bed as Michelle spoke about our babies. *I knew she'd take it hard.* I listened to her hopes and fears for a while before answering.

"Honey, you're still young." My voice was calm. "We have plenty of time. We'll have our children; I believe it, and you should too."

We lay together quietly, her head resting in its usual place on my chest. When she began rubbing her hand back and forth over my upper arm, I sensed that the question was coming. *But I know what to say to her now.*

"Jason," she whispered. "Why did God take our babies?"

I stared up backwards to where the crucifix hung above the bed. The light from the window didn't reach that far, and it was in shadow. But even though I couldn't see it in the dark, I knew it was there.

"Michelle, He didn't take them," I answered fiercely, kissing the top of her head. "He gave them to us for a little while. We wouldn't have had them with us at all if not for Him. That's what I believe."

"Do you think He'll give us another baby someday?"

"I have faith that He will. But it'll be on His timetable, not ours."

Michelle

Melanie visited again this morning. After she finished taking my vital signs and listening to the baby's heartbeat, Patty made breakfast for us. I sat near the basement door while we ate our scrambled eggs and toast. Mark allows me to stay upstairs now as long as we keep an eye out for any strangers, but no one ever comes. The only visitors to the place since I arrived have been Melanie and Brian.

The three of us sat around the table after breakfast, fanning ourselves and waiting for the fan to blow our way. Patty never complains about the heat, or about the fact that with the flick of a switch we could be sitting in air-conditioned coolness instead of humid wetness if not for the new way of doing business. The family spent a fortune having central air conditioning installed in this old house. But the law now prohibits air conditioners, so we suffer the heat, even Patty. She's such a good sport about her hardships that I find myself forgetting she's almost ninety.

As usual the talk soon turned to the baby. Patty ordered Melanie downstairs to look at the growing stash of supplies in the closet of the laundry room. We smiled at each other as we listened to Melanie's voice floating up the stairwell, exclaiming over the things your daddy picked out for you, angel.

He's sent all kinds of newborn clothes and blankets, along with packages of newborn diapers, a pink brush and comb set, bath supplies, and set of little hair bows in pastel colors. A car seat and stroller wait in the laundry room. A bright gingham elephant and a teddy bear dressed in pink sit in the stroller.

The toys and almost all of the clothes are pink and frilly and delicate. The last things to arrive were a little white dress with matching bonnet embroidered with tiny rosebuds and trimmed with white eyelet ruffles. There's also a tiny pink bib, embroidered with a single rosebud and the words: Daddy's Girl.

Patty and Melanie asked how we can be so sure you are a girl, angel, but I can't tell them because I don't understand it myself. However Jason says you're a girl, and I agree with him. In fact I'm sure you're a girl, so the pink clothes seem perfect to me. The bags they arrive in tell me they were purchased in a store almost two hours away from our house. Jason won't take any chances. He drives all that way to make sure no one from town sees him buying supplies.

As we were discussing your impending arrival, I mentioned feeling like I belong in a one hundred year-old-house. That led us to ponder what childbirth must have been like long ago, and how much medicine has changed over the course of the last hundred years.

Thank you, dear God, for Melanie. She was a labor-and-delivery nurse before the bureaucracy took over, and she knows what she's doing.

Patty told us a story then, about primitive conditions and old-fashioned medical care. She'd heard it from her mother, Adela, who'd heard it from her mother, whose name had been Orie. It was a story of the mountain. The events occurred way before Patty's birth, probably during the time of Orie's childhood.

Back then a Doc Blevins took care of the mountain community, and the story had to do with an old woman who'd ridden horseback for miles to visit the doctor. Apparently it had taken her some hours to make the trip, and when she finally entered the doctor's office he wasn't very happy with her. Patty laughed a little and said that the first question Doc Blevins asked the woman was if she'd taken a bath before coming to the office.

"And this is what she answered. She looked at Doc Blevins and proceeded to tell him that she'd started at the top and washed down as far as possible, and then began at the bottom and washed up as far as possible." Melanie and I wrinkled our noses, and I thanked God for soap and running water before Patty gave us the punch line. "So Doc Blevins told that old mountain woman to go home and wash possible, and then come back."

Melanie and I laughed until we cried. Patty went on telling more stories, and the two of us listened, fascinated. She told us about Adela's elopement.

Though it was actually Clydie's story, Patty knew it by heart. Clydie was much younger than Adela, but older than Patty.

"How old is your aunt, Patty?" I asked.

"She turned a hundred years old in May."

A hundred... Daddy, why did you have to die?

"Are you all right, Michelle?"

"Yes, I'm fine." I smiled brightly. "Go on with your story please. I love hearing you."

"All right," she replied. "Clydie was up on the mountain picking blackberries with some neighborhood children the day it happened. Clydie and her friend Vance walked up from the road and found my grandmother, Orie, sitting on the porch steps crying into her apron. When Clydie asked what was wrong, Granny Orie cried that Adela had left her a note saying she'd run away over the mountain to the town twelve miles away to be married.

"Clydie tried to comfort Granny then, and Vance—he was crushed. Even though he was only seven years old, he adored my mother. Everyone in the neighborhood loved her. Vance ran off up the road home then, hauling his berry bucket and bawling. We later heard that he pitched a fit at his momma upon arriving and being ordered to hoe turnips for an hour before supper. Vance cussed and cried as he chopped the weeds, yelling at his mother that turnips stunk.

"My mother was only seventeen when she ran off with my father," Patty went on. "My grandparents met my daddy before the elopement, but only once or twice. Clydie was devastated. She still talks about it to this day, though she was only five or six at the time. My parents moved in with my daddy's father for the first couple of years of their marriage.

When I asked how Adela's father had taken the news of her elopement, Patty replied that there wasn't much he could say against it, since he and Orie married when she was only fourteen, and that he himself had only been seventeen or eighteen.

After telling us a little more about her grandparents, Patty related other tales—those of moonshiners and farm work. Some stories were funny and others made me shiver, but no matter the subject, Patty held us spellbound.

The morning flew by. Then Sandy arrived home; she only worked till noon on Mondays. After lunch we lingered at the table, and when I returned from one of my many trips to the bathroom, Sandy recalled something she had heard from her granny. It was a cautionary tale about Adela's days in the mountain school. Sandy thought Adela was trying to get the point across to her and Liz that they should never, ever make fun of the way anyone looked or spoke.

"I think Granny was worried about Lori Ann," said Sandy. "Maybe she was afraid she'd be teased someday."

When Adela was little she attended a one room school about three miles away down the mountain. There was another little girl in school who suffered from a facial deformity of the lip and a speech impediment. According to Sandy, her grandmother referred to this deformity as a harelip when she told her granddaughters about an older girl at school who used to tease the girl with a harelip unmercifully. The events took place in the 1920s, about a hundred years ago. The little girl had to live with her deformity, since there weren't any doctors that could perform an operation to correct it the way they used to before the HCA took over healthcare.

Sandy told us her grandmother warned them to always be kind and never to tease, because of what happened later to the older girl who made fun of the girl with a harelip. Adela told Sandy and Liz that eventually the older girl grew up, married, and started having babies. And her first child was a girl born with a harelip.

I was shocked, and so was Melanie. "Really?" she whispered." Is that true?"

"Yes." Sandy nodded grimly. "I'd swear it on a stack of Bibles. Granny would never lie. She told us about it more than once, and Liz and I talked about it for years after she died. It gave us the creeps, but we believed it."

At the mention of Liz, everyone went quiet for a moment before resuming the conversation. Though I'd like to know more about Patty's other daughter, I never ask any questions. Patty rarely mentions Liz's name, and I try not to pry. However I did question Melanie once in private, and was told that Liz and the family are estranged due to ideological differences. According to Melanie, Liz—who lives in California—is a true believer in the new way of doing business, just like my mother-in-law. She cut off all contact with Patty and Sandy a few years ago. The bureaucracy seems to have left no family intact.

We went on talking, sipping Patty's iced tea while she told more stories, each funnier than the last. I suppose we got carried away, because suddenly I noticed a man looking through the back screen door at us.

Fear shot through my body. I jumped out of my chair and turned to run toward the basement before realizing it was only Mark. He peered through the screen at us with narrowed eyes. Then he came through the door and let us have it.

"What do the four of you think you're doing?" he snapped. "You're supposed to be keeping an eye out if Michelle's upstairs! I could hear you all the way around front. I walked back here without a by your leave. Anybody could have. What's the matter with you?"

"Mark, I'm sorry," I apologized. "I shouldn't have stayed up here this long."

"Michelle, you know what could happen," he replied. "There are HCA sympathizers living in the area. I've told you that. I have no reason to believe anyone suspects there's something going on back here, but you need to be careful. You're going to have your baby in less than two months, and your husband is counting on all of us to keep that hidden."

I flushed at the realization that I had been laughing and talking with friends, while Jason was back at what had once been our home, dealing with the mess we were in. I haven't seen your daddy since I arrived here, angel, and we haven't been able to talk as much as I'd like. When we do speak he tries to hide what's going on at home because he doesn't want me to worry. I'm aware of a few things though, not least of which is his estrangement from Brad. The two of them have been friends since they were babies. Jason considers Brad his brother the same way he considered Daddy his father, and now they're on the outs because of our situation. *Poor Jason... He's almost alone, with no one to talk to but me.*

"I'm sorry," I repeated. "I promise it won't happen again." The rest of them echoed me. Then Melanie rose from the table, saying she had to be going. She kissed everyone and then gave me a hug. "Michelle, don't worry, we'll be more careful from now on."

"You be careful while you're walking to the car," said Mark. "John Gillis shot another raccoon on his property last week. Watch out."

SEVENTEEN

Jason
4 Years Earlier

The Supreme Court decision came down in early June. They ruled 6-3 that civilian gun ownership was unconstitutional, the votes of two recent appointments being the deciding factor. The old man was surprised at the ruling of the female appointee. He thought she would have voted to uphold our right to self-defense, since she was presented to Americans as a strict constructionist. But even if she had it wouldn't have made any difference. A 5-4 ruling would have brought the same result.

According to the Court, Americans no longer had the right to possess firearms, a right free men had always enjoyed as long as we abided by all other laws. The old man had warned us this was coming. *And I knew he was right the whole time, even if I didn't want to believe it. Brad and Johnny knew it too.*

I ruminated over it for days on end, unable to get my mind around it. The second amendment was now null and void. I reflected on the arrogance of those who had pushed to strip us of a God-given right, understanding that they themselves would never abide by the new ruling. *They won't follow their own rule. They'll buy bodyguards to protect their families, and those bodyguards will be armed.* I'd read enough, seen enough, and heard enough by that time to have figured out the hypocrisy of the ruling class.

Two days later a law was passed, and hunting was banned across the board. Not that anyone in our family hunted—the old man and Brad played golf, and Johnny was a rabid fan of the Philadelphia Eagles. I was also fan of the Eagles, and the Phillies and Flyers as well, but my true passion was saltwater fishing. None of the four of us hunted, but that made no difference to me. Now no one could hunt.

These fucking sharks. Someday they'll pay for this.

We spent July Fourth at the old man's as usual, congregating in the garage after dinner. Brad and Nicole remained in Memphis that year, so it was just the old man and me and Johnny and the boys. The heat was extreme that night. But that was a blessing, since the women were in the house enjoying the air conditioning when the evening went all to hell.

The old man slouched back in his desk chair. Johnny and Junior sat down in a couple of ratty lawn chairs the old man kept folded against the wall, while Jamie joined me in my usual spot, leaning against the workbench. I found my thoughts returning to the Supreme Court decision, which I'd been trying unsuccessfully to get out of my thoughts for the past month.

As we listened to the revelry coming from another party down the street, the old man remarked that the story had disappeared from the mainstream news outlets. There was currently no mention of all the firearms that had been held legally up until a few weeks before. The new ban on hunting hadn't been mentioned either, and except for those of us who paid attention, the entire outrage appeared to have gone to the back of everyone's minds.

My twelve-gauge was safe in the closet next to my side of the bed, where I had created a hiding place between the side of the closet and the bathroom wall. I had it fixed so that the gun was hidden yet easily accessible, and it was loaded and waiting if ever I needed it.

I opened my third beer, lit another Lucky Strike, and smoked in silence, my mind drifting away from the conversation. I came back from my confusion about what had been a right for over two hundred and thirty years but now was not, when Junior mentioned the words: "service" and "after graduation."

What happened next was partly my fault for jumping to the wrong conclusion. Of course I assumed he'd be serving in the armed forces, even though I should have known better. I came out of my worries for a minute.

"Junior, that's great." I grinned at him. "Congratulations. The military can open all kinds of doors for you. You can see the world, too."

The silence was deafening. It should have clued me in to the fact that I had the wrong idea, but I didn't pick up on the true atmosphere until it was too late. "What branch?" I went on. "If it's the Air Force, I'll call Webby. He's a recruiter now. Maybe you can talk to him, get a few ideas about what you want to do."

I continued smiling at Junior for a minute before realizing something was wrong. Johnny's fists were clenched. The old man was perched on the edge of his chair, staring at his grandson. His face was red as a beet.

"What's going on?" I asked. Then all hell broke loose.

"Tell him, Junior," Johnny barked. He was completely hacked off. Junior stared down at the floor for a minute. Then he looked at me with defiance and said he was joining a new civilian service organization that had been dreamed up by the sharks. Apparently they'd come into St. Bonaventure in February looking for recruits. They were paying the following year's tuition in exchange for Junior's service for one year.

"Junior," I said, flushing, embarrassed that I hadn't caught on, "what the hell are you talking about? Those thugs don't do service." I dropped my cigarette and stepped on it.

"Jason, come on. They help people."

"How?" I retorted. "What exactly are you going to be doing? You tell me what that organization has ever done besides feed kids propaganda and turn them against their families."

My face was still red. I had no idea the sharks were actually entering the schools these days, though the propaganda had been infiltrating schools for at least the past fifteen years. It was built right into the curriculum and the texts, and not only in public schools.

"Johnny." I looked at him with incredulity. "They went into St. Bonaventure? A private school?"

"There's nothing to stop them anymore." Johnny's shoulders were slumped.

"Junior," I said, turning back toward him, "did you see that story on the news last week? The one where your organization was protesting at the aquarium?"

"No." He glared at me.

"Well, I did. And if that's what you're going to be doing, it isn't service. It's frigging intimidation."

Stories like that one were the reason I tended not to watch the news. The report had pissed me off royally. It showed footage of little kids crying after protesters yelled at them, simply because their families had enjoyed a day at the aquarium. The members of the "service" organization stood outside the entrance with signs depicting the suffering of sharks and whales. They shoved them right in the children's faces, chanting that they were cruel and inhuman for visiting such a place and declaring that all aquariums and zoos should be closed.

There was no doubt about which organization was doing the

protesting, either. They were all dressed alike, in khaki pants and black pullover shirts with "MCSF" emblazoned on the front. Not one of them looked to have taken a bath for at least six months.

"Don't do this, Junior. You're not that way. There has to be something else you can do."

"It's already done." He sat in the lawn chair and addressed me in a tone that suggested he considered me an idiot. "I said I'm not changing schools, and I'm not. I explained this to you back in January. This is the only way I can stay at St. Bonaventure, and I'm taking it."

"What the hell is the matter with you? Why don't you suck it up like your brother, be a man about it and go over to Kennedy? There's not a damn thing wrong with that school and you know it. You'll finish and go on to do what you want without this crap. That's the answer. It's not your mom's fault she lost her job. Why are you making it harder on her?"

"Nothing's the matter with me. It's done. I already signed the damn papers. I don't give a crap what you think. Do you think I'm an idiot? I wouldn't be caught dead in the military, especially not in the Air Force."

My jaw dropped. Jamie sucked in his breath. The old man opened his mouth to speak, but shut it again as Johnny got up from his chair and walked toward the door. He looked at me as he went by, and what I read on his face was this: *Don't bother. It's no use.* He was shaking his head as he left the garage.

I stood stiffly for a moment, imagining what would be happening to Junior if Brad were in the garage, before my thoughts returned to Webby and his service for over twenty years. The sacrifices he'd made, up to and including missing the birth of his first child because he was deployed to Afghanistan three months before the baby was due.

"Junior." I made my voice calm, but it took exceptional effort. "I ought to knock the living shit out of you." He gave me an arrogant stare then, and shrugged his shoulders at me.

That was the last straw. I finally lost it, for real. I was across the floor the next thing I knew and hauling him up out of his chair. I kicked it away absently and it flew back and folded in on itself before hitting the wall. Darts fell out of the board and bounced off the floor as I shoved Junior against the old man's refrigerator so hard that beer bottles shifted and clanged together inside. We could hear them in the silence as I got up in Junior's face. He looked back with contempt.

"You spoiled little punk," I said. "If it wasn't for your Aunt Michelle I'd beat you right into the cement, so you might want to thank her later. Anyway you're not fit to enlist. You're not fit to serve, especially in the Air Force. You're not fit to clean Webby's boots, you selfish little bastard."

I gave him another shove and walked out the door.

I came back ten minutes later, after walking around the block to get my temper under control. I could hear the yelling from the street. I ran up the driveway and went back inside.

Jamie was gone. The old man sat in his chair, drinking a double scotch-rocks, and Johnny and Junior stood nose to nose, screaming in each other's faces. I had a feeling this wasn't the first time. Neither of them noticed me.

I was surprised Junior had dared to defy his father. Johnny was no one to mess with. He was shorter than Junior, but he outweighed him by at least forty pounds. He also had a hot temper, and though Junior was yelling heatedly, Johnny was the one waving his arms as he yelled back at him.

"Junior," I hollered as loud as I could, "listen to me!" They stopped yelling and looked my way. "I shouldn't have lost my temper with you. I'm sorry." My hand rested on the old man's shoulder. I did it for him. He was already sick, and he didn't need me adding to his illness.

"Get a drink, boys," the old man said, draining his glass. I got two shot glasses and picked up the bottle on the workbench. "Do you want one?" I gestured to Johnny with the scotch. He nodded. I poured us each a shot and tipped the bottle into the old man's glass. The whiskey burned as I drank it down.

I offered Johnny and the old man a cigarette, completely ignoring Junior since he hadn't answered my apology. The three of us lit up and smoked in silence for a time, while Junior stood looking at the floor. Finally he muttered an apology, which seemed to be directed at all three of us. Then he walked out of the garage.

We had nothing to say as we finished our smokes, but afterward I squatted down next to the old man's chair and looked up at him. "Dad, I really am sorry. I didn't handle that well; he's a kid." I glanced at Johnny, hoping he'd understand why I had gone off on his son.

"Don't apologize to me," Johnny said. "You didn't say anything different from what I've been telling him for the past six months."

"What the hell happened to that boy?" the old man growled. "He's out of control."

"He didn't need my permission," Johnny said. "You remember last winter when those new regulations went through? The ones pertaining to kids' healthcare?"

I shook my head. "I don't think I heard anything." I turned to the old man. "Did you mention it?"

"No," he replied. "It went through the Friday before Michelle got sick." He was referring to the miscarriage. "I didn't want to bother you with it."

"Well," Johnny continued, "there was some amendment attached to it that nobody knew about. It seems that any child over the age of fourteen now has the full rights of emancipation. I didn't find out until a couple of weeks before school ended, when I told Junior he wasn't joining the little pricks because I'd be damned if I'd sign the papers. He laughed right in my face and then told me about this emancipation bullshit."

I sat down in the lawn chair Johnny had been sitting in earlier, remembering the tantrum my mother had thrown when she found out I was enlisting. She had said the same thing to me. It was ironic.

"So Junior's emancipated now," Johnny continued. "Jamie too."

As I sat wondering how long I'd be able to stay out of jail, I became aware that my foot was stinging. I looked down and saw that my toes were bleeding. I was wearing sandals that night, and evidently I had kicked the other lawn chair hard enough to scrape off my skin. I was lucky it was only a lawn chair; if it were anything more substantial all my toes would be broken. *I should have kicked Junior instead of the damn chair.*

"He might be emancipated," the old man said after a minute, "but I'd be damned if I'd put up with his behavior if I were you."

"I don't have much choice, Dad," Johnny replied, shaking his head. "I don't know how they did it—it's like an oxymoron. The law also says he has the right to remain under my roof if he wants to. I looked into it. There was an example made; some kid in Cherry Hill. Did you hear about it?"

"No," said the old man shortly.

"Apparently this kid's father threw him out of his house. In addition to joining this cult, he was out of control, strung out on drugs. He reported his father to the authorities, and they arrested him. The father is sitting in jail as we speak."

Michelle

After my shower I went to bed, hoping I could sleep in the heat. I turned up the speed of the fan, sighed as the air flowed over me, and listened to the monotonous hum of crickets until I dozed off.

I was awakened by a sharp musky odor. *That's a skunk.* A minute later the backdoor opened, and Mark went out to check the property in hopes of locating the skunk so he could shoot it. On top of our other concerns, the fear of rabies hangs heavy over the farm.

He had already been forced to shoot a raccoon that was acting strangely. Afterward we had all waited nervously for the HCA to show up and ask why a gun had gone off. Lucky for us they never did.

The HCA sympathizers Mark mentioned earlier agree with the gun ban. One of them had called authorities to report gunshots in the neighborhood. This resulted in the questioning of John Gillis, the farmer Mark mentioned today. He said it was all the talk at the village store. The old timers who frequent the place abhor the HCA, and most people considered them the cause of the rabies epidemic to begin with.

The bureaucrats and their sympathizers insisted guns weren't needed this summer, since they'd allowed the deer to be cleaned out the previous fall. Mark said the deer had run wild the second spring after the hunting ban. They endangered the corn crop that year, and area farmers had been at their wits end with the bureaucrats.

The corn was essential; it fed the cows. Most farmers were already overburdened with paperwork, and those that didn't go under were forced to lay off workers and raise their prices. Others were fined nonstop for minor infractions, and the deer situation was the straw that broke the camel's back. It had nearly been the cause of rioting. The farmers insisted they hadn't created the mess, and that reimbursement should be made for the seed.

The price of milk was already sky high. Farmers were losing customers, and the industry was on the verge of collapse. So after spending some time pontificating about the situation, the HCA in Harrisburg decided to allow a controlled hunt. Even the ones who'd created the mess could see that something needed to be done. The hunt was a success, sort of.

Though the deer were thinned out enough to keep them from overrunning the crops, they couldn't be used for food. That was strictly prohibited under one of the many animal rights regulations. When hunters began dragging the deer away with plans to give the meat to the hungry, they were stopped and questioned by bureaucrats. The bureaucrats ordered them to leave the deer where they had dropped under penalty of arrest. That night crews of MCSF were trucked in, and the deer were collected, dragged to an open pit, and thrown into it. Guards were set to watch the pit, and none of the venison made it into a hungry child's stomach.

According to the HCA, none of that applies now anyway—it happened over a year ago. The crisis had been averted. Milk prices had fallen to fifteen dollars a gallon. The deer population was under control for the time being, so there was no reason whatsoever for gunshots in the neighborhood.

Luckily no one reported the fact that the shots had been fired from rifles, which were banned under any circumstances. Mark reasoned that anyone foolish enough to call the authorities probably wouldn't have known the difference between the sound of a rifle and a shotgun anyway.

Guns were scary. Guns had no place in a peaceful society. Guns were dangerous, and all they were good for was murdering people. Civilized Americans had no need for guns, and people had better obey the law if they didn't want to be thrown in jail. This was the lecture Mr. Gillis received from a bureaucrat who showed up at his door along with an MCSF soldier. Who, I know from experience, may or may not have been armed.

Mr. Gillis decided to show the bureaucrat and his MCSF guard what people in this area are forced to deal with now. He led them around to the back of his house where lay the carcass of a dead raccoon. He had shot it earlier, and it was plain to be seen that it had been sick with rabies.

He told them he hadn't buried it so he'd be able to show them the evidence, before asking if they were happy now. According to the store regulars, Mr. Gillis was wearing gloves. He picked the carcass up with a shovel while the bureaucrat stood gaping, and thrust it at him. The raccoon looked completely mad, with its wild eyes and foam covered mouth drawn back. The rifle had blown its stomach open.

The bureaucrat jumped back petrified, and the kid with the gun ran back to the car. Mr. Gillis told the HCA bureaucrat to tell any subsequent callers to mind their own business, because their children were just as much at risk of being bitten as anyone else's.

EIGHTEEN

Jason
4 Years Earlier

The twins were born on September first, two girls, both healthy. Brad and Nicole followed tradition by choosing names with family connections. The first twin was named Anna Marie, after Nicole's mother and my mother-in-law. The second little girl was called Taylor Michelle. Taylor was Nicole's maiden name, and they'd chosen her middle name for her aunt, my wife. Brad finally got around to calling me after he'd gotten them home. He asked right away if Michelle was around.

"No, I'm in the shed." I lit a cigarette. I had already heard him lighting up. I asked him if he was in the house.

"No, you idiot. Nicole would kill me if I smoked in there now. I'm outside."

"Why didn't you call before?" I asked, listening to the sound of crickets coming through the open windows. Moths darted around the light outside the screen door. The breeze blew through, but it was still hot, even at ten p.m.

"I couldn't call. I was afraid to leave them alone in there."

"What?" I was shocked. "Why, what happened?"

"It was seriously messed up." Brad said. I could hear him dragging on his cigarette.

"Why?"

He went on to explain that he thought things were going along okay until the day the babies were born. They both hated the fact that they no longer had a choice about hospitals or doctors, but Nicole had been receiving decent care. She was assigned to one of the big hospitals right in the middle of Memphis. It was absorbed by the HCA over a year earlier.

"That place was always considered cutting edge." Brad's voice shook. "I was sort of relieved when we were assigned there. But damn... You won't believe what happened."

He continued his story, telling me that Nicole had gone into labor at around noon on the first. Since there were two babies, he thought the doctor might perform a cesarean, but when he brought it up Nicole reported that she'd already mentioned it.

"This was back in June," he said. "Her doctor said it wasn't necessary under any circumstances. I was pissed off when she told me, but I'm glad about it now. If she had a cesarean they might have been in there longer. I was never so glad to get out of any place in my life as I was that hospital."

"What the hell happened in there?"

Brad said everything seemed normal at first. They put Nicole in a labor room, and a nurse was checking her vital signs.

"Nicole was in a lot of pain."

"What did they give her?"

"Not an epidural. The OB on call gave her a shot right in the vaginal area. Some kind of local anesthetic; he didn't answer me when I asked him about it."

"Her doctor wasn't there?"

"No. I never laid eyes on the guy who delivered them, and

neither had Nicole. They were born in the same room she started out in."

"They didn't move her to a delivery room? Even with twins?"

"No, Wallace." He was breathing heavily. "The doctor left the room after he gave her the shot, and we didn't see him again for six hours. He came back when they called him, right before Annie was born. And they didn't give her an episiotomy. In my opinion that was a mistake."

What the hell is that?

"I'm sorry, but I don't know what that is."

"She ripped," he said quietly. Then I figured it out.

"Oh my God." I was floored. I remembered reading about it then, in one of the books Michelle had scattered around the house. "Is she all right?"

"Some ER doctor came up to the room later, after it was all over. He stitched her up. She's okay." His voice wavered. It didn't sound like Brad. "Nicole was really brave but the pain...it was bad. It seemed unnecessary."

"Do they normally do that procedure?"

"No. I don't think so. But that's not what I meant. I told you I didn't know the doctor. He had never examined Nicole. She never met him before that night. How do I know he even knew what he was doing?

"The place was crowded, and the whole floor was in chaos. He was only with Nicole when he gave her the shot and at delivery. Maybe if her doctor had been there it wouldn't have happened. And how do I know she even needed stitches? I can't explain what I mean." He paused. "If she needed stitches, why didn't the OB stitch her up?"

"I don't know. You're right. It sounds like it was truly messed up." I waited a minute before I went on to ask him about the actual birth of the babies.

"Did you see it? The births?" I took a drag on my Lucky Strike, poured myself a shot of whiskey, and drank it down. My throat was beginning to hurt. I was glad Michelle wasn't hearing this.

"I saw them," he replied. "I stayed in there the whole time. I was afraid to leave, and Nicole wouldn't have let me if I wanted to."

"What was it like?" My voice shook.

"You and Michelle will find out soon enough. How is she, is she pregnant yet?"

"Brad, for crying out loud, don't worry about us—just tell me what happened."

"Okay. Annie was born first. Nicole was hooked up to a monitor. I stayed with her while she was pushing. She was in so much pain, she screamed. That must have been when it happened; the tearing, I mean. But they said everything was fine. They let me cut the cord. Then the nurse took the baby off to the side of the room and I thought they were cleaning her up.

I stayed quiet, understanding that something had gone terribly wrong. I lit another cigarette.

"After Annie was born there was a bit of a wait. I can't quite remember what happened then; everything's hazy. I think I went back up with Nicole for a minute. She was crying, and Annie was screaming. Then the doctor seemed to panic. He said something to the nurse—something about it being turned. I wanted to go over to the baby, but I was afraid of what was going on with Nicole, so I stayed there. They were telling her to bear down, and she was straining away, giving it everything she had. She cried. She said it hurt so bad."

He paused again. His voice was filled with pain. I blinked back tears, realizing I didn't want to hear what he was going to tell me next. I didn't know why—Nicole was okay and the girls were healthy, but something had happened in that hospital room. Brad was going to tell me, and I didn't want to hear it.

"Next thing I remember was getting up and walking around the end, behind the doctor. I could see everything then. She was a mess.

There was blood everywhere. Then all of a sudden the baby was crowning. Taylor was born. The nurse took her away. Nicole was crying, so I went back up with her at the end of the bed."

He stopped then. I could hear his lighter clicking as he lit another smoke. I dreaded hearing his next words.

"Is that everything? They're all okay now, right?"

"No. Nothing's okay. I looked over at the babies, and there was some guy taking blood samples from them. And not just a drop, either."

"Oh my God." I poured another shot, wanting to be drunk. Brad was dragging on his cigarette. I thought I heard him crying, and I could hear what he was thinking in my head.

My child... Those bastards. My child.

"What did you do?"

"The son of a bitch wasn't even wearing scrubs. It scared the living shit right out of me when I saw him. He had four test tubes, two for each of them. Both babies were screaming. The nurse tried to get me to take Annie, but I shoved past her to where he was sticking a needle in Taylor and asked him what the hell was he doing. But it was too late... He had four test tubes full of my little girls' blood. Taylor only weighed five pounds, and they took all that blood out of her. She was only two minutes old."

I was holding back tears.

"Then the creepy-assed bastard looked at me and told me to get back to my wife," Brad continued. He said to sit down and not to make any trouble or I'd be sorry." His voice broke. He almost started sobbing. I waited until I thought he was calm before speaking again.

"Does Nicole know?"

"She was out of it. She was calling me, calling for the babies. I don't think she caught it."

Then he went on to tell me that after the tech left with the blood samples and Nicole had been stitched up, they moved Nicole to a private room. The babies were brought in to be with them and every-thing seemed normal, which almost made it worse.

"I felt like I was crazy. I was thinking maybe I dreamed it but I know I didn't."

"Does the old man know?"

"No, and I'm not telling him. He'd probably have a stroke. No one knows but you. Nicole's parents came to the hospital. I didn't say anything, but I didn't leave the room either. They told me to go home for a while, but I couldn't leave. I took a shower today when we got home."

"Where'd you sleep?"

"In a chair."

I drank another shot of whiskey and lit another cigarette. "What the hell are we gonna do?" I said.

"Wallace, are you drunk?"

"I hope so." I poured another shot and knocked it back.

"What do you think they'll do with those blood samples?"

I sat down on one of the old kitchen chairs I kept in the shed, feeling sick. "The old man told us that time about them getting the DNA and keeping the information on file," I reminded him.

"What the hell do they plan on doing with it?"

My answer was to gulp another shot. Then Brad changed the subject. "I'm gonna have to hang up in a minute. The monitor's on and Nicole said she'd call me when she needed me, but what happened with Junior? The old man mentioned something the other day before the babies were born."

"What did he tell you?"

"He told me what happened in the garage," he answered. "I'm just wondering why Junior didn't end up in traction. How the hell did you let him get away with that?"

"Brad, I don't know; the old man looked upset. I didn't want it to make him any sicker."

"That little creep. He's lucky I wasn't there."

"I thought the same thing that night." I laughed a little. But we're gonna have to be careful. Did the old man tell you about that kid who had his father put in jail?"

"Yeah Wallace, I know all that," he replied impatiently. "I still wish I'd been there that night. The little punk would have had my foot so far up his ass it would have come out between his ears."

I laughed again. I could see it in my mind's eye, and as far as I was concerned Junior deserved an ass kicking.

"Johnny should have beaten the shit out of him. He has no business getting involved with the HCA anyway, the little prick. Why doesn't he go get a girlfriend like we used to instead of being a wimp about going across town to Kennedy?"

"We didn't exactly have girlfriends, did we?" I said, laughing. "I don't remember many actual girlfriends."

"Yeah, you're right." Brad began laughing too.

Then my conscience gave me a twinge. *I was a pig back then.*

"Brad... Do you ever think about the possibility that maybe we shouldn't have acted the way we did when we were Junior's age?"

"What? Where's this coming from? What are you talking about?"

"Just what I said. We acted like pigs."

"We did not. We were just sowing wild oats."

"I don't know about that. How are you going to feel in twenty years if some little prick starts sowing wild oats with one of your daughters?"

I smoked my Lucky Strike and listened to the silence.

"Are you there?"

"I'm here."

"Well, what do you think?"

"I think you're drunk. That's what I think."

"So you wouldn't have any problem if in fifteen years or so some little sex-crazed punk starts coming around?"

"You know neither of us ever went after anybody that age."

"That's not the point. The point is that we acted like a couple of little creeps ourselves back then, and you know it."

Then I heard some commotion in the background, and the faint cry of a baby.

"I gotta go," said Brad. She's getting ready to feed them. One of them is screaming her head off up there. Keep me updated on Junior."

"All right." I poured another shot of whiskey. "Brad, do you have any idea how blessed you are?"

"Yeah. I know it. I'm sorry, Wallace."

"Don't be. Michelle and I were talking earlier. We're both happy for you." The whiskey burned my throat as it went down.

"Thanks. Now I gotta go."

"I'll call you next week." I hung up and poured another shot.

*　*　*

"Jason, what happened last night?"

I felt a shove on my arm and opened my eyes. Sunlight glared through the window, making my head begin to pound. Michelle was getting dressed. She pulled her running skirt up and sat down to put on socks and shoes.

"What happened?" she repeated. "You were drunk." Her movements caused the bed to shake. My stomach churned. The clock next to the bed read seven-fifteen.

"What day is it?" I asked.

"You're not funny. What happened?"

For a minute I really didn't know what day it was. Then I remembered Brad's horror story about his newborn daughters' blood being sucked out of them by some kind of government vampire, right in the hospital room with his wife still on the table. It was Saturday morning and I had to be at work by ten. I dragged myself heavily out of bed and lurched into the bathroom. My head seemed to split in two as I answered Michelle through the open door.

"Brad and I were celebrating over the phone."

"Was Brad drunk too?" She sounded annoyed. "Nicole needs his help you know."

I swallowed three aspirin. "No. I celebrated for both of us."

She came into the bathroom and looked at my face in the mirror. My eyes were bloodshot, I needed a shave, and I looked like hell.

"I guess this means you're not running with me this morning, right?

"No, but I wish I could."

"You could if you hadn't gotten drunk."

"Michelle—"

"Okay," she said shortly. "I'll be back in an hour."

Despite feeling sick as a dog, I made it through the day at work. I'd foregone cutting the grass that morning. The thought of it made me want to throw up, and all day long I regretted getting drunk. It had been years since I had a hangover as bad as that one. I couldn't even walk the four blocks to St. Catherine's after work; I had to get in the truck and drive over to talk to Father Gallucio.

No one else was around when I went inside. The door was open, so I went into the reconciliation room and confessed everything. I told him Brad's story from the previous night and followed up with my sins of missing Mass and drunkenness. Father was shocked about the babies.

"They took blood samples? I never heard they were doing anything like that."

"They're doing it." I replied. "Maybe it's not widespread yet, but it's been in the works for years. What are we going to do?" He didn't have any answer to that, and what he told me was something I already knew.

"Jason, are you finished?"

"Yes. For these sins and any others I may have forgotten, I am sorry."

"Okay. Make your act of contrition now, and then for your penance go back to the chapel and tell Our Lord everything you just told me. Say a prayer of adoration, and then pour out your heart to God."

I said the prayer, and he gave me absolution.

"Thank you, Father."

Before getting out of the truck at St. Michael's I glanced down and saw Father Gallucio's Bible shoved down between my seat and the console. I picked it up automatically, thinking maybe I ought to do everything the same way as the last time. I looked down at the Bible and almost opened it. *But he didn't tell me to read. I better not.* I sat there for a good five minutes going back and forth about it, afraid to open the book.

When I finally went inside, everything was the same. I went to the fountain, dipped my hand, and crossed myself as I walked up the aisle. I genuflected in front of the monstrance, feeling that awesome sense of power that had been there a few months earlier. As I knelt down I saw the same old lady that had been there in April kneeling in the exact same place.

No way. She can't be here. I closed my eyes for a second, and when I opened them she was still there. *It's almost exactly the same.* Only the light was different. Darkness fell later in September, and I wouldn't see the flaming colors of the sun shining through the stained glass unless I stayed much longer than the first time.

I bowed my head for a time, trying to calm my mind. *Father said to say a prayer of adoration.* There were books in the pews. I opened one and found a prayer that seemed appropriate. Then I made the sign of the cross and read the prayer before looking up at the Host. I bent my head again, listening. The water was flowing. I poured out all that was in my heart and then asked the questions.

What are we going to do? Why did Brad and Nicole have to go through that?

I looked up again, at the crucifix under the stained glass window. He was nailed there, hanging. *Hanging...hanging...hanging...* I bowed my head again. *Why? Why is there such suffering? And such arrogance?*

A memory arose, of being out in the Atlantic in choppy seas. I let my mind go back over it. The wind was picking up, rain was starting to spit, and CJ was struggling to land a huge fish. The rest of us had the idea it must have been a tuna, or possibly a marlin. We were forty miles out. The charter boat captain turned around and headed back toward the marina.

CJ was struggling. I took the pole for a while to give him a rest. Then he took it back and finally reeled it up toward the surface, fighting and struggling fiercely. But it wasn't a tuna. It was a shark. It looked to be about seven or eight feet long, and its teeth thrashed insanely as it struggled to get away from the hook in its jaw.

None of us recognized the species. Danny and Reese argued about whether or not it was a great white, but things faded into the background for me. Rain blew into my face as I stared at the shark. Its cold, empty, hateful eyes gleamed just under the surface. Then CJ ordered me to cut the line, and it swam back down to wherever it had come from. *A shark. That's what was in the room when Brad's kids were born. It didn't belong there. Why did they have to go through that? A baby's birth should be happy.*

It should have been a calm time, a time of privacy, a time of bonding for them. But the shark had intruded, showing its teeth, threatening, intimidating, oppressing.

I looked up again. He was still hanging. *Always.* The Host on the altar was surrounded by gold, like a starburst. It was golden, beautiful, wondrous. In my mind I heard Brad's voice crying and babies screaming, louder and louder and louder.

Brad never cries. Not since we were kids. Not for twenty-five years.

I was crying in silence. I looked up again. He was hanging—alone, betrayed, in agony. Brad had tried to hide his crying from me, but I could feel his pain. I saw my own drunkenness and shook my head in sorrow.

I'm sorry. I shouldn't have gotten drunk. It won't help anything. But how did this happen?

Pride, arrogance, unbelief.

Whose? Mine?

He continued to hang there. I listened and prayed.

I finally got up and turned to go. The old lady was leaving as well, and the same guy who'd been there in April was sitting in the pew five rows back with his head bowed, praying. I shook my head, confused. *What's going on? How can these same people be back here?*

I held the door for the tiny wrinkled Italian lady in black, and we walked out of the chapel. She spoke to me in broken English. "You keepa watch?" She smiled up at me.

Keep watch? What's she talking about? I didn't answer, but I smiled back at her.

"You come back. Next week. We needa people." She patted my forearm and walked away toward a car that had pulled up to the curb.

I got in the truck, still not understanding what she meant. But I doubted I'd be back next week. As I prepared to turn the key in the ignition, I glanced down at the passenger seat. The Bible was lying there, open to the head of a chapter in one of the gospels. My eyes widened at the words in bold print staring up at me: *The Calming of the Storm at Sea.*

NINETEEN

Michelle

I woke up at five-thirty this morning and went upstairs to see if Mark might want to go to the cornfield. When I looked into the kitchen and said good morning, he got the rifle and we went out. The sun wasn't quite up. The day seemed dim, and the air was close and still. The grass was so heavily covered with dew that my feet were soaked in my thongs before we even reached the corn. It's beginning to dry.

I walked ahead, brooding about Father O'Neill, whom I haven't been able to find on the radio for the past two weeks. Somehow—I don't know how—I understand that I won't be hearing him again, and I wonder what happened to him. Thinking about it causes a feeling of dread.

Mark has promised to ask the priest two towns away to come out here sometime soon so I can make my confession and receive Holy Communion before you are born, little angel. Jason wanted the priest to visit me regularly but they decided against it. It might have raised suspicions in the neighborhood to see a priest coming in and out of this place, with the knowledge that Patty's family has belonged to the Methodist church in the village for the past seventy years.

I stared up through the corn blades at the sky. It was the color of pearls, growing slightly pink, cloudless. I could see only what was directly above me, along with a bit of pasture through the rows to my left, and I was drenched in sweat before we walked a quarter mile. The light grew stronger as I looked toward the east. I went to the edge of the field and saw the sun rising through the trees at the end of the pasture. Birds sang near and far. The sound grew louder and louder until suddenly crows began cawing back and forth to each other, drowning out the other birds.

I wanted to walk further, but it was already hot, and so humid that I felt I couldn't breathe. So I turned around, hugging my pregnant belly. I made my way back to Mark, and asked him if he minded cutting the walk short this morning. As we walked back I felt another contraction and increased pressure in the top of my legs. My heavy breasts leaked through my shirt, and I kept my back to Mark.

The sun grew brighter and brighter as we walked back through the rustling corn to the edge of the field. I stopped then and looked out carefully before venturing into the open. Butterflies fluttered and hovered over the sunny yard. As I stepped out of the corn, a bumblebee buzzed past my head on its way to do something important. I headed back toward the house and the continued waiting, without my husband. Tears threatened as I listened to the sound that has come to represent heat to me—the sound of a cicada. I went back inside and down the stairs again to pick up my rosary.

Jason
4 Years Earlier

In November we flew down to Memphis with Michelle's mom and Cindy for the twins' baptisms. The old man's foot flared up right before we left, so he stayed home. Michelle and I were Taylor's godparents, and we also stood for Brad and Nicole—their marriage was blessed in the Catholic Church that day. Nicole was considering converting to Catholicism. Her brother and Cindy were Annie's godparents. It was a day of mixed emotions.

I couldn't help thinking about our situation while I stood next to the baptismal font taking my turn holding the baby and seeing Michelle take hers. We were happy for Brad and Nicole of course, but it hurt to remember our own children. Michelle still hadn't become pregnant, though we had been trying for months. It made me sad to see her cradling Taylor, because I knew she was crying inside.

As the day progressed things got worse. After the christenings we went back to Brad's for a celebration, and the two of us went out to his garage for a cigarette.

Brad started out by asking if I had noticed anything different about Nicole.

"No." I exhaled smoke while glancing toward the door to the kitchen where the women were getting the food together. We could hear them bustling and crooning to the babies. "Do you think we should go out back?" I asked. "I don't need another lecture from Michelle about cigarettes."

"Nah, we're right next to the window. We'll go back in a minute. They won't come out here—they're too busy. Now Wallace, what do you think about Nicole?"

"She looks good. Is something wrong?"

"She's taking antidepressants now."

"She looks okay to me," I replied with a shrug. "She doesn't look like she's lost too much weight; not like Michelle did."

Brad laughed and shrugged back at me. "That's true—she did keep a little on after the babies. It's okay with me." I laughed too, but in my opinion, Nicole looked a lot better now than she had before she got pregnant. Nicole was a beautiful woman, but her body always reminded me of a bundle of twigs.

"How long has she been taking meds?"

"Six weeks," he replied. The girls were two months old. "She's not like Michelle was," Brad went on. "It's more of an anxiety thing."

"Isn't that supposed to be normal after a birth?"

"Yeah." He took a drag on his Lucky Strike. "But we have an added stress."

"What?" I asked, wondering what could be any more stressful than having two screaming babies in the house keeping you up all night.

"Look." He handed me a little ID bracelet. It was from the hospital.

"What's this?"

"Look at it, Wallace," Brad repeated. He seemed upset as I examined the plastic band. It was Taylor's hospital ID bracelet. The front read: Davis, Twin B, Girl, and then Nicole's name, the date, the hospital name and room number. I saw nothing unusual until I turned it over. Then the lights began glimmering on the edge of my perception as water rushed through my head.

I stared at the bracelet, my cigarette forgotten. *Those shark bastards... they're evil.* I could hardly believe what I was reading.

"Damn them," I said, dropping my smoke and stamping it out. "What the hell do they think they're doing now?" *Am I going insane? Is that it?*

But I wasn't, and neither was Brad. We weren't the crazy ones.

"Nicole read that," Brad whispered. His hands shook as he lit another smoke. "That one and Annie's."

It was a number. *A number. Taylor's a number. Number 17-079.*

The back of the bracelet read: *FEDHCA Official, Region 4 TN*, and the date. Next was: *File #17-079 Female* and the blood type. Following that: *Davis, Nicole Victoria Taylor, birthmother.* Then their address in Memphis, and underneath, in very small print, almost too small to read: *Davis, Antonio Bradford.*

I looked at Brad in shock. He stared at the floor; seemingly ashamed of something he couldn't help. According to the people in power, his children were on file as numbers. *Son of a bitch. Numbers... What's next, tattoos?* I clenched my fists. Brad finally raised his eyes to mine. They were full of anger. I lit another cigarette.

"Nicole read it when she took them off the girls that night after I called you," he said. Smoke curled and drifted as he went on to tell me she'd figured it out; she remembered the delivery room, and he finally had to tell her about the blood samples. "She was hysterical, Wallace. She cried for three hours, scared to death, asking me what was going to happen." He flushed, sounding shaky.

"What did you tell her?"

"I told her nothing was going to happen—it's just more official bullshit. Then she asked me who I thought I was kidding."

"Does anyone else know?

"Just you," he said quietly.

"Shouldn't Nicole talk to someone?"

"She's been talking to Father Ryan about it. She has to talk to someone."

"Shouldn't she see a professional?"

"Probably. But who the hell am I gonna trust to talk to her? One of those shark bastards?"

Brad was losing control—I could see it. "You have the freaking ID cards," he sputtered. "You know damn well they tell you exactly where you have to go. Would you trust one of them with your wife?"

"No," I replied. As I considered what I might do if I were in Brad's position, the image of the hive flashed through my head. *What a royal screw up this is...those bastards.* "Do you think anything'll happen?"

"I've heard things at work. That sometimes they send people out to your house if you miss a doctor's appointment." His eyes were wild. I could hear exactly what was going through his mind: *Do you*

have a gun? Because I do. I have a freaking gun. They're my babies...
Mine and Nicole's.

"Keep your head, Brad," I said automatically. "They need you.
Don't do anything stupid."

The atmosphere was charged. The two of us were furious, yet
there was nothing we could do to change things. And with the lights
in the corners of my eyes came the truth: we were helpless. Images of
the hive, crawling with wasps now, scrolled persistently through my
head along with the rushing feeling of water, flooding out of control.
Different water. Shark infested water, bearing down in a flood.

We're helpless. The wasps are stinging now. The sharks are
circling. Then the memory of CJ's struggle to reel in that shark ran
through my mind. *But now we're the ones with the hooks in our jaws.*

Brad looked at me red-faced, the cigarette hanging out of his
mouth as he clenched and unclenched his fists. *He's getting ready to*
blow his stack...just like the old man. I put my hand on his arm, and
he shook it off with an oath. He spat the butt on the cement and
ground it out under his black dress shoe. Then he grabbed the tie
around his neck and loosened it before letting go with a string of
expletives directed at the bureaucracy.

I stood quietly, waiting for him to quit his cussing. Finally he did.
He finished off by spitting on the floor again with a final oath and
stood there trembling. I had never seen him look that way. It was
intense. "Brad, calm down," I repeated. "Don't do anything stupid."

He glared back at me, still breathing heavily with that wild look
in his eyes. They were the same as Michelle's eyes, but I'd never seen
Michelle's eyes look the way Brad's did that day.

"I'm not doing anything here," he said finally, his tone implying
the opposite.

"What do you mean?" I said sharply. "You need to watch what
you're doing. You better make sure you keep them off your back. He
looked back at me with defiance, so I gestured to him with the baby's
bracelet. "You don't want them coming around here, do you?"

He grabbed the bracelet back and lit another cigarette. We smoked in silence for a time. But finally he said, quietly, "I'm going to make sure I keep them off my back here at home, but I'm doing something about it at work."

He stared down at the ugly gray government-issue bracelet before going on to tell me about a new abortion pill that had recently been legalized. This one would work on late term babies. It hadn't been properly tested, but the sharks had muscled through more legislation and now his pharmacy was dispensing it on a regular basis. Anyone over the age of eighteen could get it without a prescription no matter how far the pregnancy had progressed. And as bad as that sounded, it wasn't the worst thing. Soon it would be legal for anyone over the age of fourteen to buy it—to get it for free actually—as long as they had an ID card.

Then he related an incident that had happened at work. Brad had been getting ready to go off shift when some shady looking guy came up to the counter. The pharmacist taking over from Brad had just signed in, and she waited on the guy. Brad noticed that the creepy guy had brought someone along with him. Some skinny little girl with a big belly was standing back in the aisle, waiting.

"She looked about fourteen or fifteen," he said in a disgusted tone. "Either these people are complete idiots, or so arrogant that they don't know what they're doing. He brought her right into the store with him."

"Maybe he thought she'd run away if he left her outside," I replied.

"Maybe. Well anyway Wallace, that hag I work with was getting ready to fill the order. So I decided to ask the son of a bitch if he was pregnant."

"Brad." I was shaking my head. "You better be careful."

"Yeah? Well, screw it. It pissed me off. The bastard ignored me anyway."

"Was that the end of it?" I asked.

"No. I went back and made my co-worker aware of the little girl. She didn't give a damn, though. She just told me it was going to be legal soon anyway."

I was speechless.

"Right," Brad said. "Can you believe that? She didn't care one way or the other. That kid looked scared to death, but that didn't seem to bother her. All she did was repeat to me that it was legal to sell it over the counter. Then I told her I didn't care what the hell was legal right now. I reminded her that it was still illegal for anyone under eighteen to use it, and that she wasn't dispensing it to any kid under my watch."

I smoked and kept quiet. "She told me my shift was over, and that she was in charge now," Brad went on. "Good thing the tech was on break at the time. I waited until she turned her back. Then I went out from behind the counter and took that piece of shit by the elbow. I walked him down the other aisle out of earshot and told him to get the hell out of the frigging store. I threatened to call the cops and told him if I ever saw him again I was gonna mess him up, the child molesting bastard. He got the little girl and walked out."

The two of us smoked in silence for a time.

"Did you call the cops?" I asked, finally.

"No. I don't trust them either." He looked at the bracelet I'd given back to him, turning it over and over in his hands.

"Do you think she'll make a complaint?"

"Hell, I'm the one with the complaint. She's the one who acted unethically."

"Are you going to make a complaint?"

He shook his head, still looking at the bracelet. "No, but I've made an enemy."

* * *

After we returned from Memphis, I began going to St. Michaels more frequently. I visited on and off over the course of the next year, trying to find answers as our family slowly disintegrated.

My father-in-law was on my mind constantly. The diabetes was out of control. His blood sugar spiked up and down dangerously, and the condition of his foot steadily worsened. His illness upset Michelle and her mom, and it scared the old man so bad that he even managed to quit smoking for real. We visited every Sunday. Michelle would go to the house after Mass to help cook dinner, and I always joined her later. We wanted to spend as much time as possible with him.

My mother was another loved one over whom I brooded. The two of us stayed in touch, but only sporadically, though Jeremy and I got together every once in a while. He was back at Mom's house every week visiting, but we didn't meet every week—only once every six weeks or so. Our conversations usually centered on Lauren, and his worries that they might split up. He complained that they were fighting a lot, that she worked too much, and that she never wanted to stay home with him. I listened to him. But I didn't confide in him about anything going on in my life.

I went to St. Michael's and told the Christ. I knelt in His Presence and laid out all my worries and fears. The old man was sick, and Michelle and I still didn't have a child. Michelle and the old man both suffered quietly and without complaint.

If he felt up to it on Sunday evenings, the old man would walk across the backyard to the garage so we could talk man to man. Once in a while he'd be forced to use a cane. Resorting to the cane always put him in a foul mood, and he'd stump through the side door and sag down into the old desk chair, throwing the cane aside. Then Johnny and I would each light a cigarette, smoke it in a hurry, and put it out, while we listened to the old man speak about important things, simple things, and family things. Other times he wasn't up to going out back, and all of us stayed inside. Nobody smoked in the house.

It was quiet in the chapel as I recalled all that was troubling me. I could say whatever I wanted to, and no matter what it was, Christ on the cross knew exactly how I felt. Sometimes I prayed for a baby. Other times I prayed for the old man the whole time, though not any formal prayers. I was never much for formal prayers, even with Michelle's example. Michelle was aware of my visits to St. Michael's, but she never went with me. It wasn't her habit. She prayed the rosary every day; that was her devotion. I wasn't structured enough to do what Michelle did. I only drove over to St. Michael's when I felt the need. Or maybe I felt drawn to Him... It's hard to explain. Though crystal clear, being with Him was always a dreamlike experience, with the flowing water in the background. I'd walk out feeling less anxious, even on those visits when I did nothing but rail at God the whole time while asking why.

Sometimes I railed and complained seeming to blame Him even though I knew it wasn't His fault. Sometimes I kept my head bowed in contemplation of what I'd read in some literature I picked up on my way out one day. That He was really there with me, in the chapel. The Son of God, come down to be with us. He was truly present in the consecrated Host, resting on the altar right in front of me. It was a difficult concept, but only when constrained to my preconceived notions and the presumptions I had held before Father Gallucio insisted on my praying in adoration for the first time.

It was different when I let my mind venture out. When I opened my mind in front of Him, I tried very hard not to let my human limitations enter in. Then I was able to grasp the truth of His presence, though at times it was difficult. I had somehow known it was true the first time I walked into the chapel the day I begged Father to tell me what to say to Michelle about the twins. He knew it was true as well, which was why he had sent me. I knew it was true every time I walked out of the chapel, feeling strengthened.

Sometimes I railed at Him about the old man, asking why? In my mind the old man didn't deserve such a fate. It was hard to accept that he wouldn't always be with us, and I pleaded and prayed for more time. But I also saw Him hanging on the cross and understood that the cross was the answer. *Neither he nor his parents sinned.*

Other times my mind was quiet and my heart felt serene while I stared at the monstrance, understanding that He was looking back at me.

3 Years Earlier

I left Saint Michael's earlier than usual one Saturday evening. It was the first week of September, exactly one year after the birth of Brad's girls. Junior had graduated back in June and was beginning to take part in what he insisted on calling service, but what I—and everyone else in the family—still considered being part of a cult.

The MCSF had set up shop in the unused firehouse downtown, and Junior was there bright and early every morning doing whatever it was they told him to do. Reese drove by one morning on his way to work. He'd taken the shortcut behind the firehouse that came out one block from the garage and said he'd seen kids unloading trucks in back of the place. He mentioned it midmorning as we sat in the break room choking down CJ's brew.

"Looked like they were unloading new computers," he said. I wondered if he knew Junior was a member. I had no idea whether or not Michelle had mentioned it to Heather.

"Did you happen to see Junior out there?" I asked. My tone was a little embarrassed. *But why hide it? If he doesn't know now he will before long.* Evidently Reese hadn't heard the news though; he looked at me like he thought I had a screw loose.

"Junior... You mean your nephew Junior?"

I nodded.

"You're kidding, right? You don't mean to tell me Junior's joined them, do you?"

"That's exactly what I'm telling you. The arrogant little punk is a true believer. He bought their bullshit—he insists they're on the level. They paid his school tuition last year, the bastards. We had it out a while back over this. The whole family's upset about it."

Reese's mouth dropped open then. He knew I wasn't joking, and the conversation ended with him telling me that no, he hadn't seen Junior doing any heavy lifting behind the firehouse. He was still shaking his head as he went back to work.

The more I thought about it the angrier I became, and that was what I'd been telling Him that evening in the chapel, minus the foul language. When I finished haranguing Our Lord about Junior I knelt quietly for a while, realizing again that He already knew. I saw Him hanging there didn't I?

He knew it all. He had *felt it,* all of it. He had experienced worse things. Way worse. Anything that anyone, anywhere at any time had ever felt—good or bad, right or wrong, sadness or joy, pain and suffering—He'd already felt. I stared at the crucifix, contemplating His agony and the knowledge that He already knew what we were going through. It had been laid on Him back when he was alone in the garden of Gethsemane, and I imagined He had experienced agonies undreamed of by me. He suffered so much on that night so long ago that it caused Him to sweat blood.

The old lady was across the aisle praying a rosary. I looked at my watch and saw that it was five forty-five. I needed to go; I had promised Michelle a night out. We'd hardly done anything fun that whole summer, and we planned to eat at a high-end steak house and go out for a drink afterward. Before I rose to leave I prayed for the old man and said a final act of contrition. On my way out I dipped my hand in the fountain and made the sign of the cross before looking back at Him one more time.

It was always a strange feeling coming out of there. Almost like I was leaving the place where I was most fully alive to go back into the world where I was forced to live. *Thank you God, for my wife.*

The guy who seemed to be there every Saturday night was

walking across the pavement from the parking lot. We nodded to each other, and I was almost past him before the words came out of my mouth: "I've seen you here before, and her as well." I gestured back to the chapel. He understood that I was referring to the old lady.

"I come every Saturday from six to seven, she's here from five till six." I stood looking at him, having no idea what he meant. Then he went on to tell me that he'd committed to being there for one hour a week, and that someone was required to be in the chapel at all times.

"How late do they stay open?" I asked. He stared back patiently for a minute before explaining that they were always open—that someone was *always* there.

"Do you mean people are here all night?" I could hardly believe it.

"Yeah, around the clock."

I had a thought then, about the old lady and the place I always took across the aisle from her, right in front of the altar.

"Was I in your seat last week?" I flushed, embarrassed.

"We don't have seats. Anyone can come." He then went on to tell me that if I was interested, I could sign up to watch for an hour a week. We didn't even introduce ourselves; he hurried on inside, saying he was late. I recalled the visit from the year before, when the old lady asked if I was keeping watch. I couldn't believe how thick I was. *If you're interested go sign up. There's a paper in there with a number to call.* I shook my head, telling myself I wasn't ready for such a commitment.

In the truck the Bible lay open on the seat again. I glanced at it reluctantly. *Matthew 26. The Agony in the Garden.* I picked up the Bible and forced myself to read on until I came to verse 40: *When he returned to his disciples he found them asleep. He said to Peter, "So you could not keep watch with me for one hour?"*

TWENTY

Michelle

My back aches constantly angel-baby, and I'm forced to lie on my side at all times if I want to get any sleep at night. The upside is feeling your movements within me. Thick wet air blows across me, stirred by the fan in the corner. Crickets hum in the distance, and I doze for a time before being awakened by another false contraction. It's nothing painful, only a feeling of pressure. There is heaviness in my breasts as well, but you're worth it. I love you. I love dreaming of holding you in my arms, with Jason's arms surrounding both of us.

Then I'm up again, needing to go to the bathroom. Afterward I collapse back on the bed and lie awake for a time listening to the night sounds and the fan. Then I'm dozing again, and dreaming of your daddy. *Why are we apart?*

I ache for him. I want to feel his arms around me, here, now, in this bed. I want you to hear his voice, angel. That deep voice, a little rougher now than it was when he was young. Its a sound I can't remember not knowing—one that means safety and struggle and unselfish love. Always, always love.

I want to see Jason. I want to see him the way he looks every third Thursday night when he comes home from Bella's with a fresh haircut. That's his only vanity, if you can even call it that. He just can't stand his hair being the slightest bit longer than the way he's worn it for years. It's standing up in front from his cowlick. The sideburns... I'm dreaming.

We're in his truck now, heading toward the beach. Someday you'll see your daddy standing next to the water in his swim trunks and sunglasses, reeling in a fish. I hope this will be one of your earliest memories. I'm watching him from my beach chair. At times he lights a cigarette and smokes it while he reels in whatever he's managed to catch.

Now we're home again. It's six-thirty in the morning. I open my eyes and look through the bathroom door at Jason. He's standing at the sink in his boxers, shaving. Steam rises as he turns on the shower.

At night I stare into his eyes, seeing many things. He smiles at me. I want to feel his hands in my hair now. Why not? Its something I've felt almost every day for the past fourteen years. His hands are strong and roughened by work. They're scarred. Faint traces of grease sometimes remain there, even though he scrubs them until the skin is coming off.

I want familiar smells, pleasant and not so pleasant. The smell of soap in the morning as I doze while he's in the shower, and fish guts on his Jack Daniel's T-shirt when he hugs me after a day on CJ's boat. The smell of gasoline, grease and oil. I want the smell of the whiskey on his breath when he comes in from the shed at night and gets into bed with me. Even the very faint smell of Lucky Strike cigarettes. That's what I want.

Jason
3 Years Earlier

The next Christmas was the old man's last. After jumping through HCA hoops to reschedule a wellness visit for the twins, Brad and Nicole drove up from Memphis with them. It was the old man's only visit with them, and after Brad had taken his family home, Michelle plastered pictures of Christmas all over the refrigerator.

The old man hadn't seen a doctor since the previous September when he'd been to the endocrinologist. They had adjusted his insulin and he'd gone on that way for a while, but after Christmas things disintegrated.

His appointments were scheduled, but the wait times were insane. The podiatrist would see him in August, and the endocrinologist again in September. The family practice informed him nothing was available until further notice.

That was the situation in January when his health began its final decline. Ten years earlier he would have been fitted in for care immediately. Now the bureaucrats had decided that there were too many younger people—those who still could contribute—to give precious time with a physician to the head of our family. They never said that of course, but we could read the writing on the wall.

Doctors were quitting right and left at the time, which added to the rationing. I certainly didn't blame them. Many doctors either couldn't or wouldn't work under the new system, back then before another law was passed prohibiting any doctor from leaving said system. We were faced with a shortage of healthcare workers, and the facts spoke for themselves. The old man wasn't surprised. He'd always known that it was only a matter of time until the madness trickled down to someone in our family. He told Johnny and me in private that if it had to be someone he was glad it was him. Upon hearing his words the two of us cried like babies.

We took him to the emergency room for the first time in mid-

March after a particularly bad day. He'd been running a fever, and it spiked that night. My mother-in-law was frantic and Michelle and Cindy were crying, so Johnny and I talked him into letting us take him. It was a ninety-minute drive. When we arrived he refused to use a wheelchair. He hobbled in on his cane.

The place was crowded. A guy in the waiting room gave the old man a seat while Johnny presented his ID to the bureaucrat sitting behind the admissions desk. Two hours later the admissions nurse sent him back to triage. We prayed that they'd admit him, but we were soon told that he was going to have to wait. Then the triage nurse came out to the waiting room and had an argument with the guy making the decisions. Johnny and I heard her telling him the old man was in bad shape and that his blood pressure was low. But her pleas fell on deaf ears.

She came to find us with tears in her eyes, saying she was sorry, but he couldn't go ahead of anyone. He would have to wait in the waiting room, and the expected wait time was forty-eight hours. We understood that it wasn't her fault, but the old man was way too bad off to sit in a chair for forty-eight hours, so Johnny and I took him back home.

Brad was in agony over his dad. But he didn't visit again after Christmas because he was being harassed at work. The pharmacist who had wanted to sell the abortion pill to the little girl was making trouble for him. She had started complaining about Brad to their supervisor a week after the incident, when she figured out Brad had gotten the little girl out of the store before she'd been able to dispense the pill to her pimp. Her complaints about Brad were many, but chief among them were three: Brad wasn't a team player, he didn't follow rules, and he was undependable.

"You? Undependable?" I said to him on the phone. "They don't believe that, do they?"

"I don't know." Brad's tone was anxious. "She has no documentation. I'm always on time, and I never leave early. The only thing she has is the incident when I ran that pig out of the store, and she was the one who was unethical in that instance." He went on to tell me that she never gave them any specific examples because there weren't any, but she complained about him every week. He was afraid he'd lose his job if he came to visit, so he was staying in Memphis."

"You'll call if anything else goes wrong, won't you?"

"I'll call."

The first package arrived the next week, followed by two more later on. All three were addressed to me. The packages had no return addresses and three different postmarks: Brownsville, TN, Dyersburg, TN, and Forrest City, Arkansas. When I opened the first one I rushed it right to the house, and my mother-in-law started the old man on the antibiotics without question. The same thing happened a month later.

The third package to arrive was wrapped as a birthday gift and placed in a cardboard box. It contained insulin and a package of hypodermic needles—the old man happened to be running short just then. There were more antibiotics, as well as other pills. The labels contained no name, no date, no pharmacy or prescribing physician. Nothing but instructions: take one pill three times a day until gone. The other container was huge and full of tiny capsules. Detailed instructions were listed along with warnings about overdose. The remaining space was covered with skull and crossbones stickers. I assumed they were narcotics; maybe even morphine. The old man didn't take any until almost the end. Our family kept quiet about the meds even among ourselves, but all of us knew exactly who was sending them.

Of course it was Brad. He confirmed it later. It was the only thing he could do for his father. It was a form of resistance; a way to make up for what he and Nicole and the rest of us were enduring. Brad had decided he'd do anything he could to throw a wrench into the new way of doing business. He was working to that end at the pharmacy, and he'd already managed to save three more young girls from the abortion pill. All three had come into the store with men, and Brad said one of them looked to be only thirteen or fourteen years old.

"Wallace, what about that? She couldn't have been more than fourteen. And I found out more about those pills. At least forty women died after taking them. They were all prostitutes, but they still deserved better."

"Where'd you hear that?"

"Not in the news, that's for damn sure. But I have my sources, and I believe them. I know what's in the damn things. And the sons of bitches pimping out those women don't give a damn now that prostitution's legal down here. If one of their whores dies it's okay with them. They just buy another little girl and put her out on the street."

"I don't know how you stand dealing with this shit. If it was me I think I'd have to go after the bastards."

"I'm dealing with it."

"Just don't get caught."

After I hung up the phone I lit another cigarette and remembered one of the last times I'd seen Michelle before leaving for basic training. It was an incident I tried to forget after I left.

Brad's parents threw a graduation party for him, and of course I was there. I was always over there, and my name had been on the cake along with Brad's. Michelle had also been there, of course. Junior was ten months old at the time, and Michelle had held him and played with him all night long; she lavished attention on both boys all their lives. I poured another shot of whiskey and drank it down, remembering the way she looked that day as she ran around the backyard with her friends, lugging Junior the whole time.

Suddenly I found myself back there again. It was one of those memories that seemed to take over, and for a few minutes I wasn't alone in the shed, but back in the old man's yard on a Saturday evening about a month before I left town, standing around what was left of the keg along with Brad and some of our closest friends.

It was two o'clock in the morning. Music came softly from the old stereo in the garage. The night was hot, muggy, and still. Mosquitoes buzzed and dive-bombed. The smell of bug repellent mixed with the pungent scent of Mrs. Davis' marigolds, growing thickly along the side of the garage. Tiny sparkly lights wound their way around the yard, and streamers dangled limply in the dimness. A colorful banner hung above the open garage doors, reading: *Congratulations St. Bonaventure Class of 2003*. Michelle had made it. She'd also done the decorating. I had noticed her earlier in the day, stringing the lights and streamers.

I was nineteen-years-old, Brad was eighteen, both of us were leaving, and this was the absolute last party before everyone went their separate ways. The old man had already taken everyone's keys. He was still awake. Every once in a while he'd wander out to make sure everything was under control. He had already told me that there was no way he'd say anything about my drinking at this point; that if I was old enough to serve my country in dangerous times, I was old enough to have a drink as long as I wasn't driving. But he made damn sure nobody else was overdoing it. *The old man's cool. He knows I'm overdoing it tonight, but he also knows he can trust me. With drinking, anyway.*

Nobody knew about my feelings for Michelle, especially the old man. *He'd kick my ass.* And nobody noticed me keeping an eye on her either, while thoughts and feelings rushed swiftly and achingly through my head. I remembered the thoughts clearly as I leaned against the workbench in my tool shed. The memory was there in its entirety. I was back there.

Look at her. Carrying that baby around all night. She'll be a good mother someday. I'm not the type to get married, but if I were she'd be the one I'd want. But that'll never happen. And I'll never marry. Not if I can't have her.

I appraised her adolescent body coolly. *She's getting there. She's bigger in the chest area than she was in September. That was the best day of my life. She's almost perfect—not too skinny. I hate skinny. I like something to grab onto, and she's definitely got that.*

Stop thinking this way. Can't happen unless she waits for me, and there's no way the old man will allow that. But she already puts every girl here to shame. In a few years she's going to be a knockout. If she waits for me we could have something. She understands me. We could have a future. Six years is a gap, sure, but so what?

Stop. She's only thirteen. No way I'm making a move on a thirteen-year-old, even if I do love her. Even if I do know she loves me. She loves me. I can feel it.

Why couldn't she have been born a few years earlier? Why am I leaving? By the time I get back she will have forgotten me. It would be wrong to expect her to wait. She's too young to make that kind of commitment, especially to me. I didn't wait for her. But what the hell did those other girls mean to me anyway? Nothing. Not a damn thing, any of them.

My life's a waste. If Brad's dad ever finds out I'm thinking about her he'll kick my ass to San Antonio. I won't need to fly to get there. But how the hell am I going to be able to forget her?

Feelings of rage began then, as that worthless bastard Joey Riley moved into my field of vision. He had been hanging around my Michelle all night long. Seeing this was equivalent to feeling a knife stabbing and twisting in my chest.

That little punk, I never could stand him. He better watch himself or he won't know what the hell hit him. I'll mess him up good. Why did Mike have to bring him over here? I'll kick Mike's ass too. Mike, you cheating bastard, you shouldn't have brought him over here. Get the hell away from her. Look my way you little punk.

Michelle and her friends from St. Catherine's were sitting under the maple tree, and Joey had slithered his way into the middle of the group. He was sitting under the tree right next to Michelle. He finally looked over toward where I was standing with my nails digging into my palms, beer forgotten. I glared at him with eyes narrowed to slits.

Sweat streamed off me in rivers, soaking my shirt. My fists were clenched at my sides.

Keep your hands off her. You're a cheating bastard just like your brother. You don't want to mess with me. You touch her and I'll make you wish you'd never seen the light of day. Leave her alone.

Joey's face was frozen. He looked scared, and with good reason. I only had to stare at him for a moment longer before he got up and moved away from Michelle. A minute later Mike and Joey took their leave.

I glanced at Michelle. Our eyes met.

Michelle, honey I'm sorry. But please don't let him touch you.

There's only you, Jason. Only you.

Then I came back to myself. When I recalled what Brad had told me I became enraged again. With the sharks there was no honor. They had no regard for the little girls and their feelings, their rights, their happiness. Girls and women were simply tools to be used by certain men who'd been given "rights" under the new way of doing business.

At least I hadn't done what these current pigs were doing. I forced myself to put Michelle out of my mind, even though I had real feelings for her. I remembered my heartache at the thought of leaving her forever and considered what I would have done if Joey—or anyone else for that matter—had touched her before I left town. *I would have torn him apart with my bare hands.*

I wasn't exactly in a positive state of mind that summer. Saying goodbye to Michelle had made me despair. But I got through the next four years somehow, and when I came back for good it was safe. Michelle was almost eighteen, not too young anymore, and her body was no longer a little girl's body. Still I drew a line. I wanted the whole experience to be different. I didn't want any memories of the woman I planned to marry to resemble those of women in my past.

I made a commitment to Michelle the night I finally told her I loved her. We always stopped before I went much further than a couple of feels here and there, except on a single occasion the summer before I married her. I don't think of it often because it was another case of my attempting to strong-arm her. But Michelle says it's a beautiful memory. She says there are no regrets because we stopped.

I had almost gotten around her. She let me take her clothes off in my bedroom. The windows were open, but the blinds were shut and no one could see into my room. Led Zeppelin was playing on the stereo. The song was *The Rain Song*—an achingly beautiful sound. Noise from the neighborhood filtered through the window—kids running around yelling, dogs barking, and cars going by on the street. It was a Saturday evening around seven o'clock, and there was still plenty of light.

Her body! My dreams never prepared me for the reality. She was perfect. She wasn't too skinny, even though she was slim; she looked healthy. I knew she was scared, but still she stood there in my room letting my eyes roam over her. Everything about her was beautiful to me. Even that mole on the underside of her left breast, and another one at the small of her back. I had never known they were there. *Just the way I knew it would be.*

I took the elastic out of her hair, and it shimmered down around her body. I took a lock of it and let it run through my hand before laying her on the bed. I stood back for a minute, trying not to feel what she was feeling—her apprehension and worry about a possible consequence.

Jason, no this is a mistake.

No. No baby, it's not.

My vow to wait was fading. I didn't listen to what my heart was telling me, not with her finally naked, and I stripped off my clothes and lay down next to her. My only saving grace was that I grabbed her by the hands. I knew she wasn't really ready, so I touched only her hands while I tried to make her want me.

I lifted her left hand to my lips and kissed it. Her eyes were big and blue and fearful. I was falling into them. I was on fire. We were facing each other, saying nothing with words. Sometimes Michelle and I needed no words.

Baby, come on.

We can't.

Why not? I'll make you feel things you've never dreamed of.

We have to wait, we promised.

Only another six months. You won't get pregnant. I'll be careful. I love you.

I love you too, but this isn't right.

I won't hurt you. Let me make you feel things, honey. Let me.

I feel it in my heart.

I'll be careful. Let me love you now. Please baby. I've loved you forever...

I closed my eyes when she let go of my hand and started reaching toward me. I waited for it. But suddenly she was gone. I opened my eyes to see her rolling away from me and jumping out of the bed. She grabbed my shirt off the floor and ran into the bathroom.

I rolled onto my back. After a minute I pulled on my jeans and went into the bathroom. She was wearing my shirt. One look at her distress made me want to sink through the floor. I took her in my arms, feeling ashamed. I looked into her tear washed eyes and smoothed her hair back from her face. *Honey, I'm sorry. You're right. We need to wait.*

The wedding was only a few months away, and we both would have regretted it if we had gone ahead. But stopping was the hardest thing I had ever done. Later I was glad she had stopped me. Our wedding night was indescribable.

I came back from the memory then and wondered why my mind had drifted into the past two times in one night. It was happening a lot lately. Maybe I was trying to get away from the old man's illness by remembering better times. But his illness—along with everything else we were facing— seemed to lead directly back to the mess we'd gotten ourselves into in America. Including the fact that Brad, a Catholic from birth, was now required by law to dispense abortion pills to fifteen year old girls who came into his workplace in the company of men in their thirties and forties.

How had it ever gotten to such a point? Those pills were dangerous. Brad knew what he was talking about. Plus, they got the damned things for free as long as they had an ID card. *Why go through the motions of having to ask a pharmacist for them?* It made no sense to me. Neither did the collective opinion of the sharks that if you didn't want to follow the law—the rules—the new way of doing business—then maybe you needed a new profession. So just get the hell out, no matter how hard you'd worked to get where you were.

But the overturning of the conscience laws was only one tip of one of the many filth-covered icebergs that the sharks had gradually foisted on us. Covering up for the sex trade and its abuse of underage girls was another one. I simply couldn't understand how any man could do what those pigs did every day of their miserable lives. It brought me back to my original thought. *I'd tear them apart. But Brad's getting around them.*

Brad's solution was to fill the orders with a placebo. I wasn't sure how he was doing it; he never mentioned the particulars over the phone. But somehow he'd been getting away with it, and when the pigs abusing the little girls in Memphis left the store, they were satisfied that their only consequence might be getting rid of a dead whore and having to look for a replacement. Brad let them think they were getting away with it, and then he called the cops anonymously. He had no way of knowing if the men were caught of course, but he gave the addresses on file.

"Maybe they were fake addresses Wallace, but maybe not. At least I'm trying."

He said he managed never to dispense the pills. He would make himself scarce if he had a suspicion an adult wanted it or tell them he was currently out if he was alone behind the counter. He knew they probably ended up getting it anyway, but still he was resisting.

"And I'm thinking something else might have happened. Maybe some of them got it elsewhere, but some of them... Maybe they changed their minds."

Brad did all of this, and still managed to hang on to his job. *But Brad's the best they have. Or else maybe he has help?*

TWENTY-ONE

Michelle

Dear Holy Mother, please ask your Divine Son to have mercy on us, and to let our child come into this world safely if it is His will. How did you feel, Blessed Mother? What did you think as you felt the contractions and knew your time was near? Did you slide off the donkey's back and struggle through the streets of Bethlehem the way I struggle through the corn, leaning on your husband? The way I lean on mine. He's not here with me, but he still gives me his strength. Hear my prayer that he can be with me soon.

What did you think, knowing you were on the verge of bringing Light into this dark world? And then being told there was no room for Him?

Jason
3 Years Earlier

Michelle became pregnant again that winter, adding some joy to our sorrow about her dad. The baby was conceived in February, on the night of Valentine's Day. I sent Michelle a big bouquet of roses, which she placed in our bedroom.

The old man also sent a bouquet for Michelle. It had been his habit for years to send flowers to all "his" girls—Michelle's mother, Cindy, Michelle, and Nicole. Even the twins received tiny buds of roses from the old man. This year the flowers were all roses; pink for Michelle because he knew they were her favorite. She also received a card, and a letter over which she sobbed inconsolably. It turned out to be the last thing he ever wrote to her.

We continued running that spring through the early months of her pregnancy. Michelle couldn't do without running by that time. She considered it therapy and said she'd go crazy if she couldn't run while praying the rosary. Running helped me deal with the old man's illness as well. I even managed to stop smoking for a while, and found that I could run further and faster. The two of us still got up early to run at daybreak. Seeing the sunrise gave us a feeling of hope.

Our happiness about the baby was overshadowed by our sadness, but we still managed to make plans for the future. Michelle was under the care of a midwife. It was my idea. Maybe.

During confession on a Saturday evening in early April, I told Father Gallucio about Michelle's pregnancy and my fear of subjecting her to the system. He gave it some thought before reaching back to the counter for another Bible.

"Do you ever read the Scriptures?" he asked. I shrugged, not wanting to tell him about my experience with the Bible after the image of the shark during adoration. "I think it would be a good idea if you spent ten or fifteen minutes a day reading," he went on. "Start with the Gospel of St. Matthew."

"Father, I don't like to read. And I can't understand the Bible."

"Don't give me that. You were almost at the top of your class, and I know what you did in the Air Force. You can understand God's word. It just takes a little concentration."

"How do you know all that?"

"I know because your father-in-law talks about you kids every time I visit him. You're his pride and joy. He talks about you as much as the rest of them, and he told me about your record. It won't hurt you Jason. It'll probably make you see things from a different perspective. So get started tonight."

"All right, Father," I replied resignedly. I knew he always won anyway. "I'll do it."

Then I confessed my sins, and after praying my penance I drove to St. Michael's. After parking the truck I got the Bible from where it had migrated under the seat. I had no idea where Matthew was located, but finally found it a quarter of the way in from the back. I focused then, and started at the beginning.

The book of the genealogy of Jesus Christ, the son of David, the son of Abraham.

It went on with a list of names, all ancestors of His, and the story was told from a different perspective. Nothing was mentioned about the angel appearing to His Mother. This one stated that the angel appeared to her husband in a dream after she was found to be pregnant with the Christ Child. Joseph had been ready to divorce her. They weren't living together yet, and he thought she'd been messing around on him.

But apparently he'd been unwilling to just throw it out there for all to see. The Jews stoned adulterous women back then, so Joseph decided to end it quietly. Then the angel came and told him not to worry—that the child had been conceived by Divine means, and that he should take the Virgin as his wife. He was also instructed not to have relations with her.

How old was he? Older than the Virgin, that's for sure. Michelle had mentioned the age of the Virgin as being around fourteen. I thought of the first little girl Brad had mentioned, and the man who brought her into the store. *One couple followed God's will, and the other is a product of man's sin. St. Joseph... How did he manage that? He died without ever laying a hand on his wife. It's a paradox.* I pondered it for a moment longer. *Where'd he get the strength?*

But I already knew the answer, and my final thought on the matter was: *I'll never be a saint.*

When I entered the chapel the old lady was in her usual spot. I genuflected and knelt across from her. It was quiet except for the sound of the fountain, and the birds in the trees outside. I didn't look up at the cross, only at the monstrance. The Christ, Body, Blood, Soul and Divinity, right here with me. I told Him about my disgust with what happened in the ER, and about my feelings of rage and sadness and helplessness. I told him about my fears for my wife and child, and then I said a prayer of adoration and bowed my head.

The fountain was soothing. The names at the beginning of the gospel flowed through my mind in a rush. They were strange Bible names—none that I recognized except for David and Abraham. Forty-two generations from Abraham to the Messiah divided into three equal sections: David's birth, the Babylonian exile, and the birth of Jesus. I kept my head bowed and listened.

I wonder what hospitals they used back then?

I looked up at Him in the monstrance.

Lots of babies were born before the advent of hospitals...right?

On my way out I turned to look back at the altar. The sun was blazing through the round window again, coloring the chapel in flames.

* * *

After taking the antibiotics Brad sent, my father-in-law stabilized for a month or so, though his illness left him weak. We continued to visit every Sunday. Michelle went throughout the week as well, whenever she could get there. Brad was sick over the fact that he was stuck in Memphis, and I promised to call him if the situation started to deteriorate. Around that time, late in April, Michelle and I had our first visit with the midwife.

Her name was Mary. Michelle heard about her from one of her friends at St. Catherine's. Mary brought testimonials, pictures of herself with families, and her credentials. I paid her cash; half down, half to be paid at the time of the baby's birth. I took it out of our savings, and I considered it money well spent. Mary didn't ask to see ID cards—in fact, she was so disgusted by the system that she only worked with families who wanted nothing to do with the HCA. Our baby would be born at home, in a safe, peaceful place, and I would make sure there weren't any HCA sharks in the room.

There would be no ultrasound and no other testing for our child. Mary was currently forming alliances with techs and other professionals to be able to offer such services to her clients, but as of that time it hadn't all come together, so our child was denied certain tests. I blamed it on the HCA. If it weren't for them our baby would have access to everything modern medicine could offer, but as it was we had to accept the facts. Births in hospitals were no longer safe, and it would be better for our baby to be born at home even if there were certain risks.

The sharks were in the process of trying to outlaw midwifery at the time, but their efforts were on the back burner, and since Mary wasn't in the yellow pages we felt reasonably safe. We found out later that the sharks had a bigger agenda at that point anyway. They were frying bigger fish at the time and must have figured they'd mop up people like us later.

* * *

The old man was dying. Though years have passed, it still hurts like it was yesterday, so I'll try to make it short.

He was so bad off one Sunday morning in late June that Johnny and I loaded him up and squealed our way to the ER again even, though he didn't want to go. We should have just let him alone...when we finally got there the experience was way worse than what happened the last time. This time, when the bureaucrat scanned his ID card nothing came up.

I recognized the guy. It was the same one who'd been there in January. The badge hanging around his neck was imprinted with the FEDHCA seal. He looked down with disdain from his desk on its elevated platform and handed Johnny the card.

"He's not in the system."

"What do you mean?" Johnny looked at him like he was speaking Chinese. The old man was in a wheelchair next to us with his bad foot propped up. He heard the whole thing.

"There's no one by that name in the system," he repeated.

"Well try it again," Johnny said, flushing as he handed the card back. "You can see that it's him from the picture. Enter the information by hand."

The bureaucrat took the card, but he was rolling his eyes while he did it, and it pissed me off. The old man noticed that as well, and put his hand on my arm. We waited while he tried again with the same result.

"There is no one by the name of John Bradford Davis in this system," the guy repeated in a scornful tone. "There are several John Davises listed, but none of them are seventy-nine years old, and none have the middle name Bradford. There is a John B. Davis listed, but he's only ten-years-old and resides in Ohio."

He handed back the card. I flushed at his words and his tone. Johnny was floored. The old man put pressure on my arm, as much as he could anyway.

"Boys, let's go," he said weakly. "It doesn't matter anymore. Let's just go."

The situation went downhill from there. I took the card out of Johnny's hand and showed the bastard behind the desk the name and the old man's photo. It was an official government ID that had been reissued in January, but that didn't make any difference to him. He was a cold bastard, and he must have been well trained. He just kept repeating what he'd already told us—that if your name wasn't in the system you couldn't receive treatment under any circumstances, and that we needed to go.

This is impossible. I couldn't believe what I was hearing, even while remembering that I myself had considered the possibility of somebody clicking a mouse and deleting a bank account when the sharks had been after CJ. Something was rushing through my brain, but this time it wasn't water. This time it was pure rage.

"What the hell are you talking about? Are you telling me you refuse to treat him?" I gestured at the old man. "Look at him. He needs help. All you freaking people ever talk about is how much you help everyone, and now you're turning him away? What the hell is wrong with you?"

"I'm very sorry," said the bureaucrat, sounding just the opposite. The waiting room was overflowing, and everyone was looking at the floor. A little boy questioned his mother and she hushed him. Nurses stepped lightly back and forth, but none of them gave us a glance. Then the triage nurse who'd argued with this very same bureaucrat back in March passed in and out of my field of vision. This time she didn't speak up for us. She didn't even look at us. Still, I noticed a tear trickling down her cheek as she moved past us.

I felt like I was losing my mind. My head was pounding as I looked at the old man, and he looked back at me.

"Jason." His voice was a weak whisper. "Let's go. Now."

Johnny seemed to be in shock as he turned the chair around. The old man's wasted body and hideously discolored and swollen leg flashed past me, seemingly in slow motion. He looked up at me with love and longing in his eyes. *Come on son...there's no help here. Take me home now... And then I'll go home.*

That was when I lost it. One minute I was staring into the old man's eyes as he ordered me to take him away from there, and the next thing I knew I had my hands on the Fed running the admissions process. I lunged around the counter and jerked the son of a bitch up by the collar and slammed him against the wall.

"You little creepy-assed screw off," I roared. "Who the hell do you think you are? I'll tear your pathetic face off—now you get somebody in here to look at him right now!" I was up in his face.

The bastard wouldn't meet my eyes. He was looking right past me, and I found out why a minute later. Someone had called security on me. Three guards ran up, and I was muscled backward and handcuffed. Then they took me down the hall to a small room.

I refused to answer their questions. The only thing I said was that they should all go out in the alley and perform a certain sexual act on each other. Nothing they asked had anything to do with the old man or his illness, and since they had refused him treatment, I felt justified in refusing to answer their questions. It went on for a while but I kept quiet, other than repeating what I'd already told them. I added that they could then perform the same act on themselves and go straight to hell afterward. Then I dared them to try to get my ID out of my wallet if they wanted to know anything else. I was still cuffed at that point, but I think they knew better than to mess with me.

"Are you finished with me?" I asked finally. "If you are I'd like to get my father and take him out of this pathetic excuse for a hospital."

I held my hands out to them. The three of them exchanged glances. I gestured again with the cuffs, looking at the guard who'd put them on me. "I'd like to get the hell out of here," I said, glaring at him. "I need to get my father back home so he can die in peace. If you're gonna hold me, maybe one of you could find enough decency to go out and tell my brother to take him home."

The guard in charge looked a little ashamed at my words, and they must have decided I wasn't worth prosecuting. They didn't call the cops. After a minute he unlocked the handcuffs and I walked out of there. Johnny had taken the old man back outside and got him settled in the four-wheel drive. I got into the passenger seat, and on the way home I called Brad to tell him he needed to get home immediately.

Brad and Nicole left the twins with her parents and flew up that night. He had more antibiotics with him along with morphine. He'd packed the drugs in his carry on and gotten it through security at the airport. He started the old man on the antibiotics as soon as he walked through the door, but it was way too late.

Father Gallucio came at midnight to give him last rites. Then Brad started him on the morphine. All of us stayed in his room, including Junior. We stayed with him all night while the women prayed the rosary over and over. Everyone kissed him and said goodbye, and he was able to die then, in peace.

TWENTY-TWO

Jason
3 Years Earlier

The next week was hellish.

After the old man left us, Michelle stayed in his bedroom with her mom, Nicole and Cindy. After Junior and Jamie left the house around eight a.m., I called Jeff Gearhart, the undertaker we used. I knew him; he had an account with CJ, and I always serviced the funeral home vehicles.

When Jeff arrived at the house and learned what had happened in the ER he hurried to tell us to call the cops immediately.

"What good is that going to do now?" I said.

"They'll want to know why he wasn't in a hospital," Jeff replied.

"But we took him." Johnny's tone was incredulous. "We just told you that." Brad was standing next to the doorway near the stairs. The sound of his mother's crying drifted down to us.

"You need to call the cops," Jeff went on urgently. "I've seen this before. They'll try to come down on you. They'll make an example of you for not staying in the ER the other time." CJ must have told him about our previous trip to the emergency room. "Believe me, I've seen it happen." The atmosphere in the room became thicker with his words.

"Maybe that was the reason they deleted him from the database," I mused. I shouldn't have said it out loud. My words almost sent Brad over the edge.

As he turned and stalked out of the room without a word, I felt the shock feeling again. The light flickered in my periphery, and Brad's thoughts came to me plainly. *I'm gonna kill him. That shark bastard, I'll fucking kill him.*

"Brad!" I yelled and ran after him. I caught him in the dining room, using the key to open the bottom drawer of the old man's desk. He yanked it open, pulled out the compact and started looking through the drawer for ammunition. Johnny came in after me, but Jeff stayed where he was. He probably figured the less he knew, the better it would be for all of us.

I walked right over to Brad and grabbed him. I yanked him up, gun and all, and told him: "No." I took the gun out of his hand before he could protest and the rage seemed to go out of him then. He started sobbing and so did I.

* * *

We did as Jeff advised and called the cops. I didn't want Michelle's mother to have to answer questions, but we had no choice, so I made the call. The cop on duty told me someone would be there in about an hour.

After I hung up the phone I found the bottle of narcotics Brad had sent earlier in the year. There were still a few left, so I broke one in half and made Brad take it. I wasn't taking any chances on him going off while the police were in the house. After he swallowed it I took what was left, along with the other drugs he brought, and flushed them. Then I took the empty containers out to the garage to hide them.

When I opened the toolbox I found a pack of Lucky Strikes half-hidden under a monkey wrench in the bottom drawer. I took it out and looked inside. There were four cigarettes. I found myself taking one out. I held it lightly in my palm. It was the old man's.

He'll never smoke another one.

I stared at the Lucky Strike. I couldn't get my mind around it. The old man was gone. I'd never see him dragging on another smoke, never see him knock back another shot of scotch, never feel him hit me upside the head again the way he used to when Brad and I got into scrapes twenty-five years ago. I could never tell him my troubles again the way I had when Michelle was so sick, and I was afraid she might waste away to nothing. He would never be able to help me figure out the best thing to do—the right thing to do—ever again.

How am I going to live without him? My child won't know him.

That knowledge was the worst. It hurt unbearably. I doubled over at the thought and cried there next to the workbench. After a few minutes I put the cigarette carefully back in the pack and replaced it in the drawer where I found it. I hid the containers in the old man's golf bag and went back to the house to wait for the cops.

Johnny, Brad and I sat in the living room with my mother-in-law while she was questioned. The officer asked what had happened, why he wasn't in the hospital, and why an HCA official wasn't present at the time of death. I don't know if he really suspected anything or whether he was just going through the motions; we couldn't tell from his attitude or his mannerisms.

My mother-in-law broke down when she tried to explain our ordeal—that no doctor would see him, and that she'd sent him to the hospital with us but they had refused to treat him. She sobbed inconsolably into her hands. Johnny spoke up then, and explained what had happened. The cop noted it down on the report without expression.

He questioned Johnny and me for another fifteen minutes before getting up to leave. I had an idea that he sympathized with us. For all I knew they could have been holding something over his head. That's how the sharks operated. It was possible that he understood our agony and our helplessness, but had been forced to question us.

The interview ended with my mother-in-law crying helplessly on Johnny's shoulder, Brad sitting silently on the couch like a zombie, and me walking the officer out. He told me he was filing a report stating there was no evidence of foul play.

* * *

That afternoon Johnny and I went down to Jeff's to make the arrangements.

Brad was in no shape to go. As soon as the cop was gone he was on the phone with his in-laws, asking to speak to the twins. A look of relief came over his face as he listened to their little voices. He called down there at least five times that day and talked to each of them in turn, asking them questions and listening to their baby replies. While he was busy with his goodbyes, Nicole told me not to worry about him. She said this was nothing unusual, and that it would pass.

Brad had committed himself to his family wholeheartedly, even to the point of having their names tattooed. The names were part of a Celtic knot design that wound its way across Brad's back from shoulder to shoulder. Nicole's name was in the center, the twins' names on either side. The lettering was almost invisible. Unless you were right up close, the names seemed just a part of the overall design, and there was plenty of room for the names of any future children. It was a great looking piece of work.

I had already told Brad about our decision to keep our child away from the HCA, and about Mary. He decided to do the same and had been looking for a midwife he could trust down in Memphis. He and Nicole both wanted more children, and they could definitely afford it at the time. But Brad wasn't worried about money. He never mentioned it, but he did mention NFP and the fact that Nicole had finally talked him into practicing it. Apparently she'd been after him ever since she converted to Catholicism, and he'd finally given in to her. He had complained about it on the phone the week before the old man died.

"How do you stand it Wallace? I can't wait a week or longer. How the hell do you do it?"

"I don't know," I said, laughing. "Don't ask me. Just deal with it."

"I am dealing with it. But I want you to know that I blame this on you. If Michelle hadn't told Nicole that you put up with it, she wouldn't think she could get me to, but every time I complain she just brings your freaking name up."

His words made me laugh even louder. "Shut the hell up," Brad snapped. "It's your fault and you know it." I continued howling, and he continued to sputter until he finally hung up on me.

But Brad was committed not only to Nicole and his daughters, but to resisting the system as well. The fact that he even considered NFP—never mind that he was actually practicing it—was proof. His transformation was total, and the resistance he showed came naturally, but there was no way he'd be able to make any decisions about the funeral. My mother-in-law also said she'd rather stay home, so it was just Johnny and me.

Johnny called St. Catherine's and scheduled the funeral for the day after the next day. Visiting hours would take place from nine a.m. until noon, after which Mass would be said. Johnny's mom had given him the old man's credit card for the funeral expenses. The old man still had money, though it wasn't in any bank, and we'd be able to pay it off quick. He'd done well with investments and had somehow been able to keep something from the sharks. In addition to investments he had a hundred thousand dollars in life insurance, but I had my doubts we'd ever see any of that. The sharks had control of pretty much everything now, including insurance companies.

That night the house was full of visitors. Aunt Rosie was there, and Bella and Lucio and the kids, along with friends of the old man and my mother-in-law, and other assorted relatives. Everyone brought food, so there was plenty to eat.

Michelle kept herself busy serving food and doing dishes along with Nicole and Cindy and Bella, and by nine-thirty everyone else had gone except the two of us. I told Michelle we'd go home shortly and left her in the living room with Nicole and her mother before heading out to the garage with Brad.

He flicked the switch next to the side door. A moth fluttered around the naked bulb hanging from the ceiling, and two or three birds sang mournfully outside in the dark as Brad and I stood quietly looking around. Everything was the same as it was yesterday. The same as it always looked: controlled chaos. The garage was the same as always...except for the fact that he was gone.

Brad and I exchanged glances, but neither of us spoke. I took a pack of Lucky Strikes from my pocket; Johnny and I had stopped at the convenience store on the way back from Gearhart's. We lit up and continued to look around, remembering and smoking in silence. The two of us smoked four cigarettes apiece in the space of fifteen minutes, in honor of the old man. It made me feel sick.

I finally put out my last cigarette, opened the bottom drawer of the grimy old toolbox, and gestured to Brad. He stared at the Lucky Strikes, half under the monkey wrench where I had replaced them exactly the way I found them. Then he broke into sobs. The two of us cried for another fifteen minutes, but neither of us touched his cigarettes. When we finally cried ourselves out I found myself leaning against the workbench. Brad was next to me. We stood there side by side, wiping our eyes.

"I'm flying back right after the funeral," he said.

"Why are you leaving so soon?"

"I have to get back to work. I have to make sure that witch doesn't get me fired. I can't take a chance on staying any longer.

"She's still after you?"

"Yeah. But she isn't gonna break me. We're in a stalemate. I think she may be ready to quit, and I need to get back ASAP just so she doesn't get any ideas. Besides, I need to see my girls. Mom's flying down with Nicole on Saturday so she can spend some time with them. Can you run me to the airport, Wallace?"

"Yeah, I'll drive your Mom and Nicole, too."

"Thanks, brother."

Brad and I talked a while longer, and after I was satisfied he was stable we went back to the house. Then Michelle and I left. She sobbed inconsolably on the way home.

* * *

The funeral is mostly a blur. I stood beside Michelle for the three hours of visitation, as all the people who had known the old man spoke to us. The line stretched out the door and around to the edge of the parking lot. It stayed the same length all morning, and the church was filled to overflowing during Mass.

My mother and Jeremy came through midmorning. Michelle hugged my mother, and Mom patted her gently before looking up at me. It was another occasion when she seemed to be looking at someone else—I never knew what she was thinking. I held out my arms, though. After a minute she hugged me, and so did Jeremy. My mother told us she was sorry about the old man before she and Jeremy left. They didn't stay for Mass.

During Mass I kept my eyes on his casket, knowing it would be in the ground soon. Afterward we followed it out and watched as it was loaded into the back of the hearse, the same one I worked on in the garage.

When the graveside service was over everyone placed flowers on top of the casket. After I laid my carnation next to Michelle's, I glanced up and noticed a figure under a tree about fifty feet away from the awning that shaded us. It was a man, gray haired, standing alone. I glanced at him as I held my sobbing wife in my arms. Our eyes met for a moment. Though he seemed vaguely familiar I couldn't place him, and no one else noticed him. When I looked back a few minutes later he was gone, and I soon forgot about him. I was too busy comforting Michelle. She didn't want to leave the casket. My mother-in-law kissed it one last time before we left the old man alone.

* * *

I drove Brad to the airport that night. His flight was leaving at nine-thirty, and he planned to be back at the pharmacy the following day by three p.m.

"What time do they need to be here Saturday?" I asked as we approached the terminal. I was referring to Nicole and his mother.

"Flight leaves at nine-fifteen," he answered.

"Okay. I'll drive them up before work that morning."

"Thanks," Brad said. I pulled up next to the curb.

"You call Saturday night and let us know they're safe on the ground."

"All right. Do you think Michelle's going to be okay?"

"Yeah. We have the baby to look forward to—don't worry about her. Are you gonna be okay?"

"Yeah. We knew it was going to happen sometime. But I'm gonna miss the old man."

"Yeah."

"All right, Wallace," Brad said. His eyes were watery as he got his carry-on out of the back of the truck. "I'll call you Saturday night."

"Be safe." I lifted a hand and nodded my head at him. He nodded back.

"All right," he repeated as he walked away.

I listened to the classic rock station out of Philly on the hour ride back, remembering the many times Brad and I had listened to it while we worked on the Trans Am.

The old man had found the Trans Am for us. He bought it and brought it home, saying that if we could get it running, he'd give us permission to drive it. Even though Brad tended to refer to the car as his, both of us understood that I was included. Brad didn't care; he shared everything with me, and I didn't care if people referred to it as Brad's car. We worked on it together, and Brad admitted he never could have gotten it running without me.

The old man knew it, too. He told both of us what he expected. He said he wasn't putting another dime out for the car, and it was up to us to pay for the parts and do the work. I was already working for CJ at the time, and before Brad started working part time at the drugstore he always found people willing to pay him for cutting their grass and other yard work. It took over a year, but we finally got the car to run, and the old man made sure Brad understood that I was to have access to it whenever I wanted. But we were together most of the time anyway, and we never had an argument about the Trans Am.

The memories shutter clicked through my head as I reflected on how much simpler everything had seemed back then, not only for us but for the old man as well. We were free back then. Twenty-five years later he had been crushed. I wiped my eyes as I drove down the back road toward St. Michael's.

The sun was almost gone when I pulled into the parking lot. It was quiet, except for a few birds off in the distance and lightning bugs flickering dreamily in the field between the chapel and St. Michael's church. Though it was after nine o'clock, a little light still hung in the western sky. The church was a dark silhouette against it.

Inside there was some other guy in the pew where the old lady usually knelt, but I hardly noticed as I genuflected in the aisle, knelt down in my usual spot, and poured out my agony. I struggled to keep quiet. It went on for a while. Michelle wasn't worried about me. She was staying with her mom and Nicole that night.

I cried, prayed, and screamed at Him in my mind, asking why? *Why did the old man become a victim? He was tough. How was it that they were able to crush him?* When I looked up at Him hanging, the answer came. *The cross is the answer.* After an hour with Him, there were always answers. Inside.

But I was in the chapel for more than an hour that night, and I asked the same questions over and over. I stared at the crucifix hanging up front. There was the answer. It was hard to accept, but it just *was*.

He knew. He suffered right along with me.

There was no answer; there was every answer. There was no reason; the reason was gone. There was no enlightenment now, at this time. A period of darkness was descending again, and somehow I knew that this time was all time for Him, as He hung there.

I took my eyes from Him hanging and looked at the monstrance. His body was exposed, seemingly as helpless as we were even though He had more power than the highest ones stepping on us at the time. He had much more power than the sharks. And He had more power than the ones who were pulling their strings—those who had betrayed us.

They had betrayed Him as well, over and over again, ever since the first betrayal in the garden of Eden. And always—every time—the same dark force was behind it. Crawling along looking for weakness to exploit. Evil was real, and Christ was still betrayed every day. And denied as well, but He took it. He put up with it patiently. He gave us an example to follow, and also a way to fight back. His way, while turning the other cheek.

You are a Mystery, a Paradox, the Alpha and the Omega, the Beginning and the End.

Answers came.

He had always been here and always would be, for all time. Always.

I am nothing.

You are everything to Me.

Men were small inconsequential ants whom He looked down upon. Ants or small animals chasing their tails, running around in circles, stupidly wasting the time He'd given us—we whom He had created, and whom He loved. He could see us frantically building, hoarding and working, and He called out to us, telling us not to do it because we were not created for this.

I am nothing...nothing...nothing.

You are everything to Me.

God was exposed, as helpless as we were yet He was also the King of Kings. He had the power.

How can this be? It's a paradox.

I Am.

Where is our Freedom? How is it that we are becoming slaves?

They are deceived.

How can they be?

They do not seek the truth. It will always be there. Truth.

Then why must we suffer?

The current evil was the same force driving the Pharisees, the elites of His day. He stood before them, already betrayed, already arrested, already beaten, already dragged through the streets. But it wasn't enough for them; they wanted Him dead. They sent Him to Pilate then, the prototype of a slimy politician, and He submitted to that and stated the fact that He'd come to testify to the Truth. He was Truth. But then came the question, the one to which we still hadn't learned the answer: *What is Truth?*

That particular set of elites had been blind, even as He performed miracles among them. *And they were supposed to be the smart ones.*

They were the educated, the rich, the intelligent and the teachers of the Law, but most of them were blind. It was still true today. It never changed throughout human perception of time and space. Not like God's time, He who felt our pain. His time was not the same as our time; His space was not the same. He was not constricted by time and space.

He felt, Him on the cross. Some people didn't realize it, but He felt. He *felt,* always, our suffering. All the time. He suffered but He also lived in Paradise, the cross leading to something else. Something indescribable in human words. Something I could feel inside, and that I knew would be mine someday if I stayed with Him. Something I prayed the old man was experiencing at that moment.

* * *

When I got up to leave there was someone else across the aisle. The fountain flowed peacefully as I walked out the door and saw the sun rising ahead of me.

I got in the truck, turned on the reading light and looked at the passenger seat where I had tossed the Bible before I went inside. By that time I had finished St. Matthew's Gospel and moved on to St. Mark. The Bible had finally lost its cover, but I had fixed it with duct tape. It was open again. I glanced down, careful not to touch it. The duct tape didn't let it lay open flat, and I wanted to make sure I was reading the right page. I put my hand between the pages and picked it up.

James, chapter four... Causes of Division. Phrases jumped off the page at me. *Where do the wars and where do the conflicts among you come from...your passions that make war... You covet but do not possess...you kill and envy but you cannot obtain; you fight and wage war... because you ask wrongly. Adulterers... Do you not know...to be a lover of the world means enmity with God... But he bestows a greater grace... God resists the proud, but gives grace to the humble.*

I drove home and took a shower and went to work.

TWENTY-THREE

Jason
3 Years Earlier

Michelle took the rest of the week off to spend time with her Mom and Nicole, but she was scheduled to work on Saturday, and she got up early to go running. I couldn't go with her that morning. I kissed her goodbye, got in the truck, and drove to the old man's to pick up my mother-in-law and Nicole. Michelle had said goodbye to them the night before.

Once their baggage was checked at the airport I walked them inside.

"You'll be okay from here, won't you?" I couldn't stay. I had to get to work.

"We'll be fine." Nicole smiled at me.

"Goodbye, Jason," said Michelle's mother. "Thank you for everything."

I hugged her. "Call Michelle and let her know when you're coming home. Johnny or I will pick you up."

"All right." She smiled sadly. I kissed them both and went on to work.

* * *

I was out in the shed when Brad finally called. It was eleven o'clock, and I had almost decided he'd forgotten. I lit a last cigarette, poured another shot and drank it down, and was just getting ready to shut off the light when the phone rang.

"Brad. What took you so long?"

"I'm on my way up," he answered, his tone dull and flat. *Brad?* It didn't sound like him.

"What? Why?"

"Mom's with me. The plane's taking off in three hours. Meet me at the airport at five-fifteen."

"What are you talking about?"

"I'm bringing her back."

"Who?" *Brad? Brad?* Then he started crying—almost screaming—worse than the night of the old man's death.

"Brad," I said sharply. No answer. "Brad. Answer me!"

He was still sobbing wildly. "Let me talk to your mom," I said. *"Mom!"* I yelled into the phone. *"What's going on?"* But there was only the sound of Brad's strangled sobbing. I couldn't hear his mother.

"Brad? Where are you?"

I waited a minute. The crying became a little less intense and he finally choked out: "In my car at the airport." I could hardly understand him.

"What's wrong?"

"It's bad. I don't want to say it."

"Just tell me." The water shock came to me along with a terrible sense of dread. I realized I was scared to death.

"Jason—" he broke off. I knew it was bad then...really bad. Brad never addressed me by my given name. I'd been Wallace to him for over twenty-five years, and there was no way at all he'd be calling me Jason if it was anything other than the end of the world. Tears sprang to my eyes. *Someone else died... Is it one of the babies?*

"Brad, just spit it out. Where's Nicole? Let her tell me. Is it one of the girls? What is it?" My hand shook as I poured another shot. Whiskey splashed over the glass.

"Nicole's dead."

My heart lurched into my stomach. I gulped down the whiskey.

"Oh my God. Brad, she can't be, what are you saying? Put your mom on the phone."

I heard him take a breath. He was quiet for a minute before speaking again.

"She's dead too... I'm bringing her back."

"*What?*" I whispered it into the phone.

"They're gone. Wallace, they're *gone*. It was a car crash."

"Oh my God... No."

Both of us broke down. We cried on the phone the way we had in the garage, but finally we stopped. Then Brad managed to tell me what had happened.

He hadn't been able to meet them at the airport because he'd been forced to deal with a fresh complaint from his co-worker that afternoon. There was no documentation of course; just the hag and her dislike of Brad. She'd had it in for him since the day he went against her on the little girl, and even the fact that his father had died didn't make her let up on him. He started to tell me about the complaint.

"You don't need to explain that unless you want to. I know she's lying about you. Just tell me the rest of it."

"Okay. She was lying again, but I had to meet with her and my supervisor. I couldn't get out of it, so I called Nicole's cell. She said she'd get her brother."

"Which one?"

"Matty. He's dead too."

"Oh my God."

Matty was only twenty-five. Brad went on to tell me that the car had gone out of control and flipped all the way over, they thought more than once, before landing in a ditch. The cops weren't sure what had happened; there was only one set of skid marks. They surmised that a deer had jumped out of the woods. Trees bordered that stretch of highway. It had been happening on a regular basis in the year following the hunting ban, but there was no way of knowing for sure. No one witnessed the accident, or if anyone had they didn't stop. Brad got the call about fifteen minutes after the meeting at work. He met his in-laws at the hospital, and they identified the bodies.

"Brad. I am so sorry." I was crying again, and so was he.

"I left her there. In the morgue. They're doing an autopsy on Matty, but I know damn well he was okay. It was only two o'clock. No way he was drunk. It was a deer. I had to leave her alone there. I didn't know what else to do—I have to bring Mom back. Her parents have the girls."

"Brad... It's all right, brother, she'll be okay there till you get back."

"My baby's gone. How can she be gone? My girls are motherless, Wallace. What the hell am I gonna do without her?"

I had no answer for him.

* * *

I told Brad I'd be waiting at the airport for him and he hung up. Then I went crazy on the punching bag, wishing it were the son of a bitch who'd been behind the hunting ban. After a while the bag wasn't giving me enough resistance so I started on the cinder block wall. I wasn't wearing gloves, and before I realized what I was doing I had bloodied my knuckles. My right hand was a mess, split open with blood dripping everywhere. *What am I going to tell Michelle?* I wrapped my hands in an old rag from under the workbench. *How am I going to tell her? God help me...*

The phone rang. It was Johnny. I hit the button with my bloody hand.

"Yeah." My voice was hoarse. Brad had called him, and he was crying now too. I told him how sorry I was about his mom.

"Does Michelle know?"

"No. Not yet. I'll tell her before I leave for the airport."

The indescribable hellishness of telling my wife that her mother was dead is something I can't put into words. I will say only that she was asleep when I finally went back to the house, and I refused to tell her in our bedroom, where we planned for our child to be born.

I kept very quiet when I entered our room. She was in a deep sleep and didn't hear me as I went to my dresser for clean clothes and then to the kitchen to wash up. I scrubbed the blood spatters from my face and arms before bandaging my own hands. It was difficult, but I did it. Then I changed into clean cargo shorts and a shirt and transferred my wallet and smokes into the pockets. I threw the bloody rag from the shed into the trash. It was three o'clock in the morning. *God help me.*

I went into the bedroom and made her get up out of bed. I pulled her out of the room before she was fully awake, but she figured out something was wrong before we got to the door. I hurried her outside while she asked me over and over about what was wrong. I managed to get her in the truck. I wanted to drive away from the house before I told her but it didn't happen. I put my arms around her and sat with her while she shrieked and cried.

* * *

I took Michelle with me to the airport. I refused to leave her alone in the state she was in, and she didn't want to go to Johnny's. After she calmed down a little she took a shower and made me stay with her. She wouldn't let me leave the bathroom. When she was ready I followed her to the truck, thinking she might be in shock. She was devastated, and I was afraid she might miscarry. *There's no way she's keeping this baby...not with all this. God. Please. Let us have our child.*

I decided that if the baby died I would find the people who had done this to us. *I'll split my freaking knuckles open for real if she loses our child. I'll make them wish they'd never seen the light of day.* We were driving up the interstate. Eighteen-wheelers seemed to fly backward on my right as I sped toward Philly. *I'll find the sons of bitches. And they'll be sorry.*

I heard the water then. It rushed in a torrent and with it came a voice that only I could hear. This experience was completely different than what I perceived in front of the Lord at St. Michael's, but it still brought Him to mind.

No. You must not do this thing.

I drove steadily, aware that there was something else with us in the truck—something big and bright. It was the same light that I had always seen in the corner of my eyes, but bigger. When I glanced over I saw only my crushed and weeping shell of a wife, yet the brightness was there, just out of my peripheral vision. It was strong—a bright and ethereal light. I paid attention.

Put these thoughts away. Such things are not in His plan for you.

But look at my wife.

Michelle sat as close to me as she could. She leaned across the console and rested her hand on my thigh. It was fine with me, but I knew why she was doing it. She was afraid of losing everything, including me. She hadn't stopped crying since I told her about the deaths.

She loses this baby they'll wish they'd never been born.

No. I tell you no. Those who live by the sword shall also die by it. Put such thoughts away immediately.

The brightness disappeared. Michelle and I were alone in the truck on the airport exit. *What was that? And what plan?* But I soon put it out of my mind along with any thought of the loss of my child, knowing Brad would need my strength for the week ahead.

* * *

Though the next week was more hellish than the previous one, at least it seemed like the end of something—the end of a sort of scourging. Nicole's funeral in Memphis marked the end of it for our family. We were whipped.

My life hadn't really been easy you understand, but up until that point my pain had at least been only my own. This time it was also my wife's. Never in my wildest dreams had I fathomed how much it would hurt to feel such anguish. The situation messed up my head. I'll try to explain it, but be warned: my actions in Memphis may seem to be those of a person on the edge of insanity.

Michelle's mother's service was private. Only the family was present at the Mass and afterward when we buried her next to the old man. Brad refused to have another public funeral. He still had to get through the funerals of Nicole and her brother.

The deaths had devastated Brad. He wasn't himself, and he insisted on a private service. He said his mother would forgive us, and suggested we hold a memorial service at some point in the future. We left for Memphis the same day we buried his mom, two hours after we put her in the ground.

Michelle stayed with Cindy. I refused to let her travel to Memphis because I was afraid any more stress would cause a miscarriage. Brad agreed with me. He told Michelle that he wanted her to stay home, and she didn't argue.

Even though I didn't trust Junior, it turned out to be for the best. Junior hadn't been fully indoctrinated at that point, and the fact that three members of his family had just been eaten by the sharks he served may have given him some food for thought. At any rate, he didn't bother Michelle while I was gone.

We took Johnny's four-wheel drive. He and I took turns driving.

Brad sat in the passenger seat, blaming himself for the accident. He said it never would have happened if he'd been there to pick them up the way he should have, seeming to forget the reason he was unable to meet them—the fact that he was being harassed at work for doing what he thought of as his job.

I finally put a stop to it, refusing to let him blame himself. We told Brad he'd done the right thing by trying to help the little girl, and that if there were any justice in the world the witch would have been sent packing the very same day it happened. But there was no justice under the sharks. What was part of the job description when Brad started his career was now against the law, just like that. The whole thing was ass-backward.

I spent most of the trip pondering the situation. I sat in the back seat looking at the back of Brad's head as we drove him home to bury his thirty-five year old wife. She'd been the mother of two babies, and she had died needlessly. *Needlessly*.

I had trouble believing the facts. To me they seemed crazy, and there were times during the drive when I thought I might be going insane. I'll list these facts, along with my thoughts about them.

Fact number one: My father-in-law had died from his diabetes due to lack of medical care. In this new day of modern healthcare in America, the old man died a horrible death in his own house, and not one of us was able to prevent it. The description of his death is something I can't bring myself to put down in words. I'll say only that his suffering was unimaginable, and that such a thing would have been unheard of twenty years earlier.

Back then he could have had it amputated, and he would have without a second thought. It would have given him another ten years, tough as he was. He'd be alive right this minute, and so would Nicole and Michelle's mom.

Which brings us to fact number two: The old man's death wasn't enough for them. The sharks were still hungry, so his wife and his son's wife and her brother were killed in a senseless accident that would never have happened if they had only left us alone.

Fact three: Everything that had happened to our family was the polar opposite of what was being jammed through the media by the drones. Examples abounded of kids and babies and moms who'd been saved by the new healthcare laws, and each and every story was the opposite of what had been jammed back before it had been enacted. Back then all the examples had been negative. Now there was no negativity except for ours. The sharks considered us collateral damage—something unavoidable during the remaking of a society, and examples of which had no place in the media.

I was forced to listen to the propaganda during parts of the drive. Johnny turned on the radio every time he got behind the wheel, and there was always a story about healthcare. It was always the same story too—that Americans were enjoying the best healthcare available, much better than that which our parents and grandparents had received.

"Turn that shit off," I snapped from the backseat.

"No. I'm driving right now, and I want it on. When you take the wheel in Roanoke you can turn it off."

He said hearing what the drones were spewing was a help to him. He knew it was lies and propaganda of course, but said the ability to listen to the lies while simultaneously remembering what had just happened was an exercise in resistance.

"Listening to their shit is strengthening my resolve. It'll keep me from ever forgetting. So shut the hell up."

I did, of course, and as the day wore on strange scenes began going through my mind. I got the idea that the drones were mutating into hideous chattering spiders spinning giant webs of lies. *But why not? They work for the sharks, don't they?* My knuckles weren't the only things that were split during that interval of time.

The drive to Memphis was one of the strangest experiences of my life up to that point. Images of what had happened to our family slashed wickedly through my head, along with images of Christ and His suffering. I could see Him being scourged as I leaned my head back and closed my eyes while Johnny drove through Virginia. I saw Him tied to the pillar in the Roman garrison, His back flayed raw by the cat-o'-nine-tails.

And then I felt our pain as we were whipped raw by images of rawhide thongs braided together like a nest of snakes. Not tipped with lead, the way whips were in Roman times, but with shark's teeth. The sharks were responsible for Brad's pain, and I could feel his anguish; we were brothers, after all. He talked to his babies on the phone and tried to answer their questions about their mother. They didn't understand, of course. They weren't even two years old.

Though I prayed a little during the drive, I wasn't really following God. I was far away from Him while I was in Memphis.

I had a gun with me. We'd divided the old man's guns up after his funeral. That was the main reason we were driving and not flying—so Brad could take his gun back to Memphis. I'd been given the old man's Colt forty-five, and it was packed in my duffel bag. I had something in mind, you see, a little resistance of my own. It felt good to think about some justice, and my experience at the funeral two days later only made me more determined.

Nicole's coffin was next to her brother's. Brad stood with a little girl on either side, holding their hands. They didn't understand what had happened to their mother, but they cried just the same. I could see the whip, looking like a twisting bunch of snakes, rising, thwacking, and drawing blood. Then I felt the scourging, as Brad raised a red rose to his lips. He laid it on Nicole's casket, picked up his girls, and walked away with tears streaming down his face.

TWENTY-FOUR

Michelle

It's dim in Patty's room, and the only sound is that of the fan in the corner as it oscillates back and forth. Patty and Melanie insisted that I come up here to rest while they're canning peaches. I'm lying on my side again, the only comfortable position I can find.

The quilt on the bed is another that belonged to Patty's mother. She tells me Orie sewed it after Adela had run away. The name of the pattern is Double Wedding Ring. Orie had saved the scrap fabric in the quilt from her worn out aprons and dresses, along with clothes Adela had worn as a child.

As I trace the scraps that form interlocking rings, I think about weddings over the years. Orie was married at fourteen. What must that have been like?

My parents had a happy marriage. *Why did it have to end?* They were married at the courthouse in West Chester five years after Daddy's return from Vietnam, and their marriage was blessed in the Church at St. Catherine's on the same day Johnny was baptized. Daddy finally converted to Catholicism the year Brad was born. There were no wedding pictures around the house when I was growing up, though. Mom had an album somewhere, but every time I asked she put me off. I finally looked at the pictures last year. She was only eighteen when she married Daddy. Johnny was born five months later, but they were friends first, Mom and Daddy. He helped her get over her brother's death.

When I look back on my own wedding I can still see Jason waiting for me by the altar with my brother standing next to him as always. Friends... *forever? Please, Brad. Won't you forgive us?* Jason was happy that day. There were no tears in his eyes.

Daddy tried to convince Jason to wear his Air Force dress blues to the wedding, but Jason declined, and of course Daddy didn't push him. So your daddy wore a tuxedo that day. He was still the best looking man I'd ever laid eyes on. Everyone knew it but Jason. He looked like a model standing up there at the altar, but he didn't know it. The concept of vanity doesn't exist for Jason. And he had eyes only for me.

I was a virgin on our wedding day, though the waiting was hard, especially for Jason. But what if we'd been born in another time, another place? Maybe we wouldn't have had to wait. Maybe I would have married at fourteen.

Brad was handsome in his tux, blonde haired and blue-eyed like me. He and Jason have been like brothers for almost forty years. I'm praying that Brad will forgive us for deceiving him. We're doing it for him. The thought of your birth, angel, and escaping to Memphis to reunite with Brad is something I let myself think about now. I want to see my brother. I want to feel his arms around my shoulders as I cry on his, asking forgiveness. I want to hear his voice telling me everything changes, except us...the three of us.

I let myself think about it now because I believe it will happen. I let myself dream of seeing Annie and Taylor. I'm dozing as the fan blows over me, seeing these things in my mind and hoping we can talk Brad into leaving Memphis with us.

We can't stay with him. Junior will look for us there, and if he so much as suspects that Brad is helping us, Annie and Taylor will be taken from Brad. I lay on the quilt, worrying about Brad, my big brother, whom I love. It's different than my love for Johnny, who is fifteen years older than I am. Brad and I have something special. But I know we can't stay with him, even though I dream of it. We can't chance staying with Brad and the girls, because if he loses his children my brother is as good as dead.

Jason
3 Years Earlier

I went to the pharmacy the day after the funerals. Brad was already back at work. He was stronger than I could ever hope to be. Johnny and I took care of the twins that day, to give Nicole's mom some time to get herself together before she had to begin caring for them full time.

The morning was exhausting. When the girls weren't crying for Nicole, they splashed in a little pool, ran around the yard playing, and asked us to push them on the swings. Johnny was in charge of Annie, and I took care of Taylor since she was my goddaughter. Unfortunately for me, Taylor's screaming capacity was much longer than her sister's. I still remember one fifteen-minute interval that seemed to go on for at least an hour. It went something like this: "Where's Mommy?" A high pitched, lisping baby voice.

"Baby-doll, let's go swing." I smiled down at her. "Uncle Jason will push you higher than before."

"Mommy," she said.

"Come on sweetie-pie. Let's play with Annie."

"Daddy." Her big blue eyes had tears in them.

"Taylor, Daddy's working. He'll be home soon. Its almost time for lunch honey, what do you want to eat? Uncle Jason will fix anything you want." I picked her up.

"Mommy. Mommy. *Mommeeeee!*" She began to scream, and I tried to comfort her. Brad had already told us what to say. "Taylor... Taylor, baby. Mommy's fine, honey. But she can't come. She's living with Jesus now. She lives in Heaven. See? Honey, look."

I took a picture from my pocket and showed it to her. It was a picture of the Blessed Mother holding her mantle up with her hands. The mantle covered various people. Brad had cut Nicole's face out of a snapshot and pasted it over one of the faces.

"Look baby...see? That's Jesus' mommy. She's everyone's mommy, and your mommy lives with her and Jesus now. She's happy with her mommy in Heaven...see honey?" She snuffled against my neck. "Taylor, don't cry...come on sweetheart. Let's play. Let's go get your car."

Johnny was able to get Annie to sleep as soon as she finished eating her lunch, but Taylor cried again for a good half hour. I held her and walked back and forth with her before I finally panicked and tried to give her to Johnny, who laughed in my face.

"Take her Johnny. She wants you...you can get her to calm down." I was holding her out in front of me as she screamed and thrashed her legs.

"Oh, no," Johnny said, laughing. "You deal with it. You're gonna have to at home soon enough."

I was glad to see Johnny laugh, you understand. I hadn't heard him laugh in months. If he found my distress amusing I was fine with it, but his laughter didn't help my shattered eardrums. I was desperate for the crying to stop, so I finally gave Taylor a lollipop, and after a few minutes she fell asleep.

I pried the lollipop out of her sticky fingers and threw it away before taking the baby to her crib. I went to the bathroom to wash up then, and changed into clean clothes before going back downstairs to get the truck keys from Johnny.

"I need some air. Give me the keys. I'll fill the gas tank and pick up some stuff for the drive home. Do you need cigarettes?"

"Yeah," he said. "If you can't find Lucky Strikes get me a pack of Camels."

I got in the truck and drove to the drugstore. I had already looked up directions online; Johnny didn't have a GPS. I wanted to see the place. I'd been wondering if it would look different than other drugstores. I thought there might be something to clue me in about the things Brad said went on in the neighborhoods surrounding the place, things he was now forced to take part in by law. *Not really though. The sharks only think they're forcing him.*

When I went inside everything appeared normal. There were only a few customers. The shelves were sparsely stocked, but that was commonplace throughout the country now and it didn't stand out at all. It could have been any other workplace. My head ached as I strolled through the aisles looking at greeting cards, cell phones, soap and pain relievers. I remembered what Brad said he had to deal with every day, but it was hard to reconcile it with the seeming normality of the store. I saw no sign of anything shady. No men accompanied by scared and scrawny-looking under aged hookers came into the store while I was roaming the aisles. Lucky for them —and me.

How the hell does Brad stand this? He worked for six years to earn a degree and now he's expected to hand poison to underage girls? Maybe it's not really happening. Maybe Brad's exaggerating. But I knew he wasn't. Brad would never lie about such a thing, especially to me. *I better get out of here before something happens. I need to think about this. Brad doesn't need me giving him any more worries. He's doing the best he can.*

I went up to the counter for a minute. Brad was busy in back. The tech had to tell him I was waiting. He was surprised to see me.

"What are you doing down here?"

"I don't know. My ears are ringing. Taylor took a while to fall asleep." Brad laughed a little at my words.

"She's okay though, isn't she?"

"Yeah," I reassured him. "But I screwed it up—taking care of her, I mean. She cried on and off all morning. I couldn't stand it anymore, so I finally gave her a lollipop to get her to be quiet."

"Whatever." Brad laughed again. "I've done it myself a few times. It won't kill her. But when she wakes up, could you please make her brush her teeth? I'll be home around five-thirty."

"Okay. What do you want for dinner? Johnny wants barbecue again."

"I don't care. Wallace, why don't you stay another day?" I could tell he was upset at the idea of an evening alone with the babies. I thought for a minute.

"Maybe we'll leave early tomorrow morning. Johnny'll be all right with that. I need some sleep anyway before trying to drive." I was still exhausted. The events of the morning had given me a new respect for anyone who stayed at home with a child. Brad looked at his watch then, and I knew he had to get back to work, so I told him everything would be under control when he got home. "I'll see you later."

I walked out of the store and back to the truck. I got behind the wheel and sat in silence for a moment. Then I was holding the gun in my hands, turning it over and over, remembering what I'd been planning. The thought of it made me break out in a sweat. It poured down in rivers, soaking my shirt. I felt sick to my stomach, remembering the words: *Do not go down that path... those who live by the sword will also die by it.*

Like I said, there were no little girls in the pharmacy. No men had come in looking to get rid of an inconvenient consequence while I was inside. But if one had, he would have been sorry. Because I had it in mind that I was going to get the son of a bitch aside somehow. I didn't know how exactly, but I'd been determined to find a way. Determined to get him where no one could see, take out the old man's gun, and pistol whip him. That was my real reason for being there. I looked down at the gun, feeling sicker than I had a minute earlier. *What in God's name was I thinking?*

I was surprised no one had noticed. I was lucky that day as I walked around the store with a suspicious bulge in the small of my back, looking for a piece of shit pimp so I could teach him a lesson.

It wasn't a small gun and it wasn't easy to conceal. If a cop had happened to see me—or even a security guard—I'd be sitting in a Memphis jail still. I know that now. But I wasn't thinking clearly while I was in Brad's store, and nothing would have made me happier right then than finding one of the scum he'd told me about, getting him aside somehow, and taking him out back where they kept the trash. It would have been sweet to tell the bastard why I was doing it before bringing the gun butt down on his molesting head. It would have been so sweet. *Those who live by the sword shall also die by it.*

I knew I was lucky. Actually, I believe I was blessed. Even though I was going against Him the whole time, I think He made sure—sure that my stupidity and hotheadedness didn't lead to my undoing.

I was under His watch. I was the one who was far away, not Him. He was always there.

Maybe He sent an angel (*This is not in His plan for you*) to prevent anyone from coming into the pharmacy. Or maybe He hid me from anyone who would have gotten suspicious. I've read of such things; incidents where His followers were hidden from harm until it was their time. He had plans for me. And by His grace nothing happened that day. *Thank you God.*

I started the engine, still in a sweat, and drove back toward Brad's, stopping for gas and loading the truck with cigarettes, water, sodas, and junk food. Michelle and Cindy had packed stuff for the trip down, but it was all gone, and Johnny and I weren't too particular about nutrition when we could get away with it. We decided to get some sleep that night and leave around four a.m.

The twins were fine that evening as long as Brad was there. He let them stay up until eight o'clock since it was our last night with them. We tried to distract them with a game of tag, but still they kept asking where mommy was. Brad answered patiently in a matter of fact tone. Somehow he managed to keep control of himself, but I could tell every question cut him like a knife. At bedtime Johnny and I hugged and kissed each of them goodbye, promising to come back to visit with Aunt Michelle and Aunt Cindy. Then Brad took them upstairs for a story. He read to them every night, and then he turned off the light and shut the door. They each had a nightlight, and they were used to falling asleep with just each other for company.

After they settled down I told Brad about what I'd been planning that afternoon. Johnny was taking a shower.

"Damn Wallace." Brad's tone was shocked. "That sounds more like something I'd do." He had a speculative look in his eye.

"Well don't get any ideas." I held up my hand. "I was acting like a frigging idiot. I can't believe I even brought the damn thing down here." I was referring to the old man's Colt.

Brad raised an eyebrow. "Well, you didn't really need the old man's gun. That piece I got off the street is big enough to cold cock any child-molesting piece of shit that happens to cross your path. You could have taken it." He still sounded speculative.

"Don't be a fool. Tell me you're not going to try anything. My stupidity was enough for both of us."

Brad kept quiet, but I could see the wheels spinning in his head. The monitor sat on the end table. We could hear the babies chattering back and forth upstairs.

"I could be in a freaking jail right now," I went on. "What would Michelle do without me?" I gestured to the monitor. Annie's high voice drifted out of it, singing some Disney princess song. Brad held my gaze, but he still didn't answer.

"Brad!" I barked. "Don't be a fool." He glared back defiantly. And then it was gone.

"All right Wallace." He sighed. "I'm not gonna try anything like that. I'm already throwing a wrench in their operation anyway. But you should have told me earlier. We could have done it together. Now you're leaving and it's too late. There was one in there this morning; maybe we could have gotten him."

"You know we can't. Our hands are tied. We have to act like the grownups. Just because they're acting like a freaking bunch of glorified teenagers, running around with everything hanging out doesn't mean we should."

"I guess so," he said with a shrug.

"Anyway, we're not supposed to deal with things that way. You know how the old man was."

"Well the old man also had a bit of a temper."

"I know. And don't mention this to Johnny. He'll probably knock me upside the head, and I don't need it. I know it was stupid."

"Okay. But the old man would have agreed with us and you know it."

"He would have agreed. But he wouldn't have gone after one of them unless they were threatening the family outright."

"They already are," Brad replied hotly. "They killed the old man and you know it—and Nicole and Mom. Not to mention Junior. The sons of bitches are brainwashing that kid."

"That's true. But there's nothing we can do right now except resist it the way we have been. And you be careful," I warned him. "Don't you dare get caught. You start getting any ideas, go sit in the church—it helps me."

"Yeah, and I can't believe that," he laughed. "You in the church every other week."

"The old man would be telling you the same thing."

"I know. I just went to confession the other day."

"Just don't do anything stupid," I repeated with finality. I gestured to the monitor again. The twins were quiet.

"All right. No one suspects anything at the store. I don't think they know how anyway; they think everyone else is just like them.

Running around with their flies unzipped and their mouths hanging open, just like you said. And that goes for the whole freaking bunch of them from the top on down."

"Yeah," I agreed. We sat there in silence then. As I reflected on the stupidity of my actions I thought about the risks Brad was running at the pharmacy and prayed his luck would hold out. *Hide him, God. He's resisting.*

We were both resisting, and anything either of us had done up to that point was in response to being pushed, whipped, and crushed by the sharks. They had it in their minds they were going to break us. *But there's no way they're breaking me...or running me.*

"They're not running me." I muttered under my breath.

"Neither of us," Brad said.

We were committed.

TWENTY-FIVE

Michelle

Blessed Mother, how did it feel to be taken away from your home in Nazareth? Was it as hard for you as it is for me? Maybe it was worse. You ended up in another country. How old was your Son when your husband received word from the angel that Herod was dead and that it was safe for you to go home?

Please turn your merciful eyes to my brother. Ask your Son to help Brad. He's alone in Memphis with only his children and their grandparents, and he doesn't know we're still family. Pray for us Holy Mother. We love Brad and we love our baby. And we love you and your Son.

Jason
3 Years Earlier

A couple of weeks after my return from Memphis I went to confession and told Father Gallucio everything. It was awkward. I had trouble admitting I had almost lost my mind over what had happened in the family.

Father lectured me for ten minutes, and that was fine with me. I deserved a dressing down. Then he dropped my penance on me.

"You need a wake-up call. Go out in the church and pray the Rosary for your penance, and while you're praying think about our Blessed Mother as she stood watching her Son dying on a cross. Think about her and what she said while He was dying."

"What did she say, Father?"

"Scripture doesn't record her words. Maybe she didn't say anything with words. But she said something just the same. And she still loves us, we who are the reason He died that way."

"Father," I protested, "Mass will be starting soon and I'm wearing work clothes." My jeans were stained with grease. "I can't go out there and pray looking like this. And I don't even know the Rosary."

He shuffled around on the counter behind him and held out a card. "Here, take this."

"But there are people out there."

"It'll teach you a lesson," he said shortly.

I considered arguing further, but I knew it wouldn't do any good. Anyway, maybe I needed to think. I could have been locked in a Memphis jail at the time instead of contemplating the humility of the Lord's Mother, so I shut up and took the card.

"Pray the Sorrowful Mysteries even though it's Saturday, and think about her," Father said, before going on to give me absolution.

"Thank you Father."

I went out, knelt in the back pew, and began praying on my fingers, following the directions on the card. People were coming in. I felt like everyone was staring at my big clumsy self, and it was hard to keep my mind on His Mother. But as I prayed I realized more fully what a narrow escape I had been blessed with.

Contemplating the Virgin and the way she had stood tall at the Cross made cringe at the memory of my actions. She didn't break down and cry like Mary Magdalene or desert Him the way all the disciples did except John. She actually stood at the foot of the cross and watched her Son as he suffered the mockery and torture before He died.

Where would Michelle be right now if I had attacked someone and got caught? What about the baby? And I'm supposed to be a man? She was stronger than any man.

I vowed never to lose control that way again. I deserved much worse than feeling like a fool, kneeling and trying to pray in front of the whole church as they came in for Mass. He had saved me from what I truly deserved.

I thought more about things on the drive to St. Michael's. Though I doubted my mother was thrilled at the prospect, she would be my child's only grandparent. Then I began wondering about my father and where he might be. We had lost touch. After he walked out he never called or visited, but he did send Christmas and birthday gifts without fail. Each gift seemed to have been chosen with a great deal of thought, especially for me.

He had always known exactly what I wanted on any given year. He sent gift cards for music and sporting goods stores and subscriptions to hot rod and sport fishing magazines. When I turned sixteen he gave me a brand new cell phone. But though he renewed the contract every year until I left for basic training, I never received a call from him on the phone. When I graduated he sent a check for five thousand dollars with the words *Congratulations Jason Michael* in the memo line. The card was signed simply: *Your loving father, Michael Wallace.*

I drove slowly down the back road toward St. Michael's, fighting off memories of the time before he left. An image of old LPs lined up on the workbench in the garage behind the house ran through my head, and my eyes started to sting. *Stop. It's over. He walked out and left me with her.*

He had left me whatever the reason, and I pushed away the

memories deliberately. I'd been doing it for years; it hurt too much. But the thought that my mother would be my baby's only grandparent hurt worse. *Why did he go? Maybe I should look for him. I can almost understand why he'd want out of there. But Mom will never tell me where he is.*

I'd never get any information out of Mom. However Jeremy had given me the return address on his graduation card from Dad, who had been living in Wichita at the time. *Maybe I'll start from Wichita. After the baby's born.*

I pulled into St. Michael's, parked the truck, and sweated in the humidity as I walked across the parking lot. We'd been having a streak of heat ever since I got back from Memphis. Thunder rumbled in the distance even though the sun was bright in the sky, but inside the chapel it was cool. I dipped my hand in the holy water, genuflected and knelt, feeling better than I had since the moment of the old man's death. After absolution, there in the peace of His presence, I felt okay.

I prayed that the old man and Michelle's mom and Nicole were with Him in His real presence the same way I was at that moment. Being there was almost like going back to when your father taught you things, and you looked up at him and reached for his hand. You had to become a child again, not letting the ideas of the world enter your mind.

The ideas of the world... Like the notion that being in His real presence wasn't possible. That was the ultimate irony; the people who most needed Him refused to open their narrow minds to the possibility of His existence. Some actually seemed to have the goal of resisting *Him,* and the ultimate goal of scrubbing Him, the creator of all, from His creation.

I wondered whether such people understood the end result of their ideas, and what they thought would happen if they were finally able to scrub all knowledge of Him. It wasn't as if it hadn't already been tried. That had happened during the previous century with predictable results. It wasn't even a hundred years earlier that Communism killed untold millions, but no one seemed worried about it except a few of us.

Do they actually think they can make it work this time around? God... Why did You take the old man away from me?

The sound of the fountain was soothing. *The old man's with Him now...he's in a better place. Way too many people down here are on board with the sharks and their agenda.*

I looked up at the monstrance and contemplated the Host, exposed and filling this place with His presence. *How do they get through each day?*

What got me through was being able to give the feelings of heartache, confusion, anger, and helplessness to Him. He hadn't given them to me, no, but He always took them off me. Being in His presence gave me the strength to persevere through all that we had to endure now. *But the sharks want to scrub Him—that's their goal.*

What am I going to do if I can't feel Your Presence here? Why won't they leave us alone?

They are deceived.

It's like swimming against the current all the time. The world is hard. God, help Brad.

Brad had called the previous evening. We talked every few days, and he always started out cussing and ended up crying. I was the only one he could talk to about Nicole.

"I still can't believe she's gone. What am I gonna do without her?"

I kept quiet and smoked, just listening. Brad continued in the same vein for a time and then said: "I'm sorry to keep laying this on you, but I gotta talk to somebody."

"I don't mind listening. Keep talking if it helps you."

"Well I think you understand what I'm talking about."

"I think I do," I agreed. "I don't know what I'd do without Michelle. How are the babies?"

"The same. They wake up in the middle of the night crying for her. I'm usually still downstairs. I can't sleep in my room."

"Just make sure you get enough sleep. Go to the doctor. Get him to prescribe something."

"Screw that. I'm not going to any shark doctor. If I need anything I'll get it myself." He changed the subject then. "I know you probably heard about the latest HCA bullshit. What do you think?"

"What bullshit?"

"That new law that's going into effect in September. You had to have heard it by now. They're calling it the post-birth abortion rule. Not in the HCA, of course."

He was right; I knew about it. Johnny and I had heard mention of it in the truck on the way home.

"Yeah, I heard. I looked it up. It seems some of the language in the bill is so vague that they interpreted it to mean they have the authority. Court cases are pending. I read that it's unconstitutional. Maybe the Supreme Court will take it eventually."

"Maybe." Brad's tone was dismissive. "But you know how much faith we can put in them. And what about what happens in the meantime?"

"The girls will be two in September. They're both healthy. Nothing's going to happen."

"Well they better get the hell off my back after that. Supposedly they leave you alone if kids make it to age two. Healthy, I mean. I heard they start in on you again when they turn four. They assign full day preschool."

"Don't worry about that. That's two years away; a lot can happen in two years. Just keep them safe until they turn two."

"Thank God they're both healthy," he said. "What do you think would happen if one of them weren't? Or if one of them had a birth defect. This whole thing is so screwed up I can hardly think about it."

"I've been thinking about it," I replied.

"I bet you have. Lucky they don't know Michelle's pregnant. The girls are healthy, and they don't know about your child. Maybe we'll be okay."

I came back to the present then, still kneeling in the chapel with my head bowed. I had never seen Brad suffer so much. I wanted to do something for him, but there was nothing to be done except listen.

My conversations with Brad these days seemed surreal when I remembered the things we used to talk about. Our years in high school and our phone conversations later had been full of nothing but the world. Now both of us struggled to resist it.

It was time for me to leave. I got my mind back on the monstrance, thanked Him one more time for delivering me from my stupidity, and left His presence. The heat hit me in the face when I walked outside. I started the truck, opened the windows, and glanced to my right. The Bible was open on the passenger seat again. I paused for a moment before placing my hand in the gap between the pages and using the paper I'd taken on the way out—the coordinator's number—as a bookmark. I put the truck in gear, and leaving the music off, I drove toward town.

How did Brad just naturally figure out the right thing to do in all circumstances?

Brad had never been to adoration, and before Nicole converted to Catholicism he barely attended Mass at all. *What caused his transformation?* He went to Mass now, of course—Nicole made him after she converted and the babies needed to go. Michelle was on me too at this point. She said we had to set a good example for the baby. I told her she was the example, and that I attended enough, but she insisted we needed to get in a routine every week, together.

Michelle understood the world. No question about that. It was the reason she'd asked if I was happy after Jeremy's New Year's Eve party. She was worried about the women at the party, even though she hadn't the slightest idea that Stacy had propositioned me.

I was ashamed to admit it even to myself, but I had considered getting together with Stacy. She was an unwanted intrusion when she joined me on the balcony, but truth be told I had enjoyed the attention, even though I was feeling hurt by my mother's behavior— or maybe precisely for that reason. I enjoyed every minute of the encounter with Stacy that night, and it hadn't been easy to pull away from her.

I didn't take my hand off her until it was absolutely necessary— right before it would have been too late. I had almost started kissing her, and I kept her business card for a while. *What if Michelle had found it? I must have been crazy.*

I had gone to confession about it of course, but as far as I knew Brad hadn't struggled with any similar situations since he married Nicole. How did he do it?

If Brad had been propositioned at a party he would have told me. There was no way he would have kept such a thing from me, even though I told no one about my own temptation except Father Gallucio. Yet it had taken me hours of reflection to come to the same conclusions Brad seemed to without even trying.

All those episodes in the drugstore... And Brad does the right thing automatically even though the whole country is upside down. What does he have that I don't?

The answer hurt me. *He has the old man's blood in his veins... that's what. He's the old man's son.* Tears stung my eyes as I pulled into the driveway. *Whose blood do I have?* I shut off the truck, wiped my eyes and went on inside, taking the Bible. I gulped two glasses of water. *The heat is nasty. Like that deployment to the Middle East.*

But no, not really. I looked around at the house. Michelle did the cleaning, cooking and almost everything else. I was a spoiled husband. The place looked great, nothing like the desert. *Thank you God, for all you have given us. Thank you for my wife.*

Thunder rumbled again as I crossed the backyard to the shed, carrying the Bible. The sun glared through the hedge, and the air was still and unmoving. Heat blasted me when I opened the door, and I hurried to get my cigarettes, leaving the book on the workbench.

I leaned against the shed, smoking. Brad was the old man's son. *Whose son are you?*

Brad and I were like brothers. He treated me like a brother and always had—he shared everything with me. And even though the old man never told me in words, I knew he had considered me his son. But still...I didn't have his blood running through my veins. *What are you thinking? Brad can't help that.*

Was I jealous of Brad? *Whose blood is running through your veins?* Was that my problem now? *No. Brad and I are too close. We haven't even argued in years...since the time he thought I was neglecting Michelle.*

If I had been the old man's blood son, I could never have married Michelle. What I was thinking was crazy. *This is bullshit. I'm not letting myself be jealous of Brad. We're brothers. I'm closer to Brad than I am to Jeremy, that's for sure.*

I decided I was thinking this way because of my confusion about my father, and resolved to put any jealousy toward Brad out of my mind.

TWENTY-SIX

Jason
3 Years Earlier

When I finished my smoke I stepped back inside the shed. I went to the workbench and picked up the Bible, feeling that sensation again, the one that was missing in Memphis—a deep down knowledge in my gut that reading it would clarify things. I opened the book to the page I had marked in the truck. *Genesis Chapter 3: The Fall of Man.*

It told of the temptation of Adam and Eve in the Garden of Eden, and the tempter, which the author called the serpent. I knew about Adam and Eve of course, but I had never read about them myself. I never thought about them in light of what had been revealed to me, and I read on, fascinated.

What I read reinforced my earlier reflection of something shadowy and perverted, an evil that needed to be resisted. It was a force that was overcoming our country, and even the whole world now. It was dark and lurking...indescribable in human terms. The serpent just gave it a form that you could picture in your mind.

Man was tempted right from the first, and we're still being tempted today.

I read what God said to the serpent, telling him that he would be condemned to crawl and eat dirt. I understood that I could easily fall into that dirt. My memory of the New Year's Eve party was an illustration of it. *How could I have even thought about cheating on Michelle?*

I pondered the fact that temptation was part of being human. God had given us a higher consciousness, and we could think for ourselves. *Animals can't make choices. Humans have freedom to choose to follow His rules...or not.* It was another mystery, another paradox.

I will put enmity between you and the woman, and between your offspring and hers; He will strike at your head, while you strike at his heel. I remembered a movie I had seen twenty-five years earlier. The movie was about Christ's passion, and the scene depicted him in the garden of Gethsemane, enduring his agony while a nasty looking snake crawled toward him. Later on he crushed that snake right under the heel of his sandal. *Just like that.* He crushed it before going on to be betrayed.

It was incredibly hot in the shed. Sweat was pouring off me and I probably stunk to high heaven, but I continued reading, not wanting to take the time to go into the house where it was cooler.

Next God's words to the woman: *I will intensify the pangs of your childbearing; in pain shall you bring forth children.* Besides the literal pain of giving birth, women these days had the added pain of having to worry about what might be in store for their children with regards to DNA samples taken from them at birth. *That's real pain...* I had listened to Brad as he agonized about the pain Nicole endured before she died. He suffered over it too. *He's probably worrying about it right now as I'm reading this. But this isn't God's doing. No way.*

God hadn't put the ideology in place to let such a thing become normal. He hadn't forced such a horrible thing on us. We had chosen it. We were suffering the natural consequences of falling away from Him, and He had to let us suffer them because He was unchanging. It had happened before in history, over and over again. Now it was happening in America because the sharks tended not to believe in God. They believed in man, period. No wonder the whole thing was spiraling. When people forgot there was something bigger than themselves they usually became arrogant.

The story then went on to say that God told the man that the ground would be cursed because of what he had done, and what I took to be God sentencing the man to toil and work for his food and shelter now that he had disobeyed. Man had been given everything he needed, but he'd been tempted and had given in to that temptation. *And then he lost it all. Everything.*

The same way I'd been tempted by Stacy. And I had thought about giving in; I'd been arrogant myself that night, even in my hurt. *Hell, it could have been any one of them up there that night except for Lauren and a couple of others. They were all loose, every damn one of them, and most of them were good looking to boot. All of them were trolling for the next piece of ass.*

How could I? How could I have let myself be tempted that way? But I had. My stomach lurched as I thought about it. What if my arrogance had continued? Stacy had wanted to sleep with me. What if I had given in to my temptation? I was hurting that night because my mother had blindsided me again. She hurt my sweet Michelle and had let me know she didn't think my wife was good enough to even be socializing with people like Stacy. What would have happened if I continued to tell myself I could get back at my mother even if she'd never know anything about it? That I could do one of the whores she admired, roll off her, and walk out the freaking door the way I had so many times in the past?

What if I'd gone ahead with it? Where would I be right now? I would have lost everything as well... just like Adam and Eve. I would have lost Michelle if it had come out. I may have even lost her because I wouldn't have been able to live with myself afterward.

It was so easy to let temptation have its way...so easy. Verse 19: *Until you return to the ground, from which you were taken; For you are dirt, and to dirt you shall return.*

We were dirt, and we would return to dirt.

I had certainly been dirt on the balcony that night, thinking about having that tramp. She would probably have let me do her right outside my brother's door if I'd been so inclined—or so stupid. No thoughts of love entered my mind while I was wondering, either. I had actually thought it wouldn't matter. That Michelle was the love of my life, and that it wouldn't hurt just this once...*just this once.* Just so I could get back at my mother who seemed not to understand that she had a daughter-in-law worth more than all the whores in that room that night. So what if Stacy was a model? She seemed to want to give it away, so why not? Why not...and that maybe I would give her a call next week.

I must have been out of my mind. Deception.

Lucky for me Michelle got upset during our lovemaking. That was what saved me. *She knew something wasn't right. She probably felt it in her gut.*

I thought about the reflection in front of Him when I had perceived humanity to be ants. I had acted like one of those ants in the week or so following the party, wondering how to do what I wanted to do. My mind went around in circles for days. It went on until I came to my senses and realized my wife was probably pregnant. Then I finally got rid of the card.

Getting back at my mother? She's not worth losing my wife. Losing her... Seeing more hurt in her eyes. Hurt that I caused. God forgive me. I wiped my face with my shirt, feeling sick. I had almost thrown it all away. *My whole life would have been over.*

God, I don't want to be perceived by You as just another ant, making wrong choices and going against you. Offending you... I'm sorry.

Not really ants; that was just my perception. We were made in His image and He loved us, but He let us run around in circles just the same.

I read on. God banished the man and his wife from the Garden. Then He set guards there to keep them out. I shivered even as sweat poured rivers down my face, realizing that I had escaped again. Even though I'd gone to confession and been lectured by Father I hadn't truly understood how close I'd been to losing everything. The thought made me want to throw up. My next thought—the thought that the old man would have been my guard—did make me throw up. I ran out of the shed and vomited up everything. *He would have been my guard! He would have guarded Michelle from me!*

I sobbed crazily, bent over and retching with my hand on the back of my tool shed. *The old man would have hated me. He would never, ever have let me back in her life!* The thought that I could have hurt the old man that way was almost unbearable. *And Michelle... Oh my God!* She would have thrown me out. We would never have had a child. I'd be alone and so would she.

Then I thought about Brad, and what he would have done.

Brad would have called me out on it. He would have made me fight him. If I had cheated on his sister and he found out he would have fought me, or maybe even asked around till he found someone he could pay to work me over. This thought wasn't that crazy, not in light of what he'd done after the cops came to his house and took his gun. Michelle meant more to Brad than any gun.

I threw up again at the realization that I had actually considered doing something that could have caused me to lose everything. Even the old man and Brad... *We're brothers. Brad needs me...he needs to talk to me.* But I knew we wouldn't be friends anymore if I had cheated. The world was spinning. I closed my eyes and took a breath, still holding onto the wall. *I could have lost Michelle. Dear God.*

Michelle meant everything to me. I had loved her since I was a kid. The thought of living without her was something I could hardly bear, and I retched again one more time, thinking about my stupidity, my arrogance and my blindness.

Then I straightened myself up and tried to get things together, thinking that it hadn't happened. By God's grace, it hadn't happened. *But it could have. I'm a fool.*

"Thank you, God. Thank you." I said it aloud. I was sorry all over again even though I'd been absolved from it after it happened. I said another act of contrition right then and there. My work boots were spattered with vomit. I wiped my mouth with the back of my hand and hurried back into the shed to finish reading.

Genesis 4: Cain and Abel. I skimmed through the passages, considering my feelings of jealousy toward Brad and shaking my head. Then I put the idea right out of my mind. There was no way I was letting envy and jealousy ruin my friendship with Brad. Brad meant more to me than my own blood brother did. If I let the temptation of jealousy get me, my whole family would be lost. *The old man loved both of us.* That was the truth. I vowed never to let my mind get away from me like that again. Temptation was all around.

Back in the house I brushed my teeth and then decided to go for a run. It would take some of the stress off. The episode had unnerved me. The reading and any revelation it brought always unnerved me, but this time I was especially spooked after realizing how close I had come to cheating.

I stripped off my soaked clothes. *Damn, they stink...* I put on running gear and went back down the hall and around to the laundry room back of the kitchen. I shoved my scuzzy clothes into the washing machine to deal with later, put on my shoes, and hurried out, wanting to get away before Michelle came home from work. She would have tried to keep me from going in the heat, and I just wanted to run. My stomach was churning but my nerves were worse, so I ran out the door and down the street in the opposite direction of the store.

* * *

While running I left the music off and pondered the episode with Stacy before coming to the conclusion that I'd been blessed again. God had decided to spare me, and I thanked Him one more time for enlightening me. I had come so close so many times to making mistakes that I would have regretted later, and I could only attribute it to Him, the Spirit who stayed with me no matter my state of mind. I resolved to resist all things that would lead me to go against His commandments.

Resistance. I liked the sound of the word. It reminded me of heroes fighting oppression. The past had been filled with them, as history could attest—recent history and ancient history as well. The Saints came to mind—those who had resisted until they died. Ancient Jews and Greeks came to mind, and American soldiers and their allies. Even some of the Boss's music came to mind. *He's Dad's favorite...*

The various women's names in the lyrics were old fashioned and pretty. *Janie... Wendy... Rosie... And Mary. That's the most beautiful...the name of the Mother of God.* I realized how much the music had influenced me as I turned around to run home. I was calm now, even though sweat was streaming off again. *Women's names... Michelle's no ordinary woman. I'll never forget it again. I'll resist.* The idea came to me then, of something I could do to cement my commitment to resist—a permanent sign representing it.

I turned on the music for the remainder of my run. Fifteen minutes later the song began playing in my ear. The memory of Dad's garage and the vinyl on the workbench rushed through my mind. *No... This can't be. It's not possible.* Images and long lost sounds flashed and shuttered, blotting out the quiet of the still, hot street. *GTO...engine stand...chipped paint and putty... That window-pane's gonna go soon, I better fix it tonight... Dirt floor...whiskey bottles and shot glasses...rain and wind. Jason Michael, go on inside, your mother's calling you... Go on son, I'll be in soon...*

I couldn't believe what I was hearing through my ear buds. It was impossible for the song to be playing. *No way. No WAY! I don't have that on here!* I imported music from my own CDs, and I didn't own that one. It wasn't on the greatest hits CD, or any of the others in my collection. I didn't take the time right then to ask myself why I didn't own it, and why some songs on it—hits—were ones I always turned off when they came on the radio. There was simply no way it could be coming through the ear buds, yet I was hearing it. It was a rocking song. *Dad liked that one. He said the guitar playing was phenomenal.* I tried to put Dad out of my mind, but the images flashed anyway. My eyes bulged behind my sunglasses, remembering. *I miss him... MISS him... Why did he leave?*

The voice was strong and rough and passionate, singing words about baptism, and crying, and fathers standing in the doorway with the same blood running in their veins.

Dad, where are you?

Heat lightning flashed.

* * *

I ran back to the house with my hair standing on end. Michelle still wasn't home, so I jumped in the shower and let the water run full force over my head in an effort to clear it. What had just happened was impossible. *But it happened. It did.* I scrubbed the sweat from my body and got out, wrapped a towel around my waist and tracked water as I walked into the bedroom. I thought I heard something from the other end of the house.

"Michelle!" I shouted down the hall.

"I'm home." I heard her voice. "What do you want to eat?"

I got dressed, ran my fingers through my hair and went down the hall. As soon as I walked into the kitchen I smelled my scuzzy clothes in the laundry room. Michelle stood looking through the cupboards with her nose wrinkling. I grabbed her and hugged her.

"Baby, don't cook tonight. It's too hot," I said into her neck. "Let's go out."

"Okay," she said, turning toward me. "What's that smell?" Her voice was muffled against my clean shirt. "It's making me sick."

"I'm sorry, honey." I tried to laugh. "I got a shower before work, but it was a long day. I thought the clothes would be okay in the washer. I'll turn it on before we go. Get changed, baby." She followed me back to our room and started changing her clothes. I got more dirty clothes out of the hamper, put them in along with the nasty ones, and turned on the washer before we left.

I put the episode out of my mind. By the time we came home it already felt like a dream and I decided to treat it like one. I couldn't think about my father. *It's too soon after the old man.* A flashing thought of the graveside and a carnation on his coffin came to mind.

I knew I would have to think about my father eventually, but not right now. I hadn't thought about him consciously for almost thirty years. *Not yet... After the baby's born, when our lives are happy again.*

That night there was a wicked thunderstorm. We lost power. It didn't come back until three o'clock the next afternoon.

TWENTY-SEVEN

Jason
2 Years Earlier

Two or three weeks after I got the idea while running, I went home and showed Michelle what I had done.

"What do you think?"

"Hmm." She stared at my forearm.

"Do you like it?"

It was another tattoo. I got it at the shop just over the state line, right next to Mom's school. The college kids patronized the place. I heard about the artist from Lucio. I described what I wanted to the guy and he designed it. We'd gone back and forth over it; I wanted it small, nothing ostentatious. Just a symbol of my commitment on the inside of my right wrist, similar to what some of the early Christians had done according to some show on PBS years ago. They had crosses tattooed to mark their commitment to Christ back when it was really dangerous. If the wrong person had laid eyes on one of those tattoos, a Christian could have ended up being eaten by lions while a crowd of Romans cheered. It was also a reminder of who would be the ultimate winner of the battles we were currently facing.

"What do you think?" I repeated.

"Wow," she replied. She understood the symbolism. "It's cool."

The artist had done a good job. It had turned out a little bigger than I wanted it but only because of the length of the snake. The head of the snake, fangs bared, was nearest my hand with a sandal crushing its neck. There was no foot in the sandal, but you could clearly see what it was; it had leather thongs trailing off it. The remainder of the snake's body zigzagged back and forth up toward my elbow with the tail ending on the inside of my arm above the elbow. The colors of the snake were muted, shading into each other. It looked like a nasty piece of work with its glittering eyes and dripping fangs, but it was also plain to be seen that the snake was helpless, crushed under that simple shoe. I was happy with it, even though it had cost me. It was worth the price to me.

"Wow," Michelle repeated. She took a picture of my arm and texted Brad, asking how he was. When he wrote back admiring the tattoo, I replied with one word: "Resistance".

* * *

After the revelations about Stacy and my father the summer was uneventful. Michelle and I got into a routine, and the days stretched into weeks as we put our lives back together little by little.

Michelle had visits with Mary, who told us that she used to practice in hospitals. I think she only spoke about it to reassure me; Michelle seemed to trust her. I had no experience with babies other than Michelle's miscarriages and Brad's girls, and I just naturally associated having them with hospitals.

But it had to be a home birth because of what had happened with the twins, who'd been tracked since birth by the HCA. Their two-year check-up had already been scheduled, and Brad had received notification stating that if he missed the appointment they would call on him at the house.

It was a scary situation. Brad worried constantly. If either of the girls were found to have something wrong, God knew what might happen now that children under age two were no longer considered persons.

Healthcare had turned into a giant death cult under the sharks. Baby care and ordinary sick visits to a pediatrician were now the opposite of what medicine was supposed to be—preventive care, treating the sick, helping them get well, and doing no harm. Now more harm was being done than good.

Mary's network included nurse practitioners and pediatricians who were bucking the system. They accepted healthy babies as patients, and treated them on a strictly cash basis. We planned to meet with the one closest to home in late October, a few weeks before Michelle's due date. All we could do was to pray for a healthy baby and hope to stay under the radar.

Even if I wanted to subject Michelle to the system she would have refused. After her father died she told me flat out that she was having the baby at home even if there were complications. She said she'd rather be dead than have to deal with what Nicole had dealt with, and that Mary was perfectly competent to deliver our baby. We were lying in bed at the time. I hugged her and told her not to think about dying.

* * *

There's nothing else to write about except the agony that followed in September. I don't want to write it. It almost killed Michelle and me. We were never the same afterward, and I thought my life was over.

I still remember the baby's face. It was a beautiful, peaceful, angelic little face that is seared in my memory. I stared at his face and prayed I would never forget it. He had a head full of thick dark hair, and his eyelashes were thick on his little cheeks. His face was a shade of blue that should be unearthly. It was the opposite of my wife's eyes, where I see many things—even him sometimes. I guess that's another paradox.

He was a fragile little thing but still beautiful to us. Even though he was so very small I could tell he would have grown up with my coloring, not Michelle's. But he didn't belong out in this hard world. He's in a better place.

This is it. I have to do it, but I think it may kill me to write it.

* * *

The sky was blue, and sunshine sparkled on the dew in the park as I ran my five miles that morning. The temperature had moderated and it was warm without the humidity, a perfect late summer day. It was September seventeenth.

I was doing a brake job when the phone went off that afternoon. I wondered why Michelle was calling. It was almost three o'clock and she should have been driving to work. When I answered the phone, day turned into night just like that. Her voice sounded panicky as she told me to get home now. Something was wrong. I asked what it was as I went up front to tell CJ I was leaving. He heard Michelle crying over the phone and asked what was wrong, but I shook my head at him and walked out again.

"Michelle, I'm coming baby. Stay on the phone, okay? What's wrong?"

"Jason," she wailed. "I'm bleeding."

Dear God. "Baby lay down. Put your feet up honey, I'll be right there."

I got in the truck, tore out of town and drove to our place, talking to her all the while. I was at the house in five minutes. When I got to the bedroom I knew it was bad. Blood trailed across the floor from the bathroom to the bed. Michelle was lying on her side with a towel underneath her, clutching her stomach. The towel was blooming red.

"Oh my God! Look at you honey." I grabbed her up and hugged her. "What should I do?"

"I called Mary. She's on her way."

"Where is she?"

"About an hour away," Michelle gasped, curling up. Blood gushed.

"An hour? We can't wait an hour." I ran to the linen closet and got more towels. The other one was seeping through so I replaced it and put another one right between her legs.

"Wait Jason, don't do anything," she pleaded. But the blood was seeping through again. It scared the hell out of me.

"Michelle, I have to call someone. I'm calling Cindy."

I entered the house number. No answer. I didn't have Cindy's cell number in my phone, so I called Johnny's but it went straight to voicemail. Michelle's purse lay on the dresser. I got her phone and found Cindy's number, but she didn't answer either so I left a message. "Cindy, can you please call us back or get over here right away—something's wrong with Michelle." I hung up in a panic.

"Baby, look at you. I'm calling 9 1 1."

"*Nooo!*" she screamed, trying to get up and falling back weakly. "Just wait Jason. You can't call them. You know where they'll take me." Her eyes were pleading.

"Honey, what if you're having the baby now?" Blood gushed and seeped through the towel between her legs. I replaced it and threw the other one into the bathroom. Michelle didn't answer my question. She was curled up in pain, whimpering as she repeated, "Just wait. Mary's coming." She sounded strange; almost half asleep.

"Michelle! Michelle?" Her eyes were rolling up. "Oh my God...honey wake up. Stay with me." I stared stupidly at the blood again. The baby wasn't due for another two months, and Michelle was losing consciousness. I had to do something. I called CJ, the only other person I could think of.

"Ceej, can you come? Something's wrong with Michelle." I was almost crying.

"Okay boy, calm down. Do you want me to call 911?"

"God, I don't know. The midwife's on her way. Michelle told me not to call 911 but she's getting worse. Just come over here."

"Okay." He hung up.

I looked around at the bedroom that had always been our sanctuary. Bloody towels were strewn on the bed and floor, and my wife lay half-conscious on the blue patterned bedspread. I patted her cheeks and begged her to stay with me as I tried to decide what to do.

The place assigned to us by the HCA was the same hospital where we'd taken the old man. *I can't take her there even if I wanted to. It's too far away, and if I call the paramedics they'll never drive that far. They're not allowed. I know where she'll end up and so does she...dear God!*

I couldn't take her to the Catholic hospital in the next state either, not anymore. It had closed eight months earlier when the sharks went after the Bishop. *I could have her there in twenty minutes... Damn the HCA!*

There'd been a fight between the Bishop and the board of directors of the Catholic hospital over abortion, and the Bishop had stood his ground. The board fought him—along with the HCA of course—and the hospital had shut down. Court cases were supposedly pending, but who knew? Everyone had already forgotten the reason for the fight. The drones had started their jamming immediately, and most people were now of the mind that the Bishop was nothing but a wicked old rich guy who wanted the hospital to close just to keep people from being treated. All he was good for now were a few jokes on late night TV. There was no help there.

I had to make a decision now. *God? Help!*

I had never wished so hard for anything in my life as I did for the old man right that minute. I wanted him to come into that room and take charge. But he wasn't there. I was in charge. Me.

"Michelle. Michelle? Answer me." She opened her eyes.

"Jason," she whispered. "Just wait. Please. I'll be okay."

I stared at her. I looked at the blood on the bedspread. And then I saw Nicole's graveside. *God! No. Don't let her die!* I panicked then. I jumped up and ran back to the linen closet for another towel. "Michelle, I'm taking you," I said. "We can't wait. You're bleeding."

"Jason, please," she whimpered as I yanked open her dresser drawers. I took off the bloody shorts and underwear and replaced them with clean ones and another towel because I couldn't bear to take her outside the way she was. She cried and struggled against me the whole time. I reconsidered and thought about calling 911 again, but there were no EMTs in town and it would be quicker for me to take her myself.

I was afraid Michelle was going to die. All I could see was Brad having to live without his wife, and I couldn't bear even the thought of living without mine. The baby was coming anyway, and I doubt the outcome would have been any different in that respect. But because I made the wrong decision, the rest of our lives would change. My faith was lost for a time, and our world was shattered.

"God," I prayed with everything in me, "Please...please? Don't take her away from me." I slid my arms underneath her and picked her up. She grabbed her rosary up off the nightstand and clutched it, crying out in pain.

"Jason, *please!* Don't take me there!"

"Honey, I don't know what else to do."

* * *

Michelle lay back in the passenger seat. Her eyes were closed and she didn't answer when I called her name. As I drove toward town, CJ came toward me in his old Suburban. He slammed on his brakes as I passed him, and I saw him in the rearview mirror turning around to follow me. I squealed through the traffic light, took a left on Main Street, and sped through downtown.

"Michelle. Michelle?" I grabbed her hand with my bloody one. *Did it feel a little cold?* "Michelle! Answer me baby." She opened her eyes. Tears overflowed.

"Jason," she whispered. "I...I wanted to be a mother."

"Honey..." My voice broke. "Let's wait and see. Maybe the baby will be okay."

I sped down route 24 and over the state line and then turned into the driveway of the women's clinic. I drove past the main entrance, looking for the emergency room. The scene in the main parking lot should have set off my antennae if nothing else did. I glanced at the cars in the lot, each with its own politically correct bumper sticker. One in particular, on the back of a late model Mercedes, read: "*Keep your rosaries off my ovaries*".

It stood out to me because Michelle was still clutching the pink crystal rosary that had been a gift from me ten years earlier. I also noticed—in the distance at the other end of the building—a woman exiting the place. She was pushing a stroller and had another child by the hand. The last thing I saw before I squealed around the corner was that woman jerking her little girl by the arm as the stroller bumped off the edge of the sidewalk.

I drove quickly around to the side and pulled up next to what I assumed was a healthcare professional, a guy standing outside a set of glass doors, smoking. I screeched to a stop and yelled out the window at him.

"My wife's in bad shape; I think our baby's coming. Get me a wheelchair." He took a last drag on his smoke and dropped it. And though I was prepared for it in a way, his first words still hit me like a brick.

"We need her ID card," he said, holding out his hand.

That was it. There were no questions about Michelle's condition and he made no move toward her. I took her ID from my pocket, got out of the truck, and handed it to him on my way around to Michelle's side. She was murmuring the Hail Mary.

* * *

I still can hardly believe I took her there. We had already talked about the clinic. It was next to the strip of stores where the tattoo parlor was located, and the college kids made use of it as well; it was a big business there.

I've gone over what I should have done at least ten thousand times since. I should have waited, or called 911, or tried to help her myself. I should have taken her to the family practice, and on and on and on. But the family practice would have sent us to the clinic anyway. The law required them to, you see.

Such places received so much funding every year that my son ought to have survived. But it's no wonder that he didn't. The sharks throw money at the butcher shops, but money can't buy human feeling and compassion. It also can't buy real doctors, and I made a terrible mistake in thinking Michelle would be treated with medicine there. It's hard to remember exactly what happened. Thoughts of that day have taken on a dreamlike quality...or that of a nightmare.

After looking at Michelle's ID the nurse or whatever he was brought us a wheelchair and took her inside. He handed her card to another man sitting at a desk. He scanned it into the computer, and it went downhill from there. Michelle was doubled over in pain.

"Her records don't list her as being pregnant." I was bent down next to Michelle, trying to soothe her.

"Can we please worry about that later?" I said. "She's not due until November twentieth. She needs help now." I admit I wasn't in the best state of mind, but still... My time in the clinic put me in mind of zombies. With the exception of one young girl whom I'll get to in a minute, that's what the employees reminded me of. Though we were in what I took to be an emergency admissions department, nobody was around but the two men. They conferred in whispers behind the desk as CJ walked in through the door. He stopped behind me and put his hand on my shoulder. I reached in my back pocket, got Michelle's driver's license, and handed it to CJ, who took it to the desk.

"Can you get a doctor out here please?" CJ's tone was cool. Neither of them answered him. The one in the chair made a call, and a few minutes later a woman arrived. She was also dressed in scrubs, and she didn't say a word to us. She just went behind the desk and looked at the computer and Michelle's IDs.

It was truly a surreal situation. Michelle's computer records stated nothing about pregnancy, therefore she could not be pregnant even though it was plain to be seen that she was in labor. This was worse than our experience in the ER with the old man. At least there were real people there. This situation was like something out of the twilight zone.

Ten minutes later I decided we had waited long enough. I got up, and CJ stood up next to me. He was a little shorter than I was, around six two. He was fifty-eight that year, but he looked ten years younger and he was nobody to mess with. The atmosphere was getting thick. CJ was about to lose it—he hated the bureaucracy as much as I did. The two of us were dressed exactly alike, in old jeans, T-shirts and work boots. My jeans had a couple of grease stains on them. My hands did as well, along with Michelle's blood.

"My wife is in labor," I said, gesturing to Michelle. "I've given you two picture IDs. You can see that it's her. This is supposed to be a facility for pregnant women. Are you going to help us or not?"

The guy behind the desk stared at me coolly. Time seemed to stretch as I stared him back in the eye. CJ stiffened and clutched my arm as the three of them exchanged nervous glances. Then Michelle doubled over again and slumped to her side in the chair. The rosary slipped to the floor. I picked it up and shoved it in my pocket.

"Michelle. *Michelle!*" I squatted down again. Her eyes opened a slit, but she seemed to be somewhere else. *Michelle? God, please don't take her away from me.*

"Please." I heard CJ's voice and felt his hand on my shoulder. "Don't worry about all that right now. Just help her—she needs help. Worry about that later."

I don't know how much longer we waited before they made the decision to let her go through, but the woman finally came around the desk and started wheeling Michelle toward a set of doors, telling me to follow her. She had no need to tell me that. There was no way I was letting Michelle out of my sight in that place.

TWENTY-EIGHT

Jason
2 Years Earlier

Michelle was having the baby. There was no going back. The period of time while she was delivering is mostly a blur, but I do remember a few things. The room we were in was bright, white, and surgical. And also dark and cruel.

I found out later that the man who delivered our son was the person in charge of the whole operation. He was supposedly a doctor. And while it may be true that he attended medical school and received training, to me he's no doctor and I try not to refer to him as such. Doctors are supposed to care for sick people, and that wasn't what he was about. What he was about was power. He barked questions and threats at me as I stared at my wife's face and prayed that she wouldn't die.

"Why isn't her pregnancy listed in her records? How is it that this woman is this far along in pregnancy and hasn't seen a doctor? Don't you know you are required by law to report any and all symptoms of pregnancy? You broke the law. You're required by law to be under the care of the FEDHCA. Your actions caused this. Do you under-stand that?"

I looked up to see him staring at my work boots and my greasy bloody hands. I in turn, looked at his hands, which were covered with surgical gloves. *If he took off those gloves his hands would be bloody.* I tried to wake Michelle, but she wasn't coming around.

I stood frozen as he examined her.

"She's almost fully dilated. She's having this baby now." His voice held no compassion. Michelle meant nothing to him. All he seemed to care about was the fact that we had tried to go against the system. He was a cold bastard. "You're in trouble," he said. "When this is finished I'm calling the authorities."

Though I've tried multiple times, I can't seem to set down a decent description of the slime that delivered my child. No descrip-tion of mine will do him justice. The only words I can think of to describe the experience in the clinic are cold, dark, and hateful. If you close your eyes and think about those words you might get an idea of what it was like in that room. If you think about the unfath-omable depths of coldness and darkness and hatefulness in certain men's hearts, you might understand how the people who worked there came across to me.

And then there was him. If you imagine a total absence of light, a smothering hatred, a complete lack of anything remotely resembling human decency and then multiply them by ten thousand you still wouldn't understand him.

By the time it was over I wished I had the old man's Colt with me. If I had he wouldn't be here anymore. I'd be locked away some-where, and Michelle and Brad would be together right now without me. I wondered again where he'd been before he came into the room, as I looked at his hands. The gloves had Michelle's blood on them.

* * *

The baby was a boy. Michelle came back to consciousness before she delivered him. After he was born I put my arms around my wife and rocked her back and forth. But for Michelle's quiet weeping there was nothing but silence. There was no sound from our son. *He was alive last night. God?*

Mary had been at our house the night before, and when I came in after work I listened to his heart beating through the stethoscope. I still don't know when he died.

"Jason, get the baby." Michelle's voice was a sobbing whisper.

I stood up. "Will he be okay?" I already knew the answer.

The abortionist gave me a scathing look. "It's too late," he said.

* * *

A few minutes later a young nurse approached us with an IV hook up. Michelle put her hands up weakly, warning the nurse away.

"It's okay," said the girl, smiling. "It's to keep her hydrated." She directed the comment at me. I looked back at her, surprised. There was empathy and true feeling in her eyes, something I hadn't yet experienced in that place. I stared at her for a long minute. *Why are you working here? What are you doing?*

"Can..." I trailed off. "Can you please help my child?" I gestured toward the side of the room, where the bastard who delivered him stood with his back to us. A startled look came into the girl's eyes then.

"You...what are you talking about?" she said. The name on her ID read "Maddy."

"My child...he's...they said it's too late. But..." I swallowed.

Michelle sobbed as the little nurse looked back at us wildly. I could hear her thoughts: *Oh my God! Of course it's too late... Why are you here if he's not supposed to be dead?*

I looked at her stricken face for a moment before saying gently, " I'm sorry. I know it's too late. But my wife... She wasn't a patient here.

This was an emergency. We live in town and I brought her here... Never mind. Just go ahead. Hook her up."

Maddy blinked back tears while she connected the IV. Michelle didn't fight her—I told her it would make her feel better—and after the drip began, the little nurse ran out of the room. A moment later a male nurse entered, carrying a syringe.

"What's that?" I asked sharply. Michelle looked at me helplessly. *No. I don't want it. I don't trust them.* Neither did I.

"It's for pain."

"No," Michelle whispered. "Jason, get me out of here."

"It's a little late for that, isn't it?" I asked. I waved him off, and he didn't argue.

* * *

A short time later the hatchet-faced robot who had assisted at the birth started to take our child out of the room.

"Let me hold him," Michelle cried out.

"Give him to me," I said, standing up. I walked toward them with my hands extended.

"He's dead." The doctor's voice was harsh. Michelle sobbed at his words.

"I know that." I glared at him. "Give him to me."

"We can't."

"Give him to me," I repeated. He shook his head at the nurse, and she started to leave the room.

"Give me my son," I said, taking a step toward him.

"Go back to your wife," he replied. "You're already in trouble; don't make it worse." It was the same thing Brad had been told. It must have been a standard talking point. *Well, this time the standard operating procedure is not going to be followed.*

"You better give me my son. Right now. *Give him to me, now!*"

But according to them he wasn't my son. "I'm calling the police," the bastard said, looking at me coldly.

That was the last straw. *I'll kill him. My life's over anyway.* I was moving toward him as the thought went through my mind. Before he could say anything else I grabbed him by his lab coat and slammed him against the wall. I got in his face, deciding I was going to beat the living shit out of him.

I was in great shape at the time, and it would be easy to beat him into the ground. I decided to start with his nose and work my way on from there. I wanted to take one of them out, and he was the perfect choice. He was what represented the worst of them, and I could see everyone I had loved and lost in his crappy little wire-rimmed glasses. I clenched my fist, raised it, pulled it back and got ready. The snake on my wrist twisted, its eyes cold and its fangs showing. *It represents this place perfectly. And my fist is going to be a stand in for His sandal today.*

The butcher didn't have time to yell, and the nurse was still standing off to the side, not knowing what to do. *Zombies.* The thought kept coming to mind. Everyone in the clinic except Maddy seemed like the living dead to me, especially the woman holding my child. *She's confused.* Michelle and I were behaving as if we were something other than numbers on government ID cards, and the nurse, or whatever the hell she was, seemed confused by it. *And that's fine with me as long as she doesn't drop my son on the floor.*

I glared down into his pathetic face and got ready. But as I pulled my fist back a little further in preparation for busting his nose wide open, something happened. I heard the words clearly: *Put down your sword!*

I glanced at my clenched fist, poised and ready to make mince-meat out of his face. I actually started to look around then, thinking someone else had come into the room. Time seemed suspended. The room was brighter than it had been. And then I heard the water, and the light shimmered just outside my peripheral vision.

My son is dead.

Your son is in Paradise. Your other children are there. All of the innocents whose lives ended here are in Paradise. Do not go down this path.

I want him dead. They are responsible for my son's death.

You must continue to shoulder your cross.

I want him gone. He's a killer.

Yes, he has taken many lives in this place. But your place is with your wife. It is not your place to judge this man. He will judge all in His time.

He will? When? They took my father from me. Now they have taken my child.

I cannot be bothered with you at this time. Your guardian was correct. You are a difficult case. And you are a fool. Your wife needs you. If you are locked away what will happen to her? Put down your sword, and trust. You will be given what you need if you trust. I must get back. Put down your sword. Now!

The light faded away. When I came back to myself my fist was still clenched, but now it was down at my side. And though the presence was gone, my mind was now clear.

I looked down at the hateful face of the abortionist, knowing I couldn't hurt him physically—not after the warning I had just been given. But I refused to leave my child in that hellhole. Michelle and I were taking our baby with us. *God? What should I do?*

That was when the name first entered my mind. And though I grasped at the thought of tipping off the media, I discounted that particular journalist immediately. *Him? No way. How am I going to contact him?*

I tried to think of someone more approachable. The names of various bloggers came to mind. *But none of them have enough reach. They'd appreciate the tip off, but not enough people would hear about it. Trust... You will be given what you need if you trust... God? Am I really to use this man's name?*

The name flashed in my head again, and I understood that I had to do just that.

The murderer was right in front of me. I began by grabbing his collar with both hands, but Michelle cried out in fear, so I let go. I held my hand back toward her so she could see Christ's sandal crushing the snake, and spoke to her, saying in a calm tone, "Its okay Michelle. It'll be all right, don't worry."

That must have made him think I was standing down. He lurched away from me toward the door. "Go on," he said to the zombie holding my son. "Do your job."

I turned to her quickly. "Do not move," I said. "Do not take my son out of this room. Do you understand me?" My voice was harsh. Michelle whimpered. Then I turned back toward the doctor and mentioned the name that had been given me.

He was on his way out—probably thinking he'd get back to business as usual—as I repeated myself and went on, "I'll contact him." He stopped in the doorway and turned back toward me before rolling his eyes and shrugging his shoulders.

"You don't know what you're talking about," he spat. "Get over there with your wife. You're going to be arrested. So shut up if you don't want things to get worse for you."

"You can put me in jail for a while, but as soon as I get out I'm blowing the whistle on this butcher shop. You know damn well they won't hold me for this—the jails are too full. They're not going to make an example of me anyway, not when they find out about you and this place."

That was a bluff. I was truly of the mind that they probably would make an example of me. Jails were full of people who had gone against the system. Criminals and gangs were running the city streets at the time, but the sharks always seemed to find room in the jails for the people who tried to resist them.

My words must have given him pause though. He hesitated, looking at me as I stared at him with eyes like slits. "Understand something," I said clearly. "I will personally go up to New York. Don't doubt that fact for a minute. As soon as I get out of jail I will go up there. I'll dog him and I'll dog his staff. I'll wait outside the elevator in the lobby up there until I get him to take an interest in this place. I don't give a damn how long it takes."

He stared back at me with hatred in his eyes. I assumed he thought I was bluffing but wasn't quite sure. "You know what he'll do," I went on. "You know that once I get him on this place he'll never let go of it." I walked a little closer. "He'll shut you down. Have no doubt about it. He's done it before."

He must have known; he looked cornered. But we weren't out of the woods yet. He was an animal, and any wild animal was at its most dangerous when cornered, even a pathetic little slimy rat like him. I knew that if I got Michelle and the baby out of this he would be after me later. But I had to fix what could be fixed. Our son was gone, that was true, but I was going to see to it that he was buried.

The man I was speaking of was the host of a TV news show. Though by that time American news organizations were nothing more than propaganda arms for the sharks, there was a single cable news network that somehow hadn't been taken over. They employed investigative journalists and producers who reported actual news. They made it a habit to ask questions, and they continued to dig until they got to the bottom of slimy situations such as this one. The host I mentioned to the abortionist was fearless. He continued to air stories such as ours even though he received death threats on a daily basis, and his show was still on the air at the time. He'd been responsible for shutting down similar operations even if they were technically not breaking the law.

The killer could see in my face that I was serious. He looked back at me, opened his mouth to speak, and then shut it.

Dear God. Please?

"If you don't bring me my son this minute I will call up there from here," I said. "I'll do it while you're calling the cops on me. I'll raise hell at that channel and I'll make them listen to me. And after I get out of jail I will personally see that this place is shut down if it's the last thing I do on this earth. Do you understand? I don't care what you do to me."

His glasses were inches away. I held his pathetic gaze for another minute. Then he shrugged his shoulders, waved his hand, and turned to the woman holding my son.

"Okay," he spat and stalked out.

I took the baby out of the red plastic container and laid him on a clean sheet resting on the counter. I wrapped him quickly and gave him to Michelle, who was holding out her arms. She whispered and crooned to him tearfully as I took the phone from my pocket. There were several missed calls— from Mary, Johnny and Cindy, Reese and Heather. The phone had been vibrating almost nonstop during the baby's birth. I hit CJ.

"No cell phones allowed back here," the zombie-nurse snapped. I ignored her. CJ answered on the first ring.

"It's me," I said. "Can you please call Jeff Gearhart for me? Ask him to come down here."

"Oh my God! Is Michelle okay, is—"

"Michelle's alive CJ. Call Jeff for me please. I'll tell you afterward."

"Okay."

I looked at my phone. I couldn't face calling Mary, not yet. I scrolled to Johnny and hit send.

"Jason," he answered sharply. "Where are you?"

"Johnny..." My voice shook. "I can't tell you now. Michelle's okay. We'll be home later."

"We're at the house. Reese and Heather are here. Cindy found Michelle's clothes, what—"

"Johnny, please. I'm hanging up. Michelle's alive. Wait for us at home."

"Leave us alone, please," I said to the zombie. She turned and walked out of the room.

Michelle rocked our child back and forth. We opened the blanket and looked at him. He was beautiful, so beautiful to us, as we kissed him and hugged him goodbye. I told him I was sorry. We said prayers —prayers parents would say with their children. Michelle was devastated but there was nothing I could do for her or my little boy. *But I can still shut them down if we get out of here.*

* * *

He finally signed for the body to be released, but I had to threaten him again before he did it. He came back into the room to inform us that under no circumstances was he breaking the law and allowing a specimen that could be used to benefit society to be removed from his clinic and taken to any undertaker. Michelle sobbed and cried as he told us he was calling the authorities, but I kept my cool.

I took the phone out of my pocket and dialed information right then and there. I asked for a New York City database. When I spoke the name of the channel into the phone he gestured wildly, stamped his foot, swore and walked out of the room. I followed him down the hall to his office where Jeff Gearhart and CJ were waiting. I continued my bluff and began dialing the number I'd been given even though I wasn't sure it would go through. And then, finally, he threw up his hands and signed on the dotted line.

Our child was taken away from that place, and Michelle refused any more treatment. Maddy came back to the room when she heard we were going home, frantic at the thought of Michelle leaving. She mentioned a blood transfusion. But Michelle told her to go away. Once our baby was gone she insisted on leaving and I carried her out myself. She was still in pain.

We went back through the double doors to where Maddy sat crying behind the desk. As I passed in front of her we looked at each other for a long moment. *You don't belong here...you don't belong here...why are you here?* She stared back as CJ opened the door. Then she was out of her chair and running after us. She glided through the door behind us, CJ followed her out, and the last I ever saw or heard of her were the words she spoke as I went toward the truck with Michelle. "I'm sorry...I'm truly sorry. But thank you." She ran swiftly up the sidewalk and around the corner toward the employee parking lot, and it seemed like her feet weren't touching the ground.

CJ followed us to the truck and helped me settle Michelle in the passenger seat. He was crying.

TWENTY-NINE

Michelle

Dear Holy Mother. I miss my little boy. Is he there with you? I pray that he is. Would you please ask your Son to look after my baby? He was innocent. His daddy and I love him and we trust your Son to take care of him even when the doubts creep in at night.

I am feeling very down and alone again as I lie awake. The nights are long and hot, seeming never-ending. How did you stand it Mother, in the days when you lived here on this earth? How did you stand all the waiting and wondering and uncertainty? Please pray for us, Jason and me. We love you and your Son. Amen

Jason
2 Years Earlier

Our lives were never the same after what happened. My agony consumed me for months, and Michelle's suffering was indescribable. I can't bear to write much more about the baby. Only—only that I knew as soon as I looked at him that he wasn't what those in the HCA would term "normal". We both knew. It was plain to be seen in his little face. His face was beautiful to us even though the Feds had decreed that such children were unfit to live in the world they were creating—this ugly world that according to them shouldn't include a child like my son.

My innocent child... He's in Paradise now. He's living with God in a better place.

Johnny and Cindy were waiting at the house when we came home after he was born, and when I could stand letting Michelle out of my arms and my sight I left her with Johnny and went out back to call Brad.

"Wallace?" He answered on the first ring.

"Yeah."

"Are you okay?"

"I wish I was dead."

"I'm on my way up. I'm at the airport."

"You're coming?"

"Where's Michelle?"

"She's in bed. Johnny's watching her."

"Get yourself a drink, Wallace."

I poured a shot of bourbon and drank it down. "I don't deserve Michelle."

"You sound terrible. Stop it. None of this is your fault."

"I almost killed her."

"You did not."

"I took her to that place."

"Well she's not dead and neither are you. She couldn't live without you so stop talking like this and get yourself back to the house. You know exactly who's responsible for this screw up."

"What about the girls?"

"I left them with Nicole's parents. They'll be fine."

"Brad..." My voice broke. "Why did this have to happen?"

"I'm sorry," he said in a measured tone. "You deserve better. So does my sister. But the sharks are the ones responsible, not you."

"But my son's dead!" I was crying wildly. Brad didn't care; we'd been listening to each other cry all summer long. "I wish it were me," I sobbed. "Why is he dead? I'll never know him now."

"Wallace." Brad's tone was sharp. "Quit talking this way. Michelle's gonna need you. Johnny told me that bastard threatened to have you arrested. That HCA shark butcher—lucky for him he didn't call the cops because if you were in jail there wouldn't be anyone to stop me from finding the son of a bitch and blowing his butchering head off." I poured another shot, knocked it back and tried to get myself under control.

"Do you hear me? Now go on back in with Michelle. I don't want you blaming yourself. It's not your fault. Thank God you were with Michelle... I wish I were on the highway when Nicole died. If I were I would have taken her to the closest place too. Go to bed. I'll be there when you get up."

* * *

Mary came to the house that evening. After she left, Michelle and I spent the first of many empty lonely nights without our child. When I came out of the bedroom the next morning Brad was there. Reese had picked him up at the airport, and Johnny let him into the house at six o'clock that morning. Johnny had stayed with us, sleeping in the computer room on the pullout couch. The two of them were in the kitchen eating bacon and eggs when I stumbled in and sat down at the table.

"Did you sleep?" Brad asked.

"Not really."

"Is Michelle awake?"

I nodded. "I told her I'd be right back. She wants something to drink."

"I'll take it," Brad said, getting up. He went to the fridge and poured a glass of orange juice. "You stay here and eat something." He walked out of the room. A minute later Michelle began crying again. I looked helplessly at Johnny for a long minute. Then I put my head down and cried too.

After a while I stopped crying and drank a cup of coffee and ate the plate of bacon and eggs Johnny had fixed for me. By the time I got to it the food was cold. Brad was still in with Michelle. I asked Johnny to go get him and to stay with her. I didn't want her left alone for even a minute. Brad came back wiping his eyes. He sat down at the table across from me.

"We have to get him buried right away before something happens," I said. "They were really pissed off down there yesterday. I'm afraid they'll call the cops. Maybe that guy'll figure out I was bluffing him. He has the law on his side."

"That shark son of a bitch had better quit while he's ahead," Brad said savagely.

"Brad, you know we have no right to bury the baby according to them."

"But he signed the release, didn't he?"

"He did, but only because I scared him into thinking he'll be shut down. He could be calling the cops on me right now. I just want him buried. Let's go to Gearhart's now. We'll get it all arranged before anything else happens. At least if they arrest me I'll know where my child is."

"Okay. But you go back to bed now. You can't do it; Johnny and I'll go."

I could hardly look at Brad. Tears dripped down on the table in front of me.

"Wallace?" Brad got up and came around the table. He grabbed me and hauled me up out of the chair. "Wallace, go back to bed. Don't worry. I'll make sure he's buried tomorrow—I'll call Father Gallucio. Go on in with Michelle now."

"I'm gonna shut that son of a bitch down if it's the last thing I do. The baby was alive the other night. I heard him. I could feel him that night—" I sat back down in the chair, stared down at the table, and cried some more. Brad stood next to me with his hand on my shoulder until I stopped.

"Brad?" I had to ask the question but I didn't look up. "Do you... Do you think it's possible that the baby was alive when he was born?"

Brad didn't answer right away. I heard him breathing harshly and felt his hand trembling on my shoulder. Then he sighed.

"I don't know." His voice was low. "All I know is what I saw in the hospital in Memphis. How Nicole was treated. And the way we had to live for the past two years. But you know damn well what happened with the old man. They killed him—no question about it. And their freaking animal rights policies killed my wife and mom. I don't care if it was a freaking accident or not—my wife's still dead. I don't give a fuck if the consequence was unintended or not. I don't give a damn if the old man would have died sooner or later anyway. I know what I know. They think they can judge who should live and who shouldn't; they're nothing but killers. And that butchering son of a bitch is working for them."

He and Johnny left for Gearhart's a few minutes later and I went back to bed.

* * *

The old man's estate had just been settled. It had been divided equally between Johnny, Brad, and Michelle, so there was plenty of money for the baby's funeral. The sharks had tried to get more than they were entitled to under the latest legislation of the death tax of course, but somehow we'd been able to win this one. Not that I cared at the time, but at least the old man would have been happy to know that we inherited some of what he'd worked to earn. It was what he had always wanted.

The funeral the next day was private. It was just the family, Jeremy and Lauren, Reese and Heather, CJ and Mrs. CJ, and Danny and his wife. Father Gallucio agreed to celebrate Mass for our son at six o'clock a.m. so we could get the baby safely in the ground before any consequences came down, if any were going to. Junior showed up about fifteen minutes before Mass started.

Brad and I were standing in the entryway. The baby laid next to us in his little white casket that had already been closed. Michelle had already said goodbye again. She was sitting in the front row with Johnny and Cindy, waiting.

Time seemed suspended as Junior came toward us. Time almost seemed to stop, as I glared at him, not fathoming how he dared to show his face. *You. You're one of them. You're part of the problem Junior.* I took a deep breath and looked helplessly at Brad. He clutched my arm as he stared back at me.

Wallace, don't. Maybe he doesn't know what he's doing. Just get through this. Michelle needs you...I'm here...your child is in Heaven.

Junior held out his hand. My face was like stone, my fists clenched at my side. A faint memory surfaced then of the night Nicole died. *Do not go down that path...do not heft your sword.* I laid my hand gently on top of my child's casket and looked at the little white crucifix on top. *God? Where are you?*

He will judge all in His time. Turn the other cheek. Stay in the path...the narrow one.

I blinked back my tears and reached my hand toward Junior. I shoved it out of the sleeve of my suit—out past the white cuff of my shirt so he would be sure to see the snake on my wrist. And what was crushing it. I looked down at him coolly as I shook his hand. "Thank you for coming, Junior."

I let go of his hand and he went into the church. I turned away. I looked back at the casket with the spray of white rosebuds on top so I wouldn't have to see him speaking to Michelle.

The funeral was so sad that I can't bear to write much more other than that my mother didn't attend. I had called the previous day after the arrangements were made to tell her what had happened. She replied that she was sorry, and then went on to tell me she'd be unable to attend the service because of work.

The funeral took place at six in the morning, and Mom worked regular business hours. But the fact that she skipped her first grand-child's funeral didn't surprise me in the least when I considered where she worked. I could feel the wheels turning in her mind during our conversation even through the phone, as she considered what might happen to her job if I were arrested. She must have figured it was too big of a chance to take. It doesn't matter anymore; I'll prob-ably never lay eyes on her again. I have forgiven her. I'm committed to Our Lord now. I don't think about her.

We buried him in the old man's plot. They let us put the coffin on top of his. It was a comfort.

* * *

Our agony continued throughout that fall. When I went back to work the following week, life was different than it had been. Michelle was taking a leave of absence from her job. In the two weeks after the funeral she escaped the crushing sorrow by sleeping late, going to bed early and taking an afternoon nap. The two of us were consumed with grief, each in our own way.

I agonized every day about what I could or should have done to prevent the baby's death. I went over the day he was born constantly, remembering that Michelle had begged me not to take her to that place. Yet I had.

I should have listened to her. He might be alive if I had. It would have been better if I had waited even if I had to deliver him myself. He would have had more of a chance; at least I could have tried to save him. Mary might have gotten there in time. Even if he died anyway it would have been better for Michelle than taking her to that hellhole.

These were the thoughts that consumed me all day every day, every waking hour. I blamed myself, and I was almost insane with anguish during that period of time.

* * *

Michelle went back to work when November came in, cold and dry and dark. We crawled under the covers of our bed every night at eight o'clock and tossed and turned until morning. Though the two of us were always tired, neither of us ever seemed to get a good night's sleep. As soon as Mary told Michelle it was safe we tried to lose ourselves in each other again, but it didn't always work out.

We were scared. We hung onto each other like we would die if we let go, but we only had intercourse when Michelle was absolutely sure there was no chance of another baby, even though that was what we both wanted most in the whole wide miserable world.

Father Gallucio had listened to Michelle's confession before the funeral along with anyone else who wanted him to, but I hadn't gone. I was so ashamed of my actions that I didn't want to confess them. But finally, about six weeks after the funeral, I went to confession because I couldn't stand staying away anymore. Father told me in no uncertain terms that under no circumstances was I to blame myself for what happened.

"You and Michelle were following the will of God, Jason." His voice was kind yet stern.

"But we broke the law, Father. And our child died."

"The law is wrong. What happened to you is criminal. You were following God's law. Is there anything else you need to confess?"

"Yes, Father, the usual. I missed Mass at least five times. And I used foul language, but only around Brad and the guys at work." I had already told him about being tempted to beat the abortionist to a pulp.

"What prevented you from attending Mass?

"Well, these past two Sundays, nothing Father. I have no excuse. Before that I had to stay with Michelle."

"Of course you had to stay with Michelle, but what were you doing the past two Sundays?"

"Sleeping."

"Mass is a Sacrament. How can you be in full communion with Our Lord if you don't receive Him in the Eucharist? Why would you deny yourself that?"

"When I'm making the decision to skip it doesn't feel like a denial to me. I just want to sleep later."

"Well, what did you gain by that extra hour of sleep?"

"A little relief. From thinking."

"The Mass can give you more than a little relief. As for the cussing, it's a habit, isn't it?"

"Yes, Father."

"Can't you break it?"

"I don't know Father. I never use God's name while I'm doing it... well maybe once in a while."

"Well, quit it. Now say your act of contrition."

I said the prayer and was given the penance of going back to St. Michael's to tell all my troubles to the Lord. But I didn't really consider that a penance—not by that time.

"Give thanks to the Lord for he is good, his mercy endures forever. I absolve you from your sins. You can go in peace."

"Thank you, Father."

I drove to St. Michael's, went into the chapel, and knelt, listening to the water. I prayed to Christ, suffering on the cross. I told Him about my child's death even though He already knew. That was something to ponder. The fact that God knew what had happened and had known it would happen was a mind-stretching paradox.

Yet we human beings had choices. Our Lord had felt my agony and Michelle's all the way back on the night He was betrayed, and yet it didn't have to be. What had happened to us hadn't been set in stone. Men had made the wrong choices, that was all. Some of them were deceived into it, and some of them knew exactly what they were doing and did it anyway, but the end result was the same: my dead son. Men hadn't followed. I was one of them, even though I tried to follow. It was something to strive for.

I knelt and listened to the fountain. It was a gentle sound, yet also a torrent in my heart, my head, and my innermost being. The sound was cool and soothing. He relieved me of my tortured thoughts, and by the time I left to go home I felt assured that my son was with Him. I understood that there was a reason for all of this even though I didn't know what it was, and I knew I would see my son again someday. *And when I do...he'll be perfect.*

That peace lasted a short while.

Two days later I finally decided to tip off that news show about the butcher running the clinic where my child died. I wanted the place investigated and hopefully shut down. Before I went to bed I logged onto the Internet to bring up the channel website, hoping to find a way to contact the show.

I couldn't log on. The website was on our favorites list and I had never had any trouble before, but this time the only page that displayed read: Web Site No Longer Available. I didn't have the actual show's website saved to favorites; anytime I wanted to look at it I just linked to it through the channel page. But there was no channel page, so I went to bed, thinking I'd try again in the morning.

The next morning the same thing happened but I didn't have time to investigate the situation because I had to get to work. Around midmorning I went to the office and logged onto the computer. There it was again: Website No longer Available. That made me suspicious. I turned on the TV CJ kept in the office and hit the channel numbers, and when the picture came up I stood gaping. Instead of the newsroom that had been on for years at that time of morning, all I saw was another zombie, talking up some hospital in DC.

It was a guided tour of the place. It was a complete and total snow job, nothing but HCA propaganda. The people who ran that news organization would never have wasted valuable airtime on such a thing. Their previous work included facts backed up by interviews with whistleblowers, and videos taken clandestinely by reporters and citizens who wanted to expose HCA abuses.

I turned it off in disgust. That evening at home I tried again. By that time they had switched from fake hospitals to healthy cooking—without meat of course. I shook my head and hit close on the remote, knowing that it was all over.

They had been scrubbed—the whole organization. I don't know to this day what happened to some of them. They're probably in Nevada, where rumor has it that the sharks have built gulags for enemies of the state.

However the guy I spoke of earlier is still countering lies with truth. Brad and I listen to him on podcasts that are usually removed from the net within a day of their release. Nobody knows where he is. There are others as well, those who formerly worked in radio and print media and have gone underground. They also continue disseminating truth, as dangerous as that is now.

THIRTY

Jason
2 Years Earlier

My peace disintegrated after I realized that the network had been scrubbed. Knowing that an entire channel had been flushed down the shark memory hole made me believe the bastard running the clinic would get away with possibly killing my child. When I looked for other journalists who might have appreciated the tipoff, I found that they had disappeared too. Many media figures that had been there in September weren't around anymore.

It seemed I had waited too long. I couldn't trust contacting the local papers. Their editorials had always been slanted toward the shark way of thinking, and for all I knew there could be worker bees on the payroll of any given newspaper.

When contemplating tipping off a news source, there was always this thought at the back of my mind: *Is that bastard abortionist going to call the cops on me? Am I going to be arrested?* He would have been within the law if he did, crazy as it might sound. I was the one who'd broken the law when I took my child out of the place and had him buried, and my only hope was that the bastard was afraid himself because we had his signature on the release form.

Michelle and I were pretty much alone. We couldn't be sure of anyone except our family and friends, none of whom had any power. They couldn't help me shut that butcher down. Maybe no one could. So we kept our heads down and clung to each other and our faith.

It's a feeling of free fall, not knowing who to trust; a mind numbing, soul twisting, agonizing feeling, almost as if the ground underneath has turned to quicksand. Once in a while I would consider contacting various online news sources but doubts would always creep in. I didn't know who might be working where.

What if they have someone inside? If one of the sharks finds out they'll come after me. Then what will happen to Michelle? She still needs me, even if I am nothing but a worthless fool.

I was waiting for the other shoe to drop, and I was under a lot of stress.

* * *

When Michelle wasn't working she sometimes spent the day with Cindy. Johnny and Cindy had sold their house and they were now living at the old man's place. They had bought out Michelle and Brad, and moved in three weeks after the baby's funeral.

Michelle liked spending time there. She said it reminded her of better times. She and Cindy were in the process of going through everything that had belonged to Mrs. Davis and deciding what would be kept and what would be donated. Johnny and Brad and I had already discussed the garage and decided that everything in it would be left just the way it was for the time being.

One evening after work I stopped by the old man's to pick up Michelle. I tried not to see the garage as I turned in the driveway. It was only five-thirty and it was already dark, but there was enough light from the street to illuminate the front yard. The red maple tree, the lilac bushes, and the hydrangeas on either side of the front porch were bare and dark and dead.

I sighed and walked up the sidewalk toward the back door. The light outside the combination laundry room-enclosed porch behind the kitchen was on. The backyard was the same as the front. The huge maple tree in the middle of the lawn reached its branches up toward the light of the quarter moon and a few glittery stars, small and cold and far away. The bench under the tree where the old man had spent a good deal of time smoking and reading the *Wall Street Journal* should have been stored in the basement by that time. *The paint's gonna weather... Johnny better get on the stick.*

I smelled sauce as I climbed the steps. I walked in the door and went through the darkened porch to the kitchen where the sauce simmered on the stove. A huge pot of water was coming to a boil, waiting for spaghetti or whatever pasta Cindy was getting ready to cook. Voices floated through the dimly lit kitchen from the dining room.

"Look, Cindy," Michelle's voice came softly. "Here's Junior's tenth grade picture. Look how cute he was."

"Yeah," Cindy agreed, sounding sad.

"What's going on with him?" Michelle asked. "Is he starting school in January?" Cindy didn't answer. "I thought he was starting in the fall," Michelle went on. "Did he decide on a school?"

"No," Cindy answered. "He's put it off again. He says he's going next year."

"He shouldn't wait another year!" Michelle exclaimed. "He's done enough for them. He should move on."

"Well, he says he is Michelle. He just wants to wait another year."

"Okay," Michelle said quietly.

"It's none of your business, anyway."

"Cindy, okay." Michelle said quickly. "I didn't mean to upset you. I'm just concerned about him."

"Well, you don't know how it's been around here ever since he started hanging around with that bunch at the firehouse." Cindy's voice was sadder yet. "He's not the same boy he used to be. I wish... I wish I'd just stood my ground. Maybe things would be different if I had."

"What... Cindy, what do you mean?"

"I thought it would fix everything," Cindy wailed. "Johnny argued with me but Junior seemed so unhappy about the prospect of transferring that I—I finally gave up and told him to go ahead and do it."

I looked into the dining room. They were standing next to the sideboard with the top drawer open; they must have been going through some things inside.

Michelle sucked in her breath. She looked like a wraith, even in her jeans and bulky turtleneck sweater. *She's losing weight again. God, why?* Cindy stood facing her with tears in her eyes, looking older than she had just a few months earlier.

"Do you mean to tell me that you gave him permission to join them?" Michelle sounded furious. "How could you?"

"Michelle, please! You weren't around... You weren't the one listening to him day and night. You weren't the one who lost her job and couldn't afford to send him to school anymore!" Cindy was yelling at Michelle. Then she started to cry. "You weren't the one he blamed," she sobbed. "Anyway you know he didn't need our permission. Please don't blame me!"

"Oh my God," Michelle cried. "Cindy, I'm sorry. I would never put blame on you—I was just surprised. Don't be so upset." She put her arms around Cindy.

I backed up quietly, not wanting them to know I had witnessed the argument. I went across the kitchen, opened the door and shut it, and walked back to the dining room.

"What's going on in here?" I asked playfully. "Cindy, that pot on the stove's about to boil. Do you want me to turn down the flame?"

"No, Jason, I'll get it," she said. They were still hugging each other. "Do you two want to stay and eat?" She wiped her eyes before giving Michelle a kiss on the cheek and coming toward the kitchen door. I moved out of her way and looked at my wife as she sagged down into a chair. *Junior, you selfish little creep. You don't give a damn about any of us, not even your own mother.*

"Michelle?" I looked in her eyes. Tears spilled over. "Honey, are you okay? Do you want to stay?"

"Stay," said Cindy's voice from the kitchen, still sounding shaky. "Junior's not coming home, and Jamie has football practice; he'll eat later. There's plenty. It's gnocchi, only frozen, but it's almost as good as Mom's."

Michelle wiped her eyes and looked back at me. *Do you want to stay?*

Yeah, Cindy's upset. So are you. Let's stay. Junior isn't home.

"Okay," Michelle called. "We'll stay. You know how much Jason loves gnocchi."

* * *

While Michelle and Cindy were doing the dishes after dinner, Johnny and I went out back for a cigarette. Both of us were smoking at the time, even though Johnny had led Cindy to believe he was quitting. I had cut back to a pack a week, but I wasn't about to quit completely. Not with the news that smoking would soon be outlawed.

The ban on tobacco would go into effect in January. The news had come out a few days earlier, and we had heard it on the radio at work. The minute I clocked out that night I went to the store and spent a hundred and fifty dollars on a carton of smokes. The sharks were in the process of shutting down the tobacco companies, but for the moment it was still legal to sell cigarettes. I was saving the money for the carton after the fact by cutting back on whiskey for a while.

Johnny and I stood in the old man's garage, out of the wind. "I think I'm gonna start rolling my own," he said, gesturing with his cigarette. His hair was thinning. He was almost bald on top, and completely gray as well.

"Screw that," I said, dragging on my smoke. My mood was dark. "I'm not. The bastards aren't forcing that on me. When they're finally outlawed there'll be a black market, and I'm gonna be one of their first customers."

"Those freaking sharks." Johnny spat on the floor. "I just saw news footage last night of some big shot congressman walking through the halls of some hospital down in Washington. The son of a bitch was smoking right in the damn hospital, and the drones didn't even try to hide it."

"Well they can kiss my ass. I'll quit when I'm good and ready to quit. What's good enough for them is good enough for me." We smoked in silence for a minute.

"How's Junior?" I said.

"The same as the last time you asked. I told him he'd better be on notice. He's down there tonight, but we're painting the trim before it gets too cold, and his little ass is spending tomorrow on the ladder with a paintbrush in his hand. He skates right up to the edge with me. He started arguing when I showed him the paint cans. He actually had the nerve to tell me he didn't have to do a damn thing."

"Well, he doesn't, does he? According to them anyway."

That was the truth. Junior could bring charges against Johnny for ordering him to do anything at all. MCSF were their own law by that time, just like the sharks.

"Well, screw *that*," Johnny said in a pissed off tone. "The little shitass doesn't contribute a dime to this place. They don't pay him anything unless he meets his recruitment requirements, but he comes home to eat every night, that's for sure. I told him I'm running my house the way I see fit, and he could go ahead and do what he had to do. Then he backed down. Said okay, he'd put in some time with a paintbrush."

I took a last drag on my cigarette, ground it out under my heel and picked up the butt, as Johnny elaborated. "I also told him to shut the hell up about that damned firehouse, and that I better never catch him bringing any of his brown shirt friends around here to brainwash his brother. There's only so much I'm willing to put up with. I'm about at the end of my rope with this shit. If he doesn't watch himself he's gonna feel my foot kicking his ass out in the street. Government be damned." Johnny finished his smoke.

"I better never hear about those brown shirt punks setting foot in this house," I said. "And whatever you do, don't mention this to Brad. You know what he'll do, don't you?"

"He'll have to get in line," Johnny said. "If I ever catch the little commies around here they won't be able to sit down for a month. And neither will Junior."

That was the end of the conversation.

* * *

The dinner with Johnny and Cindy was no different than any other meal we had shared with them, yet it seemed to be an ending of sorts. After that night the four of us began drifting apart. Though the rift was subtle, it was definitely there, even though outwardly things remained pretty much like always.

Michelle was upset about what had happened with Cindy. When we got home that night she went right to bed, dragging me with her. That put me in a bind. She said it was safe, but I wasn't sure. I almost refused her. But that would have really made her cry, so I turned out the light and things went away for a while.

Afterward we lay in the dark together. The streetlight shone dimly through the curtains onto the foot of our bed.

"Jason, how long were you in the house earlier?" Michelle's voice was muffled against my chest. Her fingers trailed back and forth over the tattoo on my bicep. "Did you hear anything?"

"Yeah. I heard the whole thing. I didn't want to upset Cindy though, so I acted like I'd just come in."

"I feel so bad about what I said. But I can't understand it. I wish she hadn't given him the okay. Do you think if maybe she hadn't he wouldn't have joined them?"

"No, baby." *Why beat around the bush?* "I don't."

My hands were in her hair that spread out across my chest. Her breasts pressed against my ribs. The weight loss had affected them as well as everything else and they were smaller now.

"I don't," I repeated. "I think Junior would have done what he wanted to do anyway. He had no respect for his mother's opinion or Johnny's. You know that." She started to cry again then.

"I'm sorry honey, to be so blunt—I know how much Junior means to you. I love him myself. But he's not the same now. He's running with the ones who made it possible for the system to push us into a corner the way they did, and it doesn't sound like he has any plans to quit running with them." She sobbed against my chest.

"Baby, I'm sorry. Cry all you want; I'll still be here. I wish things were different. I wish I had made a different decision the day the baby came. I miss him." I was crying then, too. We cried together, the same way we had almost every night since our child left us.

After a while we stopped. *She feels like a bundle of sticks.*

"I'm worried about you, Michelle. You're losing weight again. Do you have any meds left?"

"Yes. Another month's worth."

"Well, you better start taking them tonight. And call DeLuca's office. We have to get this under control."

"All right," she sniffed. I could still feel her tears on my chest. "But do you think Junior will ever come back to us? The way he used to be?"

I didn't answer right away. Junior and his organization were getting more and more cocky. They ran around town in a pack, almost but not quite terrorizing. They hung out on street corners and walked into businesses at all hours to harass the customers. It was a bad situation.

"I don't know. But I pray he will, and so should you. Now get some sleep, baby. I want you to get better." I grabbed her naked backside. "Your ass is way too skinny. I want it back the way it was. I miss it."

"Jason!" She laughed a little. "You're terrible!" She smacked my cheek a little, lovingly, playfully. "Goodnight then."

* * *

After Michelle had taken her meds and fallen asleep in my arms, I lay awake thinking about Junior.

Jamie was in his senior year at Kennedy High School. His grades were good, he was playing football, and he had taken the SATs and was in the middle of the college application process. He seemed to be doing just fine. *Junior, you little shit, why oh why couldn't you have just listened? Now look at you. What the hell are they telling those kids?*

I didn't know; I only saw the results of it. Though my nephew had always been a little headstrong, he was basically a good kid until he got involved with the MCSF. Now he was a little robotic prick, as Brad called him. Brad's description was right on target though, and I could only shake my head at the way Junior embraced the brown shirt agenda they spewed at the firehouse.

The funding for the firehouse came from my paycheck. Mine and Michelle's and Brad's and Johnny's, and every other person in the country who still worked in private enterprise. *They've got us in a vise, the shark bastards. Poor Johnny. At least I don't have to deal with Junior's bullshit the way he does.*

I sighed, remembering Junior and the fun we'd had together over the years, fishing and swimming and playing ice hockey. I shifted Michelle's sleeping body onto her pillow and tried to fall asleep, but my mind wouldn't shut down. I considered Brad and myself, and the irony of what our lives had become all because of the sharks and their power trip. He had two kids and no wife, and I had my wife and no kids.

Brad and I speculated on a weekly basis about possible ways to throw a wrench in their operation, but every idea we'd come up with so far had been impractical and probably would never have succeeded in getting past the bottom echelons of the system. So we decided to wait until one of us thought of a sure fire way to fight back. We knew it wouldn't do any good to simply disable a couple of random worker bees. Worker bees were a dime a dozen with this bunch, and paying a visit to someone at the bottom simply to put a scare in him or her would have been a stupid move.

Lucio had been hell bent on paying the principal of Sonny's school a visit until we talked him out of it. He and Bella were beside themselves a couple of weeks earlier when Sonny arrived home with propaganda given to him by members of Junior's organization who'd come into the school to speak. Sonny was only fourteen. Bella had called the house in hysterics, crying to Michelle about Lucio. He'd gone into a rage, saying it was the principal's doing that they'd been in the school at all.

Of course I agreed with Lucio that it never should have happened, but Reese and I made him see reason. We pointed out what Junior and company were getting away with these days, and told him he'd probably be arrested if he went to the school. Lucio had cussed till he was blue in the face, but he'd finally given up on the idea. He understood that he had four children to provide for, and keeping food on the table for them was more important than sending a message to some stupid-assed worker bee in the school.

THIRTY-ONE

Jason
2 Years Earlier

After my initial confession I began going back almost every Saturday. I probably drove Father Gallucio crazy with my talk about the baby. He had already absolved me and made it clear that I wasn't to blame, but it was hard to let go of the guilt. Each week he assured me that the baby was with God now before telling me to go back to the chapel to pray.

My prayers and thoughts usually went something like this: *We didn't even give him a name. The whole thing was so sudden. He was alive and waiting to come into the world when I went to work that morning, and by the time I went to bed that night he was in the funeral home waiting to be put in the ground. We should have named him.*

These thoughts rushed while I was kneeling with my head bowed. But He had already felt my pain. When I looked up at the crucifix the sound of the fountain would intensify and my heart would tell me what He was saying to me: *I know. I know how you suffer*. It was... It *is*...a certainty—a conviction, a paradox and a mystery.

It helped to know that my son was where God wanted him to be —in Paradise, with Him. Then I would go on until the next week.

* * *

One night after work as I got in the truck to go home, I noticed my Bible shoved down between my seat and the console. I hadn't picked it up in months. *Should I open it?*

I turned on the reading light and glanced down at the duct tape on the spine, waving to Reese as he backed his Chevy out of the space next to me and took off down Pine. Then I was alone. I sat for a minute staring at the locked garage bays, each with a light overtop. *Why not just open it? What else can possibly go wrong?*

I reached between the seats, picked up the book, and began leafing through to St. Mark's gospel. But I glanced down at the Prophets as I did it, stopping for some reason at Jeremiah 2. The first line at the top of the page was verse 5: *Before I formed you in the womb I knew you.*

I knew you... I knew you. My child... MY *child!* He knew him, had always known him. *Why can't I? Why can't I know him, why can't Michelle rock him, why do I have to paint the nursery this weekend?*

I sat for a time, crying. There was a very small bloodstain on the passenger seat. I had scrubbed it but I knew where it was. I looked away from it then and made the decision to trade in the truck. I could never expect Michelle to ride in it again.

She was in the kitchen when I walked in through the back of the house, standing at the stove stirring the leftovers heating in the pan. It was chili that she had fixed the day before, along with pasta. The table was already set; a candle burned in the center. I looked at her body. She looked pale and wraithlike, almost ethereal as she stood quietly at the stove, still wearing her work khakis along with an over-sized turtleneck. It was cold outside.

"Dinner's ready, Jason." She smiled at me.

I blinked back tears and rushed past her. "Okay baby, I'll be right in, let me go wash my hands." I hurried to the bathroom and washed water over my face. The plates were filled when I went back, hers with much less than mine. We sat down, made the sign of the cross and started eating.

"This is good," I said.

"Thanks."

"What did DeLuca say?" She'd called the family practice and had finally gotten in to see them that morning.

"I never saw him. I had to leave for work before they got to me. I talked to his nurse."

"What did she say?"

"He's backed up. She took my vital signs and looked at my file. She said he'd probably send the prescription to the pharmacy. Then I left."

"Did you call them?"

"Yes, honey. They had it. I picked it up after work."

"What is it?"

"The same one as before. It's fine."

She finished what was on her plate. *Thank you, God.*

After dinner I passed a couple of hours tearing wallpaper off the nursery walls. Little jungle animals stared out of the trash at me.

Michelle was waiting for me when I went to bed around ten-thirty after a smoke out back. I was out of whiskey. I brushed my teeth, got in bed next to her and turned out the light. She put her arms around me, kissed me, and rubbed her hand across the stubble on my cheek.

My response was automatic; I kissed her back, and my hands were everywhere.

"Michelle," I said after a minute. "Are you sure it's okay?"

"It's fine Jason," she murmured. I already knew it wasn't possible that night, but I had to ask.

"It's too soon for another baby," I said against her neck. "You're positive?"

"Jason, please," she was kissing me again. "I know it's okay and so do you."

"All right, honey," I breathed. I stripped off her top and felt what was under it. *She's not the same. But that doesn't matter.* "I love you more than I ever have," I whispered fiercely. "You...you're beautiful... So beautiful." I reached for her bikinis and stripped off my boxers. We got away for a while.

* * *

Around the first of December Brad told me over the phone that his coworker was wearing down. "They're getting sick of hearing her. I think my supervisor finally figured it out. He demands documentation every time, and she's got nothing."

"What took him so long?" I asked, lighting a smoke. I was standing outside in the cold and dark next to the shed. The fresh air seemed to help my moods.

"That's what I kept asking myself," Brad said. "But a certain fact has come to light. The witch was sleeping with the boss. I noticed that her claws went back every time he came into the store, but I thought she was just brown-nosing him. I had no idea he was pounding her."

"What?" I laughed. "Who told you that?"

"Sammy. He's a new tech. He was working in back and he overheard them talking." Brad laughed back at me. "Can you believe this crap?"

"What did he hear?"

"The two of them fighting. Sammy saw through her act the first week he started. He heard her ask the boss what was taking so long. That hag—she must have been getting impatient; she asked him right at the counter. The store wasn't open but she must have forgotten Sammy was in back. He told me the two of them went back and forth for a few minutes until the boss finally told her he had no authority. He said it would have to go higher up, and if she really wanted me gone she needed to show proof. Then he asked her if they were still on for that night."

"That common bitch."

"Yeah. She's a vindictive piece of work. Revenge is what she lives on."

"What does she look like?"

Brad roared with laughter. "Nothing you or I would ever touch. She looks like she's still pissed about not getting asked to the prom. She's about our age and not bad looking, but her attitude! I think she hates men. She would freaking hate you Wallace, even more than me."

"What the hell for?"

"I don't know; why the hell does she hate me so much? I had nothing against her personally. I was just doing my job." I heard him light a cigarette. "I don't know how these people think. It's like it's their way or the highway. I guess she was pissed that I didn't knuckle under. But screw that. I refuse to let these shark bastards run me."

"They want to break us." I said. I stared up at the moon, far away and cold.

"Well they're not breaking me. Those freaking sharks will never get me to knuckle under."

"Me either."

* * *

After Brad hung up I lit another smoke and stared up through the trees, thinking. I wanted my wife. Our life together was one of the things that kept me going. I exhaled smoke into the cold, looking up at the sky. The stars were pinpoints of light along with a fingernail moon, barely there. The wind cut me. I wanted to go inside and crawl under the covers with Michelle, but it wasn't going to happen, not that night. *She hasn't gained back enough weight. What if there's a baby? God, I miss her.*

I agreed with Brad that I wasn't going to let them break me, but I had to admit—if only to myself—that they had started to run me. My intimate life with my wife was almost at a complete standstill.

It had always been the strongest part of our marriage. It was always a comfort, a sacrament, and sanctity. We considered it the best thing we had going for us—the fact that we could still, after all these years, feel the way we did about each other.

I didn't care anymore about her scrawniness and her tiny breasts. I just wanted her back the way she used to be. I only cared because she was unhealthy. I understood in my mind that she'd get better eventually, but my heart told me different, and I was scared. I was so worried about her health that I was afraid to touch her. I was afraid to make love to my wife.

Me.

It was unbelievable, but it was also true. We still had intercourse, but only about twice a month because I was scared of getting her pregnant again. But I refused to even consider using artificial means. We hadn't since the first year of our marriage. There was no way in hell those sharks were forcing that on us, and we still enjoyed each other, but it was infrequent now. *They are running us. In the most intimate part of our lives.*

Michelle

Lord Jesus, the nights are still long and hot and lonely. My husband feels the same. Seems we'll be waiting forever, but I know that's not true; we just have to be patient and trust you. We know our little boy is with you along with our other precious babies. And we believe that our newest baby will stay with us this time. We believe you will keep us hidden here and that we will see Brad and the girls again. We pray for all of this and we believe. Amen.

Jason
2 Years Earlier

Michelle and I visited the grave every Sunday after Mass. Sometimes I'd go to Mass, and other times I wouldn't, but I always went to the cemetery. At least he was in the same place as the old man; it was a comfort. At least we knew where he was, and the sharks hadn't gotten his body.

The best thing that happened before the final crash was the toilet paper shortage. I don't mean I was glad to see people go without toilet paper you understand, but I laughed when we figured out the old man was right after all. He had known it was going to happen eventually.

The shortage began two weeks before Christmas and affected everyone living in the northeast from Boston to Baltimore. Nobody understood why. No one was able to explain it, and if the drones on the news had any idea what had caused it they were keeping quiet about it. For once they stuck to the facts—that there was no toilet paper available in the northeast at that time. There was also a shortage of paper towels and other such things, but the worst thing anyone had to deal with was having to do without TP. People were going ballistic over it.

All kinds of ideas floated around; rumors as to why it had happened. Danny and Reese argued about it all day long at work. Danny thought it had something to do with transportation, or lack thereof because of energy shortages.

The news was full of stories of how we were finally about to run out of fuel along with the usual stories of a substitute that was in the works and would soon be available. The drones had been running this same story every six months for the past fifteen years. After a week or so I had to turn off the drones because watching the news made me seriously question my sanity. One night after work while Michelle was in the kitchen, I sat down and turned on the TV. Imagine my amazement when what met my eyes was news footage featuring a reporter whom I knew for a fact was dead.

"Michelle!" I yelled, "come here, quick!"

"What is it?" She rushed into the living room with a dishtowel in her hand.

"Look." I pointed at the TV. "There's that guy from CRP, the one who died last year."

"Who?"

"That reporter, right there. He's dead."

"I know. He died October before last. I remember; it was the same week as my birthday. Why on earth are they showing him now with everything else going on?"

"No, Michelle. This is today's news about energy and toilet paper."

"What? No! He couldn't have mentioned toilet paper...could he?"

"No. He didn't. But the drone at the anchor desk leading up to it did and then introduced this guy."

"Are you sure?" she asked.

"Yes I'm sure," I snapped. "Oh my God...I'm sorry. But these people are driving me insane. Wait here. We'll see what happens when the anchor comes back."

She sat down next to me then, and a minute later the camera cut back to the drone reading the news of the day. She thanked the dead guy for his report before going on to parrot the talking points she'd been given: that there was a shortage of TP in the northeastern region of the country now, along with a shortage of gasoline, fuel oil, and coal fired energy in some areas. Power grids were affected in New York City, and rolling blackouts were being implemented in the Bronx and Staten Island. No reason was given as to why. The sharks were keeping mum for the moment.

Michelle and I looked at each other with incredulity.

"You saw that. Right?" I asked.

"Yes," she answered, shaking her head.

"I guess there aren't enough drones who are actually breathing to file any current reports on energy," I said in disgust. I hit the remote.

That reporter had died over a year earlier. Michelle remembered the story and so did I, even though the mainstream news outlets—including the one he had worked for—had given only a brief mention of his death. He had been a star reporter traveling all over the world for at least ten years, but once he was dead he was gone. Except for the network that was scrubbed, the drones had only given his death about thirty seconds of airtime. The host I threatened the abortionist with had run a story on him. I remembered because I had no tolerance at all for the guy who had died or his reporting. He was just the kind of little twerp who pissed me off the most: condescending to anyone he considered "Middle America" while at the same time sucking up to any shark who gave him a second look.

He died in a whorehouse in Las Vegas. He'd been found tied to the bedpost in one of the rooms upstairs with his throat slashed; yet here he was on the news a year later talking about energy. When I mentioned it the next day at work, CJ remembered the reporter being found dead but he hadn't seen the news the previous evening. Neither had anyone else.

But despite the gaslighting I knew he was dead. The drones were recycling news stories, and they seemed not to know that they had featured a reporter who'd been dead for over a year. Unless they were deliberately trying to drive people insane, which probably wasn't much of a stretch. After all, they had important work to do: informing the unwashed masses that the bureaucracy was handling the energy crisis and TP shortage in a timely manner.

Reese insisted the influence of Hollywood was behind the TP shortage. He was of the mind that they'd finally gotten what they'd been after for twenty years and had shut down the manufacture of it. Maybe he was right. Who knew?

The TP shortage happened some years ago, and we still haven't figured out why. The media drones probably knew what was going on but had been given instructions to keep their mouths shut. It didn't really matter anyway, since by that time most people didn't believe a word they said. The drones usually ignored what was really going on all over the country—the riots in Pittsburgh and Albany and the storming of some state capitol out in the Midwest.

Again, people were going ballistic. It would have been funny if it weren't so tragic. In addition to rioting and looting there was even an outbreak of cholera. I knew it for a fact even though it didn't make the news. Mrs. CJ's cousins from Baltimore told her that an entire neighborhood was quarantined after two children became sick and died. The cousins lived across town, but the husband's brother was a Baltimore City cop who heard it firsthand through work. Eighty-nine people died before the outbreak was brought under control.

Though the drones ignored the cholera outbreak, they didn't ignore the sharks, even though very few sharks were visible at the time. Most of them spent the three or four weeks at the height of the shortage in their new offices in New York City, afraid to show their faces on the street. The drones helped them along of course, entering the office buildings by night to interview sharks and shoot more footage telling people that all was well and TP was on the way. The store where Michelle worked had run out, and no one knew what to say when customers asked when the stock would be replenished.

"Are people asking you?" I said as we were getting dressed for work one morning.

"Yes. And I don't know what to tell them."

"Send them to management. It's their job to appease the customers." I sat down to lace up my work boots.

"Okay."

"Michelle, you need to be careful. People are rioting. You keep an eye on the situation, and if you notice anything out of the ordinary call me right away. Do you hear me?"

"Jason, honey, don't upset yourself."

My answer was to pull her down on my lap and hug her, worrying all the more. *There better not be any rioting around here. I'll break their freaking heads.*

I wasn't exactly in a positive state of mind at the time, and it wouldn't have bothered me in the slightest to confront some idiot looking to start a riot. It was a stupid idea, rioting. The riots were always put down, and then sanctions were brought against everyone in the area. I wasn't about to let it happen in our town. *I'll break some freaking heads.*

Do not go down that path... Those who live by the sword shall also die by it.

I won't let anyone hurt my wife.

Do not go down that path.

"All right, Michelle. But if you notice anything strange get away from the front of the store. Go to the back. Leave the damn register and call me." I was looking into her eyes.

Promise baby. I can't lose you too.

You're not going to lose me, Jason.

* * *

The old man had predicted the TP shortage and had stocked up on it the year before he got sick. There were cases of it stored in the basement at Johnny's. We had enough to get our three households through at least a year if we were careful. We had packed Brad's share in the four-wheel drive when we drove down to Memphis for Nicole's funeral. Memphis wasn't currently running a shortage, but he'd be ready for it when it came.

We found out about the old man's TP storage one Sunday at dinner when he came in late. When my mother-in-law heard that he'd been out buying TP she made some remark that rubbed him the wrong way.

"Look Marie," he snapped. "I'm five minutes late. So what?"

"Jack, it's Sunday."

"I know it's Sunday. I also know what's going to happen in this country sooner or later, and if we have to go down I'm going to be ready. We're going end up living like the Soviets—its coming. And as long as I can afford it, I'm going to make sure of one thing. This country may be descending straight into Stalinism, but I'm going to make damn sure we can wipe our asses once we get there."

Johnny and I had lost it laughing, and Michelle gagged; she was getting ready to start eating.

So our family didn't have to deal with what shortsighted people were experiencing. Namely running out, throwing up, lines at stores, and clogged plumbing. Johnny said he told Junior in no uncertain terms that he'd better not breathe a word about our supply down at the firehouse. He assumed Junior hadn't, since no one was bothering them. Jamie took wads of toilet paper to school in his backpack just in case.

I took two cases over to the garage. I told everyone to take home what they needed, and let them know there was more where that came from. Reese was so grateful he almost kissed my feet.

"Wallace, you have no idea what's been going on at my house," he said. "You saved me in the nick of time."

"What do you mean?"

"Sophie's been sick all week." Sophie was Reese and Heather's three-year-old daughter. "She's been puking up her guts... And the opposite." He made a face, gesturing with a roll of TP. "We needed this stuff, like yesterday."

"Damn it, keep away from me," I said jokingly, backing away from him. "Don't give me your damn germs. I don't need that."

"Tell me about it." He laughed. "I don't want it either, but I know it's only a matter of time. And get this Wallace. Heather... She... Heather's knocked up again. She's in the damn bathroom every fifteen minutes, and we opened our last roll today. So thank you."

I kept a poker face at the news that Heather was pregnant even though it cut me like a knife. Reese and I had already discussed the situation when he informed me, shamefaced, that his wife had run out of our house in tears the day the baby was born. She had gone home and flushed her pills down the toilet, crying that it was a shame to try to prevent another baby after seeing what Michelle did to try to hang onto one. I had been expecting the news. I had already told Reese not to try to hide it from me when it happened. Reese was one of my best friends. We had been through thick and thin together since we were fifteen years old, and I was happy for him.

"Well, I hope Sophie feels better soon, and congratulations."

"Thanks," Reese said. "How's Michelle?"

"Okay. She's back on running, seems to be feeling better."

"Wallace..." Reese sounded cautious. "Are you okay?"

"Yeah." I shrugged. "I'm fine."

"You gotta stop this. Stop blaming yourself. It wasn't your fault."

I looked at the floor.

"Wallace, I was at your house. I saw the place. For God's sake, there was blood all over the bedroom. If I ever walked in my house and found Heather that way, I'd do the same thing you did. What else could you have done?"

"Reese..." I took a breath. "I tell myself that every day."

"Well maybe you should make sure my child will have a friend the same age. What about that?"

"No," I said quickly. "Not yet."

THIRTY-TWO

Jason
2 Years Earlier

We had Christmas dinner at our place. We debated whether or not to do it with all that had happened the previous year, but Michelle said she wanted to if I would help her. Brad and the girls flew up. They were staying with us, and Michelle and I met them at the airport.

"Aunt Michelle! Hi Auntie!" Annie and Taylor ran toward us on little legs.

"Hi baby!" Michelle bent down and held out her arms. After hugging Michelle, the girls smiled and chattered happily, but we three adults were on the verge of tears for the rest of the day. It would be our first Christmas without the old man and Michelle's mom, not to mention Nicole and our baby. That week was hard for all of us. It was hard to see those two little girls in the house, and to think that our son should have been there for the twins to meet.

Michelle made an evergreen and poinsettia basket for her parents and decorated a tiny Christmas tree for the baby. We visited the cemetery after Brad arrived. We went in my new truck. Brad rode up front with me, and Michelle shared the back with the twins in their car seats.

The truck was only new to us. It was actually used, but only two years old. The cab was roomier than my old truck's, and even though the payments ended up being higher than I'd hoped, what difference did it make now? Michelle and I didn't care. It wasn't as if we had our baby with us. He didn't need any money, and I could afford the payments.

I took along some wire hooks I had made out of coat hangers to anchor the basket and tree in the ground. The baby had no marker because I hadn't been able to face ordering one. Whenever Michelle brought it up I told her we would do it in the spring. I anchored his little tree right over the place where he lay with the old man.

Michelle stood in silence with tears running down her cheeks, and Brad and I couldn't look at each other after I stood up from the grave. We all made the sign of the cross, and after a time we went home.

* * *

On Christmas Eve Michelle and I went to Midnight Mass. Brad stayed home with the twins. He would be taking them to church on Christmas morning, and he and the girls were asleep when Michelle and I got home. We exchanged gifts before going to bed.

I gave Michelle a new medal, something I knew she wanted. The Mother of God was crafted of alabaster and surrounded in blue with a delicate border of silver. I also gave her a new silver chain, a pair of diamond earrings, and a porcelain figurine of the Blessed Mother. I went to the jeweler in Philadelphia for the earrings. They set me back a good chunk of change.

Though Michelle loved the gifts, she was surprised about the expense. But lately it seemed like we never did anything fun no matter how hard we worked and saved. It had made me happy to pick out things I thought Michelle would like. I still believed I had let her down. Sometimes I thought she might be better off if she hadn't married me. *Would she be? What have I given her? Our lives are nothing but work. I wish I could take her away for a while.*

We hadn't been anywhere on vacation except our yearly trip to the beach for years because of the increasing taxation and higher cost of living under the sharks. Michelle was always satisfied with a beach weekend away now and then, but I still wished I could afford more for her.

I had my vices. I drank at least a shot or two of whiskey every night. I'd been drinking whiskey on and off ever since high school when Brad and I discovered Jack Daniel's. I still bought cigarettes whenever I could, though supplies were erratic because of the upcoming ban. *That sucks. But there's always the black market. I hope I can find the old man's brand.*

Michelle worried about what smoking might be doing to me. I felt guilty when I thought of her distress, but not enough to let it stop me from having a cigarette or two at night while I was drinking.

Michelle always looked good. She went to Bella's for her hair regularly, and she had good taste in clothes as well. She was also a shoe junkie. That was her only vice. Michelle loved new shoes, the higher the heel the better. But we always made sure we were up to date on bills before we bought anything extra, which made the idea of taking her away to a warm sunny place impossible. So I decided to spend some of what I had saved to pay for our son's birth on the gifts, thinking Michelle deserved something special after all she'd been through.

She gave me a silver crucifix. I wasn't in the habit of wearing any jewelry except for my wedding ring, and she knew it. But she said she wanted me to have a crucifix, and that she hoped I would wear it. I didn't; I put the box in my dresser drawer after Christmas. *But at least I have one now. And she gave it to me.*

In addition to the crucifix she gave me a gift card for the sporting goods store. She wanted me to have a new surf-fishing pole and thought that I should be the one to pick it out. She also gave me four pairs of Levi's that I needed for work.

Neither of us mentioned the baby, and the Christmas we had hoped to spend with him. It was something unspoken between us that night. Both of us knew that if we spoke of our child we wouldn't be able to get out of bed the next morning.

* * *

The whole family came for Christmas dinner with the exception of Junior, who was at the firehouse. That was for the best. I found it hard to look at him, and it was better for everyone if he stayed away. Cindy cooked the wedding soup that year. Johnny had helped her roll the meatballs, and half of them were way too big. We all joked sadly at the table about what his mother would have said.

Brad, Lucio, Johnny and me went out back between dinner and dessert. I kept a kerosene heater in the shed to take off the chill. There was a fifth of bourbon under the workbench—Brad's gift to me —and I still had cigarettes, so we indulged ourselves to celebrate Christmas and in honor of the old man.

Lucio was still extremely pissed off about what had happened at Sonny's school. He didn't seem to care that Johnny was present when he mentioned those creepy-assed brown shirts down at the firehouse going into schools to brainwash kids without asking permission. I felt bad for Johnny—he had no control over Junior after all. He didn't say a word during Lucio's rant, but neither did he act ashamed. I blamed the sharks for the uncomfortable silence when Lucio finished speaking.

Later, after everyone had gone, Brad and I went out to the shed again. The girls were asleep with Michelle in our bed. I slept on the living room couch that week, and Brad used the pullout bed in the computer room.

We talked openly when it was just the two of us. We had a cigarette while I filled him in on the increased brown shirt activities of Junior's organization.

"There are chapters springing up all over Memphis," Brad said.

"What are they doing down there?"

"Running the streets and going into middle schools without appointments, the same as at Sonny's school. But it's worse in Memphis. So many kids have thrown in with the cult that somebody went after them. Two brown shirts were found hanging from street-lights. It's vigilante justice."

"Damn. Lucio was ready to go to the principal's house that night. He wanted to wait for him to come outside and then jump him, but Reese and I talked him out of it."

"Good thing Bella and Lucio aren't in Memphis. They've started drafting kids right after they finish school or if they drop out.

"They're not drafting up here," I said. "Not yet, anyway. Sounds like they don't have any set rules for doing business. Jamie's graduating in June."

"Johnny told me he's not letting them get Jamie," Brad said. Then he changed the subject. "Sammy called earlier. Had a Christmas gift for me."

"What are you talking about?"

"The hag quit yesterday." He laughed.

"No shit." I whistled. "Well what do you know? I guess there is a Santa Claus."

"I waited her out and now she's gone."

We smoked in silence for a minute, but I knew what was going through his mind. *That witch couldn't break me... No one breaks me.*

"It's gonna to be easier to get around those pedophile pigs without her around," he said.

"What are you doing now?"

"When we get a shipment I take home ten pills. I steam open the cardboard, take them out of the bubble wrap and replace it with a placebo. Then I put it back together with glue. Works perfectly."

"Really?" I raised an eyebrow. "Doesn't sound perfect to me."

Brad rolled his eyes. "Well, maybe it doesn't look exactly perfect, but the whores who come in to get it are usually so strung out they wouldn't know if the container was open or not."

I shrugged.

"And the pigs who come in to get it for little girls they're screwing would give it to them even if they knew for sure it was tampered with. I still don't understand why the bastards are keeping it in drugstores. They don't need to keep it in pharmacies. There are plenty of places that'll hand them over—" He stopped as he realized what had almost come out of his mouth. "Shit," he said, red faced. I knew exactly what he was thinking: *Damn it... I can't believe what I almost said.*

I reached under the workbench for the whiskey and poured us each a shot. I handed him his as I was drinking mine. Then I poured another one and gulped it down.

"You know why they're keeping it in drugstores," I said as Brad knocked back his shot.

"Yeah. They're doing it because they can."

He was right. Even though they knew there were pharmacists with objections to dispensing those pills because of religious convictions, the HCA did it anyway. They were trying to force their will on the entire country. Rumor had it that doctors and nurses were now fired for refusing to perform abortions or to assist in them. They were also fired for refusing to help some people along to the end of their lives. The health care system was now a giant death cult, and the doctors who could be trusted to deliver a baby were being forced to quit rather than go against their deeply held beliefs. It was the same for pharmacists. Not that we would ever hear the truth on the news, but I believed the rumors. I saw Brad standing there right in front of me, didn't I?

But he was getting around them. As I took a last drag on my cigarette, I heard his voice in my head. *The shark bastards aren't gonna break me. They're not making me do anything.*

"Anyway Wallace, after one of those pigs leaves with a kid, I call the cops. I go down to the bowling alley or the bar on the corner. They still have pay phones. I hang up after I give the address."

"You better be careful. What if someone in that bar notices you coming in there and using the phone every other day?"

"I'm in the process of scouting out some shadier places where people might mind their own business."

"What about the other pharmacists?"

"The two of them are such HCA sympathizers that they're blind, and anyway, the hag is gone now. About half the store has the HCA mindset," he said, shrugging. "I just let them think I agree with them. They don't know the difference."

"What about inventory records?" I asked.

"I go in early. I know the security guard at the shopping center. I buy him cigarettes, and he looks the other way when I go in there at five o'clock in the morning on my way to the gym. It's only about once a month. I shut off the security system, change the records and get out. I use my supervisor's password, the one who's banging the bitch. I only see him once every couple of weeks; he's in charge of eight stores and they expect him to be able to stay on top of inventory for all of them. I did the same thing last year when I sent those drugs for the old man."

"How long do you think you can get away with it?"

"It's working fine so far. Sammy's not in it that far; he only sells the placebos and keeps a lookout for me." He dragged on his smoke. "Some guy came in with a twelve year old two weeks ago. He was talking right there in the store to this kid about pimping her out. He was pissed because he's losing money on her."

"No way," I replied.

"Yes, Wallace," Brad replied evenly. "That girl looked like a baby.

She couldn't have been more than twelve or thirteen. But the arrogant bastard knows he can get away with it so he didn't bother to lower his voice."

"If he's pimping her out, can't the cops arrest him?"

"I called them, but I have no idea if they even looked into it. I gave them the address we had on file, but who knows? I don't even know if it's a real address. Or even why we're required to ask for addresses anymore. The whole situation is one giant screw up.

"Do you get any normal customers in there?"

"Less and less every day." He stared into space.

"Brad... You didn't do anything about it, did you?" He looked at me sideways, dragging on his Lucky Strike. He raised an eyebrow.

"Not yet," he said.

THIRTY-THREE

Jason
2 Years Earlier

Brad and the girls flew home after Christmas, and Michelle and I went back to work. We went to Reese and Heather's place for New Year's Eve. Despite our grief, we had a nice time with our friends. It was a fun evening.

The next morning we went running together. I felt better that day than I had in weeks. Michelle was gaining weight, and running put both of us in better spirits. It was the start of a new year, and we decided to look ahead to the future. Michelle wanted another baby. She mentioned it when we got home from the park. And though I wanted another child more than anything else, I wasn't quite ready to begin trying. The memory of our son was too fresh. So I asked her to wait until spring, and she agreed.

That night I went out to the shed for a drink and a smoke before bed. As I finished my cigarette I became aware of some commotion outside and went to investigate. The sound of a car screaming to a stop was followed by a man's voice swearing. I hurried past the house and looked down the street.

A group of kids were on the corner along with a guy I didn't recognize. He got out of his car and began screaming in the face of one of the kids. His car—an old Pontiac—had bumped onto the curb under the streetlight. A big splash of something dark nearly covered the driver's side door. I realized the kids had shot him with a paintball gun.

The guy was extremely pissed off. He cursed and gestured in the face of the tallest boy. It never went any further than him screaming and waving his arms while the rest of them stood back laughing, but I heard a couple of comments to the effect that they could do whatever they damn well wanted to, and that if they felt like it they'd shoot something worse at him.

The guy's voice drifted up the street. Before he got back in his car he told the kids to get the hell out of the neighborhood and said that if he caught them around there again he was going to kick some ass. He said exactly what I was feeling. I was on the verge of taking off down there and helping him do it.

But he was leaving, and I didn't want to take them on alone. After he drove off I waited for a minute to see what they would do. I stood in the street in front of the house, looking their way.

One of them noticed me. It was dark up my way with just enough light for him to be able to see that there was someone watching them. The boy who saw me gestured to the taller one. He must have been the pack leader. He stood looking back for a minute, before flipping me off with both hands. Anger rushed. I broke out in a sweat in the twenty-degree night but I did nothing to address the little punk's disrespect. I remained standing, seemingly frozen, smelling the skunky scent of a joint they were passing right out in the open.

As I stood there watching and listening to what amounted to a legal gang marking their territory in our family-friendly neighborhood, a fleeting memory of a red sports car and my old man's grease stained, tool scarred hands went through my head. *Darkness...darkness... It's right on the edge of town. Those little punks... Junior, you better back off.*

There was nothing I would have liked better than to get my shotgun and blast it into the air while telling them to get their asses back to that firehouse if they didn't want a load of birdshot coming their way. But I didn't do it. I didn't even walk down the street and tell them to go. They didn't leave. The other guy hadn't done anything, and neither did I.

* * *

The following Sunday, Michelle and I went back to the cemetery to take the Christmas decorations off the graves. When we arrived we discovered that our child's resting place had been vandalized. The Christmas tree had been pulled out of the ground along with the hooks. We found it in a ditch next to the highway, torn out of its container with the roots exposed.

* * *

That night I took Michelle with me to St. Michael's. I had just been there the previous afternoon, but after our discovery of the vandalism I needed to go back, and I didn't want Michelle to be alone at the house if those punk kids returned to the neighborhood.

Someone I had never seen before knelt in the row across from me keeping watch, and Michelle sat two rows behind me, praying the rosary in silence. My heart was weighed down as I questioned God.

Couldn't our child have anything? He didn't have a name, he hadn't had Christmas with us, and he didn't even have a birth certificate. Why couldn't he have had a Christmas tree? Why did Michelle have to see the tree that way? Couldn't she have even a small comfort like a Christmas tree for our dead child? Why did you take him from us?

I am looking up at you, hanging. I know about your suffering. I thank you always for saving us, but I don't understand why we couldn't have even a small comfort such as a tree on our child's grave. I have read your words about servants and masters. I understand that I can't expect not to suffer; I am your servant.

But why must my wife suffer so much? Why did she have to see the roots of that tree pulled out and thrown away, and then begin crying to me on the way home that that's what they would have liked to do with our child. Why? She told me that if it hadn't been for me, they would have.

It wasn't me; I know this. It was you who sent help to guide me that day, and I thank you for that. But couldn't Michelle have been spared the sight of our child's vandalized grave?

These were the questions I asked. The holy water flowed in the fountain as I looked at the monstrance until the answers came. They came into my heart as they always did, but that night I wasn't at peace. That night I argued with Him until He seemed to be far away. And then...something else might have come to me. It's hard to write what happened because the answers weren't words, but I'll try.

Take up your cross... My yoke is easy, my burdens light.

No. This isn't easy. It's hard. It's so hard that I don't know if I can continue.

You shall find rest for yourself.

This isn't rest.

You shall find rest. Follow me... Shoulder my yoke.

I stared up and to my right at the stained glass windows. St. Joan of Arc was standing with her sword unsheathed but not raised. Unsheathed and held in her hand with the point stuck in the ground. She was Michelle's patron saint. After all, Joan was her first name: Joan Michelle Davis Wallace. She'd been named after the old man's mother, whose name had been Joan—Joan Bradford Davis. The old man's name was John Bradford Davis. Family names were important to the Davises. Johnny wasn't John Bradford; they had named him John Vincent Marione Davis, after Mrs. Davis' father and grandfather. Junior was John Vincent Jr., and Brad was Antonio Bradford for Mrs. Davis' brother.

You were with me the day my child was born, weren't you? You sent help. Why couldn't you have told me to see that he had a name?

He's here with Me.

Why not here with us? Why didn't I name him? Who was I named after? Whose blood is running through my veins?

I love you and you are Mine...you are Mine.

I knew my name—Jason Michael Wallace. I'd been named Jason because my mother wanted it; it was one of the most popular boy's names back when I was born. I was also named for my father, Michael Sean Wallace.

My mother's name was Eileen Nora Flynn Wallace. She was raised in an Irish Catholic family and had turned her back on most of them after leaving home to go to school in California. After I was confirmed she turned her back on Catholicism as well. Her blood was running through my veins along with that of Michael Sean Wallace, who had walked out on us.

It's hard. Can't Michelle be spared such pain? I can't stand it anymore.

(No...you can't stand it. You couldn't even bring yourself out of your whining and moaning long enough to contact that bigmouthed Irishman before we muzzled him. You'll never beat us, and neither will he. He's a lightweight too, even if he is under the impression that he's another Patrick. The fool. He can't drive us out, not now...this isn't ancient Ireland. There are way too many of us around these days for him to even make a pitiful dent. He can't do a damn thing no matter how much he keeps running his mouth. And neither can you, you sniveling fool...so why keep trying? You can't stand it. Lightweights like you never last. Is it worth it anyway?)

I lifted my eyes to Him hanging. Truth.

My yoke is light. Follow me... Take up your cross.

I shut my eyes.

But it's heavy.

My yoke is light.

(*Light. Light? You can't even have a crappy Christmas tree on your dead son's grave. Light. You sentimental fool.*)

I stared at the monstrance and then glanced back at Michelle, who was kneeling peacefully behind me. She wasn't crying anymore.

(*You know she will be later, though. That's a given. She'll be crying again tonight. And you know why. Because you're weak and afraid. So what if you do run twenty-five miles a week? So what if you work out on the punching bag until your arms are bulging? You may look strong but you're a lightweight, really. Especially in that way—the way it counts in any marriage. You're right in one thing though. What's she doing with you?*)

I took a deep breath, put my concentration on the monstrance, and began to pray the prayer to St. Michael the Archangel. It was the only other prayer I knew by heart besides the Our Father and the Hail Mary and the Creed. *Defend us in this day of battle...* It was the one prayer I could remember learning from my father. *You and I were named for the Archangel, Jason...* I looked at the monstrance and concentrated on the Truth.

The water of the fountain pierced my head in a rush and intensified. It seemed loud; almost like a rolling rapid in a river somewhere. I listened and looked at Him. *You are Mine. I chose you. He is happy here...ask Me and I will give you living water.*

The sound was so loud that I turned around to look, and when I did I saw my wife, smiling at me radiantly. Her face was beautiful and peaceful, her eyes so deep and blue that I began losing myself in them. The sound of the water continued to rush. It rushed and flowed, washing away my doubts.

For the time being.

On the way home Michelle picked up the Bible, and before I could stop her she turned on the reading light and read aloud: *"Do Not Throw This Freedom Away... But now that you have come to know God, or rather to be known by God, how can you turn back again to the weak and destitute elemental powers? Do you want to be slaves to them all over again? You are observing days, months, seasons, and years. I am afraid on your account that perhaps I have labored for you in vain."*

I saw her looking at me out of the corner of my eye. I stared straight ahead out at the road.

"Jason," she said in a puzzled tone. "I thought you were reading St. Luke. Are you finished? Why was the Bible open to Galatians Four?"

I didn't answer. I glanced down at my right hand, holding the steering wheel at four o'clock. My eyes came to rest on the snake's head, with its fangs twisting and dripping poison. I also saw the sandal. Then I came to understand, for a fleeting moment, a profound truth. I understood that no matter what we—His followers —had endured, or were enduring, or would endure in days to come, it had already been crushed. Once, for all. The shock feeling came to me again, and I understood that He had already won. *Just follow me... Take up your cross.*

* * *

At home we sat down in the living room. Michelle had a glass of wine, and I had a beer. She stared at me from across the room with the same look of love that had been there on our wedding night. *Do not throw this freedom away...*

You're sure, baby? There's no chance of conception?

I'm positive. Please don't worry... I need you, Jason.

I stood up and took her hand. I pulled her toward the hallway and picked her up and carried her to our room. We stared into each other's eyes before I laid her on the bed. Then I turned out the light, and we were free for a while.

Six days later, the notice arrived. Everything went dark.

ABOUT THE AUTHOR

Daniella Bova married her high school sweetheart and raised two children. She loves writing, gardening, the catholic faith, photography, and all forms of textile and fiber artistry. She lives in Pennsylvania with her husband.

 facebook.com/daniellabovawriter

amazon.com/Daniella-Bova/e/B00UNZ0SRM

Made in the USA
Middletown, DE
05 October 2023

40114113R00239